# TYGER TYGER

## BIG POPI AND LI'L FRECKLES: PART THREE

### KEVEN LESLIE

iUniverse®

# TYGER TYGER
## BIG POPI AND LI'L FRECKLES: PART THREE

iUniverse books may be ordered through booksellers or by contacting:

iUniverse
1663 Liberty Drive
Bloomington, IN 47403
www.iuniverse.com
1-800-Authors (1-800-288-4677)

Because of the dynamic nature of the Internet, any web addresses or links contained in this book may have changed since publication and may no longer be valid. The views expressed in this work are solely those of the author and do not necessarily reflect the views of the publisher, and the publisher hereby disclaims any responsibility for them.

Any people depicted in stock imagery provided by Getty Images are models, and such images are being used for illustrative purposes only.
Certain stock imagery © Getty Images.

ISBN: 978-1-5320-9659-4 (sc)
ISBN: 978-1-5320-9750-8 (e)

Library of Congress Control Number: 2020904727

Print information available on the last page.

iUniverse rev. date: 03/06/2020

# 2014; LOVE MACHINE

After Layla told me about her eighteen years without me, I was a lot more understanding about the changes in her. Those fifteen years only took a few seconds in my world because The One, who is every particle in the universe, took her spirit to a newly created realm, the eighth, where time moves at hyper-speed. She was sent back to me only after she had finally fallen in love with another man, a boy really. Anyway, my beautiful wife had to mourn her lost love and fall in love with me all over again. Not surprisingly, this only took a few days since she never really stopped, but had simply and finally moved on.

A few weeks after the ambush, I started running our daily five miles with the much younger former competitive distance runner, Layla. I had never beaten her and I probably never would, but it wouldn't be for lack of trying. I yearned, dreamed and ached for once, just once, finishing an inch ahead of her. Now, it was the first of September. I'm fifty-one and will turn fifty-two on the third of November. Layla will be twenty-three on the first. In between, November second, we will celebrate our third wedding anniversary.

Today, after weeks of recovery and training, I started my finishing pace early into the fifth and final mile long lap around our rural property. My hope was that Layla would speed up also, throwing her off her game. She didn't bite, sticking to her tried and true routine. I was a hundred yards ahead with a quarter mile to go. I was panting, but refused to let my lack of oxygen slow me down. I knew that Layla would be pouring it on about now, but I couldn't accelerate and I wouldn't slowdown. Layla passed me with less than a hundred yards left.

"Good run sweetheart," she casually said as she passed.

I was unable to reply, but still, she only beat me by fifty yards. It was my best showing ever. My grinning Li'l Freckles was waiting for me with open arms. She realized that she would be swamped in my sweat. She had never done this before. I collapsed in her arms, pulling her to the ground as I gasped for breath. She laughed as she kissed me and I rolled us over to allow my precious Layla escape from my constant rain of dripping sweat.

"Wow Popi, you almost beat me. If you live, you can brag about it, but now you've taught me that I need to up my game. Don't expect this to ever happen again."

Finally able to speak, I said, "Li'l Freckles, you might as well take up another sport. I'm going to leave you in my dust by Thanksgiving Day." Layla gave me a seriously sexy kiss.

"Good luck with that Popi." She lifted her shirt and rubbed her perfect breasts across my mouth.

I, of course, began kissing and kneading them. Layla had gotten me again. She hummed in appreciation and put her hand on my once baggy shorts. We began to get carried away before Layla moaned.

"We are out in the open, someone will see."

I looked around. She was right. I had to be strong, so I picked her up and carried her into the woods, to our bridge. I sat down on the wooden span and Layla took over, coaxing me to lie down. She pulled down my shorts and removed her own. She eased Big Popi through the gates of heaven and dazzled me with her riding skills while providing me with plenty of violent kisses as I tried to tame her wildly undulating breasts. After an exciting finale, we lay connected and talked sweetly about our wonderful love for each other. We almost fell to sleep in our embrace, but reluctantly separated when the brisk fall morning chill overtook our exercise and love created body heat. Hand in hand, we began heading to our room to wash off the runnin' and the lovin'.

It's been like this since July. Layla not only fell in love with me again, she fell in love with making love. Her eighteen year dry spell was over and her newly reawakened desires are killing me. So far, I've been keeping up, just barely. Layla has always enjoyed love making. She is a natural and truthfully, I could never tire of her, but physically, a man needs to recharge occasionally. I could almost hear the Colonel, my Dad.

"Soldier on Gyrene. You can rest in your next life."

# THE GREAT ESCAPE

Ever since Popi began writing our story, I've been adding my side to his exciting tales. It still makes me laugh when his publisher insists we label them novels even though, as far as I know, every word is true. Popi insisted that I write this part because the incredible story starts on an auspicious occasion. It was the first and only time that Popi almost beat me at our five mile morning run. I beat him by fifty meters, but this was the first time he was within two hundred and I've vowed it to be the last.

Anyway, this high holyday for Popi will always be remembered because of another remarkable occurrence. After the run and the exquisite love making in the woods, we walked hand in hand toward our back door. Half way there, we heard the sound of multiple emergency vehicles approaching from town. The two state and two county squad cars were closely followed by the entire local volunteer fire department. The walk to our showers was spent in wild speculation.

Popi said, "Maybe there's a fire at a top secret government doughnut farm."

We showered and dressed. Popi was in his fading old swimsuit and I wore old jeans and a paint spattered white button down dress shirt stolen from Popi. I was painting today. Popi and I walked into the crowded kitchen where most of the occupants were huddled around the small TV eating Claire's delicious pancakes.

Jordon said, "Popi, come watch. There are hundreds of wild animals on the loose."

I was not offended at my exclusion in the invitation. I've become inured to the common snub. When we walked into a room together, Layla's Angels, Kelly, Brooke, Charlie and Jordon, especially Jordon, saw only their Popi.

Popi got his ancient US Marine Corp cup, filled it with black bitter coffee and melted in tightly with the perky teases. I wasn't jealous. I had given the girls Carte Blanc to flirt with my husband. I got the breaking news from Claire as she added blueberries to my order. Apparently, about fifteen miles west of here, there lived a rich hermit with an illegal zoo which specialized in exotic predators, poisonous or deadly reptiles, insects, spiders and scorpions.

He had breeding pairs of Bengal tigers, African lions, Snow leopards, Grizzly bears, Gray wolves and jackals. The outlaw collector also had a single male eight hundred pound Siberian tiger. The newsman speculated that the hermit was tipped off to an impending raid, so he did the only reasonable thing that came to his damaged mind. He set his damning evidence free to roam the countryside.

By lunch time, the humorous story turned tragic. The local news had a cell phone video which started off with some fourteen year old boys tossing a football. A cute blonde kid ran out for a long pass. While the perfect pass was in the air, a pack of large dogs entered the frame from the left. Dogs, boy and ball arrived, same place same time. The boy caught the ball and was immediately mauled by the pack, which was led by two huge gray wolves. The boy was not expected to live.

Popi, of course was horrified as were we all, but Popi took it the hardest. He called Ski and asked him to make contact with the police and offer our assistance in capturing the wild beasts. Popi called a meeting of everyone on the property after sending Stump to town to buy rifles, shotguns and ammo. We met in the dining room and sat at the thirty seat mahogany table. Popi asked for quiet which was instantly granted and began his mission briefing. Popi is at his sexiest when he's preparing for battle.

"We've been informed that some federal agency has taken over the job of protecting the public from these wild animals so essentially we're on our own. Ski has told me that the feds won't try to capture the beasts, but have ordered their men to shoot them on sight."

We girls, in a choral complaint said, "Aw."

"There is nothing we can do about that, but we must be prepared to defend ourselves."

Popi, with firm, but tender words, then took away many of our personal freedoms. Nobody, especially us girls, was permitted to go outside without an armed escort and Layla's Petites personnel would be escorted to and from their cars every day. Ski brought in extra security, men with hunting experience. The security office, with its eyes from twenty outdoor cameras, would be manned twenty-four seven. The cameras all had infrared capability, from which the warm blooded animals couldn't hide.

For the next few days, we all watched the developments in the bizarre story unfold on TV. They even showed clips of some of the various animals being slaughtered. Since I couldn't get my morning run in all week, I got my exercise at night in bed with Popi. I was well aware that I was taxing his considerable romantic abilities, but it couldn't be helped. Since returning from eighteen celibate years in the eighth realm, I crave sex all day every day. So far, Popi and Big Popi have responded admirably to every call to duty. Anyway, I think Popi is secretly having the time of his life. I know I am.

With the weekend approaching, the list of marauding man eaters grew shorter every day. Friday morning we watched in horror as the two Bengal tigers were assassinated on live TV. Saturday afternoon we learned that the last of the large predators, the two gray wolves, were shot by a chicken farmer eighty miles north of here.

"Popi does this mean we can run tomorrow?" Her excitement set her pretty eyes aglow.

He reminded me that the initial reports said that there was a lone male eight hundred pound Siberian tiger which hadn't been checked off the list.

Popi called the local sheriff and asked about the man-eating discrepancy. The sheriff told us that the Feds had assured him that the beast had been sold a week before the mass escape. I could tell that Popi was a bit skeptical, but when confronted with all ten of the females in the house, he relented and lifted martial law. Popi wanted to keep the extra security for a few days, but tomorrow we could run.

# 2014; Winning Isn't Everything

I was worried about that Siberian tiger. I knew that the reporter didn't invent the big cat because the feds acknowledged its' existence. Against my better judgment, perhaps foolishly trusting the Feds, I okayed a return to our far from normal lives.

After the announcement, Layla asked, "Is something wrong Popi?" I lied.

"No darlin', I was just thinking. Will you still love me when you can no longer outrun me?"

"Of course I will." It took a second for my trusting bride to get my taunt.

That night in bed, Layla pretended to be miffed and was giving me the silent treatment. I pretended not to notice, knowing how much she hated this. I climbed under the quilt and kissed my li'l Freckles.

I said, "G'night sweetheart, sweet dreams."

I lay down with my back to my silent angel and closed my eyes for a peaceful nights' sleep. After a minute, she turned me onto my back and body-slammed me.

"I'm onto your plan Popi. You can't weasel out of your husbandly duties by making me mad." There was a hint of amusement on her stern countenance.

She kissed me hard on my mouth, biting my lip. I released a long, breezy, melodramatic sigh and proceeded to ravish my bride like she deserved to be ravished. Just as Big Popi completed his mission, the growl commenced. No, it wasn't a Siberian tiger, but something equally rare and special. She was experiencing Growler # 10 and her spirit was on her way to the sixth realm to visit her angelic boyfriend Michael. My dainty bride ceased her animalistic growl and went completely limp. She instantly acquired an angelic smile. I smiled too, as I waited for her spirit to return, fifteen minutes or so, hence.

# GROWLER # 10

Dear Popi,

I will apologize in advance for not showing this letter to you until long after my trip. It is because it contains a secret that I don't want you to know just yet. It has been only a few months since you sent me to six, but it feels like eighteen years to me since I've seen my friend Michael. When I arrived, I lay still for a couple of minutes, recovering from your perfect love. I know that I have been very demanding of you lately and you have responded admirably, never once leaving me unfulfilled.

I also know how badly you want to beat me in our runs. You will have to earn it with training and hard work instead of tricks and taunts. Your competitive nature and my stubbornness cancel each other so it all comes down to talent and tenacity. Good luck Popi.

As I lay on my soft white couch, I knew that Michael would be grinning at me in response to my obviously intense pleasure. I finally opened my eyes and was disappointed by the concern on Michael's face.

"Michael, what's wrong? You look worried." I walked to his couch.

"Layla, I've been going nuts with worry about you. I was about to go off the reservation and visit you in your dreams tonight."

I climbed onto my dear friends' lap and kissed him on his cheek, deftly avoiding his physical reaction to my peculiar spell.

"Layla, I'm worried because there's another savage killer after you. This time the killer isn't evil, in fact, he's very good." Michael hugged me and touched his lips to me hair.

"Let me guess, an eight hundred pound male Siberian tiger." He was astonished.

"How did you know?"

"Popi thought there might be a tiger unaccounted for. See, I'm very well protected." Michael smiled.

"Layla, that cat is getting very close to your property."

With a 3D image appearing in the pink and gray streaked air, Michael showed me the tiger prowling through the woods. He was so beautifully frightening.

"You need to call the authorities."

"No I can't do that. I won't be a part of the slaughter of those rare, beautiful creatures." I was worried that he would insist.

Michael seemed to be distressed by my forced, manipulative tears. Men are such suckers for those tiny drops of saltwater and Michael, one of the ten thousand who protect the seven realms, was no different in this regard.

"At least promise me that you'll tell Popi." The poor man was bargaining now.

I made the promise without specifying the timing of the dropped dime. What kind of woman lies to her best friend? Yet I'm unashamed because I'm not lying for myself. I was trying to create something positive from the immoral slaughter of innocent creatures. Fortunately, I had a sure-fire subject changer that was guaranteed to seduce Michael into forgetting about my tiger.

"Michael, I got to travel to two different realms a few weeks ago, the eighth and the seventh." He was startled silent.

I told my story of the One and my visit to his home. He was unaware of my eighteen year exile in a realm, of which he'd never heard. I told him about Leopold Bosch, my lonely life before him and my attempts to change our fates. I felt the once familiar tug of my body.

I was anxious to be back with you, Popi, because I was seriously craving sex again. I know it sounds wicked, but I can't get enough of feeling worshiped and nobody could ever worship me like you.

I had just enough time to ease my friends' mind.

"The One, Dusty, told me that he forgives you and the others for your unauthorized assistance in helping to protect me." I said this playfully, but he took it more seriously.

He hugged me tightly again and uncharacteristically whined.

"You call him by his first name?"

Before I could answer, I blinked back into your protective arms. I twisted those arms and forced you to please me again. Thank you.

Popi, please forgive me for withholding important information. I was afraid that you would put my safety above saving the tigers' life.

I love you my dear, brave Popi
PS; You need a bigger rock

# 2014; LAYLA'S NEW FAN

Layla did return. I pretended to sleep, but she sniffed out my subterfuge. We made slow passionate love. We snuggled closely and went to sleep with smiles on our faces. Layla woke me at six. She was already dressed in her running clothes, very short shorts and an I Heart Popi T-shirt with the sleeves cut off. I jumped out of bed.

"Is my Li'l Freckles anxious to run?" I was amused by her impatience.

I hugged her and she sneaked in a kiss to my cheek. She instantly felt for the spellbound Big Popi. I grabbed her dainty hand.

"Oh no you don't, you've weakened my legs enough already."

I brushed my teeth and dressed in basketball shorts with a white tank top. Layla was stretching.

"I'm going down for a cup of coffee. Are you coming sweetheart?"

"No Popi, I'm going to do some extra stretching to make sure that your new secret plan doesn't work." My angel was smugly grinning.

I guiltily said, "I have no idea what you are talking about," and sauntered out.

I don't know how in hell the minx figured out that I had been secretly training all week. I walked into the large kitchen in my silent five hundred dollar running shoes and approached the sole occupant. Claire, my beautiful ex-wife was there with her back to me, so my lips were on her neck and my hands were on her large round breasts before she realized that she was not alone.

"Walter, stop." She giggled. "Layla will catch you and scratch your eyes out."

I spun her around.

"Mon Amie, you are so beautiful. This BP&LF thing has run its' course. Run away with me."

I pulled her close with my left arm and as she began to speak. I tickled her ribs with my right. Claire's unwelcome and uncontrollable giggling stopped instantly when I planted a lingering kiss on her pretty lips. I broke the kiss.

I casually asked, "Coffee ready honey?" Her smirk was accompanied by rosy cheeked embarrassment.

"Yes, Casanova, have a seat and keep your gropes to yourself."

Claire, still with rosy cheeks, brought my mug just as Layla walked in. She, as usual, came in talking.

"Good morning Claire," Layla paused for a short second. "Has Popi been pawing you again?"

Layla turned and waited for me to defend myself. I did.

"Li'l Freckles, you're so tall. I think you may have over stretched."

Laya deflected my deflection without losing her patience, like a loving mother smiling while admonishing a mildly retarded child.

"Popi dear, Claire is a valued employee of Layla's Petites and has a constitutional right to have a safe workplace free of a hostile environment and sexual harassment." Claire nervously smiled. Layla was stern. "I think you need to take some professional sensitivity training."

"How about this, we make a little wager on todays' run. If you win, I'll take your God forsaken hippie training, but if you lose, I can flirt with Claire as much as I please." I held out my hand to Layla. "Do we have a deal?"

Claire said, "Hold on here."

Layla said, "Deal," and we shook on it, ignoring my ex-wife's protests.

We walked out the back door hand in hand. We were laughing at the absurdity of the scene especially the confused look on Claire's pretty face.

"Popi, you shouldn't tease Claire like that. She's lonely."

"Oh, I'm not teasing. I fully intend to collect on that wager. Besides, Claire needs to be reminded how beautiful and special she is. I think she only worries that you may find it inappropriate."

Layla was deep in thought for a few seconds.

"Okay Popi I believe you. For Claire's sake you better win." Then after a brief pause, she said, "Not!"

We started out at Layla's measured pace. She chatted, but I remained silent, focused on my breathing. When she stepped it up in the middle of the first lap, I followed. In the middle of mile two, I made my first move. I stretched out my stride and I was gaining a few inches with every step.

Layla helpfully said, "If you go too fast, it'll burn you out."

By the time we started the third mile, I was a hundred yards ahead, but I wasn't satisfied. I sprinted until I doubled my lead. I geared down and held that lead throughout the third and fourth mile.

I was elated. Don't get me wrong, I was tired, extremely tired, but I felt victory within my grasp. I crossed in front of the pool, the start line, and turned east to begin the final lap. I looked back. Layla had not exited the woods yet. She was still over two hundred yards behind. Layla exited the wood as I watched. When I was sure she was watching I began stretching out my stride again. I attempted to look as fresh as a daisy with unlimited energy. This was far from the truth, but propaganda can be demoralizing to an enemy.

Halfway through the lap, the course is at its highest point. After I crested the hill and began down the long gentle slope to the west bridge. I looked to my left and saw Layla approaching the summit. She was less than two hundred yards behind, but she would be running uphill for a bit. I was no longer concentrating on my breathing because all I could muster was a wheezing gasping pant. I was stumbling down the hill like a drunk in a hurry. I hit the bridge awkwardly and had to pull off a forward tuck and roll. I miraculously landed on my feet in full stride.

I was soon out of the woods, at least literally, with only two hundred yards to go. My mind was elated though my body was too exhausted to show such things. I was afraid to look back, for fear of seeing Layla poised to fly effortlessly by me. That didn't happen and I fell to the grass at the finish line. I found the energy to roll onto my side, I could watch my dejected wife lose. I was gasping for air.

I waited and fought for breath, unable to even think of standing. After a minute or so, I began to make up reasons for Layla's tardiness. Maybe she is ashamed and went straight to the house. That didn't sound like her. After another minute, I knew something was seriously wrong. I got unsteadily to my feet and began to jog toward the woods. My rubbery legs were burning. Soon, I was actually running. I was breathing in deep measured gasps. I stormed across the wooden span and saw her.

Layla was about two hundred feet up the hill with her back plastered to an ancient walnut tree. I couldn't understand the look of abject fear on her pretty freckled face until the object of her fear walked onto the running path. It was the size of a Toyota and just as foreign to these parts. The eight hundred pound Siberian tiger was walking toward Layla. It was completely focused on my beautiful, terrified wife. I somehow broke into a desperate sprint and threw my body, shoulder first, at the beasts' right shoulder. I bounced off the tiger, but at least I got his attention away from Layla. The tiger looked at me and roared, nearly causing me to empty my bladder.

I held my water and yelled, "Run!"

I stood and faced the nightmare, wondering if I could make it to the creek. Most cats despise water. The cat struck. He hit me with his lightning fast, catchers' mitt sized paw. I flew ten feet and landed in a small ditch with the air knocked out of my already burning lungs. While still grunting for breath, I saw that the tiger had already forgotten about me. He was slowly, even sensuously, walking back to

Layla who hadn't moved an inch. He obviously preferred her sweet tender flesh to my grizzled old carcass.

I forced my way to my feet and looked around for a handy weapon. I knew that anything short of a large bore firearm would prove to be ineffective. I picked up a grapefruit sized rock and staggered my way back onto the path. The ferocious cat had reached his frozen in fear dinner and was sniffing her feet. He moved his massive head up her legs, sniffing all the way.

When the tiger sniffed his way to Layla's running shorts, he lingered. I continued plodding and she continued to shiver. Each of us was playing our part in this tragic opera. He smelled her flat belly and her quivering chest and finally he was face to face with my angel. The Russian cat touched his frightening mouth to Layla's and she emitted a small squeal. The moment their faces touched, it became apparent that the huge cat was under Layla's spell.

The tiger glared at me. He was unimpressed with my choice of weapon. He turned his attention back to my terrified wife and with his huge pink tongue he licked my Li'l Freckles from her feet to her hairline. I attacked. This time, it was I who roared. I charged the great cat with the rock poised above my head. The eight hundred pound Siberian licked my wife's face one last time and slowly sauntered into the woods. I watched him go. He didn't look back, but I could feel his other senses probing me.

I awoke from my stupor and dropped the rock. I turned to Layla who lay crumpled on the ground in a faint. I scooped her up, but I refrained from kissing her. Slowly and unsteadily, I began plodding homeward. Why didn't I kiss her, you ask? I didn't want to waste any of my oxygen starved blood on Big Popi. Such is my charmed life.

Being only six-thirty on a Sunday morning, the kitchen wasn't crowded. I carried my precious burden into the brightly lit room. Claire was cooking, Ski and Rebecca were having coffee and Gabrielle and Michael were having juice and cereal. Stump was there too. All eyes turned to us.

# 2035; A Graying Superhero

I walked into the kitchen with Layla cradled in my shaky arms. She was still unconscious. I was emotionally and physically drained, knowing not what to do or say. I felt dizzy, so I handed my sweetheart to the stocky stalwart, Stump.

"You okay Mr. L?"

I said, "Yes," and fell to the floor.

I attempted to stand, but I soon surrendered to the somnolent chorus calling for me. It was beautiful, and succumbing to the insistent choir felt right. Following the calling voices was not so much a decision as a summoning, irresistible in its' righteous hum.

I was in a hazy limbo for a few seconds, but soon the veil lifted and everything was back to normal. I was at the pool, the outdoor pool, reclining on a lounge chair with a cold beer to my lips. I drained the green bottle and set it on the table. From the back door, as if she'd read my mind, Layla spoke.

"Popi are you ready for another beer?"

"Does Popi love his Li'l Freckles?"

I was swamped with a wave of déjà vu. I had been in this scene before and knew what was coming next, Layla's kiss, Big Popi's cue and a joint, the spell is unbroken. It all happened as predicted. I almost asked what year it was, but decided to hold my tongue. I don't know why, but I was worried about upsetting dream Layla. It felt important. As I said, I'd been here before, some four years ago on the night I proposed to Layla. The dream that night was just a dream, but I had used it as an omen to justify dangerous brain surgery. Now it seems as though it was a dream of a future dream. Oh well, I might as well let it play out because I certainly wasn't prepared to wake up yet.

I looked down at my chest and saw the expected gray chest hair and the, the past is not forgotten brand was right where it should be. I also checked the ugly untreated bullet wound on my upper left chest. It was almost invisible. I spotted the paper lying on the deck. I picked it up and looked at my father's watch on my left wrist. I read the date on the newspaper which was made from some unknown substance, not paper. It was one-fifty-two on June eleventh 2035, almost twenty-one years from when I awoke this morning.

I was seventy-two years old and was a bit surprised that Layla and I had made it to our golden years, as they say in laxative commercials. I should say my golden years because Layla is only forty-three in this dream. She didn't look a day over thirty. I was eager to see what I looked like. Though my chest hair was gray, my abs seemed to be well defined and I did feel quite strong. I finished my beer, a Heineken of course, and stood, which provided another hint. Getting up was effortless.

I walked into the kitchen and approached Layla. She was at the stove cooking and singing an unrecognized song in her sweet quiet voice. I walked up behind her and cupped her small, though not as small as in the waking world, breasts. She wrapped my hands in hers and pulled mine tightly to her as she tilted her head back to receive my upside down kiss.

"Li'l Freckles, I love you more today than I did on the day I proposed to you in your little girl's bedroom a hundred years ago."

After another kiss, she hummed in appreciation.

"And after a hundred years, you are still the cutest boy in the seven realms." Her smile was golden.

"Aw shucks ma'am, you're only sayin' that 'cause it's true," said my terrible John Wayne. "Li'l Freckles, what's on our agenda for today?" Layla spun around in my arms and tilted her quizzical eyes up to meet mine.

"Popi, is something wrong? We talked about this just this morning at breakfast. You are not getting out of our trip to Tunguska."

"Of course not kitten. Wherever you are, that's where I'll be. I just wanted to make sure that you had the agenda right."

What I said and what I was thinking were not identical. I thought, where the hell is Tunguska and why in hell must we go there? Layla looked dubious about my pop audit of her planning skills, but she played the game anyway.

"Okay Popi, for the last time, tonight at nine, we take the Wave to Cincinnati. At nine twenty we board the Pulse to Moscow for a midnight arrival, Cincinnati time. We sleep until noon Moscow time, and have lunch with Tigers International at two-thirty. We have a dinner and reception at the Kremlin with President Ustinov at ten." She paused to breathe.

"After breakfast, we take a three hour conventional flight to Vanavara in the Tunguska region. The various events last all day then the real work begins when we head into the forest. We'll camp for two nights at the Tigers International Siberian base camp. The trip home is the exact reverse. Do you have any questions, comments or criticisms?"

I had gleaned a great deal of intelligence from the cute, concise briefing, not least of all, Tunguska is in Russia. I don't like Russians. I also caught the reference to tigers. This was not a coincidence, I presumed.

I considered my next words carefully lest Layla learn that this life is but a dream. I felt that as soon as she realized that she wasn't real, she would disappear and I would have to awaken.

"I only have one question. What's cookin' good lookin', why the early dinner?" Layla was perplexed.

She knew that something was up, but decided to leave it alone for now.

"Not early dinner, late lunch which means we'll have a late dinner because there is no food allowed on the Pulse. Now what was it that your sainted first wife would say? Oh yeah, get the hell out of my kitchen."

I headed upstairs, anxious to depart before I tripped up again. She called Claire sainted. Does she mean that Claire is dead? I dared not ask. In my room, things were essentially the same except for the rugs on the floor and the artwork on the walls. The once blank ten foot long wall between Layla's and my bathroom doors was nearly covered in framed photos of Layla posing cheek to cheek with male tigers. I was there too, but I was touching Layla without touching the cats. She hugged and kissed them like they were her favorite tabbies. Our luggage was all packed, lined up, tagged and ready to go. How was I going to fake that I know what is going on?

I walked into my bathroom. The sink and shower were both recognizable as to their function, but the third Item didn't look like a toilet.

It was a square glossy white box on a raised platform with no controls or instructions. I studied the device from three sides, seeing no pipes or wires. When I stepped onto the six inch high platform, the thing moved, startling me and causing me to step down. I could see the headlines in the not paper.

"Ancient superhero, Popi, dies in toilet incident."

I furtively stepped back up to the menacing head. The glossy top, or part of it, popped silently up, creating an eight inch wide and twelve inch high slot, the urinal I supposed. I wondered how it knew which number, one or two. My question was answered when I turned around. I looked into the bowl and found that there was no water.

I disrobed and looked at my reflection in the large mirror. I thought, not bad for seventy-two. I didn't need a scale to know that I'd lost a bit of my former one-eighty. My hair was mostly gray on the sides, but not thinning on top as had been my dad's. My eyebrows were gray and wildly out of control. I was surprised that Layla put up with that. I looked to be in tip top shape.

I managed to use the facilities, shave and shower, all without the benefit of toilet tissue, soap, shampoo, bath towel or razor. I have to admit, it was a pleasant adventure. Clean and dry, I went to my closet to pick my traveling clothes. I was happy to find that my tastes hadn't change much though some of the materials felt different, not bad, just different. I dressed in casual black jeans, a tight black Cashmere sweater and faux alligator loafers with dark Argyle socks.

When I unrolled the socks, a small key fell to the floor. It was my lockbox key. I went back to the closet and retrieved the gray steel, fireproof safe. I wondered if I was still sending my sweetheart growling to the sixth realm to visit her angelic boyfriend Michael. In the waking world, we were up to Growler #10, due out any day now. If the rate has remained steady, I estimated that we should be up to Growler #80. Shaking the box, it didn't feel like that many. I was about to find and read Growler #10 when Layla called my phone.

"Popi, lunch is ready."

"I'll be right down, sweetheart."

The top letter had Growler # 74 written in Layla's artistic hand. I located #10. Strangely, it was sealed, although it was written twenty plus years ago. Apparently, I had never read it. Since it was written just today, waking today that is, I should have read it at some point in the intervening years. I was dreaming now so maybe whatever I read in the letter will have been created in my mind. I read it anyway and was angry with Layla for not telling me. She had risked her life and mine. I decided that I wouldn't take my anger out on dream Layla. I'd be back with waking Layla soon enough. I really wanted to find out what the hell were the Wave and the Pulse. Not to mention, what the hell is in Tunguska?

# 2014; Outrun

The cocky son-of-a-bitch just might beat me. I looked through the woods at Popi stumbling down the hill. I was trying to maintain my routine. I crested the hill just in time to see Popi trip on the bridge. I evilly laughed, thinking here is my chance to catch him. Instead, I was disappointed at his gymnastic recovery. I poured it on at my usual spot, about one hundred meters from the bridge. There was still a chance to win if Popi hit the wall.

When I was almost to the bridge, the tiger stepped into my path. I panicked and ran to my left without looking. I was unable to tear my eyes away from the gigantic beast and the tigers' eyes were hungrily locked onto me. I ran smack into a tree and turned to face my molester. I tried to sink into the rough solid bark. My fear was complete. I could not scream or move. I had thought that I was not afraid of death after facing the Wraith several times, but I was wrong. The thought of dying like this had me paralyzed.

The tiger took his time. He approached me in a slow circular arc. He left the path for a minute and just sat and stared. I could hear a low rumble coming from the cat. I hoped it wasn't from hunger. He stood. I had a thought which causes me shame to this day. Maybe Popi will come and save me. The only way that could happen would be if he sacrificed his life for mine. Even in my petrified mind, I refused to let that happen because my sanctimonious refusal to tell Popi the truth had set up this frightful feast.

The tiger stood and slowly stepped closer. I continued to shiver and felt myself drifting into a self-defensive faint. My swoon was delayed by my Popi, who appeared out of nowhere and body-slammed the huge cat. The beast didn't budge an inch, but Popi bounced off and hit the ground.

Popi stood and hollered, "Run," just before the tiger roared. The tiger, with his massive right paw, slapped him on his chest.

I started to faint again. I had the terrifying thought that the man, who I love and respect more than anyone, had just been sliced to ribbons, was thrown ten feet and was bleeding to death in the ditch.

The tiger immediately forgot about Popi and finished his approach. He was sniffing my feet. I was still frozen as the tiger sniffed his way slowly up my legs. When he reached my running shorts, he lingered. In my periphery, I saw a wonderful sight. It was Popi and he wasn't dead yet. He had a big rock in his hand and was limping back to the battle. The cat glanced at him and seemed unimpressed by the puny threat. Then the cat kissed my mouth.

The horrible beast sniffed all the way back to my feet. Popi was still five feet away with the rock wielded above his head. The tiger lowered his gigantic head and, with his rough, long wet tongue, licked me from my White Nikes' to my fearful face. Popi roared and I mercifully passed out.

I awoke with a scream, thinking I was being mauled by the tiger. I struggled in Stump's strong protective arms, so he held me closer.

He whispered, "Its' okay sweetheart, you're safe now."

"Where's Popi?" I was still shaking.

Stump, still in whispers, said, "He's here, taking a nap on the floor."

I coaxed my dear friend to put me down, knowing he didn't want to. Everyone else in the household, including five year old Michael, was gathered around Popi. I squeezed my way through the worried crowd and took my husbands' head off of Claire's lap and wrapped him into my arms. I kissed his face, every square inch.

"Popi I'm so sorry."

Claire asked, "Layla what happened out there?"

"Kurt, arm the guards and keep everyone inside. There is still one tiger loose. Don't call the authorities. Don't tell anyone."

"But Layla, what if it kills somebody?"

"He could have killed me and Popi, but he didn't, so we're going to capture him alive."

# 2014; Poor Man's Ambulance

I awoke. I was in a hospital bed. A trio of nurses was busily yet needlessly fussing with my blanket, smoothing and tucking.

When I said, "Hello ladies," one actually squealed. "Don't worry, my medical minxes, there is plenty of me to go around." I'm sure my amusement shone in my eyes.

The spokes-minx, a cute forty something bottle blonde, spoke.

"Mr. Lemon, did that skinny little wife of yours take a five iron to you or did you just have another encounter with a maniac in a garbage truck?"

"No sweetheart, it was just a small accident. Is Layla here?"

"We haven't seen her all morning, but two of your daughters are here. Should we show them in?" She was the youngest and cutest of the blanket smoothers?

"No, I'll go to them." I began to rise.

There was a small protest, but I didn't have to say a word. I think it was my impatient frown or perhaps my rugged good looks. My three Florence Nightingales showed what they really wanted when I carefully dressed in front of them. My ribs were heavily taped, but it only hurt when I made quick movements. They each had a clipboard with a blank paper. The spokes-minx explained.

"Popi, sign your name here and sign your nickname along with to Carole, with love. Now smile for your official discharge photo."

I supplied the fans needs with good humor and turned to go. I turned back.

"By the way, what's wrong with me?"

The red head who'd not spoken earlier said, "Three fractured ribs and severe dehydration."

"No lacerations?"

"No Popi," they sang in three part harmony.

I went to the waiting room and walked in on Chrissy and Mary, my two youngest daughters. Chrissy, I spoiled rotten for all of her eighteen years, but Layla and I only adopted sixteen year old Mary six months ago after I rescued her from her freakish family.

"Hello ladies. Are you my ride home?"

The girls squealed, "Daddy." They Jumped up and gave me rib squeezing hugs, which I took with only a small grimace.

"Where is Layla? Did she drop me off in the ambulance and take off?"

Chrissy said, "No Daddy. It's much worse than that." Mary completed the demoralizing tale.

"She had Kurt and Robby put you in a sleeping bag and asked us drive you here."

"What, in the back seat of your Jeep?" I was pissed off.

Chrissy said, "No Daddy, it's much worse than that." Mary, again, finished.

"They put you in the bed of your pick up."

"What about the tiger?"

"What tiger?" We drove home in record time.

# 2014; LAYLA'S GRAY RAYS

I felt horrible sending Popi to the hospital with the girls, but it couldn't be helped. I needed the rest of the men and Rebecca to facilitate the capture of the frightening cat. Claire, though she was very worried about Popi, refused to leave. Rebecca convinced a big cat expert from the Cincinnati Zoo to come and help by dropping suggestive hints, leading him to believe that the famous Li'l Freckles' appreciation would know no bounds. If I had to flirt with a creepy cat-man to safely catch my tiger, so be it. I was now thinking of him as my tiger and had secretly named him Czar.

We formulated a good plan, but Kurt thought that it was too dangerous.

"Layla honey, you'll be too exposed. I don't care what Mr. Beefcake cat whisperer says."

Mr. Beefcake was Dr. Thomas Pike, the big cat expert who was about thirty, six-three and looked like Mr. January on a worlds' hottest men calendar.

What he said was, "Siberian tigers almost never attack humans. In their habitat they are revered and are sometimes called the old wise father of the forest." Ski scoffed.

Popi would have swayed Kurt with his commanding presence and concise authoritative orders, but I had no such natural gifts. Instead of giving orders, I used my sneaky womanly guile.

"I understand Kurt. I think I'll be safe enough without you on my six. Robby can handle the shotgun and Stump can do your job with the AR-15."

"Oh no you don't, Squirt. Walter would kick my Polish butt if I wasn't there to protect you." He then said something that made me smile. "Now I know why Walter calls you a minx."

Popi had warned me years ago, that my power over men would go to my head. I think it has. I realized that I would have to make amends for my lies and bad behavior. I hadn't yet written the latest of my tales from the sixth realm, Growler #10, and was considering omitting the part where Michael warns me about my tiger. I didn't want to continue to lie, but I was afraid that Popi would feel betrayed, though I knew he would forgive me. Everyone thinks that I'm some paragon of virtue, but I emit some gray rays too.

Our plan was fairly simple and I was pushing the team to execute it as soon as possible. Before Popi was back? I don't know. We all walked to the west bridge, but only Tommy and I crossed all the way. Yes, I had to flirt a little with the cat expert. He would wield the tranquilizing dart gun from his hidden position on the slope to the stream. Robby would set up on the bridge with the twelve gauge shotgun. His primary duty was to cover our retreat, if necessary. Kurt would be the closest to me, but still on the bridge with the biggest revolver I'd ever seen.

I had the most important job, the bait. Dr. Tom wasn't convinced that my tiger would be attracted to me enough to break cover of the forest, but a few doe eyed glances made him reconsider spraying me with female tiger pee. I walked ten feet from the bridge and spread out my green Big Popi & Li'l Freckles beach towel. I dropped my cotton sun dress, revealing my tiny tiger print bikini, which I designed and made while waiting for Tommy to arrive.

I lay down on my stomach, my eyes pointed at Kurt and Robby. If

Czar showed up, my bare feet and very tiny swimsuit would hopefully, be enough to entice my new pet. We only had to wait twenty or so minutes before Czar made a hesitant appearance.

Kurt whispered, "He's here Squirt. Be ready to run." I'd never seen him so worried.

I said loudly, "Everyone, hold your fire. Don't worry, he would never hurt me."

I don't know why I was so sure. My tiger slowly approached me. I remained still, resisting the urge to peek, until I felt his warm breath on my feet. I rolled onto my back and propped myself up on my elbows.

"Well hello sweetheart. It's nice to see you again." My big smile was real, although I was a bit nervous.

I sat up and faced Czar, thinking, he is so happy to see me. The striped cat walked straight to me and kissed my face. His beautiful head was so big that I couldn't tell for sure, but I think he was aiming for my lips.

I stood, taking Czar's large handsome face and head into my arms. He licked my face. I hugged my tiger and signaled to Tommy to put my poor friend to sleep. Tommy stood and Czar heard him. He roared and leapt toward the supposed expert. Instead of firing the tranq-gun, the bumbling sexy oaf dropped his rifle and slid/fell fifteen feet into the stream.

I ignored Tommy's cries for help. Czar trotted back to me, looking mighty proud for saving me from the great white hunter. I cursed under my breath and went to the bank. I picked up the gun and shot my poor Czar in his hind quarters. Czar roared, out of sadness and betrayal. I cried at his pain and went to him. He kissed me again and fell. I lay down with him, stroking and scratching his magnificent, sad face. This is when I saw the evidence that Czar might be under my spell.

# 2014; The Body Surfer

We drove across the small two lane bridge five hundred yards from our gate.

Mary said, "Daddy stop! Some guy dressed like the Crocodile Hunter is drowning in the creek."

Had it been Chrissy who said this, I would have kept driving, but Mary doesn't joke around. I pulled over and backed the stout Ford to the bridge abutment along the nearly nonexistent, gravely shoulder. We all piled out and went to the rail. We had to cross the road to the downstream side. Sure enough, there indeed was a young man dressed like the Crocodile Hunter drowning in the creek. He was flailing his arms in the four feet deep, rapid stream. He was screaming for help.

I hopped the split rail fence and ran along the bank on the barely defined, little worn foot path. There was pastureland to my right which had me fretting about bulls. I caught up with him in a short time and ran thirty yards past him. I scrabbled down the prickly bank and took a half step into the current. The man redeemed a bit of respect with me when I felt the effect of being only shin-deep in the rushing flow.

I reached out as the large buff panicky man screamed by and

managed to snag the right epaulet on his boy-scout-like shirt. It held and the man was slammed by the current into the rocky bank to my right. The broken man lay in a blubbering heap on the muddy bank. He had been pummeled by rock and branch, so I doubted that he could climb the steep loose bank fifteen feet up the hill.

"You stay here and gather yourself while I get some rope."

"Please don't leave me."

I assured him that I'd be right back and went despite his pleas. Back at the truck, I recruited Mary and Chrissy and grabbed some stout rope from my toolbox. It took all three of us to pull the battered six-three two hundred and twenty pound man out of the gulch.

"How in hell did you end up body surfing in my creek?"

He said, "The tiger, the huge tiger charged me, the tiger, I fell."

It was my turn to panic. I threw the man over the fence, picked him up and threw him into the bed of the truck. I hurried the girls and sped to our gate, honking my horn to alert the guard. We sped up the gravel driveway and across the field. I skidded to a stop when I reached the woods near the west bridge. I debarked and ran to the bridge.

I wasn't prepared for the surreal scene I encountered. Claire and all the other women were on the near side of the creek. Robby and Ski were on the bridge. Robby was armed with a double barreled twelve gauge shotgun and Ski had his S&W fifty caliber five shot Revolver, a tiger stopper. There were only two on the far side of the bridge. Layla was there and she was hugging the other. The eight hundred pound Siberian tiger was either in seventh heaven or drugged unconscious. I, as calmly as I could, approached my unaware wife and her new friend.

"Li'l Freckles, please move away from the tiger." My wife's eyes lit up.

"Popi, I'm so glad you're back. His name is Czar and we captured him."

"Did everyone make it, Lance Corporal Li'l Freckles? Is your squad intact?" She looked at me quizzically.

"Yes sir Gunny, all present and accounted for, sir." This was accompanied by a crisp salute which I instinctively returned.

"Are you sure about that, Buck Private Li'l Freckles?" Layla's face shifted gears.

"Oh no, Dr. Tommy fell into the stream. Kurt, will you check on Dr. Beefcake?"

Dr. Beefcake, this had to be a Ski-ism. I held up my left fist in the internationally accepted signal for, stop following the silly girls' orders while I school my deceitful bride.

"Don't worry Li'l Freckles. I fished the drowning kid out of the creek half a mile downstream. How long will your new boyfriend be out?"

"I don't know Popi."

"Well then it's a good thing that I didn't let your expert die."

Just then, as if on cue, the good doctor sauntered across the bridge shirtless. He looked like and had the strut of an NFL tight end. He projected confidence with a swagger and attitude that he could never back up with action. He did look quite good playing the part. The expert walked straight to me and offered me his hand, which I shook.

"I just want to say again, thank you Mr. Lemon."

"You're welcome. How long will the cat be out?"

"How long since he was injected?" I detected a trace of fear.

Ski said, "About one minute after you panicked and went overboard, Dr. Beefcake."

"I did not panic, I slipped." He was insulted by Ski's assertion.

I said, "Okay fellas, Tom, how long?" He was suddenly nervous again.

"He'll be awake any minute now. I need my bag, but I lost it when I fell."

I glanced at Robby, who wordlessly began fulfilling my unspoken request. He went to where Tom hit the drink.

"It's halfway down. Give me a minute."

Tom turned a bit green when my son scrambled down to retrieved his bag. Nonetheless he quickly filled a hypodermic needle, approached the sleeping beast and was about to administer the drug when the tiger moved. The timid tough guy dropped the drugs and jumped back.

I said my normal, "Oh shit," but Layla ran to her new boyfriend, picked up the syringe and dosed the cat. She looked at me.

"I can't believe I flirted with that joker to get his help."

Tom was of some help when he called in a crew from the zoo to extract the majestic Czar, Layla's name for her dear kitty.

At dinner, meat loaf and mashed potatoes, I made some things clear to the occupants of my mansion. First and most importantly, that I had soundly beaten Li'l Freckles at our five mile run. Layla had the sense not to argue.

"Secondly, if any of my friends or family ever again aid in putting my wife in danger, they will not be welcome here." Ski, Layla, Rebecca and Robby all failed to make eye contact.

Layla asked,"

Do you forgive us Popi?" She was cute in her contrition.

"Robby is easy to forgive. He's in love with you. I know from personal experience, that kind of love can make you do stupid things. I'm sure you manipulated Ski by pretending that you didn't need him. Rebecca and Claire though, you should have known better. How could you believe that sending me to the hospital with two boy crazy teens was the right thing to do?"

Rebecca said, "I'm sorry, Popi, it'll never happen again." Her love for me showed in her blue eyes.

I bought Claire's excuse. "I wasn't about to leave while Robby was parading around with a big loaded shotgun."

Layla asked, "What about me Popi? Do you forgive me too?"

"Yes, I forgive you for catching the tiger, but for lying to me, I don't know." She looked worried.

"But Popi, what lie did I tell?"

"We'll talk about this in private."

After dinner, I retired to my den and put on some Stones records. I listened and sipped some fine old Scotch while I pondered her punishment. I had already figured out her motives. She felt helpless being unable to protect those escaped animals, but we all felt that. It was not a good excuse for putting us all in danger. Still, I was proud of her. Don't get me wrong, I had already forgiven Layla and would forgive her almost anything, but I felt that if I gave her a free pass, she mightn't learn from this experience. I needed something that would hurt, but not leave any telltale bruises, marks or resentment.

Though my favorite rock band failed to inspire me, I remembered something told to me by the Colonel, my dad. I was fifteen and he had caught me in a lie. I'd told him that I had to go to the Library to work on a paper, but I actually went there to meet my new girlfriend with plans to lose our virginity. Christina's dad called the Colonel looking for his daughter. When dad went to his staff car, a 1949 De Soto, so he could drive around to look for us, he found us in the back seat naked and poised for the big terrifying act. As was usual, dad connected my dishonesty to his beloved Marine Corp.

"Lance Corporal Walter, men in combat will follow a leader, who they respect, to hell and back. Once that contract is broken, he will never effectively lead them again. It is better to tell them that tomorrow we die than it is to blow smoke up their butts by saying it will be a walk in the park."

He sentenced me to one weekend in the brig on bread and water and three weeks confined to the base, effectively delaying my first time by a month or so. While reliving this thirty-six year old memory, I came up with the perfect punishment for my dear deceptive wife.

I finished my Scotch and headed for bed and an uncomfortable talk with Layla. When I got to my room, Layla wasn't there. It was only a bit after ten, so I removed the white tape from my sore ribs. I got into the shower and dressed for bed. I usually just slept in my boxers, but tonight I wore some pjs that Claire bought for me last Christmas. They were black satin and had the Stones logo on the right breast. Mick Jagger I'm not, but the night clothes were to send a message. I lay on the bed under the light blanket and turned out the lights, planning my speech.

Layla entered and rustled around in her closet before going to her shower. I was nodding off when she finally emerged. Layla turned on the light on her nightstand. When I rolled over, I saw why. She was dressed for bed, but not for sleep, in an ultra-sheer pink teddy. I could see every detail of her gorgeous body through the wispy fabric. Layla climbed onto the bed and onto me. She threw back the covers.

"Popi, why are you wearing that?" She sounded a bit nervous.

I answered her question with one of my own.

"Why are you wearing that?"

"I want you to forgive me for catching Czar without you." Layla kissed me and I kissed her back. The spell was unbroken.

"I do forgive you for that, but you knew in advance that Czar was loose and you didn't warn me. You risked all of our lives to get what you wanted." My sternness was an act.

"What makes you say that? I wouldn't risk your life for anything," said my lying angel.

"Are you going to continue lying to me? I thought you loved me more than that." Layla seemed confused or conflicted.

"I don't know how you know what you think you know, but surely you trust me enough to believe me over any other source."

"I do trust you, but I've noticed that you, my Li'l Freckles, have not denied my allegation. There is one sure way to convince me. Show me Growler #10."

# 2014; LAYLA'S SENTENCE

Popi never doubts me, but this time he acted as if he had some inside information proving my guilt. I don't like deceiving him and had made a promise to myself. I'll not lie to him again regarding this matter. Though I wouldn't lie, there were other ways to tame this tiger. I borrowed some sexy pink naughty sleepwear from Kelly. Our figures were nearly identical. I went to our bedroom and saw that Popi was under the quilt, good. I took a shower to wash off this crazy day. I blow dried my hair, something I rarely do, and put on the seductive battle gear.

I exited my bath and sensuously walked to the bed only to discover that Popi had his back to me. I turned on my lamp and he turned over staring lustfully at me. I threw back the covers, revealing his pajamas. Popi never wears pajamas. What is he trying, in his cute subtle way, to tell me?

He asked, "Why are you wearing that?"

I told him that I was looking for forgiveness. He said he had already forgiven me for catching Czar without him. I heard the unspoken but. He then proceeded to accused me of knowing in advance that the tiger was loose and nearby. Although Popi's suspicions were true, it really chafed me that he pretended to be so sure of his theory. I promised not to lie, but I wasn't going to let him bluff me into admitting to something that he couldn't possibly know much less prove. I told him that he should trust me over anyone, but he countered.

"Show me Growler #10." I told him that it wasn't written yet. "I love you so much sweetheart, so it is with great sadness that I sentence you to two days without love making."

He knew how much this would hurt me. I was craving sex all the time. Although I was very angry with him, I had never desired my Popi more. I tried fake tears, but he'd seen me use these before and was unmoved. I gave up for now and we settled into bed. Popi pulled me close and whispered beautiful words of love as he rubbed my breasts. I rolled onto my back and pulled his lips to mine. Big Popi wanted to make love, but he failed to persuade my husband. Two whole days, I'm sure I could make it, but I was extremely sexed up already and it would only get worse. While Popi slept the deep sleep of the innocent, I tossed and turned all night.

# 2035; Popi Hates Russians

I was back. Though I knew that I was in bed next to Layla, I was back. The gate guard and I were loading suit cases into back of a white, with a blue glow, streamline coach. The vehicle had no wheels. Inside the cabin, there were two red leather bench seats, which were fore of the large cargo area. The benches were facing the middle much like a diner booth without the table. There was no pilot or any other person on board. There also weren't any windows. I found this to be disconcerting and slightly claustrophobic. Layla seemed not to notice, so I managed to remain calm. I sat and Layla gave me a look that expressed confusion and concern.

"Popi, you never sit in front. What is wrong with you? Today you forgot about our trip and now you don't remember where you like to sit on the Wave."

I got up and sat on the right rear seat against the windowless fuselage. It was a fifty-fifty chance and apparently, I chose correctly because my angel smiled and sat on my lap. We got frisky for a while until I felt a mild vibration.

"It feels like we're finally getting underway sweetheart, we best strap in." Again, I got the look. "I'm just kidding Li'l Freckles."

Sure enough, we had arrived in downtown Cincinnati in less than fifteen minutes. In my time, it is an hour drive. When the door opened, I stood with Layla in my arms and carried her off the Wave. I really liked the Wave. I kissed her and lowered my wife to the clean, shiny platform. I held her in front of me until Big Popi calmed down. Layla took off to our left. Apparently, we needn't handle our luggage.

I soon saw that we were following the signs to Pulse International. When we got there, we simply stepped aboard a two seat car that had our names projected on its' side. The car looked the same, but it was half the length, though the width, height and blue glow were about the same. I sat in my usual spot and again, Layla sat on my lap.

We proceeded to get very busy. In the middle of ravishing my young wife, I had the uncomfortable thought that she's supposed to be in the penalty box for two days. To get my perverted mind back on track, I had to separate the two Layla's into two distinct people. This made it possible to deliver a surpassingly successful and acrobatic pleasing of the older, but wiser Layla. We straightened ourselves and cuddled.

Layla, with a sexy smile, said, "Well at least you haven't forgotten anything important yet."

I was about to reply with my charming line of bullshit when I felt the slight deceleration again. We couldn't possibly be in Russia already. I kept quiet. Luckily, Layla remarked on the change in speed.

"We're over land again. Did you feel it Popi?"

"Yes. Do you know why they go slower over land?" She had a theory. "I think they must go below the speed of sound over populated areas."

We arrived at Pulse International Moscow an hour later and were met by a driver.

"I am Irena. I am to stay to you all times you are in Russia. If you want things against law, you must give to me winking eyes, like joke you know."

Irena was young, maybe twenty-five. She was five-four and very beautiful. Irena was extremely innocent in appearance with long, slightly out of control, dark brown hair. Yet her eyes were bright blue, like Rebecca who I hadn't seen in this time. Hopefully all was well with her and Ski. I, of course, couldn't ask. Well anyway, Irena was quite lovely and a bit shady.

At our hotel, the Ritz-Carlton, I told the cute Russian to be back at one-thirty for our lunch engagement and that we'd need her at nine this evening to take us to the Kremlin. Layla and I were tired, so we went straight to bed. I awoke back in 2014, needing to pee. I was lying on my left side, knees bent.

Layla was on her back with her head nestled under my chin and her breasts nestled in my right hand and arm. Big Popi wasn't so much nestled in her right hand, as he was captured, gripped and yanked. I untangled from my sweet wife and staggered to the head. I went back to bed and reset us in that meaningful pose. I felt bad for her. Layla captured, gripped and yanked me again, sending me immediately back to future Layla. She was up and dressed for a run.

"Get up Popi. We have time for a run." My wife was very cute in her impatience.

"We're in Russia sweetheart. People who run in Moscow are herded up and sent to Siberia."

"Don't be silly, that's where we're going tomorrow. If you're not coming I'm going alone." Some things never change.

"Can I at least have a cup of coffee first?" My exquisite minx produced an impish grin and a steaming, not paper cup.

"Here Popi, you pour that bitter brew down while I do some stretching." She kissed my unbrushed smile.

I dressed and turned on the BBC news channel just to hear some English while I chugged the coffee. We first ran down the eight flight staircase, through the posh lobby and out onto the busy street. It was ten o'clock on a sunny Moscow morning and the tourists and shopkeepers plied their bickering, dickering trades.

I followed as Layla glided through the crowds. I think that old Walter was probably still true to the vow I made to myself on that day long ago, (this morning) after I tried to brain that humongous tiger with a rock. I vowed to never try to beat Layla again if it meant not being there to protect her. Sacred vow in place, I was there when after two miles, Layla strode across an alley and was pulled into the small side street. I rounded the corner at full speed.

A large man said, "Stop or the pretty lady dies."

The Russian thug had Layla by her silky pale blonde hair with a knife at her throat. The man looked like an American skinhead and had a confident evil grin on his menacing face. I didn't stop. In fact, I leapt across the ten feet, timing my punch, so that it carried with it my full weight and the full power of my considerable upper body strength. His nose and upper mouth was caved in, sending his liberated teeth flying. He dropped the knife and fell unconscious to the pavement, no longer a threat.

I gathered my shaken girl and turned to leave, but two new toughs barred our escape. The tall one, 6'3" 320, looked like he might be mentally challenged, judging by his nearly drooling idiotic grin. He was dressed in dirty blue jeans and a too small black T-shirt that left his large belly exposed. The short one, 5'6" 130, didn't look at all stupid or dangerous. He was wearing tan chinos and a designer blue polo shirt, both clean, as were his nails and hair.

I asked, "What do you fellas want?" My smile was a fake.

The short one replied in passable English.

"I want the girl. Give her to me and I promise you won't be hurt." Layla snickered. I picked up the knife and handed it to her.

"That's mighty sportin' of you comrade, but I think we'll pass."

Shorty tapped Baby Huey on the butt and said something in Russian. Huey's grin turned sour and he stomped toward me. I was not about to grapple with the behemoth, so I backed away and steered him away from Layla. She, knowing her part, moved slowly toward Shorty while his attention was on Huey and me.

I let the big man close the distance between us. When he was within my reach, I gave him a left to his solar plexus. I didn't want them to know that my right hand was uselessly dislocated. He gasped and I drove my right foot into his right knee. He fell and began bawling like a school girl. He sounded so childlike and pitiful that I felt bad for the dull brute.

I turned my attention to Shorty, who seemed to be flummoxed by my easy defeat of his minions. Layla was standing unseen behind him. I laughed.

"Where did the girl go?" My glee chafed him.

He looked around and Layla moved, silently avoiding his gaze. The small man pulled a gun and his head exploded, spraying me with a fine mist of warm crimson. I ran to Layla and we fled the scene, not speaking until we were back in our rooms.

"My guess is that some Russian agent is protecting us." Layla agreed.

"Well, I for one am glad they are. I really didn't want to use that knife."

I showered off Shorty's blood and brain matter, after nurse Li'l Freckles pulled three of my knuckles back into their sockets. Having only one shower, Layla joined me halfway through.

# 2014; The Zoo

I lay in bed alone. Layla had gotten up early without waking me. I wondered if she was still angry or maybe she was running without me, knowing that I needed a day or two off. I drifted to the elephant in my mental room, future Layla and Walter. I have been through enough crazy and supernatural experiences to not rule out influences from the six or seventh realm.

I could tell by Layla's reaction that the clues I got from Growler #10 were true, since I had read the detailed letter minutes after the actual incident. Okay, I'd accepted that spooky happenings were afoot, but to what end. As always, if it was to protect my Li'l Freckles, I was one hundred percent on board. I went down for coffee in my rock-n-roll jammies and grumpily greeted the assembled throng.

Jordon said, "Nurse Kelly, 500 cc black coffee stat."

Kelly brought my mug and whispered into my ear. Her lips were lightly touching my earlobe.

"Popi, I don't know what you did to Layla, but can you please apologize. She's acting totally stressed out and that's putting it mildly." Her worried hands caressed my chest.

Of course, Layla walked in from her run while Kelly had her lips on my ear.

"I'll handle it sweetie. Oh, good morning, Li'l Freckles. How was your run?"

Layla ignored me and walked to the refrigerator. She took a small bottle of orange juice and left the room. I turned back to the girls with a small smile on my innocent face and encountered half a dozen glares.

"Okay, okay, I'll handle it."

I topped off my coffee and walked briskly up the stairs. It was a blustery show of resolve for the unfortunate underlings, who would have to put up with cranky Layla for thirty-six more hours. I entered our bedroom stealthily to avoid flying objects, but luckily, Layla was in the shower. I sat on the bed and waited, knowing that my loving wife wouldn't be kind to me. Maybe getting out some of her anger on me would make it a bit easier on the innocent bystanders. She finally blew into the room in a plume of steam, a freckled goddess in white, dressed only in two towels, one a turban.

"Li'l Freckles, do you want to talk about it?" She was a bit startled.

"No, do you?" Those dark blue gray eyes started to tear up and felt my resolve waver.

"Yes dear. Come sit with me." I patted the bed.

Layla timidly crossed the room and sat on the bed three feet to my left. I slid next to her and slipped my left arm around those well-muscled shoulders.

"Honey, you know how much I love you. It hurts to see you so unhappy. Do you think I'm being overly harsh for your breach of trust?"

"First you say I lied to you without a shred of proof and now you accuse me of new supposed crimes. It's not just harsh, it's unconstitutional." Her anger didn't detract from her beauty.

I kissed my sad wife. She didn't check Big Popi's instant reaction. This was extremely rare.

I softly said, "I'll make you a deal, sweetheart. I will ask you two yes/no questions and whatever you answer, I'll believe you no matter what those answers might be. We'll make wild love right here and now." She sniffled.

"What are the questions?"

"Did you know, before our run, that there was a tiger loose and did you hold back that information because you did not trust me to take the proper action?" Layla was intrigued.

"So as long as I give you either answer to both questions, you'll forgive me and the boycott is over?"

"Yes." I could almost hear the cogs turning in her pretty head.

"I'll let you know after dinner tonight."

"Can we try to be nice to each other in the mean time?" Her sadness and anger were dissipating.

"Of course we can Popi." Layla smiled. "I love you Popi." We kissed again, this time with the exploratory grope. "Will you take me to see Czar?"

"Okay Li'l Freckles, I'll check with Ski."

I called Ski while drying off from a quick shower. He was up for the trip and asked if he could bring Rebecca.

Two hours later we were at the Cincinnati Zoo on a sunny, eighty degree day. I had been here many times over the years, but not in several. I remembered the hilly terrain, the beautiful botanical displays and mostly the white Bengal tigers. They were the most majestic and largest of the big cats, or so I thought. Czar had a hundred pounds on the biggest cat they had. We were shown to an office where we met the director and other higher ups in the organization. Mr. Edwards, the director, made the tactical mistake of thanking us for the gift of the Siberian. Layla made it perfectly clear that Czar belonged to her and her alone.

Layla left the room and I signaled Ski to follow. Being an adept multitasker, I simultaneously drew my most powerful weapon, my checkbook. I wrote a very substantial donation and told them that our intention was to take Czar back to Russia and return him to the wild. I had just invented this story because Layla and I hadn't discussed her ultimate goal for her new furry boyfriend. Although I was grateful to

Czar for not eating Layla and me, I wanted him gone, the sooner the better.

Glancing at her fancy phone, Rebecca said, "Popi, Kurt and Layla are on their way back. She's calmer and wants you to get someone to take her to her cat."

Mr. Edwards made a call for an assistant large cat handler to lead us. The assistant entered and I knew, from the moment I laid eyes on her, that she was special.

"Walter Lemon, meet Simone Walker. She's one of our up and coming naturalists in our big cat department."

Miss Walker was shorter than Layla, maybe even shorter than Jordon Woo. She was dressed like The Crocodile Hunter and made it look sexy with breasts that rivaled Claire and a derriere which would give Layla's a run for her money. Besides her height and shapely butt, Simone and Layla are physically polar opposites.

Layla's skin is pale white and decorated with beautiful tan freckles. Her hair is straight and the palest blonde possible. Simone's skin is as near black as any human skin can be, smooth and perfect. Her hair is, of course, also black, shiny and very tightly curled. Simone's face, perfectly beautiful without makeup, made her an adorable ebon angel.

Edwards said, "Simone, take care of Mr. and Mrs. Lemon. Get them anything they want. They just balanced our budget." He left with the check.

"Popi, Popi, I can't believe you're here." She jumped into my arms and planted kisses all over my face.

Rebeca grabbed her and was pulling her off of me as Layla and Ski entered. Simone saw Layla and decided that she adored her even more than me. Ski, having been in this situation many times, caught the leaping fan in midair. He waited for her to calm down before he let her go.

Layla said, "Whoa girl, we're just normal people. What's your name honey? Have you ever considered fashion modeling? You're so beautiful and I could really use a girl with your figure and face." I couldn't see Simone's blush, but I knew it was there.

"That sounds so exciting, but I could never leave my cats. They need me." Now, Layla knew that Simone was special too.

Eventually, Simone showed us to the inner sanctum of the large cats. It was in a large, long low building with barred jail cells on both sides of an eight feet wide aisle. As we walked down that runway, some of the lions, tigers and other big cats came to the bars and followed us with their predatory eyes. Simone stopped.

"What the hell? They never do this." She asked us all to walk back out the door. "Wait five full minutes then, one at a time, come in and walk the length of the room with one minute between people. Layla, you go last. I heard how the Siberian took a shine to you."

Layla was impatient, but accepted the experiment with her usual grace. I went first. Most of the animals had returned to the back of their cells. None of them reacted to me. I stood with Simone and watched Rebecca make the walk, still no reaction. Ski went next, causing neither purr nor snarl. Layla opened the door for her entrance and more than half of the prisoners rushed the bars.

I said, "My God, that's amazing, more than half the cats are drawn to Layla."

"You do call her Kitten, Walter," said Ski.

Simone said, "It's not half the cats. It's all of the males."

When Layla came to Czar's cage, the huge beast stood on his hind legs and roared. He seemed to be ten feet tall. Layla hopped the barrier and embraced her new pet through the steel bars. Simone panicked and tried to rush to her idols' rescue. I restrained her and whispered into her cute ear.

"Everything's fine, let's just watch."

We did watch in awe as my faithful wife sullied her innocent reputation with the huge handsome cat. He licked Layla's face. The spell was unbroken.

Simone said, "He adores her." That was putting it mildly.

Simone was documenting the incredible scene with her fancy phone. After half an hour, I coaxed my smitten kitten to say goodbye to her feline hunk and we all stepped outside. Simone told us that she hoped Czar would be with her long enough to mate with Sabrina, the zoos' female Siberian.

"She's in heat now, but Czar has, so far, shown no interest in her."

I asked, "Was Sabrina captured in the wild or was she raised here?"

"Tigers are no longer captured for zoos. Most are either born in a zoo or rescued as cubs, after their mothers are killed by poachers."

"I think I know a way to convince Czar to romance Sabrina."

Simone was eager to hear my plan and called for Sabrina's handler to meet us. A good looking young man soon arrived and introduced himself as Johnny Smith. Simone told him that I had a plan that I thought would get Czar to mate with Sabrina. He looked skeptical. I pulled Layla aside.

"Sweetheart, do you want Czar to mate with another woman?" Layla took a few seconds to think.

"I guess so Popi. I'll only be a little bit jealous."

"Give me your underwear. That cat loves your scent especially from there." I was pointing, indicating the nexus between her lovely legs.

"Popi, I can't take off my underwear in front of these people."

"That's okay baby, I'll do it for you."

I got on my knees, reached up her short skirt and eased my prize down to her feet. Layla stepped out of the pretty blue lacy silk. I took my pocket knife and cut the scant material between the leg holes. I handed the cloth to Johnny.

"Here son, put this around Sabrina's neck and put her together with Czar."

Johnny was staring at Layla now, imagining her naked I supposed. He took the blue silk without taking his eyes off Layla's butt. I abided this, but when he brought the dainty silk to his face and deeply inhaled, I had enough. I grabbed him by his Crocodile Hunter shirt and lifted him up.

"Boy, you better show some respect for my wife or you'll be wearing that around your neck when I throw you in the cage with Czar."

"I'm sorry sir, but she's just so smokin' hot." I couldn't argue with that.

We watched the experimental hook-up attempt on a small video screen in Simone's office. Johnny was getting Sabrina dressed for her date. He put the cloth around Sabrina's neck. The large female cat treated the young man much like Czar treated Layla, with total adoration. Czar must have caught Layla's scent and was on high alert. When ready, Johnny opened a partition between their cages and things developed very quickly. Czar ran into Sabrina's cell and with very few preliminaries, mounted the minx. He was sniffing and drooling on the blue silk. Was he imagining that she was my Layla? I don't know.

Simone hugged Layla and said, "Li'l Freckles, I want your undies."

# 2035; Tigers International

After a very satisfying love making session, I proposed that we skip our lunch meeting, stay in bed and order room service. Layla insisted that the meeting was too important. She made a believer of me when she was ready to leave five minutes before our agreed upon time of departure. Irena made us even earlier with her hair-raising dash through Moscow's dangerously chaotic traffic.

"I here will wait. Order caviar blintz, is so delicious," said the English challenged cutie.

I explained to the barely dressed hostess that we were meeting two men from Tigers International and she showed us to an outdoor table. It took several minutes to communicate that we would feel too exposed and needed a table inside. After a five minute wait, the tiger guys showed. Ted Wells was about thirty-five and Yuri Commissar was forty or so. Ted was a handsome young American man who had passion for all things relating to saving the earth. Yuri was a brutish looking Russian who earned my instant distrust.

He asked, "Mrs. Lemon is Walter your father?"

Ted did most of the talking, starting with his sincere thanks for our many years of financial support. He told us about the continuing scourge of the tiger poachers.

"Just last month, poachers killed five of our field researchers and stole their notes to help them locate the cats. These men get up to one hundred thousand dollars for each animal, almost double if they're captured alive."

I told the men about the attempt to kidnap Layla earlier today. They both seemed to be very concerned by this.

Ted said, "We'll be armed tomorrow, but until then, you must protect her Walter. Many tigers will be at risk if you are gone Layla."

I asked, "So you think these lawless killers are organized enough to cooperate in a kidnapping or assassination? I don't buy it. Do you have any proof?"

Ted said, "No."

Yuri said, "Yes."

I looked at Yuri and raised my eyebrows expectantly. He pulled a folded, rumpled scrap of paper from his inside jacket pocket and handed it to me.

The crumpled note was hand written in soft pencil. It was in Russian and signed, Doug. I excused myself and walked out the door. I met up with Irena at the car and asked the girl to decipher the hastily scribbled note.

"It says, we are pinned down, two snipers. Wolf-man and Sgt. York are dead. Catherine, Misha and I are okay so far, but Yuri, if Mitch doesn't get through it's been an honor working with you. Don't surrender, Doug."

I went back in with my transcript of the note and handed it to Layla. She read it somberly.

"This is horrible. How did you get the note Yuri?" Her brow was creased from her concern.

"The only survivor sneaked out and walked for help. He was an American named Mitch. It took him two and a half days to walk the sixty miles to my office in Vanavara. By the time we got there with reinforcements, they were all dead. Doug was bound to a chair and executed, but the girls were raped, tortured and butchered." Yuri and Ted were in tears. I now trusted them.

"How will we be protected from these madmen?"

Ted explained that the Russian army was providing transport and a Special Forces squad.

After our meal, I had the caviar blintz, we retreated to our hotel. It was just two-thirty, but we expected to have a late evening and an early wake-up for our trip to Tunguska, so we took a nap. We arose at seven and sluggishly began preparing for the gala at the Kremlin. This party seemed important a few hours ago, but now, after the events of this crazy day, it became a bothersome distraction.

Irena arrived at nine. I was on my second Scotch and prepared for almost anything but the way the Russian teen was dressed. She was in a gorgeous ball gown of exquisite beauty in ivory silk and pale green jade beads. When Layla, still in her underwear, saw the dress, she gave me a glance, which I took to be a signal that she wanted a word in private.

"Irena you make that dress look beautiful." She smiled.

"Thank you Mr. Lemon and quite dashing are you in that tuxedo." I led Layla to the large, luxurious bathroom.

"Popi, don't you recognize that dress?" She straightened my tie as she spoke.

"No dear, is it one of yours?" Again, she graced me with the worried look.

"I wore that same dress in Paris last year. It retails for over twenty thousand dollars. How can a limo driver afford it and why is she dressed for the ball anyway?"

"Let's ask her."

I went back to the sitting room, took Irena's dainty hand and pulled her to me. I led her in several ballroom steps and twirls. She was good, maybe even trained. She followed my lead to perfection.

"My Irena, are you a professional?"

"No Walter, but I'm be dancing since I was two. You are also good to dancing. You move like much younger man."

"Did you shoot that little man today?"

"I am not wanting to, but I swore to protect you and could not take chance that he have lucky day and kill you. I'm sorry."

"No, don't apologize, thank you. Who hired you to protect us?"

"I don't know man's real name. His codename is Triple D. He sends dress and invitation, so I can watch you at Kremlin. He say no to trust Russian government security."

"I can't wait to dance with you tonight sweetheart."

Fifteen minutes later, Layla emerged from the bathroom. I was spellbound and my heartrate increased.

"Popi, can you do me up?" She had no notion of the impact she was having on me.

"Li'l Freckles, you never fail to surprise me with your beauty."

"Thank you Popi, it's my back-up dress. Irena is wearing my first choice." I carefully considered my response.

"I don't know which dress I like better, but I do know they'd both look better on you." Layla smiled at my charming line of bullshit.

I kissed my dear Layla's neck before I threaded the four pearls through the loops of the graceful high collar on a dress of cascading hand stitched honeysuckle vines. Jeweled honey bees seemingly buzzed among the blossoms. It was glorious.

Much to Layla's chagrin, while she was fawned over by the aging Politburo, I danced with the beautiful Irena. Not one person at the Gala recognized me or acknowledged me in any significant way. I was okay with this.

# 2014; Sabrina and Simone

Each time I awoke, I had a tight grip on Big Popi. It seemed strange that Popi could sleep so peacefully while I punished his best friend so brutally. At six in the morning I got up to run. I left my insufferable husband to his celibate dreams. I was feeling taken advantage of, guilty, wrongfully convicted and undeserving all at once. The conflicting emotions were ricocheting off each other in my heart. In the kitchen, Claire said the wrong thing to me or maybe, in my uncharitable mood, I took it wrong.

"Good morning Layla. Going for a run? I guess Walter's taking a couple days off."

I still don't know what she meant by that. It was either innocent small talk or chiding me because Popi had cut me off. She was also cooking bacon. I felt that wonderful scent trying to seduce me into skipping my run. While sipping my highly sweetened coffee and nibbling on some dry toast, Layla's angels, all boobs and bedheads, staggered into the room. Claire was so sweet to them. She even hugged them all, almost making me gag.

"Don't pig out ladies, first fittings this afternoon," I cruelly said with a sweet smile as I jogged out the door.

The run was okay, but not as good as running with Popi who made me feel safe and boosted my self-esteem by being unable to beat me. I guess those days are gone now. I don't know if I can ever beat him again, though I tried to convince myself that I, but for Czar, would have caught up with Mr. smug. I know in my heart that is untrue.

Before re-entering the house, I sat down on a deck chair by the pool and cried. I had to pull it together because Popi seeing me this way would be devastating to me. Stump walked up to test the pool water.

"What's cookin' good lookin'?" It was an unwelcome Popi-ism. He caught me hiding my tears and pulled up a chair next to me. "What's wrong darling. Did someone hurt you?"

"Popi is mad at me because he thinks he caught me in a lie. Now he won't believe me and says that he knows it to be a fact."

"What was the lie he thinks you told?" He held my hand to comfort me.

"He says that I knew about the tiger and withheld it from him."

"Did you know, and went running anyway?" I removed my hand from his.

I bucked up, as Popi says, and resolved to ignore them all, starting with Stump. I walked through the door and they all turned accusingly to me, except Kelly who was busy nibbling my husbands' ear. Someone spoke, but I didn't listen and went straight to my shower. After a long hot ten minutes rinsing away some of my out of control emotions, I stepped into our bedroom. Popi startled me.

"Do you want to talk?" He patted the bed and I sat.

He hugged and kissed me, saying that he hated to see me sad. I unloaded on him and his accusations. He cracked. He said that if I gave either a yes or no to his two his two questions, he would believe me and would make love to me right now. I told him that I would think about it. I felt better.

Anyway, we made up, but the make-up sex would have to wait. Popi, Kurt, Rebecca and I went to the Zoo to see Czar. He was so happy to see me and I was happier to see him. We cooed and nuzzled our faces for thirty minutes without interruption. I didn't know why we were so attracted to each other, but it feels like our lives may depend upon that love.

The zoo had a female Siberian tiger called Sabrina. Simone, a gorgeous zookeeper, wanted Czar to mate with Sabrina, but he showed no interest. Popi gave my undies to Sabrina's handler, a cute guy named Johnny. He was kind of creeping me out by staring at me like he could see through my skirt. I think Popi noticed, but he said nothing, until the cute creepy guy brought my intimates to his lips. I had to smile when Popi almost clobbered him.

When Czar saw Sabrina wearing my underwear around her neck he race into her cage and immediately began to ravish her. She didn't mind one bit, but I wasn't so enthusiastic about my new boyfriend cheating on me. I'm mostly kidding about that, but there was a little twinge of jealousy. Before we went home, I gave Simone my card. I was already picturing our dresses on the cute girl.

It was my turn to cook and I felt reinvigorated by the days' events so I made eggplant parmesan, linguine with white clam sauce and Chocolate mousse. Little Michael had my tried and true grilled cheese and tomato soup. After dinner Popi and Susan cleaned up. Susan Williams, Robby's girlfriend, always volunteered for kitchen duty when Popi was scheduled for KP, as he calls it. I am no longer jealous when she or any other girls for that matter, throw themselves at my Popi. I know for a fact that he'll always be true to me. It also doesn't faze me that he enjoys it so much. He's a very handsome man and as a member of that exclusive club, he needs constant reassurance that he still has that undefinable quality which enchants the opposite sex.

I still hadn't told him my answers to his questions, preferring to wait until bed time. By his rules, no matter what I say, he will make love to me. If Popi were an illegal drug, it could be fairly said that I was jonesing for him. I hadn't thought about what I was going to say, though I had vowed not to lie. The truth seemed cold and hard, but I knew Popi could take it. Perpetuating my lies felt right, as right as lies can be. He can claim to know the truth, but it is as secret as any other in a woman's heart. No matter what I shared, the payoff would be the same. I was all about that payoff. It is embarrassing to admit how much I need that physical love from Popi.

I was ready for bed at ten so I searched out Popi. I found him in his den with Robby, Susan, Chrissy and Mary. They were playing a rousing game of Monopoly. I knew, judging by Popi's remaining property and miniscule reserve of cash, that he wouldn't be long. In my bedroom, I climbed naked under the covers, almost giddy in anticipation. I was reading when Popi entered fifteen minutes later. He took one of his patented five minute showers and was still drying his hair as he sat on the bed in his blue boxers.

"Honey, do you have a plan for Czar?" This was not the conversation I was eager to have right now.

"I want to set him free, but first it's going to take a lot of research so let's put that conversation off for a week."

"Sounds good to me, do you have anything else you want to discuss?" I tried on my most seductive smile and handed him Growler #10.

"Here Popi, this will answer your two questions."

"Thank you Li'l Freckles." He walked to his closet and deposited the unopened letter in his lock box.

"Popi, aren't you going to read it?" I was miffed.

"I already know what it says if you told the truth and if you lied, I'd rather not know." I didn't dare show my ire. I wasn't about to risk my prize.

"Okay Popi, make love to me, as promised."

My beautiful Popi did make love to me. It was everything I anticipated and so much more. He had me squirming and moaning with pleasure so intense that I think I swooned for a few seconds. All of this happened before Big Popi even made an appearance. Once that scoundrel came out, I was like a wild beast forcing sustenance from my prey. The end result was that I was in a sound sleep before my darling Big Popi and I disconnected. All my dreams were sweet.

# 2035; Shot Down in Tunguska

I was back. I had no time to reflect on the magnificent sex I had left twenty years or so behind. In fact, I barely had time to perceive that I was on a large helicopter before the explosion. On my right, a soldier spoke.

"Mr. Lemon, we are hit with missile from ground. We must get away from crash very fast." He handed me his side arm. "You take, good luck."

Layla was welded to my left arm, knowing the drill. I looked again at the cockpit and wished I hadn't. Everyone in or near the control center was dead. Irena, dressed as a Russian Army officer, lay dead and on fire. I had no time to grieve for her.

The now quiet craft began descending in an auto-rotating spiral. The two sets of rotor blades were spinning backwards thereby slowing our fall to a perhaps survivable rate. The soldier on my right was trying to open the sliding door, so we Lemon's arose to help. The stubborn door easily opened the first foot then became jammed. I instantly spotted the problem. The explosion had warped the frame.

I said, "We need something heavy to kick out the bottom and the whole thing will come off." His eyes lit up with an inspiration.

He ran to the back where others had opened the door near them and returned with a squad sized machine gun. With all due haste, he braced himself and fired until the last round from the large round clip passed through the chamber.

I, with Layla attached, walked to the door and I gave it a big kick. The large heavy door went sailing into the sky and fell toward the rapidly approaching earth. We were over a pine forest. I was debating whether it would be best to ride the flaming chopper to the ground or try to jump for a tree limb. I never got a chance to make that decision because as we hit the trees, the craft tilted toward a treetop which poked, uninvited, through our doorway. I grabbed on with my Layla adorned left arm just as the chopper fell away. I reached out my right hand to the friendly soldier who somehow found the courage to leap across six feet of space and caught my wrist.

The craft continued to fall to the forest floor and exploded on impact. Layla climbed onto her own branch and I helped the Russian find safe footing. We could feel the flames from a hundred feet below. We all knew we had to race those flames down the tree and evacuate the lifesaving giant plant before it caught fire and entrapped us in its sheltering arms.

I hollered, "Let's go," and we all skittered down regardless the scraping bark and prickly needles.

Once down, we searched for survivors, finding not a single soul. We silently, solemnly walked away, only stopping after a few hundred yards for introductions. My new friends' name was First Sargent Victor Solodnikov. He was in charge of the security squad protecting us. Victor was still committed to protecting my wife and me because he was a fan in his childhood. He said that whoever shot us down would come to finish off any survivors so the most important thing to do was to get some distance between us and the burning aircraft/tombstone.

Layla and I agreed so we walked. We were hoping to make it to the Tigers International camp which Victor estimated to be twenty-five miles to the north. Layla and Victor chatted and flirted as we walked while I tried to erase any evidence that we had passed this way. We walked six or seven hours until it got too dark to see. It was a clear cloudless night, but the pine canopy shielded us from most of the starlight and the moon was just a bright sliver.

Having no gear or supplies, we raked together some needles into a cushion to lay our weary heads. Since it was mid-June, the weather was fair, so we resisted the urge to start a fire. Victor lay down and instantly dropped off into a shallow sleep. This is very common among experienced soldiers. I made myself comfortable on my back, so that Layla could make herself comfortable sleeping half on top of me.

I lay still and reviewed the events unfolding since my arrival in 2035. With the information gained from Growler #10, I was able to force the truth from my wife. I got to travel on the Wave, a new form of transportation, at approximately 300 mph. and the Pulse at 2000 to 3000 mph. Three thugs tried to kidnap Layla and finally, we survived a fiery helicopter crash after being shot from the sky. Not much has changed. This isn't much different than my normal life. Maybe it's me. Maybe I, fifty-one year old Walter Lemon, am to blame for all the violence surrounding Layla. This didn't feel like a dream.

Eventually, Layla and I drifted off. I expected to return to 2014, but instead, I dreamed of those twenty or so people who did not walk away from the burning chopper, including the beautiful Irena, Tim Wells and Yuri Commissar, who only wanted to save some endangered tigers. I don't know how 2035 Walter Lemon feels about those dangerous beasts, but now I knew how I felt. Tim and Yuri's fight was now my fight. I expect that Layla feels the same. I needed no more proof to feel justified in exacting vengeance on these demons who will slaughter any amount of good people to acquire their illegal product. They were no better than drug cartel assassins. My thoughts quieted a bit and soon I awoke in my bed.

# CZAR

The upright man released me and the others too. There were two people among them, but their markings were different and unreadable. I ignored them and walked in the opposite direction. I walked all day which went against my nature, but I wanted to be far away from here. There was a forest here, but it was not my forest. It had some plants and prey that I had never seen before.

I missed my forest and I missed my women. I have five. I didn't care if I never saw another of the men in my family, especially my older brother Kersay. He vowed to kill me the next time we met. He doesn't have the strength or skill, but he is crafty and not to be taken lightly.

When night fell, I realized that I was hungry. I sensed some small prey or at least their trails so I settled in the brush and waited. I allowed my mind to wander wherever it may go. I wanted small prey because I would not stay around long enough to eat a deer or sheep. A real man honors his prey so letting it go to waste would be a most dishonorable thing.

We men always hunt alone while the women usually hunt in family groups. By my second summer, I felt the overwhelming urge to strike out on my own. I only return when drawn to a woman who has called out through the wind to mate. I hear the message with my nose from two or more nights away.

I heard, with my ears, a small animal skittering through the brush. It sounded like a rabbit and smelled much like a rabbit too. I remained still until Mr. Rabbit appeared, unsuspecting, right in front of me. I slowly reached out to him with my hand and pinned him to the ground. As usual, I was tempted to play with him, but I never succumb to this urge.

I killed him quickly and honored him for his tasty flesh and wished his family well, so they may be so honored if I ever came back this way again. Though Mr. Rabbit didn't fill my belly, he took away the urgent need, so I could start moving again. I didn't know where I was going, but I felt there was a purpose to my trek.

After many days resting and nights walking, I came to a stream. It was in a steep ravine and was rushing swiftly. Rushing water is the best and sweetest. While drinking, I noticed a structure built by the upright men. It was a bridge across the stream. After climbing back up the slope I went to investigate the ingenious span. That is when I finally understood my reason for coming to this strange place. All of my senses spoke to me at once and they all said the same thing.

"There is a woman nearby who is the queen of her race and she will worship me above all others as I will honor and cherish her for the rest of our lives.

My nose could judge the frequency of her passages through this area. It was odd that she comes nearly every sunrise, but not for several nights. It would soon be daylight. I rested, awaiting my queen and another Mr. Rabbit.

# 2014; DISEMBOWELED

It was the middle of the night when I came back to 2014. Layla and I were intertwined and she was lightly snoring, drooling on my chest. Since I was rudely called away from my darling Li'l Freckles before enjoying that sweet feeling you get after a wild sexual experience with the one you love. I relived it now. Big Popi awoke and tried to convince me to start some funny business, but I resisted. I willed myself back to sleep despite his tempting offer to take the blame. I know from much experience that my alter ego is very brave until the shooting starts. Layla woke me at six.

"Are you going to sleep all day or are you going to try to outrun me again."

I arose and picked up my jabbering angel. I kissed her with force.

"Li'l Freckles, you can't beat me with taunts and trickery. There is no substitute for talent and tenacity." These words were similar to what Layla had said to me in her letter, which I hadn't yet officially read. "You think that over while I go down to flirt with Claire."

True to my word, I did flirt with my ex-wife and was in an intimate embrace with her when Layla walked in talking.

"Okay Popi, I'm ready. Drop my CEO and come get your

comeuppance. Do you want to make another wager on todays' outcome?" Cockiness didn't become her.

"No way Li'l Freckles, I have everything I need." I gave Claire an unwelcomed kiss and a pat on her butt.

"I thought as much."

She walked briskly out the door. I ran well though I lost by fifty meters, never once letting my cherished Layla out of my sight.

"Wow! Good run Popi. You really have upped your game. I thought it was all smoke and mirrors."

"I've decided to stop short of killing myself to beat you. After all, it's only a run."

We went to the zoo again that afternoon. Ski and Rebecca weren't available because they were working out the logistics of our upcoming trip to Tampa for our annual BP&LF stockholders meeting. It was really a three day party. Layla asked Layla's Angels to come and meet Czar. I believed that her real agenda was to introduce them to Simone for the purpose of recruitment of the beautiful girl into her fold. I wanted to talk to her about helping to facilitate the return of Layla's feline suitor to his homeland. The girls were all overdressed for a day at the zoo, but I have to say that I would have followed them anywhere.

Simone was appropriately impressed with the sales job and was scheduled to do some test photos and preliminary fittings next week. Being September, it would be a difficult to get her ready for Paris, but if Layla wanted it enough, she would will it to happen. Layla had brought Simone a present, two pair of her soiled underwear. Simone was thrilled to get them. While Layla was showing off her new lover to the Angels, I got the beautiful Simone alone.

"You really love your cats, don't you honey?"

"More than anything Popi, but Li'l Freckles offer is also very tempting."

"If I have my way, you'll have the best of both worlds."

I told her my plan to partner with Tigers International to fight the evil threat posed by poachers of tigers throughout the world.

"I know for a fact that the problem will become far more deadly, both for the cats and those who try to protect them, in the near future. We'll need dedicated experts to do the scientific work."

"Popi, you seem to have some kind of personal stake in the safety of those tigers."

"Let's just say that some very dedicated friends of mine were killed by those bloodthirsty poachers." Simone came out of her seat and embraced me.

"I'm so sorry Popi."

I, of course, didn't tell her that those friends were killed twenty years in the future. For now, I put Simone on the BP&LF Inc. payroll to work on getting Czar back to his home and to research Tigers International efforts throughout the world. She was thrilled to be part of my plan.

"What if I decide to work for you and turn down Li'l Freckles offer?"

"That would be okay, but I think you should do both. Models don't really work too many hours and there are a lot of perks, not the least of which is becoming part of my family." She hugged me again.

"I'd like that."

We walked hand in hand to the tiger pen where we found Layla still making out with Czar and Johnny making time with the other four beauties. When the flirting man saw me, he tensed up.

"Sorry sir, again, they're so smokin' hot."

"Don't worry son, I'm not married to these girls."

Two weeks later, on a Saturday, we were flying to Moscow. On the trip were me, Layla, Ski, Simone and, of course, the mighty Czar. He was sedated, but completely conscious, so Layla spent most of the ten hour flight calming the nervous cat. Simone had been staying with us for the past week. She had successfully navigated the red tape of the Russians to get permission to repatriate Czar. I called in favors to expedite the trip out of the USA. The neophyte Nubian Angel also went about her training by the Layla's Petites staff. She told me that the hardest part, by far, was learning to walk in a multitude of heels.

Our private jet was met in Moscow by a young representative from

Tigers International. He was a good looking twenty year old with a full head of blond hair.

"I am called Yuri Commissar, to meet you is nice. My young brother and sisters are most good Big Popi and Li'l Freckles fans." Layla was pleased by this.

"Thank you Yuri, we've brought some dolls to sign and give to our biggest fans."

It was difficult speaking with the young Yuri, knowing the day of his murder. I planned, if possible, to alter that horrible day. This thought begat another. What if I learned, in my dreams, the identity of that would-be rabid killer? Would I be able to kill him twenty years before his crime? The proof must be absolute.

Yuri had us set up in an empty warehouse on the outskirts of the city to hold Czar's cage as it was illegal to bring the animal into the city. We also had rooms at a nearby hotel.

Layla said, "Popi, if Czar is staying here, so am I." She left no room for discussion.

"Me too," said Simone, "I must manage his recovery from the sedative."

I knew that I couldn't let the girls stay in the spooky space by their selves so we all stayed. Ski and Simone went into the city for sleeping and eating supplies. While they were gone, Layla and I took the opportunity to make love in a dirty office. Afterward, we were startled out of our loving embrace by a Czar's loud snarl, causing us to quickly arrange our clothes. I entered the warehouse proper. Layla was close behind me. Ski had left me a gun, one of several he had smuggled in by taping them under Czar's cage.

He said, "No one in their right mind would look there. Layla honey, will you get them for me?" Mine was a Glock nine mm.

I had left most of the lights in the large open building off, but it was bright around Czar's cage. The tiger was agitated. He was pacing his small barred enclosure and keeping his eyes on the shadowy, far side of the room. I wasn't about to ignore his senses.

I whispered, "Li'l Freckles, go to Czar, but stay on this side of him."

I gave her the gun. "I'm going to turn off the lights and when I do, you let the cat out of the cage." She looked concerned by my plan.

"Popi, what if Czar goes after you?"

"Don't worry sweetheart, he already had his chance to eat me."

I waited for Layla to get into position and calmly crossed the twenty-five feet to the electrical box, where I had earlier set up this limited lighting. I hit the three breakers and the whole building was in total darkness. As I made my way blindly back to my wife, I heard the muted sound of the cage door opening. I couldn't see or hear the big cat and by the time Layla and I were reunited, the cat was silently gone.

The intruders made themselves visible when they turned on flashlights which seemed to be attached to their hand guns. Their beams of light moved slowly toward us, spraying the dark with frantic strobe-like confusion. The men spread out left, right and center, making me think that they may be pros. The light in the center flew across the huge room and was extinguished upon contact with the concrete floor. It was Czar. I kissed Layla on the cheek.

"I'm going right."

While the other beams were pointing at the spot their comrade had occupied, I swiftly, in a low crouch, made my way toward the light on the right. By the time he got his mind back to business, I was on him. I, still in my crouch, drove my right shoulder into his solar plexus and with a great grunt, he went to the floor. I kept up my attack, clubbing his face over and over with my fists until he ceased to struggle. I felt Czar rush past me and, a few seconds later, the third gunman was neutralized by the stealthy predator.

The lights came on. I looked at the electrical box and saw Layla checking on her two men. When she saw that we were okay, she smiled a smile that completely explained why Czar and I loved her so much. She called for her cat and he came running while I checked on the bad guys. The two that Czar had taken out were dead. Their guts were spilling out onto the dirty cement floor. The one who I pummeled was unconscious, but breathing.

By the time I dragged the survivor back to the cage, Czar was back in lock-up and Layla was washing the blood from his front paws. Layla and I hugged and an amazing thing happened. The eight hundred pound Siberian tiger licked me.

Layla said with glee, "Popi! He likes you now. I'm so happy that my two big strong men can get along."

I was happy too. I now knew that the cat can and will protect our beloved Layla.

# CZAR

I did get another Mr. Rabbit and he was as delicious as his brother Rabbit. I drowsed lightly as I continued to wait for my future Queen. The sun was just beginning to rise. Normally, this was a signal to find a nice soft, dark place to sleep, but now it was time to be alert. Finally she came and I was shocked to see her. Not because she wasn't beautiful, she was, but because she was an upright woman and she was running slowly with an upright man. My future Queen was talking to the man, who was completely ignoring her. I recognized his smell from the path, although I wasn't expecting him to be with her.

I held my ground as the two upright people passed. I knew that they would be back several times. I decided that I needed to give my love a meaningful name and since her voice sounded prettier than the sound of a flock of fat pheasants in the high grass, I will call her Pheasant Song. I was pleased with my choice. When they came around again, I began to plan how to deal with the upright man. I never kill except to defend myself or to eat. The fragile upright man was no threat and eating him would be cannibalism. This was not something an honorable man would do. I must be patient.

The next time they appeared, I named the man Grrrrr. That is the sound that comes to mind when I see him. Grrrrr was a few leaps ahead of Pheasant Song. It was a surprise because she looked so fit. Maybe she was pacing herself for a long run. I was hoping that Grrrrr would extend his lead, so that I could be alone with my Pheasant Song when she passed. I would go whether he saw me or not. I had no fear of the man, but I didn't want him to ruin my time with Pheasant Song.

When the time came, Grrrrr was far ahead of my upright Princess, though he looked, smelled, sounded and felt ready to collapse. When he clumsily ran down the hill, Pheasant song wasn't in sight, though I sensed her nearing. I watched as the man clumsily tripped on the span across the stream and had to suppress my laughter at his buffoonery. Grrrrr was almost out of sight when Pheasant Song appeared at the top of the hill. She looked relaxed in her stride, but she showed worry on her speckled face. Even worried, she was a vision of pure goodness and regal beauty.

I stepped into the path four leaps in front of her. Pheasant Song turned away from me and carelessly ran into a tree. She was frightened of me. This was understandable, as I'm quite impressive, but it was not the reaction I was hoping for. My new woman was afraid, so I wanted to allay those fears by being calm and benevolent. I sat and waited for her to relax. This didn't work, so I slowly approached her. I lovingly gazed into those worried dark blue eyes, which looked as though they'd viewed more than their share of danger and triumph. I believed that she was wise beyond her few years. My Pheasant Song shivered. I was so enraptured, by the sight and smell of her, that I didn't sense that Grrrrr had returned.

The puny upright man slammed into me with all he had. I was surprised that the impact seemed to be more powerful than the size of the man would indicate. Grrrrr rose from the path and began to attack me again. My honor would not be sullied now, if I was to kill this upright man. I was worried that my Pheasant Song wouldn't forgive me for killing her friend. I hit back with my hand, but not my claws. He may be injured, but he should survive. I turned my full attention back to my adorable woman. She could have run away when the man attacked, but she chose to stay. I think she was warming to me.

I smelled her feet and along her hairless legs, savoring her sweet warm scent. I moved up her body and lingered, becoming intoxicated by the exotic smell of her. Then it got weird. As soon as my mouth came into contact with Pheasant Song's beautiful white speckled face, I felt a stirring that I had never felt before. I now knew that she had some sort of magical spell on me. Fortunately, Grrrrr had recovered enough to mount a third futile charge, this time armed with a tiny pebble.

I kissed my love one more time, starting at her feet and ending at those wonderful, enchanting eyes. The upright man charged with a weak roar. I smelled his fear, but also sensed his undeniable courage in the protection of his royal charge. I had figured out why Grrrrr was here. He must be Pheasant Song's protector. If I got my way, and I always do, Grrrrr would have to find a new purpose to his life. I calmly turned away from them, indicating my reluctance to do battle and walked casually away. I was still reading him as I retreated. I would be back soon.

I slept away the morning, dreaming of my Pheasant Song. It was still day time when hunger woke me, so I went hunting for dinner. I was looking for bigger prey because I planned to stay until my Princess became my Queen. I followed a fresh scent trail of a deer. I walked silently until I came upon her. Happily, she had no children with her. I leapt upon Mrs. Deer, crushing her neck with my teeth until she no longer struggled. Before dinner, I paid homage to her and the sustenance she would provide. I carried her back to my spot near the path. Mrs. Deer would keep me full for three nights, allowing me time to find Pheasant Song's home.

# 2014; Czar Goes Home

On our second trip to see Czar, I brought Layla's Angels. I was determined to get the exotic tiger girl, Simone, to work with us. She was a knockout, smart, beautiful and most importantly, she was dedicated to the big cats. When I went to Czar's cage, Popi and Simone stayed in her office for a bit. I introduced the girls to my new boyfriend, as Popi calls him. I don't deny it. Our closeness seems bizarre, but it also feels right and I think Popi knows that there is something big coming. That feeling automatically sends him into hyper-security mode. While this can be irritating, his exaggerated protectiveness has proved its necessity too often to ignore.

While I was communing with my tiger, Johnny the hot zoologist was communing with the hot Angels. I thought he would be a good catch for one of them. Then Popi joined us, chasing Johnny's swagger away like a gentle breeze can chase a faint wisp of French perfume. Popi reassured the young man that the girls were fair game. I talked to Simone. She agreed to some test shots and training as long as she could keep her new job working for BP&LF Inc. I didn't get the full story until the ride home. I was all for it. Having a tiger expert on our team was a great comfort.

My week was spent teaching the trade to Simone while the tailors fitted her for some of our sexiest dresses. She had never worn heels before, so I had her tending her cats in four inch stilettos. On Friday, I brought in one of the talented photographers we use and did a one girl session. When we were done, we let Simone see the digital photos on the big screen. As I knew she would be, Simone was amazed at how incredibly beautiful she and our dresses were. I could tell she was hooked.

We had an impromptu coming out party for the newest Layla's Petites model which ran into dinner and cocktail hour. The end result was that Simone had to spend the night. By the end of the weekend, she had moved all of her clothes in and suffered the hour commute to her day job. In the evenings, she worked on repatriating Czar. By Wednesday, the trip was arranged. Only four of us were permitted to escort Czar back into the wild. So, since Simone and I were going, we needed Popi and Ski, but had to leave Rebecca behind.

Early Saturday, we flew from Cincinnati to Moscow in a specially outfitted chartered jet. It did have room for a hundred passengers, but now had only four large comfy seats and a cage for a very large cat. I spent most of the flight trying to keep my jittery tiger calm. Every time Popi came close, Czar growled menacingly, so I sadly asked him to stay away. I think his feelings were hurt, but right now I was totally focused on the nervous cat.

After a long tiring flight we were taken to a warehouse outside of the city by Yuri from Tigers International. Yuri was cute and friendly, but we were all ready for bed. He had arranged hotel rooms for us, but we all refused to leave Czar all alone. Ski and Simone left to buy supplies, so I took the opportunity to make amends to Popi for snubbing him in favor of Czar and forcing him to sleep in a dirty warehouse. By the time I was done with the dear boy, he didn't have a care in the world.

We were still kissing and cooing sweet nothings to each other when Czar roared. My first thought was that he was jealous. Then I thought that Ski and Simone were back. Popi's first assumption, of course, was that I was in some kind of danger, so we had to go tactical.

We dressed and entered the huge room. Popi went first with his gun drawn. Though I wanted to, I knew from past experience that it would be a waste of time trying to talk sense into my paranoid husband.

Czar was focusing on the dark, far side of the building. Maybe there really was an intruder. Popi told me to release the tiger when he turned out the lights. I trust Popi completely, but I didn't like this idea. What if Czar were hurt? What if Czar attacked Popi? When the whole building went into complete darkness, I was still conflicted, but like a good Marine, I followed orders. Popi found his way back to me just as the bad guys turned on their flashlights. There were three of them. Popi left the gun with me and disappeared into the darkness. I feared for the lives of my two men.

One of the lights went flying through the air and shattered on the floor. I slowly walked toward the breaker box, feeling the need to see what was happening. A second light went dark and I heard the familiar sound of Popi pummeling someone. A few seconds later the third and final light fell to the floor, but remained lit. I felt the small switches and flipped as many of them as I could with two hands. When I saw that my two men were okay, I was so proud and happy that I'm sure they felt my joy and relief.

I called for Czar and he came running and gave me a big smile. Even though I knew that his intentions may not be completely platonic in nature, I returned his affection. When I guided him to his cage, he didn't resist and he seemed proud of the product of the strange spell he was under and the symbol of his affection for me. Czar's front feet were covered in blood, so I began cleaning them with bottled water and some discarded rags. Popi dragged the unconscious man to the cage and wrapped me in his arms, kissing me. Then Czar got involved by reaching his long wet tongue through the bars and licking first me then Popi.

# 2014; FREAKIN' GULAG

Though the man was still unconscious, I tied his hands and feet, just finishing as Simone and Ski noisily returned. They had food and several bags of gear for surviving a single night in this charnel house.

"Did you have to spend every Ruble I gave you? Ski, you're fired. I've got a new head of security and he'll work for ten pounds of sirloin per day."

I told them the story. Simone was frightened and Ski was pissed off.

"I leave you on your own for a few minutes and you manage to kill or maim three Ruskie citizens. Freakin' Gulag here we come."

"Calm down brother, I'd like to employ you as a crime scene clean-up specialist. It'll be just like you did in the everglades, no fuss no muss just good clean fun."

While Layla and Simone tended to Czar, I showed Ski the task at hand, the two disemboweled commandos. I called them commandos because of their identical black clothing, their identical guns equipped with flashlights and silencers, and the total absence of any clue as to their identities.

Ski didn't grow any greener than I did when he looked at the bloody remains. It was gruesome, but I didn't feel one bit sorry for the dead men. I don't know if they were out to kill us or to take Layla's feline sweetheart. It doesn't matter. An attack on one of us is an attack on us all.

It took us two hours to bury the liquidated carcasses and roughly clean up their stains on the concrete floor. Afterward, in pairs, we took turns walking to the nearby hotel for showers. Ski had brought some cans of Sterno to reheat the Thai food they had bought. It was enough to feed ten hungry men. At eleven, it was bed time. Ski volunteered to take first watch. I unrolled Layla's and my bedrolls near Czar's cage then stripped to my blue boxers and white wife beater. I lay on top of the thick brown canvass and while waiting for Layla, I dozed off.

# 2035; POPI DESERTS

I was back in 2035 and I was running. Layla was running too, on my right. Victor, on her right, was glancing back as he ran, so I looked back and wished that I hadn't. I saw headlights from three all-terrain, silent vehicles. Then the shooting started. I slowed slightly and moved directly behind my wife.

"Victor, we can't out run them so pick a place to make a stand."

"This way Walter, some rocks for cover."

Our sudden change of direction gave us a brief respite from the gunfire while the posse corrected their angles of attack. Fifty feet before reaching our objective, the firing resumed and Victor was shot in his left buttock. Layla and I stopped. I took Victor's rifle and gave it to Layla.

"Get to the rocks and cover me."

I got on one knee and, with much effort, manipulated my new friend over my right shoulder.

"Leave me, you must protect Layla." I ignored him and stood.

Victor was about my size, so my fifty foot trip to temporary safety was slow. Fortunately, Layla laid down some well-placed suppressive fire. The bad guys kept shooting, but it was less precise than it had been. I dropped Victor into the small circle of suitcase sized boulders. I kissed my dear wife, just in case it was my last chance, and exchanged my pistol for her rifle.

"Don't fire until they get close. Take a look at Victor's wound."

I took careful aim as their bullets whizzed by my face. I squeezed the trigger and one of the riders fell. His funny looking nearly silent craft continued our way, dragging its former pilot. It crashed right in front of me and stopped dead. I took aim again, but my shot was low and only managed to extinguish one of the two remaining headlamps. It was good enough to make them stop, dismount and find cover behind the trees. This gave me a few seconds to ransack the vehicle and the dead man. It was a jackpot. I commandeered another rifle with multiple extra clips, a handgun, food, water and a flare gun with four flares. Then disaster struck. I was shaken awake in 2014.

# 2014; Deadly Breasts

Someone was shaking me. It was Simone, armed with a big insecure smile.

"Popi, do you mind if I sleep next to you. I was nervous on my own. Will Layla mind?"

"The more, the merrier and I think Layla will understand."

"Understand what," my sneaky angel asked, having silently eavesdropped on us?

"I asked if I could sleep near Popi, so he can protect me."

"Of course you can dear. Popi, don't you dare grope our newest Angel. If she quits because of your old perverted ass, I'll hold you accountable."

Layla removed her pretty blue dress and lay on her bunk. She wasn't wearing a bra and I was slightly shocked, but totally filled with desire. Simone rolled out her bed roll on my left side. She took off her boots and lay down fully clothed. Layla, of course, couldn't leave well enough alone.

"Honey, I was only kidding about the old pervert thing. He is old but definitely not a pervert." Simone laughed and stood.

The Nubian vixen shed her baggy cammo pants, revealing that

magnificent derriere which was challenging the tensile strength of her tiny lacy, bright red undies. The sexy girl then took off her zoologist shirt. Simone was wearing a bra, but it was of such sheer red silky fabric that it didn't hide a thing. I quickly looked away from the incredibly sexy and dangerous vision. Her breasts were perfect, but gazing upon them for too long would surly get my eyes scratched out. I turned my back on the deadly vixen, wondering if Layla had set me up for her own amusement. I pulled my snickering wife close, my suspicions confirmed. I kissed her hard on her soft pink lips and closed my weary eyes, anxious to return to Siberia to protect the other, less serendipitous Layla.

# CZAR

By the time I got back to the waiting place, things had changed. There were many upright people gathered around the bridge. Most were women who stayed on the far bank, but there were two men armed with the upright mans cowardly weapon that loudly kills from a distance. I don't fear death, but being killed by a coward is not an honorable way to die. I knew that Pheasant Song would never let those cowardly men hurt me. She cared too much and even loved me. I sensed it with my mind.

She removed most of her pretty wrappings and lay down in the grass. My Princess was even more enchanting than she was earlier. I approached her, ignoring the menacing upright men. I kissed her feet and she stood and hugged me. Once again, the spell was unbroken. It was unheard of for me to react in this way to a woman, but it felt wonderful. A cowardly man stood near the stream and pointed his loud killing weapon at my Princess, so I leapt at him. As expected, the fool dropped his weapon, pissed himself and fell down the hill with a scream and a splash.

I trotted back to my love, hoping for another magic kiss, but she appeared unhappy. She was so unhappy that she picked up the weapon and aimed it at me. It didn't make the loud noise and it didn't kill me, but it made me very sleepy. Pheasant Song ran to me crying and blessed me with another kiss. Falling to sleep in her arms felt like nothing I'd ever felt. I also felt her pain and her love.

I awoke in a strange place. There were other men and women here and like me, they were all in barred cages. Outside the cages the upright men and women scurried about. Sometimes they stopped to stare and smile at me. One particular upright girl was very nice to me. She was small with black skin and teats that could feed a hundred babies. She called me king and said that she was Simone. It was a very pretty name for a beauty such as her.

Pheasant Song and Grrrrr came to visit. I welcomed her royally and when I hugged and kissed her, her beautiful face filled with joy. Grrrrr came close and I said his name. This was enough to keep him at a safe distance. All the other people were either desiring my Princess or very jealous of her. I've never been so proud. After Pheasant Song left, an upright man entered bearing her exotic scent. The man was a special friend to the girl in the next cage.

She was desperate to mate, but I wanted to be true to my new love. When the upright man put Pheasant Song's wrappings on the girl, I could not resist. I mated ferociously with the girl who had markings from my people, but couldn't speak my language. The experience was enhanced by my sweet Pheasant Song's aroma. While it felt incredible, I was glad that she wasn't here to witness my depravity.

The days came and went. I wanted to go home, but I could not sense where my home is. It must be a very great distance away because I could normally sense home with my mind from many nights walk away. I wasn't unhappy here. The food was good and the upright people were kind especially sweet Simone. My Pheasant Song visited me every day with her exciting magical kisses. Then the day came when my Princess coaxed me out of my cage and into a smaller cage.

We were transported at amazing speed to a strange place where I was loaded, cage and all, onto the flying machine. I was nervous and excited. I thought that my true love was taking me home where we can be happy. Pheasant Song stayed by my side the whole way and whenever I slept, which was often, she was there every time I awoke.

When the flying cage alit with a frightening commotion, we went to a strange empty space. I was beginning to feel normal and wide awake, though I found that when I pretended to be ill, I got more attention from my Pheasant Song. I was ready for her to commit to me completely, forsaking all others for her. This was not the way of my people, but it felt right. I must be patient until she is ready. The urge to be free with her was almost all consuming. An honorable man must bow to the desires of the one he loves.

The big man and Simone left the building and Pheasant Song and Grrrrr went to another room. I paced my small cage, anxious for my sweethearts' return. After a while, I sensed movement from the shadows and smelled three men approaching. I yelled in warning and they stood still for a moment, but soon they slowly came in my direction. Grrrrr and Pheasant Song returned. He was keeping her protectively behind him. I was beginning to warm to this upright man, who so obviously adored my woman.

Grrrrr gave Pheasant Song his small weapon and crossed the room, causing it to go completely dark. Pheasant Song then surprised me by opening my cell door. I didn't hesitate. I silently stalked the evil intruders. They wanted to hurt Pheasant Song. My honor would be lost if I were to allow that to happen. For even one thought of hurting her, they deserved to die. I killed the first one with one quick strike to the man's soft belly. Unlike my attack on Grrrrr, I used my main weapon, my claws.

I went in search of the other two and found Grrrrr quietly beating number two with his clawless paws. I had new admiration for the weak, but courageous upright man, who loves the woman I love. I killed the third man in much the same way as the first. The lights came on and Pheasant Song smiled a relieved loving smile at me. She made me feel great pride in my actions. She called for me and of course I came running. I couldn't help it. I was a fool for her, and would do absolutely anything for my darling Pheasant Song.

# 2035; MR. WEINER

I began to awaken. I felt two things, a pounding headache and that bounce/jolt from a moving off road-vehicle. I also felt the close physical contact with someone warm thus, hopefully, alive. I dared to open my eyes, knowing that the headache would worsen the moment I did. I was laying in the cargo bed of one of the enemies all-terrain vehicles. Victor was unconscious next to and partially on top of me. I tried to rise to make sure that it was Layla driving, but couldn't move with Victor's weight on my right arm. Since the odd vehicle made very little noise, I didn't have to yell.

"Li'l Freckles, Is that you driving this contraption over every pothole." She stopped, dismounted and ran to me. Tears of relief were streaming down her beautiful freckled face.

"Oh Popi you're okay." My dirty faced angel covered mine with sweet tearful kisses.

Victor's right leg was draped over me, creating an awkward situation when Big Popi sprang to life. Victor stirred.

"I like you too Walter, but not for wife." Layla squealed.

"Victor, you're alive." She dropped me and gave him a flurry of her celebratory kisses. Layla told the story.

"After you killed the first one and got us weapons and ammo, the bad guys knew they were out gunned. They tried to flank us left and right. Victor low crawled out the back of our fort and intercepted the one on the right. They shot each other. We had the last one pinned down thirty yards to our left. Just when I thought we had him, he surprised us with a hand grenade. Popi, you got me out of the fort just in time, but you were wounded and unconscious. The man charged us, thinking we were dead, but I came to my senses just in time and shot him dead."

As it turned out, I was not wounded by shrapnel, but by a flying rock connecting with my head. Layla somehow managed to load me into the vehicle, drove to victor and found him to be alive. She patched him up as best she could and rolled him on top of me. I don't know how a one hundred and ten pound woman is able to lift two one hundred and seventy-five pound men, but I did know Layla and her infinite inner strength.

She said, "I've been heading north for three hours, but so far, I've seen no sign of the tiger people.

Victor said, "Take us to the top of the next ridge. We'll be able to see a great distance in all directions."

Sure enough, from the ridgeline we spied the smoke from a campfire. An hour later we pulled into the busy compound of Tigers International. Victor and I were treated by the Veterinarians who sentenced him to bed, while I was released with an icepack for the large lump on my hard head. Layla and I were fed and bathed. We were told that the director would be here soon and Victor would be airlifted out on her helicopter.

Layla said, "I didn't know that Simone would be here."

The young Vet said, "She hadn't planned to be but when she heard that you two were killed in the crash, she changed her plans."

I asked a cute young tree hugger, Lacy, "Who's in charge here? Tell them to meet me in the radio room ASAP."

I took Layla's arm and Lacy's, as she was executing my request on a walky-talky. I was dragging them along with me to the communication center and HQ. There we were met by a grumpy looking forty year old scientist type who spoke decent English with a slight Russian accent.

"Mr. Lemon, you've gotten my people in an uproar. Go take a nap and let us do our jobs."

"What's your name son?"

"I'm Dr. Sergey Werner and I'm In charge of this survey. I'll only ask one more time, stay out of our way or you'll be arrested and caged."

Something was up. I may not be the easiest man to get along with, but this young punk seemed to have something personal against me.

"Look Mr. Weiner, I don't know what's gnawing at your crotch, but I need to talk to Simone immediately."

"As you know, it's Dr. Werner and that's not going to happen." He called on an intercom "Security respond to HQ. I warned you."

"You're in on this, aren't you Weiner? You tried to have my wife and I killed and now you're going to try to kill the Director."

When the idiot didn't draw his side arm, but simply tried to punch me in the throat, I knew I was wrong about his involvement. I dodged his pathetic attempt and floored him with a soft tap to his heart which left him squeaking for breath. The security guy looked more capable, so I sicced Layla on him. She had him smiling and blushing in seconds flat. Meanwhile, I was telling the young operator to get Simone on the Radio.

"Of course," the tech explained, "We haven't used radio waves for years. This is the newest technology, the Argon repeating vibrator or ARV."

"This is very important, its life or death, please hurry."

"Yes sir, Director, go for Mr. Lemon."

"Thank God you're alive, Popi. Is Laya okay too?"

"She's fine Simone. Where are you?"

"We're about thirty miles and five minutes out."

I thought, my god, that's over three hundred and fifty miles an hour.

"Listen carefully honey, we did not crash. We were shot down by a surface to air missile about twenty-five miles south of the camp."

"Oh my God, what should we do?"

"Can you patch me in with the pilot?"

"Okay Popi, Captain Whitaker is on."

"Captain, I suggest that you turn around and avoid this area."

"No can do Pops, there is nowhere else to go within our fuel range."

"Jeez son, you better hug the treetops for the rest of the flight."

After a ten second pause, he said, "Rodger, we're collecting pine cones. How will this help?"

"It'll greatly reduce the firing window for the shooter."

Simone shouted, "Oh, Popi, they just fired at us! I think they missed."

"Captain, keep it low, you better bring my girl back to me."

"Rodger that Pops we're one mike out. Holy Jesus! They missed again, compound in sight."

I quit sweating bullets and turned to the gathering crowd with a big smile on my naïve face only to run into Mr. Weiner's sucker punch. It was barely enough to knock the smile off, so when Layla kicked him in his daddy parts, I laughed. I had to figure out, like a snubbed schoolgirl, why this jackass didn't like me.

Layla and I ran out to greet the small chopper. It wasn't completely noiseless, but nearly so. The future seems to have made great strides in that regard. If only they could figure out how to put an end to the evil that men do, then I'd be impressed. Simone alit with wobbly legs and ran to us, bypassing Weiner, who also didn't take a snub well. Simone leapt into my arms and planted a large grateful kiss on my smiling lips.

"Thank you Popi, you've saved me yet again."

I guess I'll have to wait for the future past to find out how I'd saved her.

"Hello beautiful."

After greeting Layla in a similar fashion, Simone called a meeting of her staff, her security team and of course her dearest friends, Popi and Li'l Freckles. Layla, in 2035 seemed to be quite famous still, but apparently my legend has faded over the years. It's not surprising since

I was mainly known for killing evil men who wanted to hurt Layla, while she was and still is a world renowned dress designer. This didn't bother me, but I had to wonder what 2035 Walter felt about falling from the ranks of the adored international superheroes.

# 2035; LAYLA'S JOURNAL

Something is wrong with Popi. I first noticed it on the day we traveled to Russia. He was forgetting things and acting as if he wanted to ask about them, but he was hesitant to admit that he was having problems. On the other hand, he seems more vigorous and younger. He also seems to be throwing his weight around like he sometimes did while he was the most famous man in the world. It's as if he has forgotten that he's the one who spent years climbing out from under that reputation. He thought he had the gunslingers' curse which was fueling every disturbed hotshot psycho's desire to be the one to finally outdraw him.

He loved his notoriety except for the danger it put me and his other loved ones in. Popi withdrew from the public eye as best he could. He still went to Paris and New York every year, but he never appeared on stage or spoke to the press. Most meaningfully, my Popi made the ultimate sacrifice to protect me. He stopped flirting with his female fans. By around 2020 or so his plan was succeeding. He was hardly ever in the tabloids anymore and when he was, he was referred to as Layla Lemon's husband Walter.

I was no longer Li'l Freckles, but always Layla, although my dear Popi still never calls me by anything but Li'l Freckles. Anyway, after barely escaping death at the hands of presumed tiger poachers, Simone called for a strategy meeting. It was very illuminating and a little frightening, Illuminating because of the unwavering dedication of the twenty young scientists and unpaid students. When given the option of leaving, they all chose to stay.

It was frightening because an impromptu audit of arms and ammo demonstrated our precarious position. We had two automatic assault rifles, Victor's and Popi's, which he borrowed from a dead man, with four clips each. We had five hand guns, a thirty-eight revolver with six rounds, two forty-five automatics with a total of fifty rounds, Victors 9mm with twenty rounds and Dr. Werner's 40 cal. Sig Saur. There was also a Winchester 22 rifle with two hundred rounds and three dart guns with a total of twenty darts which would probably be lethal to a human.

Dr. Warner had called the Russian Army which has a small outpost four hundred miles to the east. They refused to fly for fear of the surface to air missiles, but promised to be here in force by sun up. Simone told the group that Dr. Werner, as the sole representative of the Russian government, was in charge of our defense. I detected a low groan from the crowd, giving confirmation to Popi's gut instincts about the man. The Dr. took over the briefing and managed to alienate half the crowd, causing them to insist that they be evacuated.

Dr. Werner didn't handle the revolt well, calling them cowards and telling them that they were welcome to leave, but not with any of his vehicles, supplies or weapons. Some actually began to leave so Popi stood.

"Wait, let's not do anything rash. We are stronger if we stand together. We only have to hold out for twenty hours so I'll assign you, in groups of three, defensive positions which you'll improve and man for the duration."

"Sit down and shut up or I'll put you in irons Lemon."

"Dr. Werner, you can either fight with us or against us. We have a military man in your infirmary with just the training we need to survive an attack and I propose that we put him in charge of our defense."

It was unanimous since Dr. Werner refuse to vote. Popi thought that the unpleasant man had some personal grudge against him and I was beginning to agree with him. It was why Popi suggested that Victor take charge. He didn't want anyone to get hurt or killed because of the friction between the two. Werner told the communications guy to get his boss on the ARV. After several unsuccessful tries the worried young man looked stumped.

"We can't get through. I think we're being jammed." Sergey deflated. He realized, for the first time, that we were indeed under attack and in great danger. This egoist didn't have what it takes to protect us, but luckily we had Popi and Victor. While Popi went about setting up a perimeter, I went to fill Victor in on the situation. I walked into the tent just in time to catch the young Russian patting the giggling nurse on her butt.

"Ah Layla, your timing couldn't be worse. I was about to close the deal with nurse Ivanna." He had an amused, sly gleam in his eyes.

"You, Victor, remind me of my Popi when he was much younger. No matter how badly he was shot up, he couldn't resist flirting with the pretty women."

"Layla, if I had a woman like you, I wouldn't even notice any other girls." This time he was sincere.

I told Victor the situation and Popi's fear that we would be attacked tonight before the Russian army arrived. He agreed and demonstrated his fitness to lead by jumping naked out of bed. He was about twenty-five, tall, fit and an extremely fine, manly specimen. Victor was dressed and combat ready in seconds. We walked hand in hand out of the white tent to review the defensive preparations being directed by Popi. Popi was showing one group of three how to operate the semi-automatic 45 assigned to their firing position.

"Leave the safety off. You need to be ready to fire at all times. Line up the target with the two sights with both eyes open and gently squeeze the trigger. It should almost feel like a surprise every time the weapon fires."

The two young girls were frightened, but the young man was confident. Popi told them to keep digging in and improving their position until the battle starts. He then drove two stakes deeply into the hard earth at the front of the foxhole.

"Only fire in between the two aiming stakes, this will prevent you from accidentally shooting your comrades to the left and right." Popi turned and saw Victor and me. "Victor, you're looking well. What are our chances?"

"Not good my friend, but better now that you've got these civilians working like soldiers."

I left the two soldiers to their preparations and searched out Simone. I found her in the HQ trying to reconnect with the sane world through the ARV, no luck so far. I asked Nicholai if he could track the jamming signal, so that we could find the poachers base. He told me that he was a volunteer and didn't have the technical expertise to do that.

I kissed his cheek and left the HQ with Simone and walked into the middle of an argument between Victor and Sergey.

"Dr. Werner, I need your weapon. Unless you man a fighting position, that gun is needed on the front lines."

"It's my gun and I'm supposed to be in charge so fuck off." Victor held his temper in check.

"Sergey, cowardice in combat is punishable by death." He was calm, but threatening.

Both men went for their side arms. Victor won by a large margin. Victor disarmed the bureaucrat who stormed off. Popi walked up. He was unarmed.

"Did he give up the gun?"

"Yes he did, but not without a struggle. He's going to be a problem. How are your preparations coming?"

"The forward fighting positions are ready although I've instructed them to keep improving them until the sun goes down."

Popi and Victor continued to talk strategy, but my attention was elsewhere. I was watching Dr. Sergey Werner. He was mounting the ATV that we had captured from the enemy.

"Popi, Mr. Weiner is stealing my dune buggy."

We watched Sergey begin to cross the large field at the front of the camp. He was going way faster than I had dared to drive the quiet wave machine. When he was three or four hundred meters away, gunfire erupted from the tree line and Sergey overturned the vehicle. We couldn't tell if he'd been hit. After a silent minute, Sergey got up, restarted the machine and started heading back toward us. He was smartly weaving in his wild retreat. Sergey was a hundred meters out when a small rocket, with a zigzag path, shot the vehicle out from under him.

I turned to Popi, but he was gone. He was running to the scene of the explosion. There was no gunfire on Popi's trip to rescue the man who hated him. When Popi got there the enemy began firing again. Victor ran to HQ and came back with the 22 rifle. Victor emptied a ten shot clip into the tree line, I think, to just unsettle the snipers. Popi threw the wounded man over his right shoulder and began the slow jog toward safety. Victor continued his plinking. Hopefully he was affecting the bad guys aim. Popi went down, but he didn't stay down. He eventually made it to one of our foxholes.

Instead of running to my husband, I went straight for the HQ, now the hospital, to make sure we were ready for casualties. All the while, I was sobbing and trying not to contemplate the unthinkable. I couldn't figure out why Popi would risk his life for that boor. He had kept his promise to me for many years now, a promise to not risk his life unnecessarily. Something is wrong with Popi and if he survives, I'm going to find out what.

# September 2014
## Ambush

Young Yuri Commissar came for us at daylight. We had decided not to tell him about our eventful night. We left the now conscious commando in the dirty office, tied and gagged. We rode fifty miles or so to a small civilian air strip and boarded a fifty year old four prop cargo plane. It was a five hour flight to Tunguska or rather Vanavara which is a rural outpost of trappers, hunters and reindeer herders. The airstrip at Vanavara is mud and gravel. Apparently, September is a rainy season in the Tunguska region. I was glad that Layla and Simone were busy tending to Czar and didn't have to watch the white knuckle landing.

Although the city has only a thousand citizens, more than twice that number greeted us and led us, including Czar, to an open air festival held in our honor. The plain folks treated us to music, dance and a feast of the local fare. Big Popi & Li'l Freckles posters and banners decorated every building in town, all ten of them. The men all got extremely drunk, including Ski and me. The women took Layla and

Simone off somewhere to party in the way of the womenfolk. Yuri stayed with Czar, who seemed content to be admired by the crowds.

There was no hotel in Vanavara, so we were put up in a large tent. Layla helped me get drunkenly ready for bed. She treated me like a mildly retarded child while I treated her like the sexy wife of a horny husband. I couldn't convince her that no one would notice if we quietly made love in the dormitory setting. Ski was drunk too and took my side.

"He's right Squirt. As your chief of security, I'll stand guard until you lovebirds are done."

Layla laughed, but she didn't fall for the vodka induced pitch. O-dark-thirty rang in with an ear throbbing headache. Though I attempted to hide my pain with a happy smile, Simone busted me.

"My, my Popi, you look like I feel. I've never drank so much in my life."

"That's why I usually stick with beer. Is there a shower and a cup of coffee around here?"

"Sorry Popi, but showers are forbidden for the day of deployment to the base camp. The cats can be upset from the chemical odors. There is plenty of coffee though and Layla went to get you some."

I brushed my teeth and wet down my body in the weak cold stream from a garden hose. I felt much better after my soap-less soaking. An hour later we rolled out in two old deuce and a half trucks with standard camouflage paint, except for the Tigers International logo on the doors. The lead truck carried Czars cage with Layla and Simone in the canvas covered bed. Yuri drove.

I rode in the second truck, driven by Ski. I was in the back with a few young field scientists. I really didn't want to brush up on my big cat preservation theories. I thought that I could catch up on my sleep. The kids were fans and thought it was a privilege to be on my team. I tried to explain my very limited role in the safari, but I was not believed. If they knew me, they'd know that I wasn't that humble.

The trip was only about sixty miles, but the road only went half that far. It was four bumping lurching hours later when we pulled into the camp. The camp had two log cabins and five large tents, all was orderly and quiet. Yuri pulled a medium caliber Luger pistol, causing me to draw my 9mm and Ski to unsheathe his fifty cal. cannon.

Yuri whispered, "Something is wrong here, camp is never empty. Popi, check the tents, Kurt cabin right and I will take left, the HQ."

I told the others to keep the trucks running in case we needed a hasty retreat. I checked the largest OD green tent first. There were three large, empty tiger cages, a huge surgical table and a couple of field desks full of scattered paperwork. There were no people and no signs of what may have happened to them. The other four tents were about half the size of the tiger hospital. Three were green and the fourth was white with a red cross painted on top, the people hospital I presumed. I quickly cleared these, a male bedroom, a female bedroom and a dining room. The only odd thing I found was in the white tent. It was a message written in blood, BROCKOV.

I met back up with Ski and Yuri who found nothing unusual except the lack of people.

Yuri said, "Lights are all on as was the radio. It appears everyone was interrupted last evening and generator ran out of petrol." Yuri looked to me for my report.

"The tents all looked normal except in the first aid tent."

I told them about the bloody message and everyone wanted to see it. I held Layla back.

"Li'l Freckles, we're not going to be able to stay here tonight. I think these poachers are finding it hard to get their trophies the old fashion way, so they are preying on these do-gooders to lead them to the cats." My wife was frightened.

"Popi, what are we going to do? They probably already know that Czar is here and they're willing to kill us to get him." Her blue gray eyes were beginning to weep.

"I know sweetheart. I think we need a plan that will enable us to get these innocent kids out of here and to safely release Czar. I'm hoping he can protect himself once he is in the forest."

"I'm sure he can, but I don't know if he'll be willing to leave me."

"Let's bring in the others, but I'm going to leave the final decision regarding Czar up to you." She kissed me without checking the spell. This was very rare.

"Thank you Popi. I want to protect you from killing anyone, but I want you to extend your exceptions to the rules list to include protecting Czar."

"Of course honey, he's family." I was sincere, though only because Layla loved him so much.

We gathered in the HQ and had a very lively discussion with the four young interns. I remember the two girls' names, but not the men, making me a stereotype I suppose. There was Sarah, a young busty blonde American girl, cute and a little flighty. She was from West Virginia and was a Harvard doctoral candidate. She clung to an Italian guy, who was more pleased with his situation than worried. The other girl was a pretty Russian student named Marie.

Marie and her nerdy boyfriend were volunteers from the University of Moscow. Marie was openly flirting with me. She was giving me inappropriate big smiles, fawning over my every word or movement and lightly touching me every chance she got. I didn't mind, but her boyfriend wasn't thrilled with his star struck sweetheart.

We came up with a plan. It wasn't a really good plan because it depended on the bad guys. To be successful, we needed the poachers to witness our unfolding charade and believe what they saw. We put the plan into effect immediately, starting by parking the trucks side by side.

Layla made a show of feeding her caged tiger. She climbed into the back and secured the canvass back flap. I got into the cab of the tiger hauler and Yuri took the wheel of the people hauler. On Layla's signal, I moved out in the direction of the far away woods. I stopped and Yuri pulled up tightly alongside. It took only a minute to set up the truck with a new driver, one made of stuffed clothing. I rigged the steering and throttle and evacuated the ghost truck. I quickly climbed under the side curtain of the other truck. I was helped by Marie who couldn't feel the laser beams fired at us by her nerdy boyfriend.

The situation wasn't helped when the child planted her mouth on mine as we fell to the floor. Layla was in the rear of the cargo space with her beloved and now uncaged Czar. Yuri was driving the hell out of the old diesel truck which was good, but he had the eight of us bouncing and falling all over each other. Italian guy had a secure grip on the fearful Sarah. I suspected that her fear was a ruse meant to attract the handsome boy. I peeked out the side curtain just in time to see the ghost truck plow into the forest and the eight or ten men in cautious pursuit. We had a head start.

Yuri made the four hour trip from the camp to the hardball in two and a half and we in the back had the bruises to show for it. On the road, he pulled over. The Italian kid took over the driving since he was the only one who could drive the stick besides Layla, who could not leave the wild beast alone with the others. Ski, Yuri and I dismounted to set up the ambush. I went to the back of the truck and lifted the flap, intending to get a good luck kiss from my wife. Instead, I was face to humongous face with the mighty Czar.

Czar made the low growling sound which he always made when I came near to his girlfriend. It didn't bother me anymore and became even less threatening when he licked my face. We were brothers now, in the service of our woman, Layla. She did give me that good luck kiss and Czar said goodbye with, Grrrrr. The plan was for Italian guy to drive five miles as fast as possible and pull over to release Czar into the heavy wood.

Ski set up directly in front of the trail across the roadway in a wet ditch. His first job was to aim for any vehicle engines with the S&W blunderbuss. It could supposedly penetrate an engine block. Yuri set up in the trees to the left and I was on the right of the muddy trail. We didn't have to wait long before the enemy approached. They arrived in three pickup trucks, each holding three armed men. Ski took out the first truck with one incredibly loud shot, sending plumes of steam and smoke into the blue sky and blocking the trail. These men were well trained. I knew this because they took the counterintuitive, yet correct action when encountering an ambush. They charged.

# 2014; VLADIMIR BROCKOV

I didn't like the plan. Popi needed me on his six, but I had a specialized ability to make this mission a success, the ability to control the wild eight hundred pound Siberian tiger. Kurt sat silently near Czar and me with his huge pistol cradled in his lap. He ignored the jostling and kept his unwavering scary gaze on Czar. Kurt didn't trust the friendly beast and was determined to be successful in his protection of me. I wasn't worried about him shooting my tiger accidentally. He knew how much that would hurt me and Kurt would never hurt me.

I sometimes wonder, why me? Why are so many people so devoted to me? The One told me that I was special, but only for outliving the other girls in my batch of spirits. I knew in my heart that the reason was Popi. I've begun to think that The One isn't the only magician in town because Popi has used magic of his own to save me. This came in the form of an ancient rune key. That rune saved us twice each before it was destroyed by the second bullet it had stopped from killing Popi. The point is, the ten thousand, the one hundred messengers and The One knew nothing about that magic.

Anyway, Ski was a good Marine too. He didn't like the part of the plan where he had to leave me unprotected. He knew he had to, so that we others could get away. Popi, I think, knew that Czar would sacrifice his life to keep me safe. I felt unworthy, but over and above that gloomy feeling, I felt beloved. Kurt, Yuri and Popi got out to at least delay the poachers. I of course was worried, but I had to keep a clear mind. The window for releasing Czar unseen might be small.

Antony, a cute Italian volunteer took over the driving and Sarah joined him in the cab. Simone stayed near me and Czar while the other two sat in the front of the truck bed, arguing. None of the four students had a real grasp of our situation. It's for the best. Simone was worried, but being a Big Popi & Li'l Freckles fan, she had a lot of faith in us. Antony was a really good driver, seeming to get a lot more speed out of the old truck. When he pulled over, I knew that this was the moment of truth.

I got Czar out and led him into the forest. He was happier than he had been the whole trip and I was sadder than he'd ever seen. We walked into the woods about fifty yards and stopped. I hugged my dear friend and said goodbye. He seemed as if he understood at first, but when I, in tears, turned my back on him and slowly walked away, he growled. Czar caught up with me and gently spun me around with his big paw. He looked past my tears, through my eyes and into my heartsick mind. It was a two way exchange of worried questions and emotional answers.

I knew he loved me and wanted me to be his forever and he knew that it could never be. I gave my tiger one final kiss on his black lips and we both sadly walked away. Czar was free and I had to shake off this sadness and get on with the flawed plan. I was to go another five miles and find a trappers' shed and Yuri's friend, Anatoli. He would give us shelter, hide our truck and feed us while the men walked the ten miles. Popi says that plans are just wishes. I take this to mean that one, even a good Marine, must always be prepared to alter the plan.

We spotted the wagon ruts to Anatoli's cabin. The truck barely squeezed through the tree lined track which led, after a couple of miles, to a broken down shack. We all jumped out immediately, tired of the bone rattling and diesel fumes. No one came out to greet us, so we climbed onto the rickety porch. I knocked on the homemade door and got no answer. I tried the door. It was not only unlocked, but unlockable, so I stepped into the dingy smelly house.

I saw two rooms, a living room with two lumpy unmatched sofas and a kitchen/dining room. There was a closed door to my right, perhaps a bedroom. There was electricity, but no plumbing, judging by the ten gallon water jug on the kitchen counter. I put the teakettle on and we sat on the sofas, waiting to see if Popi, Kurt and Yuri were okay. We were sipping tea when the bedroom door opened and out walked a man with an assault rifle.

He cleared the doorway, revealing two more men who were similarly armed and dressed, all wearing camouflage. They also all had dark, greasy hair and beards.

I asked, "Are you Anatoli?"

"Indeed I am, Little Freckles. You are so much more beautiful in person."

"Thank you. Can you help me find Popi?"

"I have horrible news for you my little one. Popi and the others have been killed by the poachers."

I didn't outwardly react, but inside, I was going over every possible reason for this man to lie to me. Popi was not dead. If he were, he'd be kissing my neck right now.

"You are a liar and an evil, cruel man. Are you the murderous killer of tigers and men?"

"Correct again my dear."

The gloating man gave orders to his men in Russian and they immediately searched and tied up the others, completely mauling the girls, but ignoring me. The poachers took the weeping women and the frightened men outside. The commander smiled at me and my expression. It was halfway between disdain and disgust.

"Are you really Anatoli?"

"No my little one, my name is Vladimir and you are right. I suspect that your husband is dead, but I don't know for sure. I'll not lie to you again. I must take you all to my base."

Since he wouldn't lie, I asked, "What has happened to the Tigers International people?"

"Sadly, they are dead as will be your young friends. My men need rewards for their efforts. We should have your tiger by now. My, what a magnificent specimen he is. My men get to use the women and execute the men. It's what they live for."

"My Popi and my friends are going to kill you and every one of your men. What are your plans for me?" Vladimir's face turned serious.

"You will be all mine. You will either become my perfect wife or become three night's entertainment for me and my men."

He came closer. I was looking for an opening, thinking swift kick to his crotch. Vladimir was cautious, knowing my reputation. He put his gun to the back of my head and began to handcuff me. As he closed the cold steel around my left wrist, I grabbed the rifle barrel with my right hand and spun, wresting the gun from his hand.

I fell to the dirty floor and attempted to aim the weapon, but he was on me too quickly. He took the gun from me and set it aside. He lay on top of me and forced a brutal kiss. I bit his lip, causing a big smile and a turgid expansion between his legs. No, he wasn't under my spell. He just got his sexual excitement from violence. He ripped open my shirt and covered my breasts with little bites as he pinned my shoulders with his large hands. He didn't bite hard, just hard enough for me to flinch from the pain. One of his men walked in and saw us. He quickly exited without a word. Vladimir got himself under control and flipped me onto my stomach. He finished handcuffing me.

I had two of my shirt buttons clasped secretly in my hand, after having secreted another behind the couch leg. It was a bread crumb for Popi. Vladimir stood and pulled me up with him. He didn't bother to straighten my clothes before he pushed me out the door. We got into an old pickup truck after I dropped another button. He strapped me in, not for my safety, but to help protect him from my attacks. Throughout the four hour trip, mostly on the barest of trails, the sadist reached over every few minutes and pinched my nipples until I cried out. We came to a fork in the trail and veered right.

I asked sweetly, "Vladimir, can we stop, so I can pee?"

I left my last button as he watched.

When we arrived at the camp, he said, "Home sweet home my little one, I hope you can find happiness here because you will never leave."

The camp looked like a trailer park, a dozen beat up trailer homes radiating around a huge central prefabricated barn. We were all dragged into that barn and locked into tiger cages.

"Is everyone okay," I asked?

Antony still clung to Sarah who was sobbing real tears now. Sergey was of no comfort to Marie, his girlfriend.

She asked, "Do you think it's true, is Popi dead?" I told the truth.

"If Popi is dead, how would they know? They were ten miles away from the ambush site. Cell phones don't work out here and I haven't seen any radios. They want Popi to be dead, but many others have tried and failed to kill him. I won't believe it until I see for myself. I have learned that you can never count Popi out. Even if he were dead, he'd find some way to help us."

# 2014; THE DEADLY MISCOUNT

With the lead truck stalled the three men piled out, already firing and charging Ski. Ski shot the first one as he tried a frontal assault. By the sharp percussive sound I knew my friend had used his 9mm. The other two lost a bit of their resolve and sought cover in the trees only to run into me. I killed them both. The other six men spread out on either side of the trail.

I yelled to Ski and Yuri, "Ski, cover us, we're falling back."

After getting a nod from Yuri, I turned and ran for the ditch as Ski emptied a precious clip to keep their heads down. I dove into the long mud puddle on Ski's right. I looked for Yuri, but he hadn't made it across the street.

"Where's Yuri?"

`"He didn't fall back Walter, but I didn't see him get shot."

I had to do something. I told Ski to hold his ground.

"When I flush them, put them down."

I went left, low crawling, sloshing my way for fifty yards and signaled Ski that I was ready to cross. He began firing in earnest as I belly crawled across the open twenty feet. Back in the forest, I rose and moved quickly toward the gunfire. After a minute, Ski stopped firing for a few seconds. I heard the boom of the fifty caliber cannon. They must have tried to move one of the trucks. I used the disturbance to quickly close the distance. I came upon a dead poacher, not knowing whether Ski or Yuri had killed him. I eventually came upon Yuri. He was wounded and lying in the mud, but he was alive. There were two men firing at Ski. I shot one and the other took off. A few seconds later, Ski shot him dead.

I slung my wounded friend over my shoulder and retreated the way I came. I again signaled for my crossing guard. Ski laid down even more covering fire because he knew that I wouldn't be crawling back across the road. In the ditch, I checked Yuri's wounds. He was shot in the chest and was drifting off into shock. I knew he would never wake up if he went to sleep so I lightly slapped him and told him to stay with me while I tried to stop the bleeding.

"Thank you Popi for you come for me."

I quickly ran to Ski, forgoing the soggy crawl. It worked out well because two men broke cover to get a good shot at me. They each got one free shot then my big Polish friend gunned them down. By my count, there should be one bad guy left, but if he was there, he wasn't firing. I told Ski that I had killed three and Yuri killed one.

"That leaves five. How many did you get?"

"Just four, but I saw one running to the right."

I was wondering if he had been outflanking us, while I was outflanking them. Two men sprang from the trees behind us to the left. We had miscounted, there were ten. Ski and I had to drink muddy water. We dived to the bottom of our ditch as they fired. I got back into a firing position first and shot one of the two. The other jumped into the mud hole near Yuri, who weakly grappled with the killer, blocking my shot. The bastard put his gun to my friends head and pulled the trigger. He impossibly killed the man, who I knew to be alive in 2035. I was shot out of the sky with him that future year. I shot the last poacher and continued to shoot him until my gun was empty.

By the time I came back from my paradoxical mind wandering

state, Ski pulled up in the last truck. We must link up with Layla and the others. Now that I had time to be concerned about my angel, the concern was suddenly all consuming. I did take time to recover Yuri's body and laid him gently into the truck bed. We covered the ten miles in six minutes. We found the cabin. In the only bedroom, we found a dead man, presumably Anatoli. No one else was home and we couldn't find the Tigers International truck. Something was wrong.

"Ski, if Layla was taken, she would try to leave a clue. Find It."

We were about to give up when Ski moved one of the moldy sofas and I spotted it.

"That's it, Layla's button. She was here and her shirt was ripped."

"Aw Geez Walter, you don't think?"

"No, there's no blood."

My friend accepted this and led me outside to look for another clue. While examining the freshest tire treads in the muddy ground, Ski found a second button.

"This is where she was put into a pickup truck. They headed north."

I said, "We are only an hour or so behind them. Let's go."

We did take an extra two minutes. I carried Yuri into the cabin and lay him in the bed next to his executed friend. Ski removed the break and turn signal light bulbs from the truck. We, quickly as possible, followed the faint trail. Every time we came to a crossing trail, we had to get out and check for another bread crumb. We had to go straight unless we had some compelling evidence. The third time we got out to inspect a cross trail, we found the third button. It told us to turn northeast.

After three hours we got lucky. Ski spotted headlights coming through the tree tops from behind. Even though it was dark, we had been running without lights so there was a good chance that they hadn't seen us. We quickly backed the truck into the woods and camouflaged the front with branches. When the truck passed, we saw two occupants. The passenger was swigging from a vodka bottle. In the bed of the truck was a cage, which was occupied by an unconscious tiger. He was big, not Czar big, but big. After they were three or four hundred yards ahead, we fell in behind them.

It was getting hard to stay on the muddy trail in the darkness, but Ski somehow managed. Half an hour later, the bad guys stopped. There was nothing obvious around to stop for, so we watched. Soon, an armed man exited the forest, took a swig from the bottle and waved them on.

"Ski, hide the truck while I check out the sentry."

I thought about approaching through the forest, but I decided it would be quicker and quieter to stick to the trail. Anyway, I was still covered in mud, making me hard to spot in this starlit darkness. I had my gun, but I didn't want the noise, so I kept it holstered. When I got close, I heard the guard talking on a radio. I couldn't understand them, but was relieved that they were laughing. I kept moving, while he was distracted by the noisy squawk box. As soon as the young man signed off, I attacked. I was able to disarm the sturdy punk, but he continued to fight back, blackening my right eye and kicking my right knee.

I said, "Screw this," and pulled my 9mm, with which I beat him unconscious.

Sometimes subtlety and finesse just doesn't get the job done. I left the sentry tied, gagged and unconscious. He may die without some medical assistance, but I didn't care, couldn't care. We had to follow that tiger.

# CZAR

I was thrilled to be home or at least a three night's walk away, but I was sad that my Pheasant Song and I had to part. We had connected through our minds and each explored the others innermost thoughts. That we loved each other was undeniable, but she couldn't see that we could overcome our differences. I also now knew that Pheasant Song was deeply in love with Grrrrr. How she could choose the brave, but weak upright man over me was beyond my ability to comprehend. I also knew that the reason they were in danger is because the people killers wanted me. Grrrrr had stayed behind to either draw the enemy away or fight them to the death. I liked Grrrrr, but now I was very jealous of him.

In case Grrrrr did die, I wanted to be around to help my Pheasant Song to grieve and to provide her with the love she needed to be happy. I followed her. Even though she was moving at remarkable speed, she couldn't out-pace my senses. By dusk, I tracked her to an upright mans' house. I pawed open the door and went inside. I could tell that they lingered here a while. I sensed the bloodlust of the people killers and my loves bravery. I also imprinted the pungent stink of the three killers deep in my mind. For scaring my dear Pheasant Song, I sentenced them to death.

Back outside, it was easy to pick up the scent and happily, she was traveling in the direction of my home. I really desired to show Pheasant Song my home. I walked in the forest, feeling too exposed on the open trail. After a half night's walk, I heard an upright man's truck approaching. If it was one or more of the killers who took my woman, truck or no truck, I would kill them. To my great surprise and small disappointment, it was Grrrrr and the nervous man. They, of course, didn't see or sense me watching them.

A short while later, another truck approached from behind, causing Grrrrr to halt his truck and hide it near me. They let the new truck pass. In the back of the truck was a person who I sensed was alive, but he was not moving. We all followed and watched as an upright man came out of the wood and talked to the people killers before they continued on their way. Grrrrr walked toward the hidden man who, I feel shame in admitting, I had not smelled or sensed before seeing him.

I, from the cover of the trees, followed. I was jealous of Grrrrr, but didn't want harm to come to him, at least not before we saved Pheasant Song. By the time Grrrrr got to the people killer, I was in position to kill the man If Grrrrr couldn't. When he attacked the killer, the killer fought back, giving Grrrrr a few bruises. I had to laugh at my rivals' ineptitude until the Killer made him angry. Grrrrr showed his hidden talent. He channeled his anger into a swift, unstoppable force.

When Grrrrr got into his truck, I jumped into the back. I sensed that Pheasant Song would need all of us. The nervous man drew his weapon when he saw me, but Grrrrr stopped him from using it. Grrrrr opened a small portal in the window and put his face to it.

He asked, "Czar?"

I answered my friend, "Grrrrr."

Soon, we were on our way again and it wasn't long before we came upon the people killers fort. I sensed my Pheasant Song. She was in great danger.

# 2014 LAYLA KILLS ANTONY

Vladimir stood on the long table and called for quiet. I sat next to Marie and asked her to translate. He told his gathered throng of bloodthirsty killers some disturbing things, but started with good news. Apparently, Popi, ski and Yuri's ambush was a success. They killed or seriously wounded all ten of the enemy. Then the bad news started, the bad guys killed one of ours. He didn't say which one and I refused to speculate. He said that tonight's hunt would proceed as scheduled and that there would be very special rewards for their living trophies. The three man team that brought in the first living male would have the pick of the women.

He didn't surprise me when he said, "Except the little freckled blonde, she's mine."

The forty or so men cheered and began gearing up. They all walked by our cages and hooted obscenities at the girls. I didn't understand the words, but fully recognized the meaning of their evil tongues. Some of the men carried Tigers International notebooks, presumably the sighting charts, which would help guide the bastards to their prey.

After the thirty men left for the hunt, the twelve or so who remained did their window shopping. Simone and I shared a cage, which smelled of stale tiger urine. Vladimir smiled at me while telling his men what he was going to do with me. I don't know what he said, but I saw that his henchmen were impressed.

"What will you do with the men," I said, keeping my voice as strong as I could?

"Like a gentleman, I'll honor their wishes. The men will get to watch and when I'm done with the women, they'll beg me to kill them."

Vladimir was an impressive man and not bad looking, but he reeked of evil, glowed with death. He was about six foot two. He combed his brown hair straight back and kept his beard in permanent stubble.

"You, my little one need not worry. I am totally under your spell. With a little training and time you will come to love me. I am very persuasive."

That said, the madman reached through the bars, ripped my shirt the rest of the way off and attempted to pinch me again. I grabbed his index finger and forced it back until his knuckle snapped out of the socket. The sadist must also be a masochist. His bright smile never left his evil face.

"You were so concerned with the men, so I'll do one a favor for your disrespect. One will not have to watch. You must choose the lucky man. Which is it, the homely Russian or the handsome Italian?"

"My Popi will want to kill you, but I will stop him. I'll not let him kill you until I have stripped you of every bit of manhood and humanity. Your death will be an act of mercy, a gift. You'll get to experience the evil you've done to others, man and beast." Vladimir smiled.

"The handsome Italian it is."

While Vladimir unlocked the cage door, I hugged Antony through the bars.

I whispered, "I'm sorry. Do not beg for your life. It will only give him pleasure. There will be a new life for you when you are ready. I'll take care of your family if I live. Otherwise, I'll see you in the fourth realm."

He kissed me, getting carried away. I let him, after all he is Italian, very handsome and about to die. Vladimir sent two goons to drag Antony out of the cage even though he didn't resist. If this was intended to humiliate Antony or me, it didn't work. When the young man was forced to his knees, Sarah began losing it, never having encountered such evil. I, on the other hand, remained calm. I smiled at the dear boy and he acquired a similar smile, our eyes locked onto each other.

Vladimir wasn't happy. He was missing his most beloved aspect of killing the innocent, the overpowering fear he induced and thrived on. Dismayed or not, the savage Vladimir put a bullet in my new friends' head. I tried my best to withhold my tears lest the demon find joy in them. They left us alone for a while and we girls hugged and commiserated. The homely Russian stayed aloof.

I said, "Sergey, come join us. All we have is each other."

"If you had kept your husband in line and had not allowed his seduction of my Marie, he wouldn't have stolen her away from me. I would have her to console me. Now I have no one. Dying is hard, but dying alone is brutally inhumane."

I felt bad for the dejected man, but I certainly was not going to tell him how to feel.

# 2014; THE RAID

The big cat had found us and I think he wanted to team up with us. Ski's first instinct was to shoot the ferocious beast, but I couldn't allow that. Layla would never forgive me and besides, I've seen Czar's very impressive work.

"Ski, we need him. He can kill silently in complete darkness."

"What if he turns on us, pal?"

I was able to get my friend to give the cat a chance. Ski knew our odds and had already made peace with our slim chance of survival. As for me, all I cared about was Layla. If Czar could help rescue her, it was well worth the risk of being eviscerated.

We drove to the top of a small rise and came upon the compound. There were a dozen single-wide trailer homes surrounding a very large pole barn. There was a soft yellow glow behind nearly every window making it difficult to sneak up on the base without being seen. We dismounted and hid the truck. We would be going on foot from here.

I sent Ski around to the right while Czar and I went left. Our first step was to find the generator. It must be a loud and large one to support a compound this large, yet we couldn't hear it running. It must be in an underground bunker. These people must have great faith in their sentry system because there was no one outside. The lights went out. Ski must have found and disabled the generator. His job now was to ambush whoever came to restore the power.

My next task was to give the anxious cat access to the barn. I cracked open a small door and Czar slipped in. I heard two muffled shots, from Ski I hoped. I gave the killing machine thirty seconds head start and headed into the pitch black abattoir. Having learned from Popi the cave man, I stood still and waited for my eyes to adjust. I concentrated my nose, ears and other senses, if any, to study the sounds, smells and feelings in the great room.

I still couldn't see much, so I followed my nose to the strongest scent, tiger urine. I was hoping it would lead to Layla. I came upon some cages, all empty but three. One held a sleeping tiger.

I whispered, "Li'l Freckles, is it you?"

"Oh Popi, they took Simone and Marie up the stairs on the other side of the building. They're going to rape and kill them while making Marie's boyfriend watch before they kill him."

"Okay sweetheart, who's got the keys to this kennel?"

"Vladimir, he's the head demon. He executed Antony. Please be careful Popi, he won't quit fighting until he's dead. Where are Kurt and Yuri?" I kissed my angel through the bars.

"Ski's here, but Yuri was killed."

I started to go when we heard a short scuffle to my right. Czar trotted up, dropping a large man who appeared scrawny falling from the cats' mouth.

"By the way, your other boyfriend's here."

I left the cat to guard my precious wife and started across the large barn, nearly tripping over another of Czar's kills. I came upon two men smoking and joking while leaning against a prefab metal staircase. These cocky killers weren't yet aware that they were being raided and I certainly didn't want to clue them in.

My problem was two-fold, needing to kill these two before I could proceed and needing to do this quietly without using my gun. I had a flashback to my childhood. My dad, the Colonel was teaching me strategic decision making, using the invasion at Inchon as an example.

"PFC Walter, if there is no good decision that meets all of his criteria, a Marine must make the best bad decision that meets some of his goals. Making no decision is not an option."

Time was of the essence so I put a bullet in each of their heads and ran up the stairs. There were two candlelit rooms, each apparently designed as overseer offices with windowed walls. They were overlooking the whole facility. I kicked the first door in. Two men were scrambling to redress while a third continued raping the screaming scratching Marie. I shot the two standers and pulled the other to the floor by his black greasy hair. The hysterical girl jumped into my arms.

"Popi, Popi he raped me, the bastard raped me. Kill him."

With very little hesitation, through red hazy vision, I killed the now begging man. My guilt would have to wait. The traumatized, sobbing, naked girl wouldn't let me go. Someone ran past the room and down the stairs. I had to look for Simone, so I started to move to the other room. When I turned, I saw Marie's boyfriend who was quietly staring laser beams of hatred with his eyes focused directly on me.

"Find something sharp and cut your friend loose."

I left them to work out their problems and started next door.

I didn't have to kick it because a man walked out and he was using my friend Simone as a human shield. Simone was totally naked. She was terrified, but not hysterical. She made a very poor shield for her lack of size and her determined struggling, despite the gun to her head.

"Let her go and I'll let you live." I was practically growling.

"You drop gun or I kill the little African."

"You have it wrong Boris." I took a long step forward. "My dear friend Simone is an American. You choose, prison or death?"

He chose death when he briefly moved the gun barrel from her head. When I shot him in his face he reflexively pulled the trigger. Simone fainted. I carried the petite girl into the room and lay her on the bed. I began redressing her. I had her pants, socks and shoes on. Her underwear were too ripped to be of use. I corralled her large, beautiful and uncooperative breasts into her sheer bra and was reaching under to hook it when the girl awoke with a start.

We were face to face and already in a partial embrace so, she did the natural thing. Simone wrapped her arms around my neck and pulled me into a torrid kiss, long, wet and hard. I finished hooking her bra, but handed her shirt to her. I didn't turn away as Simone put on her safari shirt, but I looked her in her pretty brown eyes.

"Did they hurt you honey?"

"It was frightening Popi. The psycho spent ten minutes describing what he was going to do to me. The man you shot was just a lackey. Vladimir ran out when you began shooting in the next room." She closed the short distance between us and embraced me. "Thank you Popi, I owe you my life."

"Stay put up here for a while sweetheart. Check on Marie and her boyfriend. Those men brutalized her and made him watch."

I hurried outside and met up with Ski. He was at the generator bunker with three dead Russians.

"Come on Compadre, no more lollygagging. We need to do a final sweep of the barn before we turn the lights back on." We did that sweep and found it all clear.

With the lights back on, I found Layla hugging the tiger as if he was her blue ribbon winning 4H project. I was only a bit jealous. I found an acetylene torch and released Layla who declared me her hero. It sounds silly, but that's what I live for. Layla followed me as I counted the dead bodies. She didn't say, but I presumed that she was looking to confirm that Vladimir was dead.

I killed six or, if the sentry died, seven. Ski killed three and Czar dismembered six. Add to that the eleven killed at the ditch, Anatoli and poor young Antony it gives us at least twenty-eight souls to recycle. Maybe they would fare better in their next lives.

We searched every trailer, finding no one home. While we were finishing up, a pickup truck arrived with another sleeping, captured tiger. We were ready for them because Layla had told me about the thirty men out hunting. After four hours, they were the ones in cages, twenty-four of them including the sentry who was semi-conscious when I retrieved him. Unfortunately their vicious leader Vladimir had escaped, probably hitching a ride with the first poachers to come in.

Before we left to return to Vanavara, Layla, who had been clinging to me since her release, looked up into my weary eyes.

"Popi, if we just leave this place here, the next bunch of psychos will just move right in." Her magical blue gray eyes were beseeching me.

I was weary, dead on my feet really, but she was right. We couldn't let that happen. Ski and I spent two more hours, using chains and the deuce and a half to drag the three cages full of people to a field a hundred yards upwind from the compound. Layla and the others filled containers with gasoline at the small fueling station near the generator and distributed some to every outbuilding. We also dragged the caged tigers, four in all, to another field near the forest line. The tigers were all conscious now and very agitated so releasing them could get hairy.

Finally, Ski supervised the torching of the killers death factory while Layla, Czar, Simone and I went to release the nervous tigers. Simone and I stayed back a bit while Layla and Czar communed with the two large male prisoners. They calmed down immediately when she touched their paws, they were instantly smitten, although not in the same perverted way ala Czar and me. The two females calmed down when the males did. Neither of the girls showed an interest in my wife.

I lowered my weapon, Ski's 50 caliber S&W, and relaxed. When Layla opened each door, the big cats leapt out. One of the males briefly turned back. Czar roared and the animals quickly ran into the forest. As the firestorm raged, Li'l Freckles had another long goodbye with our fighting partner, Czar. I approached them carefully and said my own goodbye.

I said, "Thank you big fella," and the big cat growled at me.

# 2014; Rapists

After an anxious hour, a pickup truck arrived with a sedated tiger in the back. The three bounty hunters got to work, transferring the sleeping beast to a cage, two down from mine. As soon as I saw his beautiful face, I knew it wasn't Czar. Vladimir came down the stairs at the far side of the huge barn. He was toting a brown leather gym bag. He looked at the tiger and congratulated the capture team with backslaps and laughter. The prick opened the bag and gave the men each a bottle of vodka. Vladimir turned the jovial groups' attention to the women.

Simone clung to me and in the other cage Sarah and Marie held each other. Sergey stayed slumped in his lonely corner. Vladimir was like a used car salesman, extolling the features of the three late model used women available on his lot. There was much discussion and debate among the three prize winners, but they finally settled on Marie. Vladimir opened the cage door and two of the men dragged her screaming from the cell. Her boyfriend roused himself out of his jealous funk and made a berserker-like charge at the rugged killers. He failed miserably, but at least he tried. Vladimir was so impressed that he gave orders to his men, in English.

"Bring the schoolboy, tie him up and let him watch." His smile was showed cruelty and amusement.

They dragged the two prisoners across the building and up the stairs. Sergey was compliant and Marie was kicking and screaming. I caught Vladimir salaciously staring at me and Simone.

I asked, "Aren't you going to go watch? You're a fucking pervert, that's what you do." He ignored my feeble insults.

"You two are like night and day, my little freckled blonde and my tiny adorable African. Don't worry little one, I'll not harm a single freckle on your pretty face. Not until all the others are dead."

"You're not even a man. You hurt people because you know that every person on the planet is better than you. You are to be pitied for your lack of a soul and your shame of having no one who cares about you."

My venomous harangue caused a change in Vladimir, and not a good one. I thought to myself, I think I went too far again. I was worried that he would kill Simone or Sarah for my disrespect. He put on an unconvincing power smile.

He gently said, "You are right my little one. I am despicable. I can't wait until I can start your training, but first I need to work off this sexual tension."

He gave instructions in Russian to his Lieutenant who opened and entered our cage. He wrested Simone from my arms. He put an arm around Simone's waist and began to drag her out. I jumped on his back and bit a chunk out of his right ear. I spit the bloody chunk at Vladimir and scratched at his Lieutenant's left eye. He yipped and dropped us both. Vladimir laughed and entered the cage. He wrapped his arms around me and locked my arms to my sides. His henchman took this opportunity to carry my newest Angel to the upstairs lair. Vladimir held on to me, with his lips on the back of my neck.

He whispered into my ear, "Your turn is coming soon. She won't last an hour with me."

With that, he left, dodging my kicks and claws. A sickening creepy giggle announced his departure. Sarah and I were the only ones left, each in our own cage. We clung to each other through the cold steel bars. She was losing it and I was trying to be brave. I was running out of hope. Then the horrible screaming started. I think it was Marie, but it could have been Simone. After ten minutes of that inhuman suffering I broke down. Just as my hope had run out, the power went out and I knew instinctively that it was Popi.

"Sarah, hold on, Popi's here and he's going to kill every one of these bastards." I had a hint of triumph in my unsteady voice.

We sat in the dark waiting. The screams were still coming from the high, lighted rooms. The only light we saw was coming from the two rooms upstairs and very faint. I heard a few unusual noises to my left and right. I was picturing my Popi roaming the darkness and silently killing these evil men. Then the most wonderful thing happened, Popi called my name. I went to the bars, after pulling free from Sarah, and kissed my husband.

I quickly told him all that had happened when the second most wonderful thing occurred. Czar appeared with a present for me. It was a dead guy, but it's the thought that counts. Popi gave me his damp, filthy shirt and left to rescue the girls. Czar stayed to protect me. He left once and was back a few minutes later. I think he killed another one.

I hugged and kissed my tiger as I worried about Popi. After a few minutes, two loud shots rang out and I heard someone run up the metal stair case. I could see Popi's silhouette against the faintly lit windowed door. He kicked it in. There were two quick shots and the horrifying screaming cease. After a five second pause, a third shot rang out. Someone ran down the stairs and ran outside through the small door. I was hoping that it wasn't Vladimir, but it probably was. I could hear Popi talking to someone and Simone struggling. Finally the sixth and seventh shots rang out simultaneously. Two of the three silhouettes fell. I feared for my friend and my husband.

For five minutes, nothing happened. The ominous quiet was more disturbing than the screaming and gunfire. A man walked calmly down the stairs. I was sure it was Popi, but he followed the path of the other man who escaped. Soon, Kurt entered, his silhouette unmistakable, and he was with Popi. They searched the whole building then Kurt left. I was wondering why, but then the lights came back on. Popi wheeled over a big compressed gas cart, a torch, and used it to burn off the padlocks on our two cages.

I kept hold of Popi, refusing to let him go again. I think Czar was a little hurt by this, but it couldn't be helped. It was cute the way the big cat followed us around, growling every time I kissed Popi which was frequently. Then the hunting parties started coming in, luckily, one at a time. I was forced to put on Popi's formerly white tank top. He also gave me a handgun. I got to do the most fun thing of the whole trip, forcing the tiger poachers into cages at gunpoint. One tried to grab me and I shot him in his foot.

"Get up and get in the cage or I take a knee next time." I growled like a pissed off Popi.

I could see how weary Popi and Kurt were, but I asked Popi to burn this evil place to the ground. While they moved all of the prisoners and tigers to safety, Simone and I gathered bottles and jugs of gasoline. We poured some in each trailer and had several gallons on hand to take out the huge barn. The others, Marie, Sarah and Sergey were all too broken to be of help. I would try to console them on our trip back to Vanavara. Simone, on the other hand, was not broken by her horrifying experience. She was, she admitted, on cloud nine in love with my husband.

"That's okay honey. I know he loves you too, but remember he'll always be true to me."

Our last job was to let the captured tigers go. Both of the males liked me, but the females, not so much. Popi insisted that he stand guard with Kurt's massive pistol. As the cage doors opened, they ran for the woods, obeying Czar's roared command. The time had come to finally say goodbye to my beloved Czar. We were nose to nose, eyes interlocked. My fingertips were instinctively kneading him behind his ears. I could almost hear his innermost thoughts. He knew that I chose Popi over him, but he also knew how much I love him. When the mind meld ended, Czar kissed me one last time. He turned and walked slowly into the forest, never looking back. The spell was unbroken.

# THE ABATTOIR

We all left the truck. It was not time to be patient, but stealth was a must. Grrrrr was very good at stealth, but the nervous man was a clumsy oaf. Grrrrr and I sent, I'll call him Stomper, in the opposite direction. This was smart because Stomper was only good for a distraction. We stealthy ones approached an entrance to the largest of the upright men's houses. There was bright light streaming from under the small door. We would have to go from stealthy to ferociously fast and deadly to have any chance of surviving this raid. I was prepared to die. The lights went out.

I was mistaken about Stomper. His hidden talents might just save all of our lives. Grrrrr opened the door and I quietly entered. I let my eyes adjust for a few blinks and identified several people killers. They were nearly blind, but that may not last so I quickly killed the first three I encountered. I located Pheasant song, but I didn't approach her. She was alone in a cage. I killed the upright man closest to my beloved woman. Grrrrr arrived and began wooing my girl, so I did a childish, jealous thing. I lifted the man I had just killed and carried him to Pheasant Song's cage. I dropped him at her feet and smiled. It worked.

Grrrrr left to find a more impressive present. I hugged and kissed my darling Pheasant Song, yet kept an eye on Grrrrr. I knew that Pheasant Song would not forgive me if I let her chosen man die. I saw Grrrrr approach two killers. I saw his plan to beat me in body count. I looked around and spotted two killers coming our way. While I wanted my Pheasant Song to bear witness to my heroic protection of her, I dared not let them get that close.

I trotted into the shadows and dispatched the men who dared to take my woman. They were two of the three whose scent I had memorized from the cabin where Pheasant Song was captured. I checked on the young man in the cage. He was waking up from the upright man's sleep weapon. I told him to be calm and that I and my friends would help him escape. He recognized me and called me uncle. It's a small world. Grrrrr was firing his loud weapon again, this time he was high on a ledge. Then I saw something that made me angry.

A people killer had my friend Simone in his grasp with his loud weapon to her head. Grrrrr was negotiating with him and I started heading that way. Grrrrr killed the man, but it looked like Simone may have been killed too. I went back to Pheasant Song, not wanting to see my friend dead. After the people killers were dead, except the one who ran like a frightened rabbit, Stomper entered. It was comical the way he prowled around, looking for someone to kill. He was too late to claim any credit for saving Pheasant Song and the others. He did turn out the light and turned it back on after the battle so I respected him now. Not everyone can be the hero.

Grrrrr and stomper moved all of the living prisoners to safety before burning the fort. Pheasant song and Grrrrr, along with the beautiful and thankfully living Simone, released the people. One was my brother Kersay. We ignored each other. I was weary of killing, so I would let him live unless he forced me to kill him. When Pheasant song opened his cage, he turned to confront me. It took only one shout to change his mind.

It was time to say goodbye to the love of my life. It was heartbreaking to admit, but she was right to choose Grrrrr. He has proven that he can protect her and she is devoted to the good man. We nuzzled our faces and shared our minds for a short time before I turned to go. I didn't turn to get a last look at my beautiful princess, not wanting her to see me cry. I walked toward my home. I was already sensing the call of a beautiful woman. Hopefully, she would still be desirous of me, after my two night trek. I spent those two nights reliving and reflecting on the whole long adventure I had somehow survived. I had been kidnapped by the upright men, some of whom I recently forced to pay the ultimate price for their crimes. I was taken to a faraway land where I was caged and alone. Then the mad upright man set every man and beast free.

I found the reason for all this upheaval after many nights walking, my Princess Pheasant song. I thought I was there to claim her as my queen, but in the end the true reason became clear. I could feel the subtle influence from some unseen benefactor throughout my time with my gorgeous upright woman. I may never know from whom this magic arose. Pheasant Song's magic was more powerful, but not at all subtle, so I suspected Grrrrr. My only hint was that he had a magic symbol imprinted on his battle scarred chest.

My people don't really believe in Gods, though we do honor our ancestors. I'm beginning to think there may be a spiritual world now that I have been used to protect the most holy of all women, Pheasant Song. I feel honored, blessed and maybe even a bit holy in my own right.

# POPI 2014 FLICKER

I told Marie's dour boyfriend that I wanted him to drive the deuce and a half for the first two hours back to Vanavara so Ski could take a nap in the passenger seat.

Bitterly, he asked, "So you can be alone with Marie?"

"Son, I don't want your woman. No man can steal your girl. Only you can keep her or lose her. She needs you now, so it's up to you."

He took the keys and left without a word. I had a bright flicker of recognition. I knew him now. He is Dr. Sergey Werner, Mr. Weiner from the Russian Wildlife Authority in 2035. I guess my little talk didn't work. I manipulated my tired bones into the back of the truck. They moaned like a little princess who has been asked to do a chore, but they eventually complied.

I went to the front and, using my belt, strapped my left wrist to the truck and tried to sleep. I expected and was prepared for a bumpy ride, but was not ready for the emotional bumps and potholes from the women. They clung to me, all four of them, and vented their innermost feelings. I lay as still as possible and drifted off to crying, laughing, scolding and affection from these four survivors. My last 2014 semi-conscious flickering synapse was a feeling of being loved.

# 2035; Popi Blows His Cover

"Twenty-one hundred hours," someone said upon my return.

It was Victor, apparently in answer to my question. "I reckon it won't be long now."

I was afraid of giving away the fact that I had been twenty years away. This made me wonder. Is modern day Walter in the same boat as me? Is he being sent to 2014 while I'm sleeping back there or does he remain here, still in charge and cognizant of all that occurs in this dream world? Maybe these are his dreams.

When I awaken in 2014, does he back my play or does he go rogue? Does he even exist? I even wonder, since I have been making love with his wife, is he making love to mine? Things appear to go on without me and I have to pretend that I knew what happened while I was gone. It's all too much for me to take in. Layla joined us, slipping her arm around my waist.

"We're as ready as we can be Popi. I don't know how these brave people will hold up under fire."

"None of us know until we live it," Victor said, philosophizing.

The enemy chose that moment to attack. They started with aerial flares which they fired over our position. We were in brightness while they stayed in the shadows. Next, they began an assault with coordinated, nonstop, withering small arms fire. Layla and Victor crawled to their fighting positions while I crawled to each foxhole.

"Keep down Marines. They can't keep this up for long. Hold your fire."

The barrage lasted for several terrifying minutes, hitting no one, but wounding us all. I peeked over the berm in time to see a pickup approaching with its headlights on. The truck, which was flying a white flag, stopped a hundred yards out from our twelve o'clock. Through a surprisingly clear, well-modulated loudspeaker, a man spoke.

"We don't want to harm you. Surrender your weapons and we will escort you safely back to Vanavara. Send out an unarmed representative to formalize the deal."

Layla, Victor and I locked eyes. I think Layla knew where this was going, but Victor was lost in doubt.

"I think this is trap. We can't go out there."

While I agreed with my new friend, I handed my rifle to Layla.

"Here Li'l Freckles, you got my six."

"Don't trust them Popi and don't get yourself killed." She, without tears, hugged me, eschewing an embarrassing kiss. "Come back to me Popi. I still need you." As it does every day, her love touched me.

I stepped over our inadequate earthworks and walked toward the truck. About fifteen feet from the enemy, I stopped. After a minute the drivers' side door opened and out came the ghost of the man I'd seen killed in 2014, Yuri Commissar. Of course, I now knew that this Yuri took the dead man's Identity.

"So you weren't on the helicopter. What's your real name?"

The man, who I would never call Yuri again, said, "I am called Nicholas, Nicholas Brockov and you, Mr. Walter Ranger Lemon of Cincinnati, Ohio USA, have been on our radar for many years. My brother is still quite taken with your wife."

"Let me guess, Vladimir." Nicholas laughed.

"Will you surrender your weapons?" I began slowly walking toward the cocky punk.

"Now that I know who you are and what you're capable of, that's not going to happen. Tell Vlad that we intend to hold out to the last man or woman standing and that any fire in our direction will risk hitting Layla and his brother." He laughed again.

"Me, You think you can kill me? Put your hands up or you will be shot. You'll get to see your wife with Vladimir before you die, if you surrender now."

I took a long stride toward the man and he went for a weapon at the small of his back. I rushed him. I was still a step away by the time he brought the semi-auto up to fire. I didn't hesitate. He fired as I leapt on him. I wasn't sure if I had been hit or not. It didn't matter. I was on him, on top of him and soon I was pummeling him with my fists.

A hidden man emerged from the bed of the truck with an automatic assault weapon, a Kalashnikov. I liberated Nikita's pistol and rolled right, but before I fired, Layla and Victor put three rounds into the new guys' chest. I grabbed the dead guys' rifle and extra ammo and threw Nick into the back. I drove the vehicle back across no man's land to our lines. They always underestimate my speed.

I don't know how, but the cocky maniac missed me. Though I had a new hole in my shirt, I was unscathed. Layla clung to me again. We searched the truck and found another Kalashnikov, this one with a scope, and six more clips of ammo. Victor took the rifle with the scope, giving his old weapon to Sergey.

"Walter, this is a game changer. I'll be able to kill from five hundred meters with this."

"Climb onto the HQ roof. I'm going to stake Little Nikki out in front of the firing positions to slow them down."

I secured Brockov to a folding chair and dragged him fifteen feet in front of our defensive line, facing him toward his brother. The enemy began to shoot again as I retreated. I gave orders to the troops to not fire until they had a target close enough to hit. I took Layla, lifting her from her foxhole and retreated to the HQ. I recruited my old friend Sergey and Lacy, a cute assistant Vet who was ex-US Army, to patrol the woods to our rear. Layla and I went left and Sergey and lacy right with instructions to probe the area then dig in for an ambush. With the small amount of incoming fire, I suspected the enemy was trying to infiltrate our flanks.

Layla and I found no sign that the poachers had gotten this far so we settled behind a fallen tree and waited. I told her about Yuri being a fake and that he was really Vladimir's brother.

"Did you think he was the same Yuri from twenty years ago? How could that be? You were there when he was killed."

"That was after I met this Yuri." I had blown my cover.

"That's impossible Popi, what is wrong with you? You've been acting strangely since the day we left home." The familiar concerned look graced her worried face.

"I don't know Li'l Freckles, I've been having flashbacks from the past and when I'm there I'm having premonitions about the present."

She was very worried about me, but didn't figure out the truth, that she is serial dream.

We quit our whispering when we heard muffled shuffling sounds to our left. I didn't have to tell Layla to hold her fire until the whole squad was in the kill zone. The four men walked casually by within ten feet of our hidden position. We killed two before they got off a single shot, but the third man sprayed our position with his rifle on auto. We ducked behind our tree and waited the few seconds it took to empty his thirty round clip. I stood as he scrambled to reload.

"Drop it or die." He chose death.

We gathered their firearms and ammo and went to assist Sergey and Lacy. Before we arrived, all hell broke loose both from the right flank and the camp. With Layla clinging to my shirttail, we hurried to get to Sergey. We got there just in time to see two men maneuvering to overrun their position while keeping them pinned down with suppressive fire. One bad guy lay dead on the ground and the others soon joined him when Layla and I opened up on them. Sergey stood with Lacy, still beautiful in death, in his arms. He was not a large man, so I offered to take the girls' body from him. I saw tears and rage on his tortured face.

"No Lemon, you'll not steal this one from me. She saved my life and I got her killed. Now, she will be my responsibility forever."

I gathered the weapons from the dead and followed the grim procession back to the battle. I looked across the field. There were several dead and dying men in the grass, thanks to Victor. No one on our front lines had fired yet, impressing me with their discipline. I handed out the rifles and ammo to the people with only side arms. All eight firing positions had at least one modern assault weapon now.

I told Layla and Victor that I believed that the poachers were out gunned now, but they couldn't retreat while we had Nicholas.

Layla seemed worried. "Maybe we should let him go Popi."

Victor said, "I don't know Walter. We know that they have more advance weapons like the surface to air missiles and the small rockets they shot at Dr. Werner."

"You're right Victor. Maybe Little Nikita is shielding us from their more destructive, but less precise weapons. Let's keep him." We three agreed.

We had to hold out for eight more hours presuming that the Russian Army was really coming. I hate Russians.

# 2014; THE INTERROGATION

I woke when we hit the paved road and stopped to change drivers. I peeled off the sleeping women and got out of the truck. Layla joined me and we climbed into the cab. We would be in Vanavara in two hours, then what? There was no real law in town, so it would be hours before we could try to tell our story. We had Antony's body wrapped in blankets in the back. Who knows where the nearest medical examiner might be. If I could, I would get us all on the plane and fly to Moscow where we could exert some small influence on the authorities.

We drove straight to Tigers Internationals' offices in the center of the village. Sergey got on the phone and called his bosses. The rest of us walked to the only café in town and went about the mundane task of nourishing ourselves. I restocked my system with vitamin B. Although they didn't have my beloved Heineken, the local brew wasn't bad at all. I stopped counting at eight. Simone gathered bedding from the locals who were glad to help the Tiger girl. The tigers were revered by the indigenous inhabitants.

By bed time, the police still hadn't shown, so we slept dormitory style on the two room office floor. Layla and I slept peacefully for the most part, but were frequently awakened by the nightmares of Sarah and Marie. In the morning, we were rousted by a squad of federal police. The head cop was a tall stern man who was very suspicious of our story. He sent Antony's body to Moscow for an autopsy and separated us to interview us all individually.

When it was my turn, his lieutenant led me into his defacto office, the back room of the café. He stood.

"Good morning Mr." He hesitated. "Is it Lemon, like the fruit?"

"Yes sir, like the fruit. What is your name?"

"I am Colonel Ivan Petrochinko. Tell me why you come to my country and why all of those people are dead."

"Have you sent people to the Poachers base yet?"

"Mr. Lemon, please let me be clear. This is my official interview, and I have my process, so answer my questions."

I uncharacteristically said, "Yes sir," knowing that Ivan would make a much better friend than an enemy.

The interrogation lasted two hours, but I took it like a man and answered truthfully for the most part. I dishonored Yuri Commissar.

I said, "Yuri provided the weapons," when Ivan asked the question.

I think he would understand. I also downplayed Czar's role lest he be tracked down as a man eater. I don't know how many laws I may have broken, but it was all in defense of innocent people and against murdering criminals. Righteous is righteous, I felt no guilt and it showed. In the end Ivan summed it up.

"Mr. Lemon, I would have to be an idiot to believe even half of what you have told me." The stern man paused, shaking his head slowly. "Yet I do believe you. Your transport to Moscow will be cleared to leave."

"Thank you Colonel. This may become international news. Would you like to have your picture taken with my wife and me?" The man who had claimed not to know my name seemed to get a bit embarrassed.

He softly said, "That would make me a hero to my daughters, thank you."

Layla of course insisted that we clean up and acquire clean clothes. While she was able to borrow some Siberian Haute Couture, I had to choose from the spare Tigers International bush uniforms, think Boy Scouts. The photo session went well. Layla looked adorable in a black peasant skirt and plain red blouse, skipping the black babushka. I felt like Dudley Doright protecting the lovely Nell.

After a farewell meal at the café, we boarded the same antique airplane that brought us here three days ago. We were all in need of R&R, but had to suffer a bit longer. The girls were all still very clingy and Sergey was still in a moody funk. The only one who seemed unaffected by our two days of hell was Ski. How I wished that ability for myself, that instant emotional recovery.

All I could think about were the dead and wounded. Not the bad guys, we'd been generous by capturing as many as we could. My bruised mind refused to make an exception for the three rapists who I executed though they were all unarmed and one surrendered. My rescue squad of three was too small to handle the taking of prisoners during the assault. When the battle was over, we showed more mercy than they deserved. The dead and wounded I fretted over were the good guys. All of our survivors were wounded in some way, even Ski though he'd never admit it.

Layla felt responsible for the death of the Italian kid, Antony. She was not persuaded when I told her that it was her duty to resist and fight the evil Vladimir.

"If I had not insulted him so much, Antony may have lived to be rescued." I felt bad for my brave angel.

She would have to own this and resolve it in her beautiful heart. Sarah witnessed her friend get executed and couldn't get the picture out of her head. I wanted to tell her it would someday leave on its' own, but I refused to lie to the poor girl. As for Marie and her grumpy boyfriend, they would bear their emotional scars forever.

Then of course there are Yuri and Lacy, oh wait, Lacy won't be killed for twenty years, but Yuri was a dear courageous young man committed to the tigers. The ambush was my plan, but Ski and Yuri knew we might be killed. Ski and I had a very personal stake in risking our lives, Layla. Yuri barely knew any of us yet he stood with us like we were brothers. He is my brother now and I'll do anything to take care of his loved ones. I finished my self-flagellation just in time for the noisy landing in Moscow. Layla stirred from her troubled sleep in my lap.

"Are we here Popi?"

"Yes Li'l Freckles, we're here."

We had kept our hotel rooms which Yuri had arranged for us, but since they were cheap and dingy, I phoned the Ritz-Carlton and got rooms for our whole group. They all wanted to stay a few days to decompress, except Werner whose hatred of me continued to grow. When Marie gave me her first smile since being brutally raped, he grudgingly relented. I told them all to buy some clothes in the hotel shops and charge it to my room.

In our new fancy room, I let Layla use the phone first. She talked to Ted, her head designer, Claire, Gabrielle, Mary and Charlie who was, thank God, the only Angel present. By the time Layla finished her hour long call, I had stripped her naked and had dropped my own clothes. I decided that my important call could wait. We hadn't made love in days and didn't waste time with preliminaries. I had a humorous thought, I'm just like Czar going after Sabrina. My tigress was even more in need of this than me and showed it in her wild abandon. Quickly spent, we talked and listened to each other. Our worries and confessions were instantly forgiven. Our bonds of love grew ever stronger from the admitted frailties and failures.

We both felt so much better after our lovin' and talkin' that we were ready for round two. It was slower, softer and extraordinary. I could almost feel the bright red beams of love happily deserting my dear Li'l Freckles and drifting to the sixth realm with a few gray wisps sparking as they followed, skittering along.

We are charmed yet also cursed. After spending time with dream 2035 Layla, It seems we survive and are happy, but how many others have died from simply being in our sphere of existence? Anyway, that's enough bellyaching. I made my call, to Triple D.

"I've got some bad news for you DeeDee." I gave him the names and he took it like a man.

"I just thank God that you guys are safe."

"Yeah we're fine, but still a little shaken up."

"Walter, did you have to kill anyone?" It was the worst kept secret in the seven realms, my psychological problems from all the killing.

"I'm afraid so, but two of my friends were killed and another, Marie, was brutally sexually assaulted. I'm not feeling any regrets about the men I killed, but the two who got away are haunting me."

"We'll hunt them down brother. What are their names?"

"Vladimir Brockov and his younger brother Nickolas, they are both insane scum. I want you to focus on Nicholas on the low-down. Layla, Ski and the Russian authorities don't know about Vladimir's brother."

"It's down-low Walter. How do you know about Him?"

"Get to work DeeDee."

I felt better knowing that Triple D would be taking care of those three students, Simone and the families of Yuri and Antony. I had an afterthought, and Anatoli. Though I'd never met him, he died because Brockov was after Layla, Czar and me.

I knew that Ski would be calling Rebecca and was sure that she would be tracking Vladimir Brockov. I didn't like holding back important information from Layla and Ski, but I was afraid of three things. First, Rebecca and Ski depended on international law enforcement databases which Vladimir may be able to access. Secondly, from his thinly veiled threat in 2035 dream world, Nicholas knows where I live. Lastly, I had information that I couldn't logically have.

Between Rebecca and DeeDee they were as good as caught, so how is it that he has another shot at us twenty years from now? If we do find and kill them, surely it will be enough to change our future. Maybe I can still save Lacy and any others who might die in our pitched battle which may be raging as I sit in this luxury Hotel room. Of course that means all those dead poachers would live too.

Layla and I hosted a fancy dinner in the hotel restaurant. I didn't get to sit next to Layla because Marie and Simone were bookending me fiercely. As usual, these days, Layla understood. I wish the same could be said for young Werner. He did sit on Marie's left and maintained close contact with his girl. Layla had told me about the nerds' heroic attempt to rescue his wayward girlfriend. This reminded me of my son David's pitiful attempt to save Layla from Paco and how proud of him I was for his bravery.

# 2014; LAYLA DREAMS

We flew home on our sleek charter jet. We'd left Czar's cage in our haste to escape the poachers so the plane was nearly empty and devoid of seats. The four large leather seats were one short because we were giving Sarah a ride to Cincinnati where she would be met by her parents who would take her back to their home in West Virginia. The shortage of seats was not a big problem because Simone and I took turns sitting on Popi's lap.

Unfortunately, Frank and Betsy Hargrove were unaware of the perils of speaking to the press. We were ambushed at the airport by a gaggle of heartless distorters. Popi successfully ignored the baiting questions until a young newsman shoved me to get his microphone into Popi's face.

"Popi, is it true that you executed an unarmed man who begged for his life?" Popi pulled me even tighter to him.

"Is it true that I kicked the ass of a rude and nosy scumbag who laid his hands on my wife?"

"Will you answer my question?"

Popi grabbed the man by his cheap suit and lifted him into the air. He was briefly face to face with the menace and whispered something unheard before tossing the frightened punk to the floor. He stopped and turned to face the crowd.

"We've had a very trying few days and are in need of some recovery time. If you want the gory details, you must find other sources beyond these poor folks who only want to take their daughter home."

Frank and Betsy were profuse in their apologies and their sincere thanks for rescuing Sarah. Sarah was angry.

"Mother, how could you? I told you that in confidence."

"It's okay sweetheart, no one really believes these jokers. It just adds to my legend anyway." Popi was over it.

We said our goodbyes to the Hargrove's and drove the long hour home where we received exuberant welcomes from our family. They wanted to hear the story, but that would have to wait. Popi and I were ready for bed.

After making steamy love, I asked my grinning husband, "What did you whisper to that reporter?"

"I told him not to put himself in the position of begging me to spare his life."

I fell to sleep quickly wrapped in Popi's strong protective arms. I had a troubling dream. I was strolling through the sixth realm, totally naked as usual. I was imagining various flowers and picking them as they appeared. I have no idea if this is possible or not. After I had gathered a large bouquet, I turned back and headed home. I don't know how I knew the way or why the sixth realm was my home. When I got there, all the whiteness disappeared although the pink streaked air remained. I carried my flowers through the gate and up the gravel driveway which felt like plush carpet underfoot. I climbed onto our porch and through our front door.

Popi was there and he wasted no time wrapping me in his powerful protective arms. Without a word, he kissed me. I automatically checked for the spell even before the long kiss, filled with secret meaning, ended. The spell was unbroken, but something else was wrong. Popi was much older. His hair was showing serious gray along his temples and his eyebrows were bushy and completely gray. He had well used laugh lines radiating from the corners of his bright brown soulful eyes.

"Popi, you look so old, still sexy, but old."

"I know Li'l Freckles I've been to the future. I have some bad news. Brockov killed me in 2035, so I have to kill him before then."

This jolted me awake. I was unable to drift off again until I turned on my light and checked Popi's face.

# 2035; Popi's Wake

Back on the front, the firing was sporadic. I think Vladimir was still waiting for his sapper teams to attack us from behind. When that didn't happen he broke out the smoke. He soon had the whole battlefield in a thick blue haze. Visibility was down to ten or fifteen feet. How would this help Vladimir? He would have difficulty killing us if he couldn't see us. I think I knew. He could sneak up on us to rescue his brother. I got Layla settled into a firing position with the fancy Radio operator, Nicolai.

I gave young Nicolai a few whispered words of encouragement and set about with my plan to ambush whoever came to save Nicholas Brockov. If I was lucky, Vladimir himself would lead the mission. The smoke was dissipating, but still thick enough to low crawl unseen to the best seat in the house, Brockov's. I didn't have to wait long before the ghostly shadows appeared, only two. I didn't prolong things. From six feet away, I shot them both twice and quickly withdrew.

I checked each foxhole and checked the occupant's ammo and morale. Our people weren't firing much and that didn't bother me at all. Victor and I would do most of the killing, me at the front and he from his roost on the HQ roof. As I slithered up to Layla's hole, she popped up and killed a shadow with three to the chest. I complimented her, but when I saw her tortured face, I felt great sadness that she had to go through this. In fact, all of these innocent people would, if they survived, be scarred for the rest of their lives.

Nicolai was dead. I pulled the poor boy out of the hole and laid him down. My thoughts betrayed me by reminding me of my last words to the nice young man.

"Boy, if anything happens to my wife, I'm holding you responsible."

I felt a great deal of guilt for the threat and responsible for his death. The enemy ceased the smoke-out and began a mini-barrage of mortar fire. They had run out of options, having failed at every tactic they had tried. Now they would try to bombard us with high explosive ordinance without killing the brother, good luck with that.

They did get lucky when the third round scored a direct hit on the HQ. I ran in search of Victor. I found him twenty-five feet from the blazing structure. He was dead and still holding the deadly rifle with the scope. I had no time to mourn for my heroic friend. I took the weapon and returned to the fray. I crawled into a foxhole with Werner and a terrified young zoologist. I lay my rifle on the berm and searched out the mortar crew, eventually finding them set up ten feet beyond the tree line.

Two men manned the mortar tube, one with binoculars and another adjusting the range and dropping the rocket shaped rounds into the tube. My rifle pulled a little to the left, instead of hitting the bombardier in the left eye as aimed, my round struck him in his right eye as he loaded his next round. He fell dead onto the tube, knocking it over as the weapon fired. The mortar was propelled along the ground skipping twice before exploding a few yards in front of the restrained Nicholas Brockov. He was nearly disintegrated.

I sent Werner and the frightened young girl to find a safer position. I knew that Vladimir would only be concerned with killing me. I often have that effect on the psychopaths I regularly encounter. A camouflaged pickup truck pulled in front of the mortar position. I killed the driver, but soon they were sending the rockets our way again. Really I should say my way because they were bracketing my position. The fourth round was very close. I saw a bright flash and was suddenly standing outside my hole.

It took me a minute to figure out that I was dead, a victim of a direct hit. I wondered why I didn't awaken back in 2014. I'm a practical man, these worries could wait. I needed to find a way to kill Vladimir Brockov.

I commanded the fourth realm, "Take me to Brockov," and instantly I was face to face with the insane punk. He looked worried.

"Did we get him? Is Lemon dead?" his nervousness bordered on agony.

No one around him knew for sure. Mad Vlad (there I go giving my enemies horrible nicknames again) had about fifteen men left though five or so seemed to be seriously wounded. One of his men ran up and excitedly told the crazy Russian some apparently good news. It was in Russian, but I expect it was the news of my death. He smiled then laughed and clapped his lieutenant on his back. I was pissed, but soon it was my turn to smile. The Russian Army was here with two tanks and two platoons of angry infantry. Vladimir and four of his men took to the pine forest on foot.

I knew I couldn't do anything to stop him, so I walked back to the battlefield. It was eerily quiet. The Russian Army spread out and rounded up what was left of Mad Vlad's company, mostly the wounded. Werner and Simone were walking hand in hand toward the unit commander who had already set up a folding table and chairs, an impromptu HQ. Most of the tiger people were hugging their foxhole mates, but Layla was standing over a smoldering crater, my final resting place.

She was sobbing so hard that from this distance she seemed to be in the midst of a great belly laugh. I went to her and put my arm around her grief wracked shoulders. I kissed her dirty neck and Layla paused in her grief.

"Popi I love you. Your beautiful body is gone. Please don't go to five, not right away. Please stay with me for a while."

I kissed her and she closed her eyes and smiled. Even muddied, bloodied and filthy faced, she is the most wondrous sight in the seven realms.

I did stay through the challenging hearing with a panel of judges. The young prosecutor took an instant dislike of me, but had an obvious love for my widowed wife. He let his assistant, a severe humorless matron, do the dirty work.

"Mrs. Lemon, don't you think killing twenty-four Russian citizens is excessive, maybe even murderous?" There was a note of scorn on the homely woman's sour face.

"Some of those people were my friends and one was my beloved husband. People like my Popi and First Sargent Victor Solodnikov are God sent heroes who saved as many lives as they possibly could, sacrificing theirs." Enough said, they were released without charge.

The flight home, on a conventional jet, was uneventful and was only noteworthy because there was another spirit on the plane. She was an old, Russian woman who kept glancing at me. I finally spoke up.

"Ma'am, are you going to USA?"

"Da, my sister Sonia I see."

It was difficult, but I taught her how to travel in the fourth realm. She thanked me. "You nice man, take me to Sonia," and she was gone.

I sat next to Layla for the rest of the flight, frequently kissing her graceful neck, eliciting a sweet smile each time.

Back home, we were met by dozens of friends and family. I got to see all of my grandchildren for the first time. Rose and David had a preteen girl and a teenage boy. David and Greta had three, two boys and a girl. Robby and Susan also had two boys and a girl. Chrissy and Chet had only one boy. He is ten and named Ranger Richards. Mary had a six year old girl and a ten year old boy. Her husband seemed to be devoted to her. Ski and Rebecca were here. I was relieved to see that they were okay, but there was no sign of Claire. I refused to declare her dead without positive proof.

DeeDee and Jordon Woo were there and like in Layla's eighth realm adventure, they were married with two kids. Unlike in the eighth realm, there weren't as many of the kids named after me since I had not died until long after they were born. Robby's oldest was named after me and Stump and Sally did have a Walter among their brood of four. Mary's kids were Walter Ski Crocket and Rebecca Rose Crocket. The Rose was for David Rose, all in honor of her rescue team.

It felt oddly wrong listening in, like a needy eavesdropper, to the hallowed words of comfort and the glowingly inaccurate tales of the fallen hero. I didn't hover too closely to the beloved mourners. I knew this homage was really for them to come to terms with a loved ones' death. Several lamented about the horrible nature of my demise. I'm here to tell you. I've experienced death before, so you can trust me. There are worse ways to die than from a direct hit from a mortar round. That there is nothing left to bury is icing on the cake.

After midnight, after everyone tipsily tiptoed off to bed, I began to worry. I had been awake for twenty-four hours before being killed and now, after death it's been about seventy-two more. I, of course, was not tired because spirits don't really sleep. The problem is, if I don't sleep, how can I return to 2014? If time moves at the same speed in both my life and my dream life, I've been away far too long. Why doesn't Layla wake me? Here I go again, thinking too deeply into the contradictory pitfalls of time/dream travel. I had to stop lest my worried mind explode.

I had one thing left to do before leaving this future dream world. I need to leave Layla a message. I went to our bed and watched my angel in her fitful sleep. She is so beautiful even in her worry and sorrow. I willed myself into her dreams. We were back in her foxhole. When she ducked, I ducked. Layla popped back up and saw that I was dead. I spoke and suddenly she could see me. She threw herself at me and kissed my filthy face.

"Popi, get your ass back to your body and come back to me." She was panicky.

"Li'l Freckles I can't, you are dreaming and my body is gone." She shook her head.

"No Popi, you must not leave me."

"Honey, I need you to start a journal, beginning with the day we left for Russia. Will you do that for me sweetheart?"

Before she could answer, without warning, I was pulled back to my old body, my pre-dead body.

# STUCK IN 2014

"Popi, Popi, wake up. My, sweetheart you were so sound asleep. I've been shaking you for five minutes."

I awoke, groggily relieved. I sat up and became aware of Big Popi who was wide awake.

"Shaking me or making out with me?"

She smiled coyly and said, "Maybe a little of both."

We went for a run, cleaned up and went straight to the security office after filling my coffee cup. Layla was anxious to get back to work, but I insisted she attend this meeting. Ski, Rebecca and Simone were waiting with warm welcomes. Rebecca was clinging to Ski just as Layla was clinging to me.

"Thank you Popi for bringing him home to me again."

"I didn't have to rescue your big Pollock even once. In fact I'd say the tiger was the superhero this time." Ski agreed.

"Amen to that, brother." I got down to business.

"I am going to hunt down and kill Mad Vlad. Rebecca, I have two assignments for you. Get with Layla and give us the best portrait possible. Work with Triple D and get a worldwide manhunt started." Layla and Rebecca went off to work on the sketch. I also knew in great detail what the scourge looked like, but twenty years older. I would have a hard time explaining how and when I had met him.

"Simone, I want you to stay on top of all tiger poaching around the world, looking for Brockov's signature extreme violence. Feed any leads directly to Ski."

"Yes Popi, may I go see my cats today?"

"Of course sweetheart, family first, say hello to Sabrina for me."

It was just me and Ski now. I said, "How you doing brother?"

"You know me Walter, one day at a time. I'm ready to go after that asshole."

"And you know me Ski, I don't have the skills to track Mad Vlad, but I know what to do when we find him. I need you-all to be strong for as long as it takes."

I had an embarrassing urge to hug my stalwart friend because I knew how he felt inside, the burn of hatred and need for retribution. I thought what the hell and gave in to that urge.

"We'll get him Walter, hopefully before he kills again."

Kurt didn't make promises lightly and when he does, you can carve it in stone. We planned, in secret, Vladimir Brockov's murder. Rebecca and Layla returned and as usual Layla entered talking.

"Popi, I want to hire Rebecca as an artist. She is amazing."

Layla handed me the drawing as Rebecca blushed at the praise. The man on the paper was definitely Vladimir Brockov twenty years younger than when my spirit was face to face with him a few days ago.

"Rebecca honey, Li'l Freckles is right, but I need you to help catch this demon before you even think of changing careers."

"We'll get him Popi."

I left them and walked my sweet wife up the attic stairs to her work station where we parted with a very prolonged and public kiss.

I whispered, "I love you Li'l Freckles. Promise you'll never leave me."

"I've tried life without you Popi, and it kinda sucked."

I went about my day, antsy from the routine I love so much. With my mission in the hands of the experts, there was little else to do but stew about the evil men still loose on the world. I read the paper, made of real paper, and drank cup after cup of coffee by the indoor pool. My brooding was made easier by the frequent interruptions by the many beautiful women on their breaks.

Layla's Angels were all here for the start of the winter fashion season leading up to Paris and New York fashion weeks in January and February. This was Layla's busiest time of the year. While no one could ever replace Layla in my heart, I must admit that watching the five lovely, sexy models swim and their constant flirting improved my mood.

I filled my time by taking over Ski and Rebecca's mail duties. We still received hundreds of fan letters every day which had to be picked up at the local post office and sorted from the junk mail and bills. I took the fan letters to the high school where student volunteers, in order to raise funds for their clubs, answered them with a form letter and faux autographed photos of Big Popi & Li'l Freckles. The household bills, I sent to Claire who took care of our finances. All of this took quite a bit longer than it did for Ski and Rebecca because I frequently got caught up in the silly fan letters. I still can't get over how these young boys and girls adored us.

The days and weeks crept by without change. Layla worked and I filled my time with mundane chores. The team reported the disappointing results of their investigation. Ski felt my growing frustration.

"He's gone to ground Walter. The Russians are after him, so the prick won't surface until the heat dies down."

"I think you're right. Maybe we should back off a little. He may be feeling the pressure from our investigation too." Ski was mulling this over.

"We could pull back our assets on the ground in Europe for a few weeks, but keep up our cyber intelligence gathering."

"Whatever you think Ski. A psycho like Vladimir won't go long without satisfying his sick hunger. Maybe we could analyze spikes in crimes against women."

Ski liked that idea. It felt good to at least help with suggestions since I had no real idea how these things could be accomplished. My biggest frustrations were not from the fruitless investigation. They occurred in bed at night. No, my love life was fine, in fact fantastic, but my sleep was dreamless. 2035 Layla must think that I had left her without saying goodbye. I don't know why this upset me so, but it did. I needed to get back to comfort her and to read her journal. I wanted to find out if I could effect changes in the future by my actions in 2014 and to prove this by memorizing her journal and recording it in 2014. I know, it's confusing, but if I could change things, I could save a lot of lives and protect Layla from so much pain and trauma. Maybe tonight I'll dream.

# Layla's Journal June 11 to June 20 2035

I don't know why Popi wanted me to start this journal or why he wanted me to start from June eleventh. It was a normal day which we spent packing for our trip to Moscow and Tunguska. Popi didn't complain, not even once although he still didn't like Russians very much. I think this is because of Popi's long dead father who was a dyed in the wool anti-communist. My first hint that things were not normal came when Popi seemed to be forgetting things we had just talked about.

At first, I thought he was trying to get out of the trip, but we'd been going every other year for many years and Popi was an avid supporter of Tigers International. Throughout the trip, Popi was acting odd. It was as if he'd been rejuvenated. The way he made fantastically physical love to me on the Pulse made me weak in the knees. As did the thwarting of the kidnap attempt, reminding me of all those times he saved me many years ago.

He was once again brash, cocky and full of charming confidence. He then proceeded to prove that something was seriously wrong. He began to shamelessly flirt with our beautiful young Russian driver and she was buying it. I felt feelings of jealousy that I hadn't felt in more than fifteen years. Popi had willingly shed his super hero persona many years ago, but I always knew that he had it tucked safely away in his heart, the heart of a tiger. He resurrected that heroic soul when the flaming helicopter was falling from the sky.

Popi, I'm sorry, but I can't do this. Reliving this is taking a horrible toll on me. My heart is broken and retelling the story of your death is too much to bear. I haven't felt your presence for months now. Did you go to five without saying goodbye or have I just lost the ability to sense your loving touches and kisses? Everyone is gone now, reclaiming their peaceful lives while I stay all alone in this monstrous mausoleum. It no longer feels like our home, the one we have loved and shared for these many years. I know that you want me to be happy, so you'll understand. This story is punishing me, torturing me. Go live another extraordinary life and I'll wait for you on six. I'll always love you.

# 2035; New Plan/Wish

I was finally back. It was the middle of the night, dark and quiet. I walked up the stairs and through Layla's bedroom door. I could have just willed myself to instantly go to Layla or anywhere else for that matter, but it felt more human to walk. Layla lay sleeping, completely covered by our favorite quilt.

Spirits have some amazing powers, but can be completely humbled by the need to move even the smallest of physical objects on the third realm. I had to be content with caressing my Li'l Freckles through the blanket and kissing her exposed face and hair.

She stirred without waking and said, "Popi."

I went in search of the journal I'd requested. It wasn't in the bedroom, so I walked to her attic work station. It lay on her desk, under a pair of scissors. Moving the scissors and opening that book were monumental tasks, taking over forty minutes. The payoff for my labors was not what I'd hoped. Layla couldn't complete the story. Her pain saddened me and made me think twice about contacting her. She would get over losing me in time, but not if I kept a hold on her. I needed a new plan.

I decided that I would have to leave my grieving dream wife one more message. One that she could write about and one that didn't involve direct contact with my sad angel. I spent three hours making a mess in the kitchen. With much effort, I managed to tip over the canister of white flour on the granite countertop. The easy part was writing the message in the fine powder.

"I love you Li'l Freckles. The spell is unbroken. Write about Claire."

Hopefully, Layla could tell me what happened to my beloved ex-wife. Why wasn't Claire in our lives anymore? Was she dead and gone, or was she living her life apart from the chaos of BP&LF? With my labor complete, I returned to Layla's lonely room and watched her sleep until I was pulled back.

# Cynwrig & Fiedlimid; The Past is not Forgotten, Remembered

I was pulled, but not back to my relatively sane 2014. I was just an observer in the head of a teenager. The other people, dressed in coarsely woven wool, were running in all directions. My host was yelling for information. Finally a friend stopped and anxiously told the story. The words I heard were strange and foreign, but I also had access to the boy's mental assessment of those guttural coughs and grunts. Apparently, according to Eibhear, son of the armorer, they were being invaded by strange, ferocious men from the sea. They could be here within half a day. All the villages in the area were mustering fighting forces to meet the enemy before they reached Ulaid, our town. Eibhear had called us Cynwrig. The name sounded strange at first, but now felt right.

He ran home. While Cynwrig was running, I was observing. I saw many similar homes, maybe fifty, all circular with thatch roofs and walls of sod. They ranged in diameter from ten to twenty feet. Each structure was supported by a tall central post. We entered one of the smaller homes and excitedly greeted his mother. She was attractive and seemed too young to be the mother of Fourteen year old Cynwrig, pretty ten year old Aine and four month old Braeden. When he told mom the rumor and that he was going to join the men to protect our town, she cried. This caused a chain reaction of tears in his brother and sister.

We left to find his father. He was named Donn after the Lord of the dead and would be at his hilltop workshop. Donn is the high Druid priest of Ulaid. He would be consulting with the elders about the coming battle. No major decision was made without his Father and Cynwrig was in training to take over for him. The top of the hill was dominated by a structure which looked a lot like the village homes, but immense. It had many poles supporting the roof and looked to be large enough to hold the entire population of Ulaid.

By the time Cynwrig and I got there, the first wave of men began trotting off for the battle. Most of the men, young and old, were armed with bronze axes, bronze knives and iron tipped spears. Iron was superior, but rare. We went into Donn's work shop and foundry. He only worked in gold, silver, copper, tin and bronze, making blessed jewelry and tributes to our patron gods and goddesses.

"Father, I must go to defend the Tuath."

I probed for the meaning of Tuath and found it meant something akin to Kingdom.

"I've told Daragh and the others that their efforts would fail and the North men would burn Ulaid. They will rape and kill our women. He is more worried about his legacy than the lives of his people."

Cynwrig respected and believed his father, but was not swayed.

"Even knowing that I'll probably die, I must go." He too, was concerned about his manhood.

"I know son, but wait while I arm you."

"Daragh will provide weapons, even iron tipped spears."

"Son, Iron is strong, but it has no magic. Take this sword and dagger."

Cynwrig's father gave him a beautiful bronze short sword and long dagger. The swords' hilt was decorated with a God figure which Cynwrig recognized as Camulus, God of war. The dagger bore the likeness of Belisama the goddess of light and forge. Both weapons' blades were covered with mysterious graven runes. I probed Cynwrig's mind for their meanings. He didn't know. Cynwrig strapped on the wide leather belt. It fit perfectly.

"Father, when did you make these?"

"I began them four days ago when I keened the coming war. I have one more weapon for you. If you survive the battle, you will need it after you come back to Ulaid to bury your family."

"Father, we have many brave men. We will stop the invaders long before they reach Ulaid."

"This last weapon, you must wear over your heart."

Donn went to his small forge and retrieve a bronze pole with a knob on the end. My first thought was that it looked like a miniature golf club. The oblong knob end had been in the fire though it did not glow red, but silver.

"Raise your shirt Cynwrig my son."

Cynwrig didn't question him and without hesitation, he lifted his sheepskin shirt to reveal a skinny chest. Just before Donn held the hot metal to our chest, I recognized the rune which was about to be seared onto our flesh. It was the past is not forgotten symbol. He flinched a bit, but did not cry out when the rune was branded on his chest in much the same place where I have worn it for years.

Donn said, "When you find your way back home and honor your family, you may recite the incantation that I will give you. You will go back three days in time for a very short time, no longer than it takes to shear a sheep. You will be sent one winter into the future. You may bring one and only one person with you by clinging to them mightily."

Donn gave the magical words. I dare not print them. He hugged his firstborn and sent us off to war. Cynwrig had one more important duty, his farewell to his girlfriend. He walked back down to the village and to a small home.

Cynwrig left his new weapons outside and entered. "Fiedlimid, it is I Cynwrig."

I heard her name as Fiedlimid, but from his mind I heard Evergood. The girl entered from a curtained room at the back of the house. She ran into our arms and embraced us.

"Cynwrig, have you heard about the war. I'm so happy that you are not going to fight." I felt her love for the young Cynwrig.

"Yes my darling Evergood, I've heard, but I must go to protect Ulaid and the tuath, to protect you."

Fiedlimid was a short pretty redhead, reminding me of Layla because of her adorable freckled face. She was around thirteen and was taking her first tentative steps toward womanhood. She showed her fiery personality when he told her we were going to join the fight.

"You bog maddened men! You would rather kill each other than stay home and care for your families where you belong. We women must remain behind to worry and grieve. I'll not grieve for you Cynwrig. You can go, but I'll not grieve for you after you've deserted me." Li'l Evergood was crying now.

"My little Breck, do not talk this way to your husband."

"Husband!" She was stunned silent for a second.

"I love you Fiedlimid. If I survive, will you marry me?"

"If you survive, I'll consider it, but if you are killed I'll not forgive you, nor will I grieve."

We kissed our future bride and held each other for several pleasant moments. We had to go to meet up with the last of the men marching off to find glory or death. I searched Cynwrig's mind for the meaning of the pet name Breck and found that it meant freckled face. The next time I would see our little Breck, she would be dead, mutilated and desecrated.

# Layla's Journal July 15 2035: Claire

I first met Claire Lemon when I was in the fourth grade. David Lemon was in my class. Every Friday throughout the school year, one student brought a parent in to talk about their work and lives. Mine, of course, refused to miss a couple hours of work. One Friday, David's mom came. I pretty much knew before I met her that she would be special because David was so smart, nice and polite. When Claire came into the room, everything paused. She was so young and beautiful. I don't remember much about her talk, but I do remember the delicious brownies she brought.

I don't remember seeing Claire again until my freshmen year. I asked David to take me to the homecoming dance. He brought me home for dinner to meet his mom and siblings. His father couldn't be there. I was nervous at first, but they were all so nice. It didn't take long to fit in. I didn't get to talk to Claire one on one until weeks later. I asked her some probing Questions about her son and her husband.

"Claire, do you think that David and I have any chance? I mean, he's so damn smart. Do you think he will get bored with me?"

"David is brilliant, but there are other types of brilliance. You are literally brilliant. You shine, mind, body and soul. There is no way that a man as smart as David couldn't see that in you. He will instinctually know that he must treasure and nurture your relationship to give you the happiness you deserve."

"Thank you Claire. I've got one more difficult question. Do you know of any reason that your husband wouldn't like me? I ask because David seems to be intentionally preventing me from getting to know Mr. Lemon." Claire found it impossible to contain her amusement at this.

"Layla, Walter is a wonderful man. He is a great husband and father, but he has a few subtle flaws. He is way too handsome, smart and charming for his own good. Women throw themselves at him, but he is devoted to me only. I trust him with my heart and my life, but to a guy like David, he is a reminder of all his social shortcomings."

"I think David is plenty charming and handsome."

"Yes, and he wants to keep it that way. He'll get over it once he is sure that you are committed to him. I think it's all so cute."

David's jealousy of his father went on for years. Although Claire was aware of the situation, Walter didn't have a clue. On the rare occasions when I saw him, he was kind, witty and, of course, still very handsome, but never the least bit improper, unless you consider him calling me beautiful improper. One day, after my second year at UC, Claire asked if I had accepted her invitation to join them on their vacation. She knew by my reaction that I had not gotten the invite. Claire didn't know what to say, so I spoke.

"Don't say anything to Davey. If after dating for five years, he doesn't want me along, it's his prerogative and his loss."

I suspect that Claire said something to Davey because the very next day he invited me to come along to Tampa with his family. I wanted to play it cool and refuse his reluctant offer, but I had never been out of Ohio in my whole life.

I guess this is the time to come completely clean, so I'll admit that I wanted to get to know Walter Lemon. It wasn't something I'd characterize as sexual desire. It was more like being intrigued by this handsome and mysterious man. Claire was thrilled and I did want to get to know her better too.

Even before Popi saved me from the three killers, my feelings had changed. Now it was desire, especially since I learned about the peculiar spell. Claire had been so secure in her marriage for such a long time that she couldn't see that I had stolen her husband.

I would have to say that I really didn't get to know Claire well until I invited her to live with us when some serial pervert attacked her and Chrissy in their home in Cincinnati. Even though they were divorced and she knew by then that Popi and I were engaged, she treated me like family. She even helped me plan our wedding. Claire not only became our house manager, she became the business manager for Layla's Petites. To me, this didn't make sense because Claire had the chance to keep Popi if she would only quit her high powered job. She couldn't do it, but she later quit that job to become my CEO.

She has never kept it a secret that she was still in love with Popi, maybe even more in love than she had been before the divorce. Yet she always supported me, my marriage and my company. I don't think I have ever met another woman who could possibly do that, including me.

# Cynwrig & Fiedlimid

There were only twelve of us in the last squad. Four were old and infirm and five were under the age of twelve. The other two were older than him by a few winters, so he would follow their lead. If I could exert any influence on my host Cynwrig, I would advise him to run and catch up to the real fighting men. These brave, but incompetent men and boys will be unable to watch your six. We were worried about the battle. He was worried about dying of course, but above that concern was the fear of discovering that he was a coward.

Again, if I could talk to Cynwrig, I would assure him that most men in this position would have those same worries. Cynwrig did get exasperated with the slow pace of his squad and volunteered to scout ahead. The inexperienced leader seemed confused.

"We are stronger if we stay together." His befuddled eyes did not inspire confidence.

I was proud of Cynwrig when he said what I might have said, "Our real power is in what we know about our enemy. Now we know nothing, but I can give you that power of knowledge before the enemy even knows that we exist." We ran ahead.

We heard the sounds of the battle before we saw. Dying screams sound the same in any language so the horrible noise gave us no clues. We crawled to the next rise and looked down at the violent scene. The men of Ulaid had the enemy outnumbered three to one at the beginning of the battle, but our citizen army was dying at an estimated rate of ten to one. At least fifty of his neighbors and citizens from neighboring villages lay dead or dying while five or six of the larger more powerful professional soldiers had fallen.

These evil invaders wore metallic armor on their heads, chest and knees. Their greatest weapon was not a weapon at all. The iron reinforced wooden shields were used to fend off our spears and swords. The enemy worked as small teams, so when a few were surrounded they fought back to back, killing from all sides. He had promised to bring back news of the battle, but he could not tell them to run away and would not urge them to rush to their deaths. Cynwrig didn't rush to his death. We walked.

Cynwrig's racing mind belied his grim stoic countenance. He was thinking of his parents, siblings and of course his beloved Fiedlimid. He knew that if he and his unprepared countrymen couldn't stop these demon invaders, the women and children will be at the mercy of the godless killers. We attempted to take in the whole violent conflict. I was surprised by how quiet the battle was. Most of the yelling seemed to be from the soldiers communicating to their comrades. Then, of course, were the dying screams of our townsfolk being hacked to death.

Once Cynwrig was amongst the fray, he didn't hesitate. He came upon an enemy who was tangled up with two of the good guys and ran his sword through his neck. He found another and killed him too. This time, he stole the dead man's shield. He was surprised by the weight. The boy used his new tool to good effect, killing two more before the enemy overran the villagers' line. It was now a free-for-all and many of the citizen soldiers broke and ran. The enemy didn't follow the faint of heart, but instead, they went into a deadly frenzy on the brave men who had remained.

Cynwrig held his ground and continued to make the demons pay with their blood. I could feel that he was changed and, should he survive, would forever fight to reclaim all he had lost in the past few minutes. A massive invader confronted us with a swinging iron axe. Cynwrig raised his shield to protect his head and thrust his sword deeply into the giant's gut. The weight of that swinging axe drove the heavy shield into our skull, stunning Cynwrig and driving him to the bloody ground. I was still thinking straight, but still impotent. Another large, dangerous man drove his long iron sword through our chest.

# THE MAD VLAD
# MURDER CLUB

I had a lot of irons in the fire. I was lying awake before sunup, having returned from Bronze Age Europe, maybe Ireland. I don't know what lesson I was supposed to take from the violent trip. Cynwrig was dead and evil wins, not exactly Aesop's fables. I had too many irons in the fire. 2035 Layla was suffering. 2014 Layla was, for the first time since I've known her, harboring a guilty conscience. It was over the death of young Anthony. She thinks that she goaded Brockov into executing the boy.

Then there was Claire. Claire who I still love and who I believe still loves me. Now when I see her, many times each day, all I can think about is losing her. She is the mother of my children, my first real love. I need 2035 Layla to tell me how and when my Claire is lost to me. Maybe I can change her fate and mine. I, of course, wanted most of all to change the worlds' fate by killing Vladimir and Nicholas Brockov, the sooner the better.

Layla stirred and the day began. I went running with Li'l Freckles, my Breck, never once letting her out of my sight until we were back in our kitchen. Claire was there, looking beautiful, prepping for breakfast. I went to her and gave her a kiss on her cheek. She didn't shy away from my sweaty face.

"Thank you Walter, what was that for."

"Just a pitiful show of my love for you," I kissed her again.

Layla and I went off to shower. When we went back downstairs, I was barefoot and bare-chested, wearing only my famous swimsuit. Layla was in black tights under a pretty, short red dress.

My princess asked, "What's wrong Popi? You seemed stressed."

"Nothing urgent baby, I just have too many irons in the fire, we'll talk tonight."

The kitchen was hopping when we arrived. Nearly everyone in the house was there. Robby and Susan were in a day early for the weekend. The Angels were here as was Stump, Ski and Rebecca. The only ones missing were Chrissy and Mary who were in school and Michael who was playing outside with his Mother. My bar stool, paper and coffee were waiting for me.

I was lost in the paper amidst the laughing chit chat when I came upon a story in the international news section. It was a short story with a tasteless headline, Jacques la Ripper loose in Brussels. Seven young girls have been kidnapped, raped and murdered in the last fourteen days. The girls' mutilated bodies were dumped exactly two days after each was taken. The girls were all waitresses or barmaids.

I remained quiet and calm, but inside, my blood was boiling. I didn't know if this monster was my monster, but it almost didn't matter, almost. I bided my time in relative calm and waited for all the busy people to go about their various duties until it was just Claire and me. I helped her clean the kitchen and she finally had time to relax after fixing breakfast for sixteen. Again, I had to cover my emotional response to the thought of losing her. I used my most advanced tactic, good only against pretty women, I comically flirted.

"Claire honey, I'm trying to lose a few pounds, so I didn't eat any of your fine breakfast."

"Oh no you don't, my Walter alarm just went off. You never eat breakfast."

"No honey, I'm serious. Since I can't eat, I was wondering if it would be okay if I just sniffed your apron bib."

"Sure Walter let me take it off."

I stood and wrapped my arms around her. I sat, spun her in my arms and pulled my ex-wife onto my lap.

"That won't be necessary."

After a few fun minutes of flirting with Claire, I tracked down Ski in his office.

"Read this." I handed the article to him.

After a long moment, he said, "If he's in Belgium, he's off our radar. We've been concentrating on Eastern Europe. Belgium is a hard place for a Russian to blend in."

"Unless he has someone helping him there, Ski, I want to make this our top Priority. Even if it's not him, it is someone just like him."

"Okay Walter, I'll give you an update this evening."

I knew Ski was skeptical. He has a deep rooted fear of tunnel vision. Don't ever ask to hear the story. It'll make you cry. I went to my den to make an important call.

"Hello DeeDee. How goes the investigation?"

"We're coming up empty in the former SSR's, the Balkans and Eastern Europe. I'm thinking next is France, Germany and Spain."

"I agree with your instincts, but I want you to focus all your resources to Belgium, Brussels to be exact. There is a mad dog serial killer there who just might be Vladimir and his psychotic little brother."

"Walter, you do know that Nicholas is only seventeen, don't you?"

"Let me know what you find DeeDee."

Seventeen, Nicholas Brockov is only seventeen in 2014. How could I be so stupid? This is why I should never hold anything back from my team. These good people have first class minds and their interaction increases the chances that one shot up old cowboy won't screw the pooch. I decided then and there to bring in Layla tonight and the rest tomorrow. I just need a way to do that without sounding like a delusional crackpot. Maybe Layla can help me with that. I spent the rest of my day in more pleasant pursuits. I spent two hours sitting with Michael and half an hour flirting with Claire when she came to relieve me.

Claire asked, "Walter, what is wrong with you? You've been so nice and sweet to me, it's scaring me."

"I love you Claire, I always have and now I have Layla's permission to show you, up to a point." Claire was unconvinced.

"You won that bet months ago. What has changed in the last few days?"

"My adventures in tiger country have made me aware again of how tenuous life can be. So I've decided to live my short allotment of time appreciating the things that bring me joy and trying to return some of that joy. If you really want off my most beloved list, I guess I can do that." She frowned.

"Don't you dare." My charming line of bullshit saves the day again.

I spent the rest of the day with Stump, overhauling the tractor. It was nice being able to teach the young man a little about diesel mechanics. We were elated when we turned it over. The forty year old American machine was purring like a well-loved woman.

I went to clean up for dinner at five and walked up the creaky stairs at six. I, of course, found Layla hard at work all alone in her ten thousand square foot design studio. I don't know why she seems even sexier in her reading glasses. Her vision is perfect, but she uses them to see even closer and better. Layla feels that everything she makes deserves that minutely detailed attention. The only thing in my life that I give that much care was Layla herself.

"Li'l freckles." She started a bit.

"Hi Popi, is it Six already?"

"Fraid so sweetheart, will you come to dinner with your neglected husband?"

"Will you carry me? I'm too exhausted to make it on my own." She cutely feigned exhaustion.

"I will, but only if I can steal a kiss or two."

I did steal that kiss which turned into a grope which morphed into passionate desk top lovin', the best kind. We were late for dinner and everyone stared at us with knowing smirks. If only they knew the true extent of my devotion to my darling Breck, my sexy fiery wife, they'd be consumed with envy.

After dinner, Ski called me to his office, Layla came along. As soon as we entered, I could tell he had something by Rebecca's nervous and squirming attempts to hide her excitement. Ski was better at it.

"We may have gotten our first break. It seems that Vladimir has a little brother. He's just a kid, but maybe he's helping his big brother. We have a rumor that Nicholas Brockov is attending a fancy private prep school in France."

"That's great Ski, you know that's pretty close to Brussels."

Layla asked, "Why Brussels?"

Rebecca said, "Because they have a vicious killer on the loose who's mutilating young women there."

I went to sleep that night with Layla wrapped tightly in my arms. I was thinking about the other irons I had in the fire. I was hoping to dream of 2035, but I was too excited about Brussels. I was champing at the bit to get after Vladimir and his juvenile, monstrous little brother. Nicholas' age was problematic. Mad Vlad deserved to die for his crimes in this time, but Little Nikki might be redeemable. That is, after all, what I've wanted for myself, to restrict the killing to the most evil and not painting death with such a broad brush. There is some chance that the kid is not yet the man he will someday be.

When I finally did dream, I dreamed of an erotic encounter with my ex-wife. Strangely, this was the first ever, no, not my first bawdy dream. I've been regularly having wild sex dreams since I was twelve, but this was my first one about Claire. We were in the kitchen. I was reading the paper with Layla on the stool to my right and Claire on the stool to my left.

Layla asked, "Popi, do you know what day it is?" Her eyes glimmered with amusement.

"I think it is Tuesday sweetheart."

Everyone in the room, in unison, said the same thing, "Men!"

I looked around and saw that the room contained only females.

"No Popi, its ex-wives day. You must spend the whole day with Claire and do anything she asks."

I was astounded, "Anything?"

"Let your conscience be your guide." The amusement was gone.

Claire took me by the hand and led me to her bedroom, five. Inside, she didn't waste any time. My beautiful ex-wife stripped and lay on her bed.

"Make love to me Walter." Her words felt like an order.

She was as beautiful as I remembered and since I knew that I was dreaming, I didn't hesitate. I used my entire considerable repertoire of woman pleasing moves and ravished her until she begged me to stop. I want to make it clear to you, dear readers, that in the waking world, no woman has ever asked me to stop because she couldn't take anymore pleasure. Dream Walter is such a better lover than me. Lying entwined and entangled, Claire kissed me again.

"I've always loved you Walter and I've always known that you love me too, but tell me the truth, am I going to die?" She didn't seem worried, so I told the truth because she deserved it.

"Claire, I do love you. You are second only to Layla in my heart. I don't know for sure if you're going to die, but I've been to the future and you're not there." Claire began to reinvigorate Big Popi, or Little Walter, in her vernacular, with her talented mouth. "I'm trying to find out when and how you die to see if there is something I can do to change your fate."

She had Little Walter in a high state of readiness and climbed aboard.

"If fate could be changed then it's not really fate. It's a series of decisions and decisions should not be changed without the expectation that a better outcome is probable." Her pleasure shined through her matter of fact statement.

I wanted to ponder these wise words for a while, but with the sexy woman riding Big Popi and her luxurious breasts in my face needing my personal attention, I chose to enjoy the dream moment instead of worrying about mere life or death issues.

I awoke with Layla quietly pleasuring me with her incredible mouth. It was not a difficult transition between pleasuring my beautiful Claire and making love to my enchanted wife. When we were exhausted Layla continued kissing my face.

"Popi, tell me your dirty dream." Her worry was palpable.

"I dreamed that you told me it was ex-wives day and that I should do whatever Claire wanted."

"And she wanted you to make love to her, of course."

"Of course, who wouldn't?" Layla was momentarily miffed, but she thought about it for a few seconds.

"Popi, I would never give you permission to screw anyone." She was stern.

"I know that honey. It was just a dirty dream and not my hearts' desire."

"Why have you been so lovey dovey to Claire lately? Do you want her back? Are you tired of me?" Her sternness had turned to insecurity.

"Li'l Freckles, I'm supposed to be the insecure one. You are so special to me and I can't believe that I'm enough for you. I have been fixated on Claire for several days because I've been dreaming about the future and she's not there. I'm afraid that we are going to lose her."

As I had been intending, I told the long complicated story of my dream life including our battle with Mad Vlad, his brother and my death. Then I told her about our mourning family with Claire being absent. I didn't tell her that I was depending on her future self to tell me how and when Claire was lost. I also didn't tell my trusted, beautiful wife about Cynwrig and Fiedlimid. It didn't, at the time, seem relevant and I was still unsettled by the disturbing adventure.

Layla had nothing to say, so she coerced me to make love to her again. With my dream lovin' and the real lovin', I felt like I was at it all night long. I'm not complaining. It was only two in the morning so there was still a chance that I would dream.

# CYNWRIG & FIEDLIMID

I was back inside Cynwrig's head. The boy was groaning. I began trying to monitor the lads' vital signs. He seemed to be breathing okay and his heartbeat was strong and steady. His eyes were still closed, blinding me, but I could feel his mind beginning to reawaken. His sexy dreams of Fiedlimid were fading, replaced by fear, anger and most of all, pain. I couldn't feel his physical pain, but was privy to the distress levels it produced. I could also still hear the dying sounds of the fallen men.

Cynwrig was jostled awake and his eyes sprung open. It was his squad who had finally made it to the battle site. They picked him up and moved him a short distance, away from the dead and dying. He held onto his short sword and long dagger, refusing to part with the killing instruments which had served him so well. His cowardly comrades examined our wounds and declared them to be survivable. The enemy sword had slipped off Cynwrig's ribcage leaving a horrific bloody wound, but his core was intact.

Cynwrig was torn, these men were the lowest of the soldiers and were not to be expected to defend the tuath, but they were also the last line of defense for Ulaid. When he found out that they had hidden and let the evil demons pass unopposed to pillage Ulaid, he was less understanding.

"You cowards, you dawdle here while those demons rape our women and burn our homes."

He turned his back on his unit and began quickly limping toward his family and his beloved Fiedlimid. He was about three hours into his sacred journey when he saw the smoke arising from the southwest horizon. He stopped to pray to his patron gods, rubbing the bloody runes on his dented bronze sword as he beseeched them to protect his loved ones.

Two hours later we entered Ulaid. It was really just the land where his village had stood. Every structure was burned to the ground. Only the center posts still stood. Small children were wandering, eyes glazed in shock, throughout the piles of ash and amongst the bodies of the old men and women. Some of the younger women still lived, but were so savagely beaten that they couldn't even cover their naked, brutalized bodies.

Cynwrig was falling into shock himself, but he refused to let it sway him from his dreadful course. He came to his family's' pile of ash and found his little sister Aine sitting on the dirty, smoldering ground next to her dead mother. Aine was crying and rocking her baby brother who was also crying in her small arms. His mother was naked and hacked to death.

"Little sister, where is father?"

Aine didn't rejoice at the sound of her big brother's voice, but simply pointed to our right. Ten feet in that direction, Cynwrig found Donn. He was, of course, dead, his head split by axe or sword. Cynwrig walked zombie-like to Fiedlimid's pile of ashes. Her mother was alive, but in a trance, hugging her younger, crying children.

"Where is she?"

He knew she would know, even in her tortured state, who he meant. Again, the silent pointing finger, so we followed the shaking signal. I wish I could say that, like Lacy, Cynwrig's little Breck was beautiful even in death, but I shall not tell that soothing lie. Fiedlimid was naked, still clutching a small bronze knife. Her slender body was covered in blood and flies. She had been beaten, repeatedly raped and ultimately decapitated or nearly so. Even with that horrific trauma, miraculously, the expression on her murdered face was almost serene.

Cynwrig knelt at his beloveds' side and tried to wipe the blood from her pale lips with his dirty, bloody hand. Seeing the futility of this, he leaned in and kissed those lips, closing his eyes. He shed no tears, having also seen the futility in that, but I, in spirit, was bawling. The boy, a man now, rose and walked back to his sister and brother. He picked them up into his weary arms, hugging them, kissing them. He did this wordlessly, knowing not how to craft something to say which would make it better. He carried his family to Fielimid's mother.

"Balis, Aine will be your daughter now and little Braeden is your grandson. I will bury our dead. We spent the next four hours digging graves. The cowards, men who had fled the battle, insuring the success of the enemy's charge, began drifting in. Cynwrig held back his anger and kept digging, refusing their assistance several times. Near the limit of his physical endurance, he had an epiphany. In the end, only the cowards are left to rebuild.

Cynwrig presided over the funerals after cleaning up in the creek. He was missing all of the ceremonial items commonly used in the sacred proceedings. No shrouds were to be found to wrap the dead. No blessed religious tokens were had to accompany the souls of his people. Not even a single drop of lambs' blood was available as an offering to the goddesses of the afterlife. The demons had destroyed, burned or stolen everything of value in the whole town. Yet the funeral, before the survivors, was poignant and meaningful.

A group of townsmen hailed us as we walked up the hill. Cynwrig drew his sword and turned to face them. From his position on the higher ground, he loomed above them.

"What do you want?"

I probed Cynwrig's mind and found he had hatred for these men who he'd known all his life. His best friend Eibhear's father, the armorer, stepped forward.

"Cynwrig, we want you to be high Priest. We witnessed your

courage in battle and think you are ready to carry on your father's work." Cynwrig became enraged.

"I'll not minister to men such as you who will run and hide while your wives and daughters are raped and murdered."

The six men, though shamefaced, drew their weapons. Cynwrig's laughter was not from amusement. It was more from evil glee at the thought of killing these despicable men. They had all suffered the same losses as he, but unlike him, they held their lives as dear. He advanced on them, unafraid. They, of course, wanted no part of the half mad young man and quickly, without another word, departed.

Cynwrig continued to the top of the hill and found the remains of his father's forge. He stirred the ash and found the strange gray metal rune with which he had been branded. He could not leave his fathers' magic to be misused by men such as these. We walked away, down the other side of the hill and into the bog, deftly walking the wooden, floating planks which were the only path through the smelly, fetid earth. When he'd made many turns, he climbed upon a rare piece of solid ground, his secret place. He lay down on the soft grass and finally let go. He allowed himself to cry and once given that permission, the tears streamed in rivulets until, mercifully, he slept.

# Layla's Journal;
## July 30 2035

Claire almost got a chance to get Popi back when all of my memories of him were stolen. To make matters worse, the evil Mr. Charles brainwashed me into hating my beloved Popi. Popi had told me once that if he lost me, he would ask Claire to take him back. In my state of mind at the time, I wouldn't have put up a fight. Yet when Popi cured me of my hatred for him, she hugged me.

"I knew you would come back to us Layla. You and Walter were made for each other." She is, without a doubt, the best person I know.

Claire always worked tirelessly for Layla's Petites. Her business savvy and organizational skills were a very large part in building a successful company. In late December 2014, she asked to fly, two weeks early, to Paris to see her boyfriend, Henri Remy.

I said, "Of course you can Claire. I know you'll be too busy during and after the Paris shows."

"Thank you Layla. I knew you would understand." We hugged and planned her trip, making a list of things we needed to do in her absence.

At 5:05 p.m. on January seventh 2015, four days after Claire had left, a crying Inspector Remy called my cell phone. He said that Claire had been taken from his home while he was at work. He asked me to tell Popi because he didn't have it in his heart to break the news to him.

"I'll be expecting his call. Meanwhile we are doing everything humanly possible to get her back."

I called Popi and asked him to meet me in his den in ten minutes. He didn't try to pry a hint out of me, knowing, I think, that it was bad. I knew that Popi would be crushed with worry, but he had to be told. Popi had been worried about Claire for weeks and tried to convince her not to go. The source of his worry was in his dreams of the future. Claire wasn't there. Claire, even though she'd seen some miraculous events, still had the heart of an avowed skeptic and was unpersuaded. I had to wait outside his hidden door. Popi came and embraced me.

"What is it Li'l Freckles?" He unlocked his door and I guided him to his couch.

"Popi, Henri called. He told me that Claire has been kidnapped."

Popi's reaction wasn't what I was expecting. In fact, this was the moment in those early years of our beautiful marriage that I learned that I can't see deeply into his heart. After my expected knockout blow, Popi picked up his cell phone and pushed one button.

"Ski, it's time. Make sure the plane is ready, Yeah, an hour and a half." He put down his phone. "Honey, Ski and I are going to Paris this evening. Rebecca's staying here to help you guys get ready for Paris."

"Popi, aren't you going to tell me the rest?"

"I'm sorry baby I can't, it might change things." I understood that he wanted to tell me, but couldn't. I couldn't figure out why. "Li'l Freckles, no matter what happens in the next few days, you must go on with your fashion schedule. Claire's life may depend upon it."

We hugged and he kissed me goodbye. I felt a sense of dread and foreboding which lasted for a long, long time.

# January 1st

We had a big party on New Years' Eve. All the beautiful girls brought dates except Gabrielle who never dated and Claire whose boyfriend lived in France. Gabrielle didn't leave the property enough to even meet a man. Everyone was dressed to the nines. The Angels, including Simone, danced for hours to the music of a raucous Punk-rock band that I had flown in from New York City. They were pretty good and the young people loved them.

I walked out of the ballroom to give my ears a rest from the driving bass and ran into Claire. I hooked her arm and guided us to the kitchen where I got us each a beer.

"I'm an old rocker, but that is way too loud for me."

"All the girls are having the time of their lives. Walter, I'm leaving for Paris on the third. I want to spend a couple of weeks with Henri before the real work starts."

"Claire honey, who will protect you? I'm going to hire a bodyguard."

"I'll be fine Walter, no one even recognizes me when I'm alone."

I told her that I had a bad feeling about this and even told a bit about my dreams and her absence, but she was determined.

"I'll not live my life in fear of your voodoo warnings." I knew my ex-wife very well and was smart enough to give in.

"Okay sweetheart, just be careful. I don't think these people will survive without your pancakes."

We went back to the party and even danced. I didn't allow my worries prevent a good time, but I was anxious to dream tonight. I hoped that my drunkenness wouldn't hurt my chances. At two-thirty the band was supposed to leave, but the doe-eyed pleading from women as beautiful as these bought us an extra set. I found Layla.

"Sweetheart, I'm dragging these old bones to bed." She was tipsy.

"Okay old timer, but you can bet that I'm gonna wake your cute butt up after the party."

"I wouldn't have any other way."

I had to take a shower, having sweat profusely on the crowded dancefloor. I was soon naked in bed dozing. Even in sleep, I was trying to steer myself to 2035 by force of will. This rarely works so I was not surprised when I awoke inside of Cynwrig's mind.

# CYNWRIG AND FIEDLIMID

My first thought was a feeling of impatience. I didn't have time for this. After considering this, I had a change of heart. Cynwrig was likely going to try to save one of his dead loved ones today by using his father's magic. While I knew this was all a dream, it may be something else too, something that may prove useful in my own life. Cynwrig awoke. After relieving himself into the bog, he grabbed his sword and knife. The boy walked the floating path back to Ulaid. When we left the swamp and started up the hill, I could see that the large town hall was still a pile of ashes.

Halfway up the hill, he looked toward the heavens and said the unprintable words given to him by Donn. Nothing happened. Cynwrig looked at his wound and found it was gone. The brand was still present on his chest. I was not surprised at this, but Cynwrig was. I noticed his bronze sword. The runes which were carved onto the blade were also gone. Donn wasn't finished making it. We looked up the hill and saw the town hall had returned. He walked to his father's shop and entered. Donn was working on the sword that hung from Cynwrig's waist, carving the runes.

"Father, you were right." Donn looked up from his work and smiled.

"Son, you have survived. What about your mother and the young ones?"

"Aine and Braeden are unharmed, but Mother and you are dead."

"Who will you save?"

Without shame, he said, "Fiedlimid." Donn smiled at this.

"You must hurry. I think I saw her at the cook fire a moment ago. Try to go from a hidden place, but hurry."

He hugged his father. When the plain sword at Cynwrig's waist nudged into the sword on the work bench, sparks flew with a high voltage crackle.

Cynwrig found his little Breck at what was apparently the communal kitchen. Two goats were roasting and a large bronze pot full of vegetables was boiling. I could also smell fresh bread baking, though I couldn't see it. He walked unseen to Fiedlimid. Her back was to him. I could feel his overwhelming joy at the sight of her alive and well. He wrapped his long arms around her waist.

"What's for dinner my little Breck?" Fiedlimid spun in his arms.

"First you must tell me how beautiful I am, in my new dress."

She was quite fetching and her dress was very pretty too, at least compared to other women's attire.

"I would hate to cause your perfect little head to swell from my expressions of admiration for you." Fiedlimid smiled, apparently satisfied with his deflection. "Evergood, I need you to come with me so we may speak in private."

"You rascal, you just want to steal a kiss."

"Of course that is true, but I also have something important to ask you."

They walked hand in hand down the hill and to Fiedlimid's house where she had her own room created by a curtain. Inside that small space, Cynwrig wrapped his little Breck in a tight embrace and kissed her as he held her mightily as instructed.

"Fiedlimid, I love you. Will you be my wife?"

"How can I marry you if you crush the life out of me?"

"I'm sorry my love, but I cannot let go lest I lose you and die from that loss."

"I love you too my dear Cynwrig and I would be proud to be your wife."

She kissed him hard on his smiling mouth and he kissed back, holding her tightly as he waited for the magic which he knew was coming. It came without warning and I was forcefully ejected from his mind, back to my bed.

# Secret Armor

I pulled Layla tightly to me, though not nearly as tight as Cynwrig held his Evergood. My darling wife stirred a bit.

She said, "Popi," in her beautiful slumber.

I kissed her neck and whispered, "I'll love you forever my little Breck."

I lay there, unable to sleep, worrying about that beautiful young couple. Did they make it? If they did, I was pretty sure that Poor Fiedlimid would be mad at Cynwrig for not being able to say goodbye to her family. I think they did make it and was pretty sure that their love for each other would get them through. I had no doubt that the brave young man would be able to protect his darling Fiedlimid.

I was able to go back to sleep, but did not dream. I didn't know whether 2035 Layla had the key to saving Claire. Even if she did, it might be many years before I could act on that magical intelligence.

Layla slept in, she didn't wake me until seven ready to run. I was not looking forward to running five miles, but I was too proud to admit this to my young bride. I dressed and went to the kitchen while she stretched. Claire was sleeping in too. There was no fresh coffee, but I was able to reheat yesterdays' leftovers.

The run was painful. Fortunately, Layla was slowed by last nights over indulgence too, so I finished my standard fifty yards behind. I met with Ski and Rebecca for an update on the search for Mad Vlad.

"Walter, I think we've located Nickolas. He's going to some snooty private prep school in Paris. We've got round the clock eyes on him."

"Great Ski, do we have anything new on the Brussels' Butcher?" I'd just made up that name. I must not use it in public.

"Only that he's stopped. He'll pop up somewhere. We just have to follow the dead girls."

On that happy note, I left to pursue my peace, my favorite thing and my solace. In other words drinking coffee, reading the newspaper and watching the pretty girls at the pool. Today it was a new cast of beauties. First it was Chrissy and Mary. They flirted with me just like Layla's Angels and I reacted much like I did with the others. They are, all of these beautiful women, like daughters to me. Except, of course, Layla for whom my sentiments were far from fatherly. She made the thought of being truly sexually attracted to another impossible. Still, I appreciated ogling that exquisite feminine form which I, in this humble mansion, have been blessed with in abundance.

Up next were Jordon and Simone on a break from Layla's sweatshop. There were no holidays two weeks before Paris week. They ignored me and went straight to the two meter springboard. Jordon, a tiny Asian athlete who was barely covered in a shiny bronze bikini, went first. She was talking the whole time.

"Watch Simone, it's easy once you control your fear." She sprang off the board without her preparatory bounce and performed a simple head first dive. "You go, I know you can."

Simone hesitantly edged to the end of the board, her nerves were apparent. Simone was adorable in a white bikini which provided a striking contrast to her ebon flesh. Her large, for her size, breasts were overflowing and quivering. She was terrified and Jordon was no help.

She said, "Jump," in her cute, commanding voice.

Simone tried to dive head first, but bailed out in mid-air, flailing into a full body flop. Showing a dearth of empathy, I laughed, not just a ha-ha or a muted snicker, but a full belly laugh. Jordon glared at me.

"Popi! It's not funny. The poor thing is afraid of heights."

"I'm sorry Simone. I thought you meant to do that just to cheer me up."

They each sat on an arm of my deck chair and kissed my cheeks. They waved their sexy chests in front of my face, finding joy in my discomfort. I found joy, not only in their superb physical forms, but in their simple devotion to their Popi. Life is good. Good except for the looming specter of the soulless killer and the foreboding worry about the safety of my beloved ex-wife. I've always been able to find some joy in even the most trying of times. It's my secret armor against the chaos of my world.

Claire would be leaving the day after tomorrow and I was in a near panic. I had been dreaming of 2035 nearly every night, but now when I really needed to in the worst way, I couldn't beg borrow or steal passage on that ship. I was thinking of calling Henri Remy and asking him to cancel Claire's visit. I didn't think he would even consider it with my dreams as the only proof. I had one bit of leverage. I believe that I can predict that he'll soon have a serial killing beast in his jurisdiction. I would let Ski decide if there is any merit to that plan. I'm done going solo. On the third, I drove Claire to the airport. I didn't try to talk her out of going.

"Claire, you know how much I love you. I want you to take me seriously when I ask you to be on high alert to danger."

"Walter, I'll be with Henri the whole time. He's more than capable of protecting me."

"I know, but he won't have the foreboding sense of danger that I'm experiencing which means that he may not be prepared."

Before she joined the security line, I kissed her. Worried that it may be our last kiss, I strove to make it spectacular. By her dreamy gaze afterward, I was successful.

"Walter, don't worry, I'll be fine." Her voice was husky from the kiss and her love for me.

On my drive home, against Ski's advice, I called Remy.

"Hello Walter, is anything wrong? Is Clarissa well?"

"Yes Henri, she's fine. I just put her on the plane. She'll be there in about ten hours."

"Trey bon, is there something else my friend."

"Yes Henri, I want you to protect her like the irreplaceable work of art that she is. I'm worried that my enemies from Russia will want to hurt me by targeting the people that I love."

"Thank you Walter, I'll make sure that Claire will have a security detail when I can't be there."

"Thank you Henri, have fun." I felt better.

On January sixth, we had a breakthrough. Ski's men in Paris sent him some photos from their very expensive surveillance of Nickolas Brockov. In one series from last night, the good looking seemingly normal young man was caught meeting a darker man in a park. The larger and presumably older man was wearing a hooded jacket and kept his face hidden in shadow. The man hugged Nickolas and gave him a brown leather satchel which looked like a gym bag. They hugged again and Nickolas returned to his dormitory.

"Ski, did they follow the man?" I was excited.

"No Walter, the agent was alone and had instructions to stick with Nick."

"Is the plane ready?"

"Almost, the pilot is flying in from Houston tonight. Walter, I know it's your money, but we're two million into this thing, before you count the jet."

I knew he was right, but I'd never forgive myself if I lost Claire due to fiscal responsibility.

"Lock in the jet and pilot for three days. We'll revisit the finances after that."

"Will do Walter, oh, I almost forgot, Henri Remy just called me. He asked about your mental stability."

I went about my day and shut my mind to the constant questioning of myself, why can't I dream? I was learning from my disappointment that the great amount of internal pressure may be having a negative effect. I blocked it out and tried to relax. At least I could stop worrying about Bronze Age Ireland, one iron out of the fire.

The only problem is that now I find that I have to keep Layla out of the loop. I can't take the chance that what I tell her now changes the actions of her future self. Every time I ponder the intricacies of time/dream travel, I get a headache.

In bed that night, after the headache curing love making, I purposely got Layla talking about her work. I knew how excited she was before Paris. I don't know if she kept talking after I drifted off to her sweet sirens' song of fashion talk, but she may well have. First I dreamed a silly sex dream involving two of Layla's Angels, but I rejected that. Then I dreamed of Claire again. This was not an erotic encounter, but a horrible nightmare of my beautiful ex-wife being tied to a bed, tortured and mutilated. I was a helpless observer and her screams startled me awake.

It took a while to drift off again. My persistence finally paid off and I found myself or rather my spirit in 2035. I wasted no time and willed myself to Layla's desk. The book was unobstructed this time, so it only took twenty minutes to open it to the latest pages. She had gotten my message and wrote glowingly of her relationship with Claire. I tried to memorize the whole three pages of heartfelt prose, but the most important part was burned into my brain. At 5:05 in the afternoon of January 10th 2015, Inspector Remy called crying. Claire had been murdered in his home at one o'clock this morning.

I couldn't resist going to Layla's room. I kissed and fondled her as best I could, but she didn't stir. It was probably a good thing that I couldn't contact her, but it sure didn't feel like a good thing. It felt sad. Still I lay next to her and pretended to sleep until I returned to my time with the secret information. Back in bed with present Layla, I tried to go back to my rejected dream of the two Angels, but was unable. Instead, I kissed and fondled my little Breck, relishing the warmth of her.

# JANUARY 7ᵀᴴ D DAY

Layla predictably awakened and seduced me. She was still demanding all the lovemaking I could reasonably be expected to produce. Someday I would tell her how much I enjoyed these days, but for now I feigned inevitable surrender to her exquisite charms. I knew that she knew, but it was a sexy unspoken game. We fell into sleep entangled and intertwined with the tactile treat of her breast in my hand and the familiar aroma of my true loves clean hair pleasing my olfactory senses and thus my mind.

Apparently, we didn't move an inch the whole night. When Layla's quiet alarm sounded at sunup, we were still in that comfortable position. Layla tried to slip away from me discreetly, without waking me, and I pretended that she was successful. She walked naked to her bathroom before my hidden gaze. I was still enraptured by her perfect body. When she returned, I had to close my eyes to maintain my charade, missing the second reel of this blockbuster.

She maneuvered herself back into her former position, even placing my hand on her breast. Then she kissed me. Big Popi was awakened and knew what to do. With assistance from Layla, he found his way through the gates of heaven and we enjoyed some slow, lazy morning love, barely changing positions. She had set me up, but I pretended not to notice. When she was satisfied, but before Big Popi was finished, Layla stopped and rose from the bed.

"Popi get up and ready to run." Her grin was both impish and smug.

"But honey, I wasn't through." Was I whining?

"Now tonight, maybe I won't have to trick or cajole you into pleasing me."

Layla and I ran. I was so excited about my developing plan that I didn't notice at first that I was ahead of her, with more in my tank, when she poured it on for the last quarter mile. I reached inside myself, though not too deeply, and started stretching out my stride. Layla had to dig deep to beat me by ten yards.

"Wow Popi, I almost didn't have enough today. You're actually getting faster."

"I guess it's out of the question to consider that you may be getting slower."

"Bite your tongue Popi."

After breakfast, every man for himself with Claire gone, Layla went straight to work and so did I. I skipped my morning routine and went to work on my complicated plan. I have toyed with mimicry for many years and did a passable job with impersonations of iconic movie stars of the forties, fifties and sixties. The man I wanted to impersonate was no star. He was a French police inspector. I had Peter Sellers as Inspector Clouseau in my repertoire, but I needed him to be crying.

My son Robby has an extensive collection of BP&LF videos, but he was in school. So I did something that I have never done to any of my children. I searched his room. After two hours of reviewing his video archive, I found what I was looking for. It was news footage of Remy speaking at the funeral of Christian Du Champs, the young Gendarme who was killed by Hideous Hellen while he was assigned to protect Layla and me. Remy was in a very emotional state. He was choked up and crying. I took the video to my den and practiced for hours. That afternoon, I called Triple D.

"DeeDee, I need to make a call to someone in Ohio, but I need the caller ID to indicate that the call is coming from Paris, France."

"I'll have to consult with one of my techs so I'll call you back in an hour."

"Thanks DeeDee, you're learning, you didn't even ask why."

"Would you tell me if I asked?" I laughed.

"Not likely my friend."

"Walter, we have a new set of dolls coming out on Saturday. This set comes with a stuffed tiger. Presale estimates are through the roof."

"Whatever you think DeeDee, call me."

I guess I can get Ski to stop worrying about my out of control spending.

# REMY CALLS

I woke up at six desiring sex, but didn't want to go through another of Popi's cute protests of being overburdened. We both knew that it was an act and most of the time I enjoyed it, but this morning I had a new strategy for avoiding the game. I wish you could have seen the look on his face when I got out of bed before Big Popi was satisfied. I think Popi must be right about sex before running weakening his legs, he very nearly beat me. It seems my little prank may have had some negative consequences.

Popi is still extremely worried about Claire, but he won't talk about it with me. He also won't talk, in any significant detail, about his dreams of the future me. Last night when I tried to draw him out, he sneakily changed the subject to our new line for Paris. I, of course, couldn't help myself from telling him about our inspired collection, Simone's readiness and my excitement about it all. The son of a bitch fell to sleep on me.

After our near disastrous run, I had to make my own breakfast. I really miss Claire. The rest of the household has been going to the diner every morning, but that wasn't an option for me and Popi. The other customers and even the staff wouldn't let us have any peace. Popi only had coffee.

Besides our near daily runs, Popi has a grueling exercise routine that he performs twice a day. When he is in hyper-protective mode, like now, he increases this to three. If it weren't for his beer, he wouldn't have enough calories to sustain his magnificent body. He must have been in this mode for many days, unnoticed by me, because his abs are cut sharper than I have ever seen them and his biceps have recently grown by a solid inch. There has been a corresponding increase in his vigor in bed, but I thought that might be my doing. Whatever the reasons, the results should be enjoyed and not questioned. Popi taught me that.

My days have been filled with frantic work. Popi doesn't like when I work too much, but he understands, especially this time of year. The downside to total immersion in ones' profession is the disconnection with your love ones and the sacrifices. I've only played with Michael for ten minutes a day for a week. I haven't pressured Popi to let me into his worries. I'm just too focused on Layla's Petites. I'm not really too concerned with Popi because he always does the right thing. As of late, he can be depended upon to limit his dangerous rage and avoid any unnecessary death.

I skipped Lunch and worked through the afternoon. While sitting at my workstation and working on a brand new creation in gray satin, my cell rang. Very few people have that number and almost all of them live or work in this house. I always pick up. The caller ID indicated that it was Inspector Remy in Paris. He had never called me before so with no small amount of dread, I answered.

"Hello? Henri is Claire Okay?" Henri Remy was crying and hard to understand.

"Clarissa has been taken. I came home from work and found her missing." The poor man was choked up.

He asked me to tell Popi because he couldn't bring himself to have that conversation.

"I'll tell him. You must get her back, we'll pay anything."

"And I'll do anything to bring her home."

I looked at my clock. It was 5:05 p.m. I disconnected with Remy. I wasn't comforting with him. How could he leave her alone? I made the call to Popi and, not wanting to tell him over the phone, asked him to meet me in his den in ten minutes. He didn't pry for a hint or clue, probably suspecting that it was bad news, maybe even knowing that it involved Claire. I got there a minute before Popi who hurriedly unlocked the hidden door.

"What is it Li'l Freckles?"

I remained silent as I led us to his couch and sat us down. I knew he would be crushed and angry. I was preparing myself to talk him down or at least direct his energies toward positive action.

"Popi, Inspector Remy just called me. He said that Claire has been kidnapped." I waited for his response, with bated breath.

Popi didn't panic. In fact he seemed calm and prepared for this horrible news. He called Kurt.

"It's time. Is the plane ready? We leave in two hours." Popi looked at my confused expression. "Li'l Freckles, Ski and I are flying to Paris tonight." He pulled me close. "Rebeca's going to stay to help you out. I have to go." He kissed me, but that wasn't enough.

"Popi, aren't you going to tell me what the hell is going on?"

"I'm sorry Li'l Freckles, I can't. The less you know, the better the chances of saving Claire."

"How can that be? Don't leave me hanging like this."

"Please don't ask honey. No matter what happens in the next few days, don't let it interfere with your Paris shows. Let Ted Know. The show goes on no matter what." With that he was gone.

I wasn't angry that he couldn't trust me with his plan. He thought it was for the best and, although I didn't understand now, I trusted my Popi. He would explain when he could. What bothered me was the fact that I didn't see this coming. I couldn't see into Popi's heart as well as I had believed and it made me worry that one really truly may never know who the love of her life is, in his innermost thoughts.

# SAVING CLAIRE

On the eighth, we landed at De Gaulle. It was six in the morning local time. I told everything to Ski on the trip over, even about Cynwrig and Fiedlimid and the magical words that, along with the strange rune, gave them a second chance. Ski didn't believe a word of it, but he would and I knew that I could depend on him to follow my crazy plan.

"Walter, now I'm beginning to wonder about your mental state. What exactly did Remy say when he called?"

"Oh yeah, that's another thing. Remy didn't call. It was me pretending to be him. He won't be making that call until the tenth. I got us a head start."

It was very difficult leaving Layla out of the loop. I could see the hurt in her stormy dark blue gray eyes. I can't pretend to understand the possible effects from telling her the whole story, but I had a deep pang in my gut that said, Lance Corporal Walter, if you think it's' right, it probably is. Don't muddle things with cover-your-ass bull. Everyone has a different mission. No one Marine has all the information. Just do your job. It was my Father, the Colonel, reaching out to me, as he frequently does, with his childhood teachings. I have about a million of these in my scrambled memory banks. I would do my job.

It was early morning Thursday so the Airport was not crowded and was mostly peopled with business travelers, not my typical fan base. That, plus the absence of Li'l Freckles and some cheesy dark glasses prevented my cover from being blown. The only one who recognized me was the customs agent who asked me to sign her paycheck envelope. We were checked into the hotel closest to Remy's apartment by eight. We went out for breakfast. I went back to our room while Ski left to procure us some weapons.

We ate lunch in our room then took a nap. We left to reconnoiter Remy's place. We had waited until dusk and walked the ten blocks to our target location and strolled by the building while pretending to be involved in an animated conversation. We were surreptitiously looking for a surveillance team. When we were a block past Remy's place, we paused.

"Did you spot him Walter?"

"No I didn't see anyone loitering."

"He was in a tree across the street. I think he might have been Nicholas."

Ski and I went around the next block and approached the building from the rear. Ski couldn't find anyone watching the back.

"It's not surprising. As long as the target is unaware that he's being watched, one man is plenty." We went back to our shared room.

"Ski, we don't know exactly what time Remy will go to work tomorrow night so we need to be in position very early. After he leaves, can you get us into his building unseen?"

"I doubt it. He may have a security system. I think our best play is to make contact with Claire and have her let us in the back door."

"Is there any chance that they are monitoring her calls?"

"You're right, we can't take the chance."

We planned until midnight, going over every element of the simple plan multiple times. There would be no room for error. In my whole life, no plan I was ever involved with went right. I always seem to do what comes naturally to me when things inevitably go awry. Still, planning was necessary. It got one ready for battle.

If our plan fizzled, it was all on me and I was more than willing to take that weight. If Vladimir and Nickolas didn't show, my credibility would be at an all-time low. If I was right, what then? Does that make me some poor mans' seer, Rasputin with a Heineken? I don't know.

The next day was torture, having nothing to do and me unwilling to venture out in public. I was afraid of blowing my cover. I did not want Brockov to know that I was in Paris. I exercised, watched TV and drank beer. Thankfully, the hotel bar had Heineken. We took a long nap in the afternoon, knowing we were in for a long uncomfortable stakeout. We woke at six. I called room service and got coffee for four. By nine, we were in the shadows in back of Remy's building.

We settled in for a possibly long wait, which we suffered in complete silence. We waited for hours, making me wonder if Remy had changed his plans to leave Claire alone. Finally, at one in the morning Remy pulled out from the garage beneath his building. He looked happy. As soon as he began to turn, I quickly extricated my stiff frame from behind the smelly trashcans and rolled under the closing door. I was in. I walked up to the door to the first floor and found that the stout door was locked.

There was no landing on this side so it took several attempts to break it open with my shoulder. We were ten minutes in and I was worried. I found the back door and let Ski in, finding a stout lock, but no electronic security system. On the small landing, was another locked door. Unlike on TV, it took Ski over five minutes to pick the lock. Once he did, we were faced with two more locked doors, one labeled with a small brass 1. It only took four minutes to nervously watch Ski circumvent the other one. Of course we faced the same situation on the second floor landing.

Five minutes later we stood at apartment threes' back door. I knocked. There was no reply so I knocked again, louder. Fifteen seconds later, Ski pulled out his tools, but I pulled my gun.

I said, "Screw this," and threw my shoulder against the sturdy door.

My adrenalin levels must have been intensely high because the jamb shattered, the hinges gave way and the whole chaotic scene, including me and the door, flopped to the floor of Remy's living room. Ski helped me up.

"Are we a little impatient Walter?"

The living room, dining room and kitchen were all open and Claire wasn't here. There were two other doors plus an open half bathroom. Ski kicked down the door to the left as I bulled through the one on the right. These doors weren't nearly as strong as the others so I was in relative control as I entered. That control evaporated when I tried to comprehend what I was seeing. Claire was completely naked. Even in her mid-forties, she is very beautiful and sexy.

My dear Claire was tied to the bed. She was supine, with each wrist and ankle tightly tied to a bedpost. In her mouth, was a black rubber ball which was strapped around her head. She saw me with her horrified eyes and began shaking her head desperately. I turned, almost in time to prevent being stabbed. I threw out my left arm in self-defense, but was only able to block the knife with the palm of my hand. I didn't have time to get woozy from the sight of that bloody blade skewering my hand.

I closed my fist on the hilt of that large knife. I pulled the attacker toward me and punched him on his chin. He staggered and spun around. I wrapped my right arm around his throat. Before I clamped down on his neck, I closed my eyes and pulled the blade from my hand. My vision was blurred with deep red, my killing colors. Ski was there. I was choking the life out of Mad Vlad and Ski was trying to stop me. He was unable to break my grip and unwilling to strike me, so he whispered into my ear.

"It's not him Walter, it's his brother Nickolas."

This semi-worked and I released my chokehold on the apparently dead boy. My killing colors began to recede and I went to Claire while Ski attempted to revive teenage killer. Claire was crying, but the terror was disappearing from her eyes. I had to take my dear ex-wife into my arms even before I released her. I removed the gag and kissed her.

"Did he hurt you baby?"

"I'll never be able to thank you enough. That bastard found great joy in telling me what he was going to do to me. I guess it's a lucky thing, but at the time, if I could have willed myself to death, I would have."

I cut her loose and she covered her lovely body with a blanket. I sat on the bed hugging her as Ski continued to resuscitate the demon. Neither Claire nor I was rooting for the boy, but after a few minutes he coughed. I had already decided that Nickolas wasn't going to survive the day, but I hadn't told Ski yet. Maybe some good will come from his briefly extended life. Maybe I can get him to give up his brother. In my experience, bullies and psychos are cowards and are incapable of withstanding the evil that they dish out. Claire left the room to dress.

"Good job Ski. Little Nikki tried to check out before paying his bill." Nikki still didn't look so good. When I said, "Strip him down Ski and tie him to the bed," Ski glared at me like I was insane.

"Walter, you know I can't do that.

"Okay, I think I can handle this puny squirt."

I grasped the boys' hand and threw him on the bed where I pulled off his expensive Italian shoes. He tried to kick me, so I removed his socks and broke one of his toes. I was unmoved by his squeal of pain. I pulled off his baggy pants and his drawers. He slipped away to the far side of the bed. Claire walked in looking cool and cute in tight leggings under an oversized pale blue cable knit sweater.

"Look honey, little Mr. Rape, Torture and Murder thinks he can get away from us." I pulled my gun and handed it to Claire. "Take this sweetheart and convince this young man to follow orders."

Claire hated guns and had never in her life even handled one, but she eagerly took it from me. I didn't know what would happen, but I turned my back on them and faced Ski.

"Maybe you should make yourself scarce for a while."

"Listen Walter, if you kill that boy you'll never forgive yourself."

"What's one more, dark dream to me? I live with dozens of ghosts every day. Little Nikki won't even make the top ten on my hit parade."

"Okay pal, I'll make breakfast." Ski wasn't happy.

Back in the bedroom, Claire had the boy naked and tied to the bed. It looked as if she had strapped him even tighter than he had tied her. Her anger had not yet run its course.

"Claire, write me a list of the things he said he'd do to you." She reluctantly returned my gun and went to find pen and paper. "The only way you live through the day is if you rat out Vladimir."

"Fuck your ass you American shit eater."

"If you survive round one, I'm gonna wash your potty-mouth out with soap."

The killer was scared. Claire returned with her list and a first aid kit, with which she disinfected and wrapped my hand. I asked her to rescue breakfast from Ski.

"Walter, I want to watch."

"I know honey, but when your hatred wears off, please believe me, you'll wish you hadn't." She relented.

"Okay Walter, I trust you more than ever. I'll never disregard you're warnings again."

Claire kissed me and left, with a vengeful glare at Nickolas Brockov. I looked him in the eye, trying to gauge his level of fear. He was scared, but I could tell that he didn't believe that I had it in me to stoop to his level. He would soon see what I was capable of. I was reading Claire's list. It was disturbingly detailed and descriptive.

"Nikki, Nikki, Nikki, were you really going to do all these horrible things?" The boy was mute, so I examined the toe I had broken earlier. I pulled it and he squealed. "Lesson one, when I ask you a question boy, answer me. Now tell me," I went to the disgusting last item on the nice, beautiful woman's list. "Were you really going to amputate her pussy and take it home, so you could fuck her for a week?"

"No sir, I was just trying to scare her." The boy was wising up.

"Son, I really don't like blood too much, so I'm going to stick with the less messy items."

I took his brown Leather satchel and dropped the twenty pound bag on his un-muscled gut. I grinned at the involuntary whoosh escaping his now quivering mouth. In the bag, were four different knives, a motorcycle battery and a wicked looking whip. There were also several empty plastic containers, which led me to believe that he was indeed going to save his depraved samples for sick trophies.

I picked up the smallest container and the largest knife. I held the container next to the boy's shrunken genitals.

"This will do nicely, plenty of room. Tell me, Little Nikki, where is Vladimir?

"I don't know. I haven't seen him for weeks." Again, I tweaked his toe.

"I have photos of you meeting with him in a park, from three days ago." I started to reach for his sore toe again.

"Wait, please, that same day he flew out of the country." There were tears in the kid's eyes.

"Where did he go?"

"I can't tell you. He'll kill me." Nicholas was believable.

"You'll be no less dead if I kill you."

"If I die either way, I'd rather die protecting my brother." He showed a hint of pride.

"Loyalty, I respect that." I jammed the rubber ball into his mouth and strapped it on tightly. "Even if you change your mind, I'm going to complete number one on the list. Afterward, I'll give you another chance." I studied item one, reading aloud. "He said he was going to punch my big tits until they are black and blue, then he would hook my nipples up to his battery." I glare at the frightened boy. "What kind of sicko would want to hurt those beautiful breasts?"

I climbed onto the bed and straddled his hips. Boxing practice began. I threw one two combination punches to the panicking boys chest, holding back just enough to prevent broken ribs and dislocated knuckles. Some thirty punches later, I climbed off of him. His whole chest was bruised.

I removed the motorcycle battery and the two wires which were tipped with copper alligator clips. I clipped them onto his flaccid nipples. Nikki screamed, but it was barely audible.

"If you think that hurts, just wait until I light 'em up?" I pretended glee.

The terrified boy was struggling and shaking his head back and forth vigorously as I connected the first wire. I held the second wire poised an inch away from the terminal and looked the boy in the eye.

"I suppose you're ready to talk." He overwhelmingly indicated that he was. "Well, round one is almost over, so soon you'll have another chance to do the right thing."

I touched the wire to the battery. Little Nikki screamed and arched his back in a horrifying display of inhuman pain. I pulled the wire for a second, but as soon as his body relaxed I hit him again. I put the battery back in the bag and disconnected the clips from his slightly charred nipples. Nikki was crying a steady stream of tears and when I removed the gag, he added bawling to his feelings of pain and despair.

"Have you had enough or do I have to go to round two?"

"No, No please stop. I'll tell you anything." He was shivering in his fear.

"Where is your brother?"

"He flew to the US to kill your wife." His teary face showed shame.

"When will he attack?"

"I don't know. I texted him when Mrs. Big Tit's boyfriend left."

# A Letter From
# Mad Vlad

I ran to the kitchen where Claire had taken over breakfast.

"Ski, Vladimir is going after Layla. Get the cops to the house quickly then call Rebecca." He made the call.

"The cops are on the way." When he made the next call, he said, "She's not answering. Neither is the gate."

"I'm taking the jet. You stay and keep calling. Try to clean up this mess. You can blame me if you have to."

"Walter, is the boy dead?"

"No, of course not Ski, I never was going to kill him," I lied, "I only wanted him to believe that I was." I took the rental car keys, kissed Claire and left with a profound foreboding brewing in my mind.

I was in the air within the hour. I had bypassed customs, so if we were landing in New York as planned, I would be arrested. A fifty thousand dollar bribe goes a long way even with a well-paid private pilot, so we were flying directly to Dayton where I had some pull. He said that even with the headwind, he could cut an hour off the normal flight time. Still, it would be about six hours. None of my calls home got through, so I stewed and fretted for the safety of my wife and family. I was able to talk to Ski and Claire. Remy was there now and I could hear him ranting in the background.

"Claire put Henri on."

He grabbed the phone and started yelling in French while I waited for him to calm down. I didn't try to mollify the angry Gendarme.

"Listen Remy, you brought this on yourself. You said you would provide a security detail, but you lied. I had to do your job of protecting Claire now you must do what is necessary to make sure that punk pays." I hung up on him.

It was four in the morning when I landed in Ohio and half an hour later, I was home. As expected, the roadway and grounds were swarming with cops. The ones at the gate wouldn't look me in the eye as they waved me through. One immediately called someone on his radio. I was trying to steel myself for the expected tragic news. The County Sheriff, my friend Dale Gleason, was waiting for me on the front porch, grimly unprepared for this most wretched part of his sworn duty.

"Tell me Dale and don't leave anything out."

Walt, she's dead. Some vicious monster has killed your beautiful wife."

"Was anybody else hurt?"

"No, the beast sneaked in through the dress shop and laid in wait in the master bedroom. He ambushed Layla as she left her shower."

"I want to see her."

"Please Walt, don't ask me to show you. You'll be better off without that picture in your memory."

"I must see."

"The bastard left a note for you."

The Sheriff opened a manila folder containing a clear plastic evidence envelope which held a piece of Layla's personal stationary marred by a clumsily handwritten message. It was stained with blood.

Dear Popi

In Russia, I promised our little one that I wouldn't harm a single freckle on her exquisite face and I have kept that Promise. I was disappointed that you weren't here to watch the beautiful festivities, but we managed without you. You probably haven't heard yet so it is my regrettable duty to inform you of your other wife's similar fate in Paris this morning.

I have glimpsed the many adorable girls in your fine house. If you keep coming after me, I'll soon be back to perform my acts of love on your harem. I can't wait. I'll see you soon. One more thing, our little freckled one called for you over and over, "Popi, Popi."

With love and respect always, Vladimir Brockov

"If it was your wife or daughter, you would have to see. Don't deny me or I'll feel like I abandoned her when she needed me." This got a surprisingly tender response from the tough cop.

"Okay Walt, but please forgive me for giving in and exposing you to this act of evil." The sheriff chased everyone out of the room and stood outside the door. "Don't touch anything and please don't lift the blanket."

I slowly entered the room I had always called my happiest place on Earth. The room was in disarray. Layla put up a fight and no one had heard. The other occupants of my castle would carry this horror forever. I walked to the bed. Layla was there, covered by one of those red blankets that cops keep in the trunks of their cars to cover bloody roadside victims.

My angels' face was uncovered and true to Vladimir's word, her face was unmarred. She was wearing her unique smile that she only wore on her trips to the sixth realm to visit her angelic boyfriend Michael. I was happy that she had gotten out of her body, hopefully before suffering too much of Vladimir's torture. My wife was unbelievably beautiful in death.

I kissed my true loves pale lips before lifting the blanket. Big Popi was unmoved, the spell was broken. Under that red veil, was a sight too gruesome to describe here, too sickening and despicable to inflict upon you, my dear readers. There was not a square inch of her perfect body unaffected by the monsters' knives. He may have taken trophies. I finally cried. I could no longer steel myself against the pain and loss. I was seriously in need of, at least, the touch of her spirit, but remained disappointed. I covered my little Breck. I was hoping that Cynwrig was a helpless passenger in my head. He being the only one I knew who would understand how I felt.

The Sheriff must have thought it odd that I hadn't completely broken down, knowing how much I love Layla. I was still able to function. The astute readers among you of course know why. I still had hope that I could save my Li'l Freckles using the magic of Donn the way Cynwrig saved his beloved Fiedlimid. I had been prepared to use it to save Claire, but we were able to rescue her with more conventional methods. I needed some alone time to plan, but when I went downstairs, I was mobbed by the women of the house. They were all in near hysterical grief.

I didn't need to say anything. I just had to hold them and cry with them. Their debilitating grief was breaking my already broken heart, but firming my resolve to get this right. I absolutely had to find a way to calmly plan my next moves. I was worried that the unknown intricacies of changing the natural timeline would have unwanted consequences.

I did something that I'm not proud of to gain separation from these dear people. I pretended to collapse. Robby was here now as was Susan. My son, who loved Layla as much as I, picked me up from the floor. He carried my limp body and laid me gently on the sofa, in the grand entryway of our mansion.

My plan didn't work. All of my loved ones refused to leave me alone. They maintained contact, sobbing and kissing my face, so I feigned recovery. Sheriff Gleason, Dale, observed all of this and came to my rescue.

"Walt, I need to get your statement while everything is fresh in your mind. Is there someplace where we can talk in private?"

"Okay Dale, let's go to my den."

I hugged everyone again and led Dale to my hidden room. I told him the incomplete truth about my trip to Paris and the rescue of Claire, not giving him the supernatural details. Dale Gleason was a simple man with very good instincts and a logical, deductive mind. I knew that he wouldn't be taken in by lies, so I stuck to the truth. I told him of my foreboding feelings, but not my dreams.

"Dale, I knew in my heart that Brockov would come after me. I thought that Layla would be safe in our home, but was very worried about Claire. Being half right is no consolation."

"Walt, I've got some more bad news. The Feds just sent me a warrant for your arrest for suspected smuggling. It seems that in your haste to get here, you broke several laws. I have to take you in."

Dale asked me to turn around. I could see how much it hurt him to place me in handcuffs. I knew that I couldn't let him take me away, at least not far enough that I couldn't find Layla in the time it takes to shear a sheep. The Sheriff led me out through the shocked throng of mourners. I didn't speak until Robby barred our way.

"What's going on dad?" Even in shock, he was worried about me.

"Don't worry son, I broke some laws to get here from France."

"What should I do?"

"With Layla gone, nothing matters. Just get through this the best you can and don't worry about me."

"Everyone is going to think you had something to do with this."

"Nothing matters son." The loss of Layla and now of his father, warped his handsome face into a disfiguring mask of grief.

The Sheriff led me to his Squad car and put me in the back seat.

"Walt, wait here for a few minutes while I give instructions to my men."

I was finally alone. When I say the magic words, what will happen? If it works, I believe that I'll go back three days and I'll be in this same spot three days ago, but what will the rest of the world do? Will they be transported to their three day old locations? It seems probable. What about Claire. She'll be in peril again. I had an idea that may save her, but I couldn't act on it in this time because nothing I do here will be remembered.

When Cynwrig said the words we traveled to the approximate same time of day. It was just a bit before six now on the tenth of January. At six on the seventh Layla and I would be in bed. I didn't believe that I would be next to her, but if I was, I knew that I must not touch me. There would be a violent electrical reaction like with Cynwrig's sword. My phone would be on my night stand, my wallet and watch too. I must steer clear of these. I was ready as I'd ever be. I had nothing to lose and everything to gain. I would have to depend on Ski to do the right things.

I saw Dale returning and willed myself into a state of calmness. I recited the magic incantation which I had been rehearsing in my head for a week. When Cynwrig said those words, it was difficult to detect any change, but when I said those same words I fell on my ass. The car was gone as were the handcuffs. I picked myself off the concrete and headed inside. I, of course, went straight to Layla. She was drowsily feeling around the bed, looking for her disappeared Popi, I presume.

"Popi, what's wrong? Can't you sleep?"

"There is no time to sleep Li'l Freckles. Throw on a robe we must wake Ski and Rebecca."

# POOF

My name is Kurt Staniskowski, my friends call me Ski. My gorgeous fiancée Rebecca and I were sound asleep at six in the morning on January 7th 2015. We were awakened by someone kicking our door in. I am never far from one of my many guns, so I was armed and prepared to kill the would-be intruder. When I flung open the door, Walter barged in. He had a wild look in his eyes, but this wasn't the strangest thing. He had Layla in his arms and appeared to be crushing the life out of her as she struggled to get away. I didn't know what to think.

Rebecca got out of bed naked and slowly put on her robe, not bothering to shield her nudity from our irrational friend. This bothers me a little because I think she would trade me for him, at the drop of a hammer. Fortunately, Walter has Layla who is to me the most beautiful and special woman on the planet. Yet, I love Rebecca so much that I wouldn't trade her for anyone, even Layla. Walter is about my age, but he looks way younger than his fifty-two years. I'm a few pounds heavier than him and I look like a thug, while he looks like a male model, so I can understand Rebecca's attraction, but that don't mean I have to like it.

With all that said, I love and respect Walter more than anybody in the world. He is my best friend and we have both risked our lives for each other and for Layla and Rebecca. Most of you have read the books, so you know the stories. Most of those stories are provable to be true, but they all contain elements of spooky stuff that I can't explain and can't really believe. Just because I can't explain something doesn't make it supernatural. Rebecca believes every word. Her Popi can do no wrong or tell no lie.

Getting back to the story at hand, Walter burst through our door with Layla barely dressed and flashing her lovely breasts.

I said, "What the hell?"

He said, "No questions, just listen."

Walter seemed to be in a terrific hurry. He told us in rapid fire fashion that Claire would be tortured and killed in the early hours of the tenth in Paris by a seventeen year old psycho named Nicholas Brockov. Then he said that little Nikki's big brother Vladimir was on his way here to kill Layla on the evening of the ninth at about the same time, accounting for the time difference. Layla was still struggling in Walter's crushing grip.

"How do you know, Popi?"

I was unkind to my dear friend. "Walter, you have lost your mind."

"You'll believe me in a minute." Rebecca, of course, believed every word. Walter gave some more details and said one final thing. "Make sure you go ahead with Paris and New York."

Without a sound or warning of any kind, Walter and Layla disappeared into thin air.

"Popi, Popi come back to us," was all Rebecca could say, like people vaporizing before her was an everyday occurrence.

I hadn't much to add to that and Walter was right. It was a minute later and I did believe him. The Houdini act added a lot of weight to his predictions, so I decided then and there to take them as gospel.

I wasn't about to go to Europe with a madman coming and Layla in danger even though she wasn't here to kill. I called the man who I trust as much as I trust Walter, my old partner David Rose. Rosy was the Chief of D's in Tampa and was the smartest detective I knew. He is also Walter and Claire's future son in law.

"Ski, I'm on the first plane to Paris. Tell me everything you know, even the spooky stuff." I told him everything and it was all spooky stuff to me. "Ski, one more thing, I'm doing this my way."

"As Walter would say, I wouldn't have it any other way."

It was in Rosy's hands now. By my way, he meant that the dirt-bag didn't have to die to have a positive outcome. He was referring to Walter not me. Walter is as nice a guy as you'll ever meet and it takes a lot to anger him. Once angered, he can become a killer, a mad, crazy, unstoppable killer. That being said, he always seems to be right. There is an army of people, not silly fans, who would do or give anything for the man and I'm one of them. He's my best friend. I will deal with the threat on Layla my way. What I'm gonna do for and give to Walter Lemon is that I'm gonna trap and kill Vladimir fuckin' Brockov.

To accomplish this, I was gonna need someone to help with the computer. Becca would be fully employed helping Layla's Petites get ready for Paris which was less than two weeks away. My only choices were Chrissy and Mary. They are both still in high school and both pretty smart. I chose to ask Mary because she was more serious while Chrissy was more of a social mover and shaker. She was fully savoring her senior year. Plus she has an hour commute to school while Mary's was a five minute drive. Never have I used such criteria for hiring an operative.

The whole household would be up soon. It would be difficult to explain what has happened. The ones who live here were somewhat inured to these minor miracles surrounding Walter and Layla, but the employees, the designers and seamstresses were about to experience it for themselves, for the first time. I decided to make Claire's pancakes for everybody. I had her recipe and I'm a pretty good cook. Walter told me just the other day that my breakfast really stuck to his ribs. That's a good thing, right?

My hotcakes didn't go over too good and neither did my story about Layla and Walter's absence. The women were in an uproar and I was caught up in their passionate disbelief. Rebecca rescued me by corroborating my unbelievable story and by adding the last thing that their Popi said before going poof.

"Make sure that you go on with Paris and New York."

It seems that I had left out the most important part. The girls were still worried, but they used those last words as a rallying cry and went to work on making it so. Tragedy averted, I caught Mary before she left for school.

"Mary I need your help to catch the man who is after Layla."

The cute kid wiped the tears from her pretty eyes. "I'll do anything to help. What do you need?"

"I need you to do research on the computer for me. I'll have a better idea after you get home from school."

"Okay Kurt, I'll see you at three." She kissed my cheek "You've got to save them."

"We will sweetheart."

I've never really wanted kids, but in that moment I finally saw what they were all about, an unbreakable bond of love.

My next task was to recruit my undercover agent. There was only one candidate for this job, Kelly. She was the only one who could convincingly pull off Layla. She was nearly her spitting image. I called her cell and asked her to come to my office when she had a few minutes. She agreed and was here in two minutes.

"Honey, I want you to be Layla for the next three days. That psycho may be watching us by now and I want him to think that all is normal with Layla."

"What should I do?"

"Wear her clothes, take off your make-up and sleep in her room."

# KELLY UNDERCOVER

When Kurt asked me to help trap the killer who was after Layla, I didn't hesitate. Popi, Kurt and Layla are, to me, among the greatest people in the world. Popi and Kurt saved my life on the plane trip to the Philippines. Kurt killed the gunman who held a gun to my head and Popi of course saved us all by impossibly landing that huge Jet in the ocean. So like I say, I would do anything for them. Layla has never saved my life, but she has given me my dream job.

I've walked the runways of Paris, Milan, New York and many other exotic places. I was a short smalltime model with a blasé career until Popi picked me and Layla hired me. As an added benefit, because we look so much alike, she designs her favorite dresses with me in mind. Of course that is why Kurt asked me to help. Layla and I have the exact same measurements, blue eyes and light blonde hair. It allows me to think of myself as very beautiful because I can see how incredibly beautiful she is.

I've worn makeup since I was a skinny twelve year old, but Layla never wears anything except mascara. Her eyelashes, like mine, are white and don't show up on film. Not wearing makeup was frightening for me. I have nice skin, but still, I feel naked without it. I told everyone at work what I would be doing and they were worried that I would be in danger. Ted, who is a dear older man, took me aside.

"Kelly, are you sure you want to put yourself at risk? I don't think Layla would approve."

"I'm a little worried about it, but I know in my heart that Layla would do it for me. You're right, she wouldn't approve. She wouldn't ask me to do something that she would not hesitate to do for any of us. I'm scared, but I want to repay, in some small measure, the bravery they have shown on my behalf." Ted hugged me.

"I'm very proud of you Layla."

I went to Layla's room and showered, removing all of my make-up, remembering not to blow dry my hair. Layla often came to work with damp hair because she thought that blow drying damaged her gorgeous slow growing, shiny pale blond hair. I wanted to shave my legs, but oddly, Layla didn't have a razor. I shuffled through her underwear drawer. She had such a big selection of pretty undies, but hardly any bras. Neither of us really needed the support, but I was uncomfortable without one. I mean, what if there was a chilly draft. I would be mortified to catch someone looking at my stiff nipples. I decided to take one for the team and go commando.

Even before I went through Layla's closet, I thought about her style. She could be extremely glamourous for going out in public, but for work she kept it simple, feminine and very cute. I picked a short blue mini dress over black leggings. I saw her huge and beautiful emerald engagement ring on her dressing table and put it on. I briefly fantasized about Popi putting that ring on my finger. The simple platinum wedding band was still on Layla's finger. She never took it off. I finished my costume with a light coat of her mascara. But for my lack of freckles, I was Layla.

I sat at Layla's desk and pretended to do what she does. I can barely draw a bath, but I worked with her sketch pad. Kurt told me not to betray the ruse because we may be observed or monitored at any and all times. It felt strange, but everyone played the game, knowing the seriousness of the situation. I took Layla's mid-day break to visit

Gabrielle's five-year-old son, Michael. When I entered his room the cute boy ran to me.

"Lala, Lala," he pulled up short, "You're not Lala, you're Kelly."

I whispered into the child's ear, "I know sweetie. Layla couldn't come today so she asked me to play with you."

He accepted this and we had a good time playing.

That night, I walked around the bedroom preparing for bed. I really didn't know what Layla slept in, so I looked through her hamper. The best I could figure, she slept naked. It felt wicked, but I have to say that I enjoyed it. I had steamy dreams of Popi being fooled and making fantastic love to me thinking I was his wife. It's certainly not unusual fantasizing about making love to Popi, but the extra element of him believing I was Layla, had me squirming with desire.

The next day, I followed Layla's routine as closely as I could but, as I told Kurt, I'm no runner so running five miles is out of the question.

"That's okay squirt. You'd be too exposed anyway."

While I seldom run, I do exercise extensively every day. We all do because the food around here is so good that it is necessary to burn off a lot of calories to fit into the tightly tailored clothes. I loved to swim laps in the pool and couldn't wait to wear Layla's iconic tan bikini. I did and got many curious looks from my employees.

# READY

Kelly was doing a great job and everyone in the house was aiding the charade. I saw her from twenty feet away and was shocked at how convincingly she had adopted Layla's looks, mannerisms and even her voice. I spent the morning planning. Desk work is not for me. I wanted a target but he was still two days away. I tried to run a system scan on the security system. I was in over my head, but no worries, Mary came to my rescue. She took over and found that there had been a breach starting at eight this morning.

"Should I kick him out?" I thought about it for a solid minute.

"No honey, let's let him believe we are at his mercy."

I was happy to hear that Mad Vlad didn't have eyes and ears on us yesterday. We were more prepared now. Still, it's hard to not be creeped out at the thought of that monster spying on all these young girls. Most of our cameras are outside. Inside, we had coverage only in the kitchen, the pool and the front entryway. Mary and I agreed not to tell anyone that they were definitely being watched lest they become self-conscious and blow our plan. In deference to the civilians, I did make a small change and had an armed security guard protecting Layla's Petites personnel to and from their cars.

I didn't have much else to do but wait. The eighth and ninth crawled by. I knew it was the calm before the storm. Rosy will be calling this evening with his report on the events in Paris. I was worried. Walter didn't say when Vladimir would break in, but he did say that he would come in through the design studio. This meant it would be after six when most of the people went home. This time of year Layla often stayed another hour and had a late dinner. The timeline was defining itself and the window for the punks' entry has shrunk to between seven and nine. The call came at seven forty-five. I was in the bathroom, ready.

# VACATION INTERRUPTED

Henri and I were having a wonderful time. He is such a dear man and we had each professed our love for the other. At noon on the ninth I got a terrific surprise in the form of a ring at the door. I answered in my rudimentary French through the intercom.

"Bonjour Mama, it's me, Rose."

I rang her in and greeted her on the landing with a big hug.

"It's so good to see you. You look so beautiful. Why are you in Paris? You're glowing, are you pregnant?"

Rose answered the string of excited questions sounding just like her father.

"It's good to see you too. You also look lovely. David has business here and I made him bring me. Yes, I'm six weeks pregnant."

I squealed and wrapped my tall daughter in my arms. I was thrilled and so would Walter be.

"Does your father know?"

"No he doesn't and I want to keep it secret for a few more weeks."

Then my brilliant daughter did a silly thing. She reached into her purse and pulled out a thin stack of index cards while keeping up her small talk. She held up the first one. It read, don't let on. We are being watched and bugged. Keep talking and read.

I said, "Henri will be back soon," while I read, Nicholas Brockov is coming for you tonight. Invite us out to dinner tonight so we can plan.

"Rose, can Henri and I take you guys to dinner tonight?"

The last card read, don't discuss this with Henri until we're at the restaurant.

"That sounds great mom. I've gotta go to meet David. Call me later and we'll meet at the restaurant. I love you mom. Don't tell anyone except Henri about the baby." We hugged again and Rose left me alone with my worries.

I kept my word to Rose and did not discuss the situation with Henri. I didn't really believe that we were bugged or that we were under any kind of surveillance for that matter. Still, I hadn't heard from Walter. He was very worried about me, over the top worried. I had never discussed with Henri what I call Walter's fractured fairy tales, the unexplainable things he accomplishes. Henri is a very pragmatic man, so I didn't think he would appreciate the unknowable.

Henri picked the restaurant, his favorite. David and Rose were already there and we were promptly seated. Henri ordered two bottles of wine as I hugged David. Henri kissed Rose on each cheek and firmly shook the detective's hand.

"David, what brings you and your enchanting wife to my beautiful city?"

"It's not good. We've uncovered a threat on Claire."

I looked around and saw that Rose was watching me as if she were poised to catch me if I fell. The story that David told, though frightening, was based on not a single fact. I detected the signature of Walter.

"David, how could you fall for Walter's paranoid dreams and predictions?"

He solemnly said, "Claire, keep listening, you'll believe in a minute."

I was right that all the information came from Walter, but the twist shocked me. After giving all the details he had, Walter, with

Layla struggling in his arms, disappeared before Kurt and Rebecca's eyes. As big a skeptic as I am, it sounded just like another fractured fairy tale. Henri, not being inured to these Walter tales was trying hard not to scoff.

"When will this happen?"

Rose answered. "At 1:00 in the morning on the tenth when you leave for work." I had them now.

"Henri isn't going to work tomorrow." I looked at Henri. Something was wrong.

"I didn't yet tell you Clarissa, I must go to work for a few hours tonight to greet some Moroccan VIP."

Rose, David and I couldn't persuade Henri Remy to believe, so I guided them to a win/win solution. This is what I've been doing professionally for nearly twenty-five years, but really for my whole life. I was always the peacemaker and the deal maker.

"Henri dear, they don't expect you to believe. They just want you, in an act of loving over-caution, to give them the backdoor key, so they can sneak in and protect me from Walter's fantastic delusions."

"Put like that, a petite bit of excess in the name of love is always acceptable."

We all lightened up and managed to have a very nice reunion. We were all still worried about the health, welfare and whereabouts of Walter and Layla. We left and went our separate ways, separated by only ten blocks since they were staying at a third class hotel nearby. Henri and I were a bit tipsy when we went to bed, having opened another bottle of wine upon arriving home. We talked about the investigation, mostly his respect for David Rose. This suggested that he had checked him out. Anyway, we were entirely in the mood and my considerate and charming lover left me smiling into my sleep which was not spoiled by my steamy dreams of Walter.

Henri got up at midnight and began preparing for his late night assignment. He never used an alarm clock and was never late for anything, especially work. I got up and made coffee and set out Henri's favorite pastry. No, it wasn't from some fancy French bakery. It was called a Hostess Snowball and was a cream filled cake covered with marshmallow and coconut. It came in three varieties white, chocolate and Pink. Henri only ate the pink. I've never mentioned all of Henri's quirks before. I hope he won't be angry. It's not that I'm embarrassed, but Walter is always looking for ammo against Henri. It was because of jealousy, but because he felt that Henri failed to adequately protect Layla on our first trip to Paris.

We spent a few minutes planning our beautiful life together. He was retiring in two years and we planned to marry and retire to the country, where his family had a large estate with ancient vineyards. With his small fortune and retirement income and my large BP&LF Inc. money plus the six million dollar divorce settlement from Walter, we should have a carefree life. At one, with a big kiss, Henri left for work.

Just minutes after Henri left, there was a knock at the door. I hadn't seen David or Rose but, on faith, I knew that they were here.

"Who is it?"

"Delivery for Mrs. Big Tits Lemon," he said in a choirboy voice.

I rang Rose's phone and got only static. I picked up the house phone and got no dial tone. I believed now. The intruder began drilling the door lock, taking less than a minute to breach the sturdy wooden front door. He kicked it open and stepped in with a huge grin on his cute face, my God, he was just a boy.

"I'm here to make love to you, Mrs. Big Tits."

The boy dropped his drill, but not his brown leather bag. He chased me into my room. David was standing there with his gun drawn. He directed me to move behind him. When the boy turned the corner, his gleeful expression turned into an angry mask of hate and fear. He threw his heavy bag at David while drawing a large knife. David allowed him only one step toward us before he shot him twice in his skinny chest.

I was gripping David's arm tightly as he went to check on the boy. As he tried to kick the knife away from the kids' hand, the boy came alive. He spun on his hands and kicked David's and my legs out from under us. We went down hard, landing on our butts. David didn't relinquish his gun. The boy rose up and leapt toward the fallen detective with the butcher knife raised. David calmly put three rounds into the boy's head, his cute face.

In death, the young man seemed so small and harmless. I couldn't help but wonder what this normal looking handsome child must have gone through in his short life to turn him into this heartless evil killer. David didn't bother checking him for signs of life. This monster was dead.

I asked, "Where is Rose?" His smile was a bit crooked.

"Oh Claire, you don't think I would bring your daughter and grandchild to a shootout, do you?"

David found the small device that was interfering with the cell phones in Nickolas' pocket. I called Henri and he called Rose.

"Henri's on the way. He said don't touch anything." David laughed.

"Rose is on her way up. I have to call Ski."

"I wonder what he has in the bag." He kissed my cheek tenderly.

"You better look quickly or you may never know."

I did look and to this day, when I think about the contents of that brown leather bag, I get shivers of fear. I overheard his side of the call to Kurt.

"It's done, the boy is dead good luck on your end."

He exposed the boy's ballistic vest, took a picture of the dead boy with his phone and sent it to Kurt.

Rose came in through the broken front door and we hugged and cried. A few minutes later Henri arrived. He first hugged and kissed me then showed his appreciation to Rose and David.

"I will never forget what you have done for me, saving my beautiful Clarissa. Walter called me before Claire even arrived and warned me that she was in danger. I jealously thought he was trying to sabotage our relationship. I'm so sorry."

I said, "Henri, Walter is incapable of jealousy and he never lies about important things."

"He told me to protect you like an irreplaceable work of art that is you. I'm so sorry I didn't do that. Will you forgive me?"

I, of course did.

The crime scene people came and ran us out of the apartment, after relieving David of his gun. To Henri's dismay, I flew home that evening. He was cutely worried that I hadn't forgiven him.

"No Henri, I do forgive you, but my children's father is missing and I need to be there. I'll be back soon because Walter said that it was important that we go on with Layla's Petites' Paris shows." He accepted this.

"I promise you my Cherie, I'll never be jealous of Walter again even when you cry out his name in your sleep."

I was embarrassed, but not surprised, I dream about Walter a lot. I flew home with Rose because David offered to stay behind to help Henri with his investigation.

# BEING LAYLA

I woke up early on the ninth in full erotic orgasm. This had never happened before. I was screaming Popi's name. I lay there shaking, mortified that a dream, even about the sexy man, could give me such fantastically wicked pleasure. I soon got over my embarrassment and simply enjoyed the afterglow. I think this was the last missing part of my evolution into becoming Layla.

I got up and donned another of her iconic bikinis. This one was the tiny and sexy tiger striped suit that Layla used to lure in her tiger. I admired myself in the mirror. I was Layla. I went swimming before breakfast and caught Robby and Stump lustfully staring at me. Robby's girlfriend was staring too, not with lust, but deep green jealousy.

This was the big day. If Popi was right, some Russian madman would attempt to kill me tonight, believing I was Layla. Although I was enjoying my role, I would be glad when this was over. Even when the assassination failed, it wouldn't be over until Popi and Layla were back. None of us knew when that would be or even if it would ever be. This uncertainty made us all sad yet we would do as his last words implored. We would carry on with Paris and New York. After that, I don't think that I can continue with my happy positive attitude and my dream career as one of Layla's Angels.

I went on with my day, not only as Layla, but also a fashion model. Ted had finished Layla's latest creation, a gorgeous evening gown in gray satin. It clung to me like Popi did in my dreams last night. When I put it on everyone applauded. Though I felt very beautiful in that dress, I think they were really clapping for Layla and possibly for the end of an era. This wonderful dress may be Layla's last.

Before lunch, I met with Kurt and his new assistant, Mary. Mary had swept the Security office for bugs, lord knows how the cute sixteen year old learned how to do that. Anyway, Kurt declared it to be a safe zone and we were able to openly plan tonight's trap. I was the bait. It was a dangerous and inglorious role to be sure, but I was proud to play any part in the righteous plan. Whether or not Layla and Popi could be saved, that monster had to be stopped and I would suffer any peril to make that happen. I know, that sounds like mighty tough talk for the bait.

Mary told me that in the middle of the night the phone lines had been cut and a foreign signal was jamming all cell phone communications. This was stage three of the attack, first the surveillance, next the plot to murder Claire and now our isolation in preparation for the killer's entry to our formerly safe haven. Stage four would begin tonight. Unbeknownst to the psycho, we were ready for him.

After six, I, one at a time, began my goodnight wishes to my employees. Each one gave me a touch and a look that said, be careful and good luck. I kept my eye on the door to the outside stairs because Popi believed that this is how Vladimir would enter. At seven, I went down stairs and had a late dinner. Several of the early diners stayed on to keep me company. Robby and Stump were still fascinated by my Layla act. I think I was witnessing the beginnings of an uncomfortable double infatuation. I couldn't think about that now, although I thought they were both really cute.

I was supposed to do kitchen duty tonight. By I, I mean I Kelly. I felt guilty, so I went to the kitchen. I was falling out of character. Layla always went about chores as if they were some sort of blessing.

All smiles and comfortable chit chat. If she was alone she'd sing. Her soft voice was so sweet that it could make a hidden eavesdropper cry. Kelly, on the other hand, grumpily did the barest minimum to earn her citizenship in Popi's family. Chrissy was there finishing up, so I happily jumped back into Layla.

"Hi Chrissy, didn't you do KP yesterday?" She wrapped me in her long arms and hugged me. My face was uncomfortably smushed against her world class breasts.

She said, "It was Kelly's turn, but she's been crazy busy and must have forgotten, so I decided to cut her a break."

"That's so sweet Honey." We hugged again. "You're the best."

The second hug wasn't so uncomfortable, so I wasn't weirded out when number three spontaneously erupted.

"I love you Layla."

She nuzzled her lips in my hair as I accepted the comfort from Layla's dearest female friend. I didn't feel like a fraud. Just like with Stump and Robby, I was providing them all with a small bit of solace.

We parted. Kelly I was feeling much closer to Chrissy and Layla I was ready for my evening shower. I had been successfully hiding my nerves so far. At the top of the wide marble staircase, I ran into Mary who was dressed to swim.

"Hi Mom, wanna swim?"

"No thank you sweetheart. I'm ready for a shower and a good book." We hugged.

"I love you Mama."

"I love you too Mary." I was beginning to realize that there weren't enough hugs in my life, Kelly's life.

I glanced at my phone to check the time, forgetting that the damn thing wasn't working. It must be at least 8:15. At my door I took a deep breath. I shouldn't see anything odd and I shouldn't look for anything odd. I walked in softly singing that song that had made me cry. I resisted doing Kelly's bath ritual of gathering my clothes before entering the bath room. I have it on good authority that Layla always leaves the bathroom in two towels, one in a turban around her damp hair.

I walked directly into the bathroom, praying that Kurt would be there. He was and I breathed. The training kicked in and I started my new job as the sound effects coordinator. I turned on the water and brushed my teeth. I recommenced my singing, this time an upbeat Beyoncé. As I was singing about putting a ring on it, I noticed the large expensive emerald on my ring finger. I took it off and put it back where I had found it two days ago. I hadn't removed it in all that time and taking it off now made me a little sad.

I flushed the toilet and turned on the shower. I eventually turned the shower off and fiddled around for a minute. Kurt gave me a gun and steered me into the shower, but I peeked. He walked to the door and whipped it open.

Vladimir Brockov was standing there with a quickly retreating smile on his handsome face. He had something strange in his hands, a short length of rope with two wooden handles. I think he wanted to strangle me. Kurt didn't hesitate. He punched the Russian on the chin, knocking him down.

"Flinch, go ahead and flinch. I will shoot you dead pal."

I walked around Kurt to get a better look at the cautiously still man. He looked at my face and angrily shouted.

"You are not my little freckled one." He tried to kick Kurt's gun.

Kurt didn't move, not a muscle except the one for his trigger finger. The three gun shots were louder than anything I'd ever heard. Kurt already knew about Nickolas' bullet stopping vest, so he avoided the monsters chest. The first round pierced the Russians' throat. The others cut a path through Vladimir's left eye and the left side of his skull which separated from the rest of his head. I hugged the detective and he hugged me back. This hugging thing is something that I, Kelly I, could get used to.

Mary came in. I was expecting another hug, but I was disappointed. Mary searched the dead man's pockets and retrieved a small electronic device. She turned it off and Kurt made a call,

"Hey Dale, we caught some dirt bag breaking in." He paused for a few seconds. "Well, the thing is, he got all the way to Layla's room and he made me put him down. Okay, we'll be here."

Outside the room, everyone was there and I got a mega dose of my new addiction. They all called me Kelly, except Robby and Stump. I was Kelly now and yes, I'm proud of myself. It made me think, one can only feel the way I felt now by taking that risk to do great things and succeeding. Kurt topped off my tank of pride.

"Nice job squirt." We were face to face with his big hands on my shoulders.

"Thank you Kurt."

"Do me a big favor kid, call me Ski." He pulled me into a tight hug.

I felt like the Lemon family Citizen of the Year.

# CLAIRE TAKES CARE OF BUSINESS

From the plane, I called the house and Kurt answered. The news was good. Both of the Brockov brothers were dead. I'm not one to celebrate death, but I was glad that Vladimir wasn't captured. I, without any facts, blame him for turning his cute young brother into a sadistic, merciless killer.

The police were gone by the time we got home and so were the happy celebrating people I heard on the phone last night. In the end, they realized that Layla and their Popi were still gone and no one knew if they would ever return. All the Layla's Petites people were very businesslike. It was the tenth of January, a Saturday, and just a week before we flew to Paris. I jumped right in and kept everyone on track. Simone needed the most help. This would be her first show of any kind and it would happen in the high pressure atmosphere of the fashion capitol of the world.

Triple D called my cell and I told him about Walter and Layla's disappearance. That's not accurate. I told him that they had left to parts unknown, not that they had literally disappeared. He was upset, but not pessimistic.

"Walter has scared me so many times that now I just assume that he'll make a miraculous comeback. The new dolls hit the stores this morning. They are selling like your famous hotcakes."

"That's wonderful. I'm going to borrow your attitude about Walter. He can be guaranteed to do one thing, protect Layla."

I had the dear young man send a doll set for each member of the household and Layla's Petites staff. They may cheer us up.

The news that Walter and Layla were missing got out through the county coroner's office. They held a public inquest into the death of Vladimir Brockov. The news people hounded us. We didn't have any briefings to prep our people for spin control. I just trusted that none of us would spill any spooky stories. We only had to put up with the chaos for a few days before we had to put up with the chaos of Paris. Ted came along for the first time to be the creative director, normally Layla's job. Things went well. The clothes were magnificent and the Angels were radiantly, adorably beautiful. Still, the crowds were worried and disappointed at the absence of Big Popi and Li'l Freckles.

Kurt was a nervous wreck. He was so worried about all of us. Without Walter to be the yin to his yang, he put all of the pressure on his very broad shoulders. We all instinctively knew not to take any risks, so that Kurt wouldn't have a breakdown. The post Paris sales were very good. Ted decided on his own to mass produce the tiger patterned bikini that Layla had whipped up to catch her tiger. It sold for fifty dollars and all of our profits, $21.00 per unit, went to Tigers International. It was a master stroke. We sold six million of those tiny, sexy suits. The good will from that unselfish act was priceless.

A month later, we were all doing the same things in New York. Kelly, Kurt and I took time to go on the talk show circuit. We carefully rehearsed what we should and shouldn't say. We told the story of Popi warning us about the Brockov's before he left and the exciting tales of their deaths. Kelly was also tasked with modeling that tiger bikini and was met with tremendous applause. She was certainly beautiful and I think everyone saw Layla in her. When we got back home, we all had a chance to breathe. The Angels all went to their own homes, having a month off. I wrote them each a substantial bonus check for all they had been through.

The days, weeks and months went by uneventfully, much of the joy we all took from one and other was missing from our lives, but we carried on. Eventually, it was fall again and Ted and I were considering whether or not to go ahead with Paris fashion week. If we were to cancel, it would literally mean the end of Layla's Petites. Sales generated from Paris and New York represented forty percent of our sales. These were contract sales, guaranteed money. The clothes were good, but we were missing the quirky, inspired creations from Layla.

We, in the end, decided to wait until after the high holy days to make a final decision. This is what we called the first three days of November, Layla's birthday, Walter and Layla's anniversary and Walter's birthday. Until then, we scrambled to prepare for another chaotic fashion season. On October twenty-first, The FBI, the State Police and the IRS raided our home, with several search warrants. They were looking for evidence that we had murdered Layla and Walter to steal their money and her business.

Stump was arrested for punching out a weasel of an IRS agent who all but accused him of murdering his beloved Layla. They were here for twenty-four hours. They interviewed us all separately and left us each with a subpoena. They took a lot of business records and all of Kurt's weapons. The only thing that worried me was Walter's lockbox which contained the letters from Layla's sex induced trips to another realm. Kurt was hot under the collar and immediately called Triple D. He went to town to buy new weapons.

The Design shop was sealed. We were not permitted to continue preparations for Paris. Some decisions just seem to make themselves. The next day about a hundred people showed up at our gates. They had dogs and earthmoving equipment along with new search warrants for the property. Then the press and public came in force. There were two camps of fans, one believing we were victims of a rabid government run amok and the other shouting for our heads on pikes for depriving them of their adored Big Popi & Li'l Freckles. I called Paula Reynolds and Simon Gertz.

They arrived the next day along with Triple D who had Legal paperwork of his own, an injunction and order to cease and desist from a federal judge forbidding law enforcement from further harassment of the extended Lemon family. Layla's Petites was open for business. This did little to ease the intrusion of the press and the fans. Paula talked to them outside of our gate. She told of our worries about Popi and Li'l Freckles and how hurt we were from the accusations against us. Simon used his pen. He wrote of our struggles, made worse by the publics and governments unfounded charges. Most of the fans were gone by the next day, but the press, of course, couldn't be shamed from a possibly huge story.

The high holy days passed and so did Thanksgiving. Kurt and Rebecca were still here as were Chrissy and Mary. I was moving to Paris to be with Henri in a few weeks. Stump had moved in with his girlfriend Sally who had just inherited the local feed store from her father.

Rose and David got married a few days before Christmas. The whole remaining family was there in Tampa for the large, cop filled ceremony. It was sad that Walter couldn't be there. In a poignant moment, the beautiful bride tearfully asked us all to toast Walter and Layla, the most spectacular man and woman in the Seven Realms. Many of us cried.

# January 7th Again

I was in my favorite place on earth, in bed wrapped in my Popi's strong arms. I was sleeping peacefully, but something changed. It was as if Popi had vanished and I fell, face first, to the mattress. I was slowly waking and trying to feel around in the dark for Popi. He walked into the room fully dressed.

"Popi, what's wrong? Can't you sleep?" He walked to the bed.

He was crying a little, but had a sweet smile on his handsome face. He scooped me into his big strong arms and crushed me to his rock hard chest.

"Popi, you're hurting me. Let me go." His adoring smile didn't match his actions.

"I can't let you go. We must hurry. I have to talk to Ski."

"Popi put me down." Instead, he picked up my short white terry robe from my dresser.

"Put this on."

He released my arms, but still kept a tight hold of me. I demanded that he let me go and tell me what was bothering him.

"There is no time for questions, so put on the robe or I take you to Ski naked."

I slipped my arms into the robe, but with his tight grip, I couldn't properly wrap it around me. At Kurt and Rebecca's door he began kicking it impatiently.

"Popi," I was getting angry, "Tell me this instant."

"I have to talk to Ski before we leave." I was shocked.

"Leave?"

Ski opened the door with a big gun in his hand. He started to speak, but Popi interrupted while barging in.

"No time for questions, just listen."

Ski may have been listening, but I was doing my best to escape that iron grip, giving Ski a free show as my robe failed to cover me. Popi said that Claire would be killed by Nickolas in the early morning hours of the tenth in Paris and that I would be tortured and killed by Vladimir on the evening of the ninth. I quit struggling.

"Popi, how do you know?"

Ski asked, "Walter have you lost your mind?" He didn't answer, but continued.

"He'll come in through the design shop and ambush her as she exits her bathroom."

Kurt reiterated, "Have you lost your fucking mind?"

Popi said, "You'll believe me in a minute."

Rebecca spoke for the first time as she slowly covered her perfect naked body.

"I believe you Popi."

I thought, of course you do, because she loved my Popi so completely that she thought he could do no wrong.

Popi said one more thing. "Make sure you go ahead with Paris and New York, no matter what."

He said this as if I wouldn't be there, but I wouldn't miss it for anything. Then the strangest thing possible happened and I began to believe Popi. Kurt and Rebeca disappeared into thin air. Popi released his painful grip, but he didn't put me down. Instead he began kissing me, first on the lips then the rest of my face. I felt for Big Popi and the spell was extremely unbroken. Even with all of my questions, I began kissing back. Popi laid me on the bed and kissed and caressed my whole body. I began undoing his pants. He stripped faster than I thought possible and continued his savage attack, much the same as Czar attacked Sabrina.

Popi picked me up again. Big Popi didn't lose a stride, and continued making wild love to me while standing. This was only the second time he had done this and I wondered why. The first time was when we had been separated for three months, but now, we had made love only a few hours ago, or so I thought. With Popi's large hands on my butt and my arms around his neck he bounced me up and down, sending me into a dizzily screaming fit. When I came to, I was in the sixth realm.

# GROWLER #12

Dear Popi

I knew I was on six, but as usual I needed a moment to gather myself, if you know what I mean Popi. Before that moment had passed, Michael picked me up and kissed me. When that extended kiss broke, he began a steady stream of sloppy little kisses all over my face. It felt different than when you, a few minutes ago, did the exact same thing.

"Michael stop, what's gotten into you?"

"Layla, where have you been?" He kissed me some more.

"What do you mean? I've been in Ohio since I saw you in September."

"Oh no honey, I last saw you here in September 2014."

"Yes Michael, a little over three months ago."

I realized that for the first time in six, I was not completely naked. My robe was hanging loosely and uselessly on my shoulders.

"The last time I looked in on you, which I do many times a day, was five in the morning on January seventh 2015." I was wondering why he was being so dense.

"That's today, only an hour or so ago. Thank you Michael for looking in on me."

"My pleasure dear one, todays' date is December 25th 2015."

"Michael that's impossible, that would mean that I've lost almost a year. How can that be?"

"I was really hoping that you could tell me."

It seems that you, Popi, for some unknown reason on January 7th 2015, took me fifty weeks into the future. We had the where, when and who, but not the how, why and what the hell is going on.

"Yes sir, I'll ask."

"Who are you talking to Michael?" He looked worried.

"Layla, one of the Messengers asked me to ask you." The man was speechless and so was I for a moment.

"It won't hurt to ask, go ahead dear."

"Mr. Lincoln wants to know if you or Walter has some kind of magical spells or potions or maybe a talisman or something of that nature."

He was embarrassed to ask because he thought that the sixth and seventh realms knew everything. I had to say in my mind, don't Lie Layla, Gandhi will be disappointed.

"Popi has an amulet which he thought was magical."

"The one I held in my hand, the one with the rune?"

"Yes, the past is not forgotten, it was destroyed by a bullet. That being said, I think Popi tends to be able to access some mysterious power in times of need. He doesn't know it, but I think he's had it all his life. It didn't really come to the forefront until he met me. It's a part of why I love him so. Together we are magical."

"Will you ask him?"

"You just did sweetheart, I'll let you know next time I see you."

I kissed his cheek, feeling the tug of my body and the poke of Big Michael. I was happily back in your arms, my strong, handsome, and magical husband.

Forever yours, Li'l Freckles

# CHRISTMAS

I had a lot of questions for Popi, but when I found myself back in his arms it was a matter of first things first. I didn't have to cajole, beg or trick Popi into making love to me again, he was all over me. I just relaxed and enjoyed as my Popi ravished his Li'l Freckles. Afterward, we became aware that we had made a mess of Kurt and Rebecca's bedroom.

Popi said, "Let's try to sneak to our room."

"Popi, its Christmas day! I wonder what time it is."

"I'm sorry Li'l Freckles. I didn't get you anything."

We did successfully sneak into our room without being seen. It's a good thing because Popi was still naked and I had lost my robe during the ravishing. We left a mess in Rebecca's room, but ours was even worse. The area rug was gone and there were three ugly gashes in the oak floor outside my bathroom.

Popi said, "I think that means that Mad Vlad is dead."

We showered before sitting down to talk. It took two hours to listen to the incredible convoluted story. It had so many sides to it and the timeline ranged from prehistoric Ireland to 2035 Ohio and Russia. Popi finally told me about 2035 Layla. He was afraid that telling me earlier might compromise his amazing plan to protect us from the Brockov's. He told me that Vladimir had somehow foiled his plan by sending his brother to kill Claire while Popi left me unprotected at home. Popi refused to tell me in any detail exactly what the demon had done to me for fear that his heart would break. Can you believe how sweet my dear Popi is?

It being Christmas, we dressed festively or at least I did. My red sequined mini-dress with matching platforms made me feel ready to celebrate our triumphant return. Popi looked nice too, but as usual he wore black. It was a beautiful tight cashmere sweater, so I approved. He almost never wore anything bright or colorful. His palette ran to gray, black and an occasional blue. On the bright side, my specialty, it did make my choices stand out. We took a deep breath and left our room, steeling ourselves for the inevitable fuss from our dear friends and family.

We searched the entire 40,000 square feet of our house plus the basement and the attic. We were alone, nobody was home. Popi even called for Lilly, but got no response. Where could everyone be? We finally had to make some calls. It turns out that most of them were in Tampa for Rose and David's wedding. They were staying to celebrate Christmas. I promised that we would be there tomorrow. We talked for two hours. Popi and I didn't have much to add to their stories of their time without us because nothing happened in our lives for the last year.

"In fact," I told the speaker phone, "If Kurt and Rebecca hadn't been there, we wouldn't have known that anything had changed."

I knew that Popi was sad at missing another of his children's wedding. He missed David and Greta's while in the hands of terrorists. This one was worse because he had promised to give Rose away and dance at hers. I called my mom and dad. They acted as if they didn't know that we were missing. They thought that I was just angry at them. I didn't know what was up with that, surely they'd read it in the National Tattletale.

I called my five models while Popi called Triple D. I asked Simone about Paris. She told me in vivid detail of how nervous she was and how thrilled she was when it went so well.

Simone proudly proclaimed, "I didn't trip even once."

It brought back fond memories of my first Paris show. When I had talked to them all, Popi told me that Triple D was doing flip flops. He said that the Tiger doll set had set records in sales. He wants us to check our accounts, but we should sit down first.

Popi said, "Just what we need, more money. Li'l Freckles, I tasked DeeDee with fulfilling your cavalier promise to be in Tampa tomorrow. It's Christmas, so we'll be extremely lucky to get a seat." I wrapped my arms around my man.

"Extremely lucky is one of my super powers."

Finally, I called Ted. "Hello Ted, it's me Layla. Have you missed me?"

"Layla, Layla, my god I can't believe it. Where have you been? Thank God, are you alright? Is Walter back too? Where are you now?"

Popi has a cute habit of ticking off his answers to my excited strings of questions in an equally rapid fire manor. I've adopted this habit.

"I don't know where I've been. I'm fine. Yes, Popi's back too and I'm at home."

"We've missed you so, so much, especially in Paris and New York."

"How did those weeks go?"

"They went okay, but the joy wasn't there. According to Claire, sales wise, we had a good season."

"Thank you, Ted, for keeping the team together. How about this year, are we ready?" My dear friend and mentor was crying now.

"We're as ready as we can be. I completed some of your designs from your sketchbook, but only three, so we're definitely short on your inspiration."

"I guess I'll have to break out my swamp dress."

The swamp dress is the silly nick name for the most beautiful and expensive dress that I've ever created. It portrayed a living pond scene in Egyptian cotton, Japanese silk, Irish lace and semi-precious stone beadwork.

Triple D was able to get us to Tampa the next morning. Rose and David put off their honeymoon for three days to celebrate the return of her prodigal Father and me. I'm not her stepmother, she's three years older than me, but we're still very close. We approached the beach where a Luau in our honor was being held. From a hundred yards away, we saw Chrissy and Mary running toward us. I think they were shouting, but they were downwind, so I couldn't hear. As they got closer, I saw that Mary could easily have beaten the much larger Chrissy. She was honoring the order of things out of respect for her sister.

They reached us and we were swarmed by the squealing teenage girls. Popi Lifted Chrissy and with a tight hug, spun them around. I heard his whispers.

"I missed you my precious Princess."

I swapped an excited Mary for exuberant Chrissy. She picked me up and kissed me on my surprised lips. Again, I heard Popi's whispered greeting to his newest daughter.

"I love you my brave strong Mary and I always will."

We walked to the campfire. Strangely, no one came out from the circle to greet us save two. Rose came to her father.

"Welcome back daddy I want you to meet David Walter Rose, your Grandson."

Of course, we were thrilled. Popi didn't give up the beautiful redheaded baby boy for almost an hour. I was next and I think I beat Popi's record. Popi refused to tell anybody what he knew about our disappearance. Though he had told me everything, I was hesitant to repeat his supernatural tale. Those few days on the beach were some of the best days of my life. No one noticed what was different about Popi even though he was shirtless most of the time. His, the past is not forgotten, brand was missing from his chest.

Of course, life goes on and I had to get back to work. We went to Paris and had a wonderful time. With only five dresses of my own design I felt a little guilty until Kelly walked on stage in my swamp dress and the thousands of people stood as one for a five minute ovation. I cried. Though it retailed for over 15,000 dollars, we got one hundred and ten orders for that handmade dress between Paris and New York. That one dress paid for travel expenses for the year, including the private jet.

The New York talk shows hounded us for interviews, so we finally relented, knowing it would be difficult, especially for me, being an inept liar. Fortunately, Popi can lie well enough for the both of us. He claimed to have no knowledge of where we were and how we got there.

He said, "I think we were pulled into another realm for our own safety by some supernatural force and sent back with no memory of that place and those beings."

Popi knows that the closer to the truth, the more believable the lie. The Ex-comedian host made numerous jokes and even had us laughing, but the audience seemed to believe our unbelievable tales. Maybe they were just happy to have us back. No amount of probing could persuade Popi to recant any part of his story.

As usual, there was a relaxing month after New York fashion week. Romantically, Popi and I had switched places. Now, he absolutely cannot get enough of me and I'm having great fun in using his lame tactics for denying him sex, though always, just like him, unsuccessfully. My beautiful, sexy, sweet husband loves me more than ever and I love him the same as ever. I can't conceive of a love greater than what I have for my Popi.

**The end**

# PART TWO

# THE GRAVEDIGGER, THE UNDERTAKER AND THE PREACHER

# DISTRAUGHT WOMEN

After New York Fashion week, Layla and I tried our very hardest to get our lives back to, if not normal, at least our old crazy and happy existence. For me this was made more difficult by all of the beautiful women in my life. The usual flirting had turned to uncomfortable touching and attempts to seduce me.

I wasn't surprised by Layla's Angels. They had always been very forward with me, but the others, Susan Williams, Claire and Gabrielle had me at a loss for what to do. Of course Claire could not be blamed because I often touched her that way. I didn't want to cause any upset in my home, so I ignored the pleasantly perilous petting in hopes that, with time, it would go away on its own.

Gabrielle had never shown any sexual attraction toward me in the past, but the other day I came upon her in the laundry room. She didn't see or hear me approach and she was very embarrassed that I had caught her crying.

"Oh Popi, you startled me."

Gabrielle spoke perfect English with the sexiest French accent you could possibly imagine. She is a 5' 7" brunette with soft, long wavy hair. She's a slim thirty year old with a youthful, beautiful face. Her eyes were her lure, of the palest blue. A man could get lost in those eyes especially if they were weeping. I took her, lure and all, into my arms.

"What is wrong Cheri and what can I do to make you smile again?"

The tragic girl wrapped me in a tight clutch.

"Oh Popi, I almost lost you again and I can't go another second ignoring my love for you."

I stroked her long wavy hair as she cried onto my chest.

"It's okay sweetheart, I love you too."

This proved to be a tactical error because she pulled my face to her and locked her soft and determined lips onto mine. I succumbed to her charms for several seconds, including cupping her small breasts. I started calculating my exit strategy and by the time the kiss broke, I was ready.

"Gabrielle, our love must be kept in our hearts. We will know the truth, but we must resist our desires to engage in that heavenly forbidden act of love."

My charming line of bullshit, normally infallible, failed to completely solve the problem.

"Yes Popi, of course you're right." The beautiful woman hugged and kissed me again. She got even for my groping of her by groping Big Popi. "Goodnight my forbidden lover." At least I got her to smile.

I have experienced this before with several of the young women in my house. I think it has less to do with me and more to do with the way women deal with loss. Hopefully this storm would pass. I had to find something to do that kept me too busy to interact so much with these sweet peripheral victims of the violence that surrounds Layla and me. I checked with Ski.

"Geez Walter, I'm not too busy myself." I saw the lightbulbs' glow cross his face. "There is one thing that I'm behind on, but I don't know if you'll enjoy it."

"Anything partner, I'm dying here." Was I pleading?

Ski went to the small closet and came back with a paper grocery bag overflowing with fan letters.

"These are the letters returned by your high school operatives for threat assessment." His voice was all business, but his eyes shone with amusement.

I asked, "Operatives? Those kids were just supposed to send out fan club junk, not read and rate them."

"Well I thought they were a good resource so I deputized them into my security team." His poker face was starting to crack.

There had to be three or four hundred letters in that bag.

"Ski, do all of these people want to hurt Layla and me?"

"No of course not pal, only five or six percent of them." He openly chuckled.

"I feel so much better now. Okay, I'll take a run at them."

"I usually sort them into three piles, cute and harmless, disturbing, but no action needed and Psycho killer in training."

I left with my weeks work in my arms. I had no inkling of what I was getting myself into. How I long for those sweet innocent, naïve days before I took on that nightmare. I took my homework to my den, my most private place, and started reading. I had read many sappy fan letters before and always came away amused, but confused by the devotion these young people had for Layla, me, or both of us. The very first letter shocked me.

My dearest Popi

Hi Popi, I've been madly in love with you since I was thirteen. I'm ready for you now. I'm much older now and am finally old enough to be your woman. I have protected my virginity just for you, my dear handsome hero. I dream of our first time every night, knowing how gentle and considerate you will be. It makes me so hot and excited just thinking of your passion as you teach me your ways. I can't wait until my sexy body is all yours. (See enclosed photo) I yearn for the ecstatic pleasure of your pure love.

In my dreams, your extraordinary romantic abilities are superhuman. If they're normal in real life,

I'll be completely okay with that. My breasts are a lot bigger than those of that bitch you married so I hope you're okay with that. If not, I'd be more than willing to have surgery to change them to any size and shape that you desire. Can we meet soon? I'm ready to devote my life to you. No other girl will ever love you like I do. I would kill or die for you.

Your devoted lover, Cici Devers
PS, I've heard that your wife can't have children. I assure you, I'm very fertile.

I was stupefied and made the mistake of pulling and looking at the disturbing picture the girl included. It showed Cici, naked from the waist up. Indeed she was very beautiful. I tore the image up and considered putting the letter in the Psycho pile, but in the end, it ended up in the no action box.

I now knew how difficult this task would be, but I'm a good Marine. I never give up a mission because it is difficult. I also realized that these letters were here because they were all unusual in some fashion. Hopefully, they were not all this disturbing because I'd spent fifteen minutes on this one short sad letter. If they all took this long, my weeks' work just turned into a torturous month.

I randomly picked another letter. It was another addressed only to me and was from James Patrick in Lebanon Kansas.

Dear Walter

My name is James and I think your nick name is kinda lame so I'll call you Walter. A man's name is his birthright and should be treasured. Through reading your first two books, I know that you were named after your father, The Colonel. He sounds like a glorious man so it makes no sense that you would dishonor him by shedding the given name of his choice. We all sometimes make bad choices and this one is easily fixable and forgivable.

The reason I'm writing is to profess my love for you. I know that you are not yet gay. This is fixable and forgivable too. When I fantasize about you, you are always hesitant to show me the love which your old standards deem forbidden. When I undress us, and begin to caress you, you always respond, belying the reluctance on your nervous face. When I perform that most loving act, you respond with involuntary moans of pleasure.

Finally, after you are satisfied you are reborn and transformed into the total man you always secretly wanted to become. Then you do for me that which was always considered to be taboo in your mind. You become instantly an expert at the penultimate act of love. It will take time and a building of trust before we are ready for the ultimate pleasurable thing which I have never done. I'm saving myself for you.

You'll always be Walter to me, my love and I can hardly wait for your transformation. Like you, I'm all man and I'm the man for you.

OXOX, James.

Day one and I couldn't take any more for now. I was still determined to complete my mission, but decided that I needed help. I would try to get Layla involved. I went up to my room and put on my fancy old swimsuit, deciding to do my normal routine of drinking coffee, reading my paper and ogling the pretty girls at the indoor pool. These are the things that I was avoiding to limit my time with the overwrought women of my house. True to form lately, my plans backfired.

Claire was there, swimming in a black one piece. Claire always wore a one piece, being insecure about her fantastic body. At forty-eight, she still looked young and gorgeous. I last saw her naked about a year ago in Paris, though it was only a few weeks ago to me. She was strapped to Henri's bed in preparation for being tortured and murdered by Little Nikki. I still had that disturbing yet stunningly erotic vision firmly entrenched in my cluttered mind where all sexy images stay forever. In that memory, her angelic face was distorted by horror and a gag, but the rest of her was nearly perfect.

Claire's breasts were large for her small frame and still firm and exquisite, while quivering in fear. Her tiny bit of belly was of course invisible while being stretched out on her back, but I knew that even while standing, it was cute and really, barely there. I think that living among all these young attractive models and of course, Layla, has her over sensitized to her perceived flaws.

I sat in my usual deck chair and began reading the days' news. Layla calls it my inky old news because anything that has happened since early yesterday afternoon wouldn't be in it and she ruined one of her hundreds of favorite sweaters while sitting on my lap and making out with me while I read.

Anyway, Claire eventually noticed me. She came and sat on my lap like the others often do. Claire kissed me on the cheek as a test I think.

"I still remember the kiss you gave me at the airport." Her tone was sultry.

"I've been told that all my kisses are memorable." I was wary of the direction of this conversation.

"Walter, do you ever dream about me?" Oh my, what should I say?

I tried to deflect. "When I thought you were in danger, I dreamed of life without you."

"No, I mean one of your fantastic sex dreams." I was cornered.

Claire was now rubbing my chest, right where the rune symbol used to be, and nearly nibbling my ear. I had to come clean.

"I had an erotic dream of you a few weeks before we disappeared. Do you want to hear about it? Layla wasn't amused."

"No, that won't be necessary. I dream about you nearly every night lately."

"All good dreams I hope."

"For me, they're very good, but in bed with Henri, a little bit concerning."

"But Claire, you never talk in your sleep."

"I do now. I've been thinking about you while I'm awake now. I want you to make love to me one more time. Will you do that for me?"

This was the first time in thirty years since I met Claire that she has said or done anything the least bit improper or unethical.

I cruelly said, "Yes Claire, of course I will, after you bring me a signed permission slip from Layla." She left in a huff.

At dinner that night, Beef Stroganoff with asparagus and homemade sourdough bread, I decided to get the problem out into the open.

"We have a problem in paradise. I'm not going to mention any names, but some of you ladies have been crossing the line between flirting and seduction. If I were single, I would be proud to have any of you as my girl, but if things don't change, all flirting of any kind will be discontinued. I don't want that so don't force me to make that choice."

Layla spoke first, surprising me.

"That goes for me too."

I distinctly saw Robby and Stump drop their gazes to their plates. Claire, Gabrielle and Susan refused to make eye contact.

In bed that night, after my Li'l Freckles and I worked off some of the sexual tension, I showed my grinning wife the letters. I had her reach into the sack of doom and pick a letter. She chose one addressed to her. It had a photo and Layla flashed it at me. The boy looked like a normal kid, if such a thing exists. My innocent wife read aloud. I just lie there and irresponsibly let this disaster happen.

My dearest Li'l Freckles

My name is Anthony and I'm fourteen. I know that you're in your twenties now and way too old for me to be your boyfriend. I read in the National Tattletale that you and that man Lemon have adopted a fifteen year old girl. If I were to become an orphan, you could adopt me. The only problem is Lemon. I hate him and if he were to expect me call him dad, I just can't guess what I'd do.

Once we were mother and son, we could be alone. Our love would grow and grow with every day. By the time we became lovers, the Lemon problem would go away, I promise. When I turn sixteen, you can sign away your rights to me and we could legally marry in some states. Then I would be your protector, lover and your husband instead of Lemon.

On a lighter topic, my girl Ginny begged me to take her to the school dance. I told her that I would, if she would dye and style her hair like yours. I swiped my mom's credit card and took Ginny to the mall. I bought her a Layla's Petites dress. It was the one you wore on that Jackass jokers' show last month, you know the one, pink with sequins. We danced every dance and enjoyed ourselves immensely.

We left early and walked to my house. Adolf and Ava were out so I hit the liquor cabinet. In my room, we listened to some John Legend because the silly girl loves him. We began to get frisky. I rubbed her cute butt, not nearly as cute as yours, as I kissed her. When I unzipped Ginny's dress and ran my hand up her thigh, she went cold on me. I kicked her out and made her walk home alone, the bitch is afraid of the dark. On Monday I told everyone at school that I had hit that. When she heard, she had to go to the nurse and left school early. It was a hoot.

I can't wait until I'm pleasuring you with my huge manly equipment. I'll be gentle because I know you are used to Lemon's old and pitifully small Mr. Limpy. I promise you, it will be epic. I would be very appreciative if you would refrain from screwing Lemon until we are together. I'm well worth the wait. I've written my cell number below so call me any time. I love you, my future mother and wife.

Forever yours Terrible T

"Popi, this kid is horrible what can we do to stop him?"

"He can't be all bad. He loves your cute butt." I rocked her over and kissed that cute posterior.

"I'm serious, he might kill his parents."

"We are supposed to assess the level of threat, so this goes into the immediate action required pile."

"Okay Popi, that's enough fan mail for tonight. Now get little Mr. Limpy over here and pleasure me like Terrible T would like to. Big Popi, though insulted, managed to put whatever Anthony had to shame.

# TAINTED LOVE

Popi got me addicted to those dreadful letters. As I understand it, these are three hundred out of twenty thousand sweet, normal fan letters. Even though it hurt to hear us being torn down by the others biggest fans, we just couldn't look away. It was like a deadly accident scene, good people enthralled by disaster. The first letter I read last night scared me a bit. The boy, Anthony, was actually planning to murder his parents and Popi to be with me. The next day, Popi faxed the letter to the sick kid's father.

"Popi, did Adolf or Ava fax you back?" Popi chuckled.

"Don't they teach you kid's history anymore? Adolf and Ava are Hitler and his mistress."

You learn something every day. Popi told me that he had read five letters today and that they were all off a bit, but none of them required any action. So, of course, I was pulled in again. Popi pulled the first one. It was addressed to him, but was from one of my fans.

Popi

What kind of childish name is Popi? You are a worn out old clown who has captured and held the most heavenly woman in the world, against her will I'd bet. I don't know what kind of evil hold you have on her, but I'm putting you on notice. You will release my Li'l Freckles immediately or I'm coming after you with everything I've got. She is one of God's greatest creations and you're an old perverted rapist.

I have a crew of gay thugs who would really enjoy raping you over and over. I think that would drive a macho pig like you to suicide unless you are too much of a coward. Speaking of cowardice, what kind of man despoils an angelic goddess, forcing sex on her nightly, if your books are to be believed? I'll tell you who, a cruel bully who revels in his insane need to ruin everything good and pure in this world.

I'm coming for you and if I let you live, I'll make sure that you will be unable to rape another woman. I'll stuff and mount your disgusting manhood. Don't worry. I'll display it in a place of honor above my bed, where I'll be making sweet sensual love to your wife.

With no love and zero respect, your worst
nightmare, Suzanne

The letter was typewritten, so I was shocked that it was from a girl. Popi told me that he had read a similar, though nonviolent, one sent to him written by a boy. I wasn't put off by the thought of a girl loving me, but was by the violent hatred of Popi. We discussed what action might or might not be required and agreed that I would write Suzanne a letter. I wanted her to know that it was alright to love me, but not okay to threaten the man I love. I would remind her that we are all born into our sexual preferences and should not allow people to shame us or try to change what is in our hearts.

Popi picked the next one. It was addressed to me and from a boy named Mark.

Dear Li'l Freckles

I'm sure you hear it all the time. You are the most beautiful and sexy girl ever created. My name is Mark and I'm no hero like your husband. Let's be honest here, he's not going to be around forever. The way he attracts trouble, it could happen any time and you should be prepared. An exquisite woman like you shouldn't be without a loving man. As for protection, with your millions, we can afford to hire professional bodyguards to insure our safety.

Even if the old man lingers for years, we could have an affair behind his back. With his fading mental faculties, he won't suspect a thing especially since I'll befriend him. I can be quite charming in a needy sort of way. He'll be mentoring me, while I'm hooking up with his wife. I don't have a lot of experience, sexually I mean, but I'm sure that in the presence of your gorgeous, glorious nakedness, it will come naturally to me.

In a few years or less when your husband dies, we will be able to announce our love to the world. That will be the happiest day of my life. Don't worry. I'll be able to cry at his funeral. I can cry on demand, as I did a few weeks ago when my mom died. I'll never understand why she's gone and my drunken dad lives on. Life isn't fair. I need you to respond to me quickly because I can't stand many more of his beatings.

If your husband were to find us out, would he hurt me or even kill me? I don't care. I would risk everything to be your man. I can't wait to get your letter. I'm about to turn fifteen, but I'm a little small for my age. You are so petite that I think we'd be a perfect fit. I've tried to picture you making love to that large brute of a man, but find it hard to imagine how that works. Doesn't he smother you? Can he even kiss you while he's inside of you? What I can picture is you and me, the perfect interlocking puzzle pieces of love.

Hurry my love, Mark

Just like last night, the letter struck a familiar chord with me. At first, Mark seemed to be a standard star struck fan with an active imagination, but near the end of the letter he revealed himself. He was another abused and neglected soul who had recently suffered a grave loss. At first I disliked him, but after I saw into his fragile mind, my heart melted for him. Tomorrow, I will call the child protective service in Boston. I would overnight a registered letter to Mark, promising that help was on the way. Also like last night, all the sex talk had me desirous of my Popi.

"Come smother me Popi."

My old, feeble minded man did leave me breathless, no smothering involved.

# THAT CRACKPOT SCARES THE HELL OUT OF ME

Layla and I were slowly working our way through the sack of letters. Most, like Ski said, were just smitten fans with potty-mouths. The fifteen year olds seemed to be the most sexual and the most violent. In many cases, it was obviously all bravado, but some of the boys and girls seemed to be genuinely disturbed. We had handled about one third of the sack and taken some kind of action on four so far. Today, at my desk, I read the first one that frightened me.

Dear Walter

The name and return address on this envelope are fakes. Read on and you'll see why. I'm telling you this because I have great respect for you and don't want you to waste your time trying to track me down. My real first name is Pete and I've been married to the mother of my three kids for thirty years. I was born ten days after you, but look at least ten years older. I think I know the secret formula for your youth and vigor, Layla.

Marie is no Layla. I pretend to love her, but really, I haven't cared a thing about her for many years. I've had to find creative ways to hold on to my virility. Once a year, during the month of May, I take a girl for my own pleasure. I started this hobby in 2001, so last May I had my fourteenth affair. This year, Marie left me and has filed for divorce because she found my stash of pictures and souvenirs from my sinful acts.

I choose my lovers from parks, college campuses and other places where young people gather. I don't take them immediately. I identify them and research them for two weeks. Once I know them, I can spot the weaknesses in their protective systems. They all have at least one time in their routines when they are most vulnerable and that is when I strike. I like to put them to sleep with ether to get them into my van. I keep my new lovers for as long as I can. My record is ten days.

Of course, when I'm through with these angels, I can't just let them go no matter how much they promise me that they won't tell. I've experimented with several methods for solving the pesky witness problem. My favorite way is to strangle them while making love to them for the last time. My goal, timing their death to my ejaculation, is very difficult and not always successful. Of course, when they die a little early, I'm not deterred one bit. The hard part is leaving them in a place where everyone can see just what sluts they are.

The reason I'm writing you is to give you fair warning. I've never done this before, but since I admire you, I thought you deserved to know that I've chosen your Layla to be my next conquest. On a happier note, my wife is gone and my kids are grown, so I'll have a lot more time to spend with your adorable wife. I'm even thinking of trying to keep her for the entire time between girls. It can take that long to completely get to know someone as exquisite as her.

As the old saying goes, mi casa es su casa, so it only stands to reason that su slut es mi slut. Tell her I'm coming, so she can fantasize about my forceful worship. Although Layla dresses very sexily, I'd prefer that she dress a bit younger. I have the tape of you two on the Dr. Joe Marks Show. That red leather mini skirt with a white button down and red leather tie made me mad with desire. I have spent many nights pleasuring myself to that film clip. You are a very lucky man to be able to tap that slut anytime you like. I'd be hitting that ass ten times a day. Someday very soon, I will. I'll send you pictures.

Your biggest fan, Pete

I took that letter, made a copy and slid the original into a plastic document protector, along with the envelope. It had been handled by several people, but may still hold traces of Pete. Though I didn't want to show it to Layla, she needed to know. I decided to wait until I investigated a bit further. I don't really have much pull with the FBI, but I needed their evidence labs to check that threatening letter. I called the only Special Agent that I knew would take my call, Don Briggs.

I've known Don for a couple of years. He helped me capture Mr. Charles, Malcolm and Meagan. He lost nine of his agents in that battle and suffered a broken neck for his assistance. Needless to say, he's not my biggest fan, but he is a stock holder. I'd heard that he was in charge of the Baltimore, Maryland office. I still had his old cell number, so I called and he actually picked up.

"What the hell do you want Walter. My neck hurts from just saying your name."

"Gee Don, where's the love? How are you doing and how is SA Templeton?"

Templeton was the only other FBI agent who survived Malcolm and Meagan's raid on my house.

"He's okay. I've heard that he's selling sports cars in LA."

"What made you go back to crime fighting?"

"I considered giving it up, but it's in my blood. Let's get to the point. I'll tell you in advance, the answer is not only no, but no fucking way." I read him Pete's letter and he softened a bit. "That's pretty disturbing, but it's probably just someone yanking your chain. Almost all of these types of things are from effete losers who get their jollies from terrorizing people like you, rich jackasses."

"Don, I just want you to submit the letter for testing. I agree, it's probably nothing, but I have to know for sure. Is this asshole coming after Layla?" He thought for a moment.

"Okay Walter, overnight me the letter. I'll get it checked out, but don't draw me back into your troubles."

"Thank you, Don, I owe you one."

"I'm collecting now, lose my number."

I'm not surprised at his anger and was happy with his limited offer, though I'd been hoping for a better reception. I paid eleven hundred dollars to have the letter hand delivered that afternoon by Stump.

The fact is, Ski and I captured Malcolm and Meagan for him and the FBI let them escape. He brought a squad of agents to recapture the two dangerous escapees. He lost nine of his ten men and the bad guys were killed or captured by Layla and me. I was beaten to a pulp and Layla was strapped to a bomb. I should be the angry one. That was really unkind. Those brave men died trying to protect my darling Layla. I was just venting in my mind. I decided to put Pete out of my mind until Don got back to me. I won't frighten Layla with the details. After all, he's probably just a crackpot. Who the hell am I kidding? That crackpot scares the hell out of me.

That night in bed, I showed Layla the copy of the letter and studied her reactions. She showed no obvious signs of fear, but her face grew stern as she finished the short missive.

"Popi, do you believe this guy? Is he really coming after me?" Her brow was furrowed.

"I don't know, but he scares me. I sent the letter to the FBI. What do you think?"

"He scares me a little bit, but he'll need way more than two weeks to find a weak spot in my routine."

"Mad Vlad did." The memory of Layla's savagely murdered body seeped into my thoughts.

"One thing I can tell about our Pete, he's no Vladimir Brockov."

"It could be days before." I was about to finish with, "Don gets back to me," but I was interrupted by my cell phone. It was SSA Briggs. I put him on speaker.

"Hello Don, Layla and I were just talking about you."

"I've got good news and bad news." His delivery was deadpan.

Layla said, "Good first."

"Okay honey, we found a finger print on the letter and got a hit on CODIS."

"That's great Don. Who is he?"

"That's the bad news. His print matches prints found in two unsolved homicides."

I asked, "Does that mean that you're going to take the case?" I was hoping that another, less rude, agent would be assigned.

"The moment that print hit, my fate was sealed. Twenty minutes later, before I told anyone, the Director called me. He told me to drop everything, get a team together and catch that creep." Briggs was not happy.

"Sorry about your misfortune buddy. If you need me, you know where to find me." Briggs fought back.

"Oh no you don't Walter that postmark was from Indianapolis, less than a hundred miles from you. We're setting up at your house."

I was about to deny him access, but Layla is, of course, much kinder than me.

"How many beds do you need?"

"Thank you Layla, we'll be three men and a woman."

Before sleep, Layla read more letters. I suspect she was searching for another sexy one. If that was the case, with her third one, she was successful.

Dear Layla

I dream of you every night. These are the happiest times of my life. My name is Jason Witt and I just turned seventeen. In my dreams, I am man enough for you, but in real life, I'm just a normal guy. I decided to write you on the off chance that you are unhappy with your husband and would be open to getting to know me. I'm tall and athletic and most girls think I'm sexy. I sent a pic so you can judge for yourself.

(Layla paused to look at the picture. The kid was tall, athletic and pretty buff without his shirt in a laid back pose. He was wearing a toboggan cap that read, I love Li'l Freckles.)

I have some experience with women, but still haven't gone all the way. I've had some chances, but not with anyone I respect. I'm looking for a girl who I'd be proud to have for a wife and mother of my children. I've heard that you can't have children. I assume that your old man is just shooting blanks. How old is he, sixty? Anyway, I have to give him his props because he has you and he has saved you many times. I thank him for that.

Last night, having just finished your husband's second book, I dreamed that we were on a tropical island. We were stranded and all alone, but I didn't have a care in the world. Our first night, you came to my crude bed of leaves and cuddled naked with me.

You kissed my ear and whispered, "Make love to me Jason."

We kissed, our tongues dancing. I kissed my way down your exquisite body, only stopping at your expectant pussy. With my lips and tongue, I explored every delicious fold and crevice. You writhed and moaned until you exploded into a spectacular orgasm.

You took my huge and hard penis into your sexy mouth and soon took me to the peak of pleasure, greedily savoring my seed. I kiss you deeply without hesitation, enjoying the traces of my manly juices. I rolled on top of you, fondling your magnificent breasts. My raging hard-on remained ready. When you took him into your soft little hands to guide him into your eager pussy you whispered.

"Be gentle with me Jason."

I was gentle at first, but when you began to go wild with passion, I followed right along. After a couple hours of animalistic fucking, you screamed my name with unrestrained desire and extreme pleasure. As you were convulsing for fifteen minutes, I continued pleasuring you until I erupted like a volcano of fiery love for you. Just as I was falling to sleep, you curled up tightly with me and whispered into my ear.

"I love you Jason." I took this as a sign that I should write you and declare my love.

Your biggest fan, Jason

Layla, looking stern, said, "Popi, it seems that I have set the bar way too low for you. Do you think you can pleasure me for two hours and make me convulse for fifteen minutes or do I have to call Jason?" I smiled.

"Let's start with the dancing tongues and work our way up to marathon animalistic sex. I'm old."

Big Popi and I did our utmost to keep the boy from our door. I wanted to put that letter into the disturbing, but no action pile, but Layla insisted it go to the cute and harmless pile.

# THE FEDS

I'm a little bit ashamed of myself. Popi and I don't really need any help with our remarkable love life. I adore him and he worships me. We rarely go a day without sex, but still, I find these warped fan letters are making me extremely turned on and Popi knows it. He's been trying his best to reenact the fantasies of the teenage wannabes. Of course some of these acts are totally unrealistic and some of their physical attributes greatly exaggerated. I have only had one lover, Popi, but I really can't even imagine a better one at any age.

Popi wasn't happy that I invited Don and his team to stay with us, but I believe it is the best way to keep the resentful man from locking us out of the investigation. Besides, Popi and Don Briggs have some type of incomprehensibly complicated man stuff to work out. If they were women, I would advise them to tell each other their true feelings. I've found from my limited experience that this doesn't work with men. The best I can figure, men work on an unfathomable pheromone system.

Don's team showed up a few days later. Popi offered Don his hand, but the agent didn't take it. It was worse than I'd thought. Don was very nice to me, giving me a small hug. He introduced his three team members.

"Layla and Walter Lemon meet SA Jon Hoskins, SA Mike Latham and SA Sophie Templeton."

Popi's body language changed when he heard Sophie's name, declaring his interest. Sophie is a very pretty woman of about thirty. She has long natural blonde hair which she wears in a severely taut ponytail. Sophie was wearing only a small amount makeup, mascara and a dab of pale red lipstick. Her nose and upper cheeks are lightly and attractively freckled. Her only apparent flaw was her cheaply made and poorly tailored dark gray business suit. Popi took her right hand gently into both of his.

"Templeton, are you related to Sam Templeton?"

"Yes Popi, he is my twin brother." Her smile was inviting.

She was a fan, she was cute, and she had those beautiful freckles. I hated her.

"How is Sam?" Sophie resumed her professional demeanor after an impatient glare from Don.

"He's okay Mr. Lemon. We'll talk later."

"I'd like that." I bet he would.

The son of a bitch just met this woman and he's already made a date with her. I hoped that my gray flannel nightgown was clean.

We showed Don and his team to the ballroom, where they could set up their many cases of gear, and to their bedrooms, ten, eleven and twelve. They were the furthest from the front stairs. When the FBI all went about their business, I cornered Popi.

"Why were you flirting with that whore?" The SOB laughed and I almost went, "Popi," on him.

"Flirting, I was just checking on one of our stock holders." He correctly read my expression and continued, "Sam Templeton, Sophie's twin brother, is the other agent who survived Malcolm and Meagan's raid."

As with every other time that I've had a fiery flight of jealousy over Popi and another woman, I was embarrassingly wrong. I don't know why these things happen, but I seem to have no control. I also didn't know why Popi gets so much amusement from my irrational mistrust. Again, a man thing and a woman thing collide, resulting in her angst and his hilarity.

"I'm sorry Popi," I wrapped him in my arms, "But why do you think it's so funny?"

"It's funny because you still don't know how special you are." He kissed me, long and passionately. The spell was unbroken. "There isn't a man in the seven realms who would cheat on you."

When Popi asks me to write chapters of his books, he always asks me to cut down on the mushy stuff, but I need to tell just how sweet he is at his core. The people who really know him see this, but his fans think of him as the irascible, cynical and tough as nails he-man. I think he sees himself this way, but there is an incomplete truth to that perception. I want to offset that image by showing them how sweet, caring and tender he can be. To his credit, he never edits my stories.

# LILLY, AS TOLD TO WALTER IN HIS DREAMS

I have, for years, been interacting with Walter through his dreams. I've been in the dreams of everyone in this house, but Popi is the only one who always knows that he's dreaming. Whatever crazy things that are going on in his slumber, he always stops what he is doing and talks to me. This makes me feel alive again for a few moments. I treasure that glorious feeling.

Coincidental with Walter's encounter with the magnificent Czar in September 2014, I was blocked from Walter's nightly adventures. I could tell he was actively dreaming, but I couldn't break the usually easy barrier. Then, back in January 2015, Walter and Layla disappeared. We were all devastated. I knew there were unfamiliar forces at work, but didn't know if they were good or evil.

I hung on for several months, keeping up an energy sapping search for any sign of my beloved friends. They were the only ones able to see or hear me. The family was falling apart, not the Lemons, but most of these others were here for Walter and Layla. I couldn't watch anymore, so I accepted my longstanding invitation to six. I never before thought

I could afford to leave Walter alone, Layla too, but mostly Walter because he was always finding new ways to risk his life.

On six, I not only got to meet my father, I got to reconnect with dozens of my fathers from my hundreds of previous lives. The flood of memories of over a million of days, throughout my forty-five hundred years, was crippling at first. After a few days, I learned to focus my mind to block out all but what I wish to remember at the time. Needless to say, it was very time consuming. Some of my lives were full of promise, but abruptly cut short. I've died nearly every way that I can conceive. Others, I lived to my passionate fullest, in more ways than one, if you catch my drift.

I was able to check up on three whenever I wanted, but as the months passed I checked less and less. Nearly a year after they'd gone, I got a five alarm hit on my Popi and Li'l Freckles radar. By the time I located them, they of course were making desperate, sexy love and soon Layla was visiting six. I made up my mind then and there to go back to four. It wasn't an easy call because I'd now have to live another life before I was qualified to return to six. On its' face, not a bad thing, but really a big gamble because if I lived that life inside a psycho, it could be a long time before I qualified again. To be back with my loved ones, it was worth the risk.

I had some loose ends to clear up before I left six. I called for Peter Gibson. I would have called for Angie Wilson too, but the whore still lives. She owns the diner in town. I was dating Peter when I was eighteen. I caught him sneaking around with Angie, so I confronted him. He was very nasty when he broke up with me seconds before I could break up with him. I got so angry that I drove to one of the area farms and hired four Mexican pickers to beat the poor boy half to death. He, knowing it was my doing, never spoke to me again.

I was in my eighteen year old disguise and not surprisingly, Peter showed up looking young and sexy too. We were both dressed ala 1954. The spark was still there,

"Peter, it's so nice to see you." I gave him my most coquettish smile.

"Hi Lilly, This isn't a trap is it?" He exuded wariness.

"No, of course not sweetheart, I wanted to apologize for my violent behavior."

"I forgive you Lilly. You were right to be mad. Although I loved you, I believed that I could play the field and you would never know."

"I loved you too Peter. I planned to punish you for a while then take you back, but when you took that whore to the summer fair, I went psychotic."

We spent the week reliving the life that might have been, mostly in bed. Making love in the sixth realm is almost as good as in life on three, almost. When our brief love affair had run its course, I went back to four. I had to wait for Walter and Layla to go to sleep, not wanting to interrupt their nightly Olympics of love. Walter knew that I often watched, but Layla hadn't a clue. I tried to enter his dreams, finding no resistance. Walter was dreaming of an evil faceless man who was strangling a young girl as he raped her. I didn't interrupt until after Popi beat the man to death.

He resuscitated and released the beautiful victim who fell instantly in love with him. The revived girl began to sexually assault her hero, pulling off his shirt. He started to respond to her greedy gropes. This, of course, was my cue.

"Hello Walter, it's good to have you back." Walter shrugged off the sexed up bimbo.

"Lilly, I was worried that I'd never see you again."

He took me into his manly arms and hugged me to his hard body. We kissed and I turned to putty, leaving a Lilly-like impression on him, oh my, what a man.

"I've been on vacation on six."

"Are you coming back to us honey?" His dreamy eyes begged me to answer yes.

"Of course I am Walter. One can stand only so much perfection."

The handsome man went on to tell me all he knew about his comings and goings for the last year. I am not easily shocked, but that he had used magic, unknown to the sixth and seventh realms, filled me with awe. I now understood how he brought Layla back in time to cure her cancer in 2011. I noticed his missing scar from the rune and rubbed the spot.

"Do you think the missing rune means that you have lost you're time traveling privileges?"

"I reckon so sweetheart." I kissed him again and excused myself to greet Layla.

Layla's dream was a bit more boring. She was at work, playing dress up with her models. They would appear in their sexy underwear and she waved her hands, magically dressing them in beautiful dresses. The child had something that I've wished for myself, a calling.

"Hello Layla, I've missed you."

Layla had a difficult time responding. Like most people, she didn't realize that she was dreaming. Soon her excitement of seeing me overcame her need to continue this dream. She ran to me and enfolded me into a fond embrace.

"Lilly, I'm so glad you're here. We thought you might have gone to five." Her excitement warmed my heart.

"No dear, I was in six waiting for you to return. Your Popi told me what happened."

"Did he tell you about Pete?" She frowned at the mention of this man.

"No, who is Pete?"

She told me that Pete was another sicko who was after her and that the FBI was set up in our ball room. They were even staying in the house. I wasn't happy that the Feds were here. The last time was a disaster. It took months to rid the house of their confused spirits. I kissed Layla goodbye and went right to work, probing the dreams of the four sleeping agents. Two were dreaming of Layla and two were dreaming of Walter.

The two dreaming of Layla were in the same room, ten. Layla told me the first ones name by calling out in passionate ecstasy.

"Jon, Jon, please don't stop, fuck me harder, Jon."

The other was Mike, but I didn't find out his name until the next morning. He was dreaming that Layla was forcing him to make love to her at gun point.

"Please, Mrs. Lemon, don't make me do this. I love my wife."

"Pleasure me or die," said his version of Li'l Freckles.

He, without guilt, did as he was ordered.

In eleven, I found Don Briggs. He was nearly killed here a while back. I forced my way through his strong mental barrier and into his dreams. He was dreaming of Walter, not in a good way. He seems to have some hard feelings over the death of his men. He didn't exactly blame Walter, but felt that if he had never met him his life wouldn't be so full of smothering guilt. Guilt at the loss of those young men was weighing heavily on his spirit. This is what I felt. What I saw was not so poignant.

Briggs was punching Popi. He was landing shots that in real life could never even come close to Walter's handsome face. Walter was slowly and weakly trying to dodge or fend off the feds angry fists, to no avail. No words were spoken save Walter's grunts of pain. I couldn't watch anymore so I left the disturbed man to his fantasy beat-down of my dear friend. Since the four agents were using three rooms, I fully expected twelve to be occupied by a woman.

She was very pretty. Her face looked innocent in sleep, especially when framed by her long and lovely flaxen hair. The girl was very open to my intrusion into her private slumber. She was running through a field of wildflowers, laughing. She wore a light summery dress in soft yellow cotton and was barefoot. She looked back toward her pursuer, a shirtless Walter Lemon. He caught her and took her into those magnificent arms. He spun them round and round, ending in a long kiss. When she dropped her dress, I left her to her excellent dream.

My take on the girl was generally good. I sensed kindness, dedication to her job and an overwhelming desire to be a force for good. I also felt that she was very insecure about her standing in the male dominated career which she adored. She was also unsure of her desirability as a woman. If I dared to communicate with her, I would assure her that she was absolutely gorgeous and could do anything those hairy apes could do. Of the four agents, only Briggs worried me.

# Fifty Square Miles

By the last week of April, I was weary of the FBI. Jon, Mike and Sophie were kind and respectful, but Briggs was becoming insufferable. His snide, derogatory comments were wearing thin, so I, in my irritated state, decided it was time for a showdown with the unpleasant Fed. After dinner, I cornered him.

"Briggs, I need to talk to you in private. Let's go to my office."

"Walter, I don't have time for your foolishness." His tone was dismissive.

"Make the time. This is a pivotal point in your career."

"That sounds suspiciously like a threat. What are you gonna do, fire me? Oh wait, I don't work for you." His team was gathered around us now.

"Okay, have it your way, we'll hash this out in front of your crew." Briggs looked around and reconsidered.

"I hear your fancy office is nice. Do you have any booze in there?"

The only one who had seen my office was Sophie. I led him to the hidden room and to the overstuffed split cowhide chair. I procured a bottle of my finest Scotch whiskey and two glasses. I settled on the matching sofa.

"Don, I want you to either get it off your chest or recuse yourself from this investigation."

"You know what Jagger said, you can't always get what you want." He thought for a moment and continued. "I know you're some powerful star, but there is nothing you can say to get me off this case."

"Well Briggs, you leave me no choice. I want you out in the morning."

"You'll be impeding a federal investigation." He wasn't worried yet.

"No, I'm going to have you fired and ask for a professional detective instead of an emotional wreck." He began to show both worry and anger.

"If you do that, I'm going to kick your rich spoiled ass."

"Finally, some passion, I'll take that over disrespect anytime. Is that what you want? Do you want to kick my ass? Go ahead, but it'll not be as easy as in your dreams." Lilly had whispered into my ear this morning.

I finished my drink in one gulp and stood. Don Briggs did the same. I knew that he couldn't strike me first so I threw a soft right jab to his jaw. The younger, stouter agent threw a flurry of out of control punches, scoring with a roundhouse to my left ear. This got my fire going and my return flurry to his chest, left right left right left, stunned him. After experiencing my speed, he changed tactics and wrapped his arms around me in a weak take-down attempt. I shrugged him off and kicked him in the gut just below his ribs, flooring him. I stood over him, calming down.

"Was it all you hoped it would be?"

"Not even close, help me up."

"Why do you blame me for the loss of those men?"

We decided to have another drink before round two. He finally answered my question.

"Walter, I don't blame you. I blame only myself because instead of doing the cautious thing and evacuating, I fell for your macho legend. Backing down from that aura of heroic bravery you put off, would make me feel like a coward."

"If that's the case, maybe I am to blame. If everyone were to do the cautious thing, who will fight the evil? We'd be forever running from them."

It took a few more doses of thirty year old Scotch, but we got it all out. We were both better men for our bare fisted confessions. When we left the sound-proof room, we surprised Jon, Mike and Sophie. They clumsily pretended to be busy, not fooling anyone.

Don said, "Walter and I kissed and made up, so you can all get back to work." They scattered.

With things settled between Don and me, there was peace in my home. The agents were busily sifting through leads. They had an advanced computer program that sorted all the seemingly insignificant details into time lines and logical sequences then spit out probabilities. They use this data to focus their investigation. Don told me that the DNA on the fan letter was a match for six other murders of young women. The oldest one of these was from 2001. It seems that Pete was being truthful.

The computer also calculated Pete's comfort zone and the probable area of his home. From where the eight known victims were taken and where Pete displayed their remains, the cyber cop calculated that he lived and hunted in, not Indianapolis, but north Cincinnati. This is where I, Layla and my whole family grew up. Pete's victims came from three states, Ohio, Kentucky and Indiana. Not only did the unfeeling machine narrow down Pete's location to fifty square miles, it found the other six girls murdered by the psycho.

"Walter, fifty square miles doesn't sound that big, but there are over two million people in our primary zone."

"How many men in our zone named Peter, were born on November 13th 1963?"

Sophie said, "Just two, but they have both been ruled out. Even assuming that his name and birth date are true, we can't assume that he was born here." I thought this over.

"You're right sweetheart, I mean Special Agent. How hard would it be to check for the last name Peterson?" Jon, who was at the terminal, began typing.

After a few seconds, he said, "Seventy-four males named Peterson or similar names were born on that day and reside in our general area."

Don said, "Good idea Walter, let's run them down."

Don explained that it would take a few days to do the leg work. He actually encouraged me to keep offering suggestions, but not to be disappointed if his team shot my ideas down.

"They're all very experienced at what they do." It felt good to be actively involved.

# THIRD REALM
# PROTECTOR 1ST CLASS

Somehow, magically I suppose, Popi and Don Briggs are best buds again. Popi hasn't said a word and I haven't asked. Popi doesn't lie to me and I could ask, but I want him to want to tell me. Anyway, I was happy that they worked it out. Popi was noticeably more relaxed when he came to bed. I had just finished reading his draft of his third novel. It has the working title still, in bold, at the top of page one. If it lasts, it will be the first time one of his titles has lasted wire to wire. The book is called Tyger, Tyger and I loved it. I contributed to it quite a bit. Popi showered and came straight to bed.

"Did you finish it Li'l Freckles? Did you like it?" I withheld my critique until he was nearly squirming.

"Popi I loved it. It's your best yet. I couldn't put it down." He smiled. It was golden like an innocent child on Christmas morning.

"I couldn't have told the story without you. I hope that someday, people will see the real message. I hope my readers see the love story amid the violence and find a love of their own." This of course melted me even further.

Soon we had created another chapter in this epic. Afterward, I picked some letters as Popi laid his head on my belly, with a grinning sleepy-eyed satisfied look on his handsome face. The letter review was my project now. It's not because Popi gave up, but because I took it over. I was fascinated by the overpowering emotions contained within the disturbingly juicy communications. It was a lot like my mother's fascination with the bizarre gossipy tabloids. Fortunately, I didn't believe most of the teens' letters were based on real expectations that Popi or I would be agreeable to their desires.

Dear Layla Lemon

I hope this letter finds you in good health and great cheer. It is my sworn duty to look out for you. I know you are special and that the future of the planet depends upon your survival. Your aura of goodness attracts the most evil souls that walk the Earth. Walter Ranger Lemon was assigned to keep you safe and he has been fairly successful at the job. That's right, job. I'm sure he has developed some feelings for you during his tour, but he is a professional. He knows he can't let himself get too close, lest he compromise his mission by becoming emotionally involved.

The only problem with this is that the most spectacular and important woman alive is without the full depth of her husband's love. Since you were innocent when he first saved you, it's the only love you have ever known. That's where I come in. I'm an amateur protector with allegiance to no man and only one woman, you. I will have no conflict of interest. I can show you the full spectrum of love that you desire and require to become the Goddess you are destined to be.

I have been read in to the mission personally by the One himself and have completed all the necessary training in the sixth realm. I'm prepared to die for you, of course, this being one of the minimum requirements for service. Most importantly, I'm prepared to live for you. Your happiness is paramount. I won't keep you locked up in that red brick prison. We can go anywhere without fear. My presence will make anyone with evil intentions flee in terror.

My biggest talent is my physical appearance. No one will suspect my killing power because I have the ability to disguise myself to be completely unnoticeable. I've been working on this ability for many years, never once breaking cover. Even the evil agent at my cover school, Grant Logan, didn't recognize the danger he was in when I let him believe that he had hurt me the other day. He was too stupid to see that my tears were fake. I could not risk being outed as a Third Realm Protector First Class.

I want to spend a moment discussing our love life. You have been making love to your husband for so long that I'll have to bring you along slowly. If I started with my A-game, it might prove to be fatal to a sensitive Goddess like you. I will have to start with baby steps like holding your tiny tender hand, kissing the back with my well trained lips. After a few days of this, we'll try kissing and I'll caress your perfect breasts through your soft sweater. Within a year, I will be all yours and you will then know what real love is.

Please call for me before you leave the relative safety of your beautiful estate. We can run and like Lemon, I'll let you win every time. By the way, Grant Logan was killed in a fiery car crash on the highway today. No one suspects and no one will.

My cover parents live very close to you, so I've been keeping a close eye on you whenever I can. I mostly just watch you run. I must say that I am always dazzled by your beauty. You run through those woods like a majestic gazelle with a sexy bounce to your lovely derriere and supple breasts. I can't wait until you are bouncing for me alone.

Your humble servant, TRP 1st Class Jacob Smoot
(cover name)

I was really enjoying Jacob's letter until the last few paragraphs. He had me feeling concern for him and his transparent description of his bullying.

"Popi, did this kid kill the bully and is he really watching us run?"

"Oh yeah, he's watching and I know exactly where his duck blind is."

"Where is it, Popi?"

"He has to be in the tree line just before the path enters the woods to the east." Uh oh, Popi instantly transitioned into Hyper-protective mode.

"How do you know?"

"It is the best vantage point to catch sight of your bouncy butt and your bouncy boobs." I laughed at this.

Popi and I decided to employ Ski and his security team to find the voyeurs' nest as we ran tomorrow. I wanted to meet this Jacob Smoot. I think I'll know whether he's a lonely nerd or a deranged killer. It's one of my natural gifts, reading people. I've been fooled a time or two, but not often. I decided to try one more letter, hoping to cleanse the bad taste that Jacob had left in my thoughts. I wished for a cute and harmless.

Dear Li'l Freckles

In my village, you would be queen, my queen. My name is Ramone and I'm a few years younger than you. My father is the richest man in the district, so I could provide for you. I have paid a witch to place many spells on Senor Lemon, so I expect him to be dead soon. When he is gone, you will be free to be my queen. I pledge thirty head of cattle and one thousand acres of land, some of it cleared, for your dowry. Our wedding ceremony will last three days and everyone within many miles will join in the blessed celebration.

On the third night we will be left alone for the consummation of our union. I will peel away your voluminous wedding gown until all of your charms are laid bare before me. I will lift you and lay your exquisite purring body on a bed of tropical blooms. When I undress, you will happily witness my manly form and possibly swoon from eager anticipation. I will then visit every inch of your supple body with my worshipping lips, making you squirm with desire and ready for the holy act. My already impressive manhood will grow to maximum proportions. Just before I enter your holy realm, I will whisper my sincere words of devotion.

I will finish with a simple I love you, my precious Li'l Freckles. When we tenderly engage in the beautiful loving act, I will never cease in my adoring kisses to your angelic face and proud pointy nipples. When I suckle at your sacred fount, I will drink in your beautiful spirit. This first physical expression of our permanent connection will be only the beginning of a love for the ages. You will forever be my queen and I would never even think of another. Having tasted perfection, all others would pale in comparison to my dear Queen Li'l Freckles. Please don't wait too long to reply. There are many eager young women who await your decision.

Your king, Ramone Pizzatta

Wow! I had hit the jackpot. I was looking for a romantic letter and had gotten all I had wished for and more. The sweet boy was just as delusional as most of the others, but he had turned me on without using a single foul word or vulgarity.

"Popi, I'm seriously considering Ramone's offer. How do you feel?" I placed my hand on his forehead. "I think you feel a little feverish."

So it began, Popi's defense of his claims on me. He even offered forty cows and two thousand acres. I accepted his generous offer, a bird in the hand as it were. We celebrated and it didn't take three days.

# MOUSE TRAP

I awoke before Layla. This is a very rare thing. I know myself enough to profile my behavior. It means that I'm worried, more specifically, worried about Layla's safety. I really believed the boy was harmless, but I've learned from terrifying experience, that getting complacent can be deadly. I got up at five and visited Ski in his office.

"Well well Pretty boy, to what do I owe this honor? You only see five in the morning when you stay up all night."

"It's an ungodly hour, but Layla has a stalker."

I gave my friend the letter. He snickered several times.

"Are you sure that he's not really some spooky super protector first class who is about to put you out of a job?"

"I've learned not to rule anything out, but I'm pretty sure that jacking off to my wife's bouncy butt won't satisfy this kid forever. This ends today."

Ski outlined his simple plan. All Layla and I had to do was run. I told Ski that both Layla and I wanted to interview the troubled boy.

"Okay Walter, but don't forget that he's a juvenile."

"Don't worry. Layla will probably want to adopt him."

At five-thirty, I slipped back into bed and wrapped myself around a stirring Li'l Freckles. She kissed me.

"Mmm, your breath tastes good." She fell back to sleep with my tasty breath on her sweet smile.

The next thing I knew, she was shaking me, waking me. She was dressed to run. She was wearing her sexiest running shorts and a white, tight and sleeveless T-shirt that had a picture of me, with I love Popi, printed across her chest. I dressed as usual in my long UC basketball shorts. Unusually, I decided to run shirtless, wanting the boy to see just what his competition brought to the fight, 180 pounds of muscle and power.

I was trying not to be seen scanning the brush for him and for the first three laps I saw no sign of him. On the fourth lap past his suspected position, I saw a slight movement. By the next pass, the security guards had him prone on the ground. Layla insisted that we finish our run and afterward, coerced me to shower and change before we went to the security office to meet with TRP 1st Class Smoot.

I dressed in my usual morning attire, my fancy blue swimsuit, but added a black Li'l Freckles T-shirt for decorum. Layla dressed for work in a short black skirt with her white blouse tucked in. She looked cute, but I had to do up one more button to hide her small hint of cleavage.

"No use in rewarding his bad behavior."

I got my coffee and we went hand in hand into a bizarre scene. Smoot was a gangling, skinny six feet two, pimply faced teen. He was dressed in a Marine snipers' Gilly suit. It was no wonder he was hard to spot. He was weeping. Layla went to him and offered her hand. The boy took her little hand into his catchers' mitt sized paw.

"It's an honor Ma'am."

"Have you been spying on me Jacob?" She kept her voice calm and kind.

"Yes'm, I'm so sorry." Their hands were still connected.

"Jacob, did you kill that bully?"

"I'm not sure ma'am. I prayed awful hard for him to die, but I didn't do anything else to make it happen." His tears resumed.

"I believe you Jacob. You must know that I'm a married woman, so I'm not available to you or any other man."

"Yes'm I do." He was caressing he hand with his thumb.

"It's nice to meet you and I hope Popi isn't too hard on you, but please take it like the strong man you'll someday be. Promise me Jacob."

"Yes ma'am, I promise, thank you." His tears stopped and his relief was apparent.

I could see the way my special wife boosted the boys' self-esteem. She boosted mine with a sweet kiss and left without another word, forcing me to sit until Big Popi got himself under control. My sexy minx was trying to use her spell to quench any violent feelings in me. This is the first time that I know of, that she used her power prophylactically. I ignored the nervous boy.

"Ski, what did the kid have on him?" Ski was still amused.

"It's in the box." He pointed to my left. "The only thing of note is the very expensive digital camera and telescopic lens. He also has a wallet with forty dollars and a school ID. He also had this small pocket knife." Ski held up the knife.

"Smoot," I glared at the kid.

He stuttered, "Yes sir?" He didn't start crying again, but he was close.

"What were you going to do with the knife?"

"I've been carving Layla's and my initials into the trees." His eyes were downcast.

This finally convinced me that the kid was not a danger to my family. I quickly scanned through the digital images on his fancy camera. They showed extreme close-ups of every part of Layla's beautiful face and body, from this mornings' run. I kept scrolling and found that he had similar photos from other runs going back six weeks or so. I glared at the boy again.

"Follow me." I led him to my office, sat him down with my imposing desk between us. "How old are you Jacob?"

"I'll be sixteen in two weeks."

"You go to the same school as my daughter Mary. Do you know her?"

"Yes sir, she's very pretty, but she's still nice to us rejects."

"Son, if you think of yourself that way, so will other people."

"We don't mind the names, but we are terrified of the violence the jocks put us through."

"How many are in your reject circle of friends, son?" I had shifted to a gentler tone.

"There are eight of us, but at least three more who think they're normal and are in denial."

# Gravity's Law

I wanted to speak to the boy first, before Popi scared him to death. He was dressed in a flowing cloak of rags in greens, browns and black. Popi told me later that it was a homemade sniper suit and a very good one. I immediately knew he was not a threat because, never mind Popi, Jacob Smoot was scared to death of me. I tried to give him a little encouragement and forgiveness and turned him over to Popi. I went to work.

At dinner, Popi asked, "Mary do you know a kid named Jacob Smoot?"

"Yes, Daddy, he looks and dresses like a farm boy, but he's a math and science wiz."

"Did you know that he and his friends were being bullied?"

"Yes I did, and I'll answer your next question before you ask it. I've filled out fifteen reports and turned them in to Assistant Principal Dyer."

"Good girl. Did you happen to keep a record of these forms for yourself?"

"Of course I did, just like you taught me, document any contact with the Government."

"Make me a copy sweetheart. I'm going to school with you tomorrow." Mary looked nervous.

"Tomorrow's not real good for me Daddy. I have to be there at six."

Popi looked up and down the long table and picked the last person, with whom I wanted to run.

"Sophie, do you run?"

"I try to run three miles every day Popi." She was eager to please my man.

"How would you like to protect Layla on her run tomorrow?" Sophie tried to hide her disappointment that she'd be running with me, instead of Popi.

Sounds fun, would that be okay, Layla. I didn't like it, but I didn't let on.

"We can get to know each other at least until you can't keep up." Sophie predictably pushed back.

"I may surprise you. You better bring you're A-game."

That night in bed I asked, "Popi, why did you pick Sophie to run with me?"

"I thought she would be the one who is most likely to be able to keep up with you. Would you rather someone else run with you?"

"I'd rather have you run with me. Do you not see the way she looks at you? She's in love with you." He thought about this for a few moments.

"No, I don't see it, but if I ruled out the assistance of everyone in this house who was in love with one of us, we'd have no one to help protect us."

I had no argument for that, so I picked a letter for Popi to read to me.

Dear Popi

I'm looking for a job. I've enclosed my résumé so you can see that I'm very qualified as a cook, housekeeper and personal assistant. I am 28 years old and extremely fit. Many men think I'm beautiful too. I've enclosed a picture so you can judge for yourself. Your wife is very pretty, but she is way too young to be the complete package of wife, lover and caregiver. I've been married three times so I'm very experienced at taking care of a man.

You are a strong, handsome man who could cure me of my fear of falling in love again. I don't believe in divorce, so I would never try to break up your marriage. Instead, I propose that you integrate me into your family as a mentor and trusted teacher for your wife. I'll keep your servants working hard at their jobs. I'll take control of your kitchen and diet. I'm a licensed dietician and nutritionist. I can also manage your household finances. The most important thing I can do for you and your wife is to manage your love life.

I'm skilled at pleasing both men and women. Since you are both are very attractive, though I prefer men, I am very excited about the prospect of making love to Layla. I believe that we can be a new type of marriage where we are all dedicated to pleasing each other. For providing these unique services, I require monetary compensation, of course. I'm thinking in the two to three million dollar range. I think you'll agree that I'm worth it at twice that price.

Yours truly, Gloria Thompson

Popi looked at the photo, shielding it from me.

"Ooh La La wow! Can I buy her Li'l Freckles or better yet, will you buy her for me for my birthday?" I grabbed for the picture which he held out of my short reach.

"Popi let me see. I'll not buy her for you sight unseen." I made another grab for it.

He showed me the beautiful woman's naked picture. I looked long and hard at the voluptuous woman whose pretty face, large natural breasts, washboard abs, slim hips and long sexy legs made a striking impression. I was almost in tears.

"Do you think she's prettier than me, Popi?"

"Not even close honey. You are the most beautiful woman in the seven realms, but she does have one quality that you don't possess."

A tear welled up and obeying gravity's law, fell from my right eye and beaded up on my cheek.

"What Popi?"

"She is crazier than a shit-house rat." Popi's big grin calmed me.

This of course cheered me up instantly and led to the most enchantingly tender love making I've ever experienced. That is saying a lot.

# LOIS, HORACE AND ELI

My Rolex woke me at five. I stole a few soft kisses from Layla as I gently untangled myself from my Sleeping Beauty. I showered then shaved twice. I was playing a character today. I wanted to emit an aura of power. Not mere physical power, I didn't need to play a part for that, but overwhelming social/political power. I had no gift or inclination for that power.

I put on some expensive cologne, a very rare thing, and dressed in my Italian silk, dark blue three piece suit. I looked in the mirror and trimmed my eyebrows. I wondered if Layla would notice. I slipped on my Alligator loafers, the real ones, over dark blue stockings. Finally, all put together, I bent down and kissed Layla on her already smiling lips. She opened her eyes and pulled me into an extension of the sweet kiss.

My wife, my dear wife looked into my eyes and rubbed her tiny thumbs across my manicured brows.

"I'd hate to be that assistant Principal." I gave her one more kiss.

I went down to the kitchen, only Claire was there.

"My Walter, I'm glad I'm not that assistant Principal." She accidentally showed a glimmer of desire in her pretty eyes.

"Has Mary been down yet?"

"I'm here, Ooh trey chic daddy. You're not going to get me expelled today, are you?"

"Who can predict the fortunes of war my dear?"

Mary and I walked hand and hand to the principal's office where Mary introduced me to the secretary, Lois. The fifty-something lady nearly fell out of her chair in order to get into close contact with me.

"Popi, Mr. Lemon, it's so nice to finally meet you, my, what a nice suit. Is it silk?"

"Yes, sweetheart, beautiful and discerning too." I took her hand and caressed it.

Mary said, "You seem to have everything well in hand daddy. I've gotta go."

"Have a nice day sweetheart," I kissed her pretty cheek.

"Miss Hamilton, I need to see the Principal. Is he available?"

"He won't be here for ten minutes or so. You can wait in his office."

People, both students and teachers were beginning to crowd into the office.

"Since my presence seems to be disrupting things, I'll take you up on that generous offer. Is there any black coffee beautiful?"

Lois fawned over me, "Anything for you Popi." Mary had filled me in on the scary old lady on the short drive.

"Lois is tough as nails daddy, not even you can charm her."

I was about halfway through my bitter, but appreciated mug when Mr. Horace Welling, the Principal, strode into the room trying to portray impatient confidence, but his tells said he was worried about the impending meeting.

"Mr. Lemon, what can I do for you?"

"Call me Walter." We shook hands. His was damp. "Horace, I understand that you have an anti-bully procedure."

"Has someone been bothering Mary?" His concern was real.

"No, not her, but some of her friends have suffered violence from other students."

The relieved man told me that his Assistant Principal, Eli Dyer, was in charge of the zero tolerance anti-bullying protocol.

"Eli assures me that he keeps a tight rein on the problem. His last report included no incidents in the last month."

Horace led me to Eli's office. He lightly rapped and we entered. Assistant Principal Dyer stood and extended his hand without introduction.

"Mr. Lemon it's an honor. I was beginning to think that you were a myth." Mr. Welling went to leave.

"Horace, I'd like you to stay for a few more minutes."

"Of course Walter." I turned to Dyer.

Eli was in his early forties and looked more like a football coach than an administrator. His blond hair was in a crewcut.

"Eli, are you familiar with form number 304-12B."

"Yes of course, it's what we use to record and report any acts of violence or hazing."

"Do you keep these reports?"

"Sure, forever, what's wrong? Has something happened to Mary?"

"Yes, Mary has reported bullying no less than fifteen times since the school year began and feels that nothing has been done." Horace was shocked.

"Eli is this true?"

"Sir, I don't necessarily get back to the witness. There are privacy issues involved." Eli was sweating already.

He must know that he is caught. Horace knew too and he was backing me.

"Eli, you haven't reported fifteen incidents in the three years since I entrusted you to this position."

"Let me guess Dyer," I was getting riled up and made a mental note to stay cool. "You only act on reports that don't involve student athletes." I turned to Horace who was seething.

"Call me if you need me. I trust you'll deal with this."

"To be sure I will Popi, Mr. Lemon." I shook his hand.

"Popi's fine, good day."

Dyer said, "I'm gonna kick your punk ass Lemon." I ignored this and kept walking, but he continued. "I hope your little Princess doesn't have a run-in with my men." As the familiar crimson veil formed across my vision, Horace spoke.

"Did you just threaten a student?"

I crossed the small room until I was face to face with the now unemployed civil servant. He sneered at me.

"You best back off Lemon. You don't want any part of this."

I had already sized up Eli Dyer. Yes, he was strong, weight room strong, but he had no idea what he was in for. I slapped him like Scarlet slapped Rhett. He tried to block me, but he wasn't even close. He threw a vicious jab at my chin. I slipped his powerful punch and slapped the other side of his face. He grew irate at the insulting way that I was kicking his ass.

He attacked, trying to bull rush me into the wall. I slapped him twice and tripped him to the floor. His face was bright red and he was still sputtering mad. I grabbed the two hundred pound man by his cheap suits' lapels and lifted him up. I slammed him against the wall and pulled close. I put my lips to his ear and whispered/growled.

"Don't force me into making you disappear." He stopped struggling. My phone rang. It was Sophie.

# Sophie's Run

When I saw how Popi was dressed for his meeting at the high school, I actually felt sorry for the Assistant Principal. He even trimmed his bushy eyebrows. I got up at six and dressed to run. I stretched for ten minutes, a bit longer than usual, because I refused to lose to the beautiful agent. Yes, she was seven years older than me, but that means nothing. Besides, she's twenty-three years younger than Popi who is still a challenge to beat. The best news is that Sophie only runs three miles a day. The pace is very different.

She was waiting for me when I entered the kitchen, dressed of course, cuter than me. Her short tight pink running shorts showed off her long legs and perfect butt. The snug matching halter showed off her other sexy assets. I was beginning to dislike her again.

"Good morning Sophie. That outfit is really cute. Are you ready?"

"Ready as I'll ever be, what should I call you, Layla, Li'l Freckles or Mrs. Lemon?"

"Call me Layla. Only my crazy fans call me Li'l freckles and, of course, Popi."

"How did you two come up with the nicknames?" We were running now.

"You'll have to read Popi's first book for that."

"I did but that's fiction isn't it?"

"I stand by every word."

"Really," Sophie's pretty face was overtaken by a cloud of introspection.

After a moment, I said, "Sophie, a penny for your thoughts." She abruptly came back to the here and now, having acquired a red glow of embarrassment.

"I'm sorry, I was just thinking of all that wild sex with that spectacular man. I'm very jealous."

"There are some downsides to being married to the perfect man, for instance, having to watch all those beautiful women fantasizing about my husband."

"I'm sorry Layla. Is it that obvious? I'll admit it. I've had a serious crush on Popi since Sam was wounded by those psychos."

"I'm used to it."

We began our second mile in silence. By the time we began the fifth lap, Sophie was breathing hard and unable to keep up. At the top of the hill, she was fifty yards behind. I was happy. My happiness was short lived. A large fat man barreled out of the woods and tried to grab me. I slipped out of his grasp and kicked him in the shin. He yelped in pain and slapped me backhand across my face.

I yelled, "Sophie!" I tried to run toward the agent.

The man caught the neck of my T-shirt and pulled me to the ground. On my back, I kicked out with both feet, aiming for his crotch. I missed. He picked me up off the path, wrapped me in his arms and began to carry me into the woods. Sophie arrived.

"Freeze you Puke, put her down."

The man stopped, but he didn't put me down.

He said, "Put down the gun or I snap her neck."

I knew she wouldn't and rightly so. Sophie was looking for an opening to shoot the smelly bastard as she slowly walked our way. I began scratching at his eyes. He was holding me with his big left arm around my chest with my back against his large belly and my feet were a foot off the ground. I had to reach over my shoulders to get to his face. I wished that my nails were longer. I connected, poking him in his right eye. The rest of my nails clawed at his cheeks.

He screamed, as Popi might say, like a little girl. He knew now that he couldn't hold me. He roared again and threw me at Sophie. The panting agent either caught me or failed to dodge me, depending on point of view. Anyway, we both hit the ground. The man piled his foul smelling body on top of us. I was briefly face to face with the scourge. His right eye was closed and bleeding.

"How do you like me now, you prick?"

He was after Sophie's gun. I crawled from the middle of the pile and stood. I kicked the big slob in the head three times. He ignored me and wrested the semi auto handgun from Sophie's hands. The Prick didn't hesitate, not even for a split second. He shot at me from four feet away and missed. I ran for about twenty yards as he fired three more wild shots. I'll wager that he had never before fired a gun or maybe his injured eye saved my life.

I ducked behind a tree and yelled, "Just let her go and we won't follow you."

He didn't respond and I watched him go about his work. He had Sophie in a secure left armed headlock. With the gun in his right hand, he managed to pull a plastic sandwich bag from his back pocket. He ripped it open with his teeth. He, with some difficulty, removed what looked like a damp washcloth. He put this over Sophie's mouth and nose. He wanted to put her to sleep. I couldn't let that happen, so I picked up a rock and ran at them. He had too much going on to react very quickly, but ten steps away he dropped the rag and fired at me again. I took cover again and pulled out my phone, finding it broken. I made eye contact with Sophie. She still seemed to be alert.

"My phone is broken, throw me yours.

The man was bending to retrieve his drugged rag, but he was listening. When she threw the phone he nudged her shoulder with his big ugly head. It only made it halfway. He was waiting for me to step into the open to get the phone. Since this delayed him from dosing the agent, I was patient. As soon as he placed the rag on the poor girls face, I sprang back onto the path, rock still in hand.

I feinted toward the phone, but veered straight at him. Three steps away, as he fumbled the rag again and tried to bring the gun to bear, I threw the rock. It hit the beast solidly on his forehead. I retreated, scooping up the phone. Back in hiding, I checked the phone. It was asking for a password. I peeked out, drawing fire.

"What's your password?" If a person in Sophie's position could look sheepish, she did.

"Popi,"

I called Popi. He told me to protect myself, but keep them in sight.

"I'm five minutes away. Call Ski then Briggs. I love you Li'l Freckles."

I made the calls, but there was a price to pay for that time. The third time the bastard tried to suffocate Sophie, he was successful. He threw her over his shoulder and backed into the woods. I followed. Twenty feet into the woods, he mounted a four wheeled ATV. He lay Sophie across his lap and drove away after shooting at me a few more times.

Kurt got here first, how he managed, I don't know. Next, Jon and Popi tied, arriving from opposite directions. Last was Don, huffing and puffing. Mike stayed back to man the computers. Jon stayed to collect evidence. Don, to no avail, tried to talk Popi out of following the ATV on foot.

"He's heading north. He'd have needed to cut at least three fences to get here from the hardpan. Ole Pete must be heading to County Line road. That's where he's parked his van."

"Pete, that bastard was Pete?" I took Popi by his left wrist and looked at his watch, the first of May.

# THE GRAVEDIGGER

I followed the trail of Pete's vehicle through forest, thicket and finally field. The nine strands of barbed wire he cut had to slow him down. At County line road, he had abandoned the ATV. There were tire tracks from the van in the soft damp shoulder. I called Briggs and told him what I'd found.

"Wait there Walt. I'll send Jon to you."

"Don, we can't waste time following your sluggish procedures. I'm riding that Yamaha back the way I came."

"Damn it Lemon." I hung up.

When I got back home, all three Feds were racing to their cars.

"What's going on Don? He spoke without slowing down.

"The computer spit out three places to hit. I'll call you."

Inside, I met up with Layla, Ski and Rebecca who were standing around the genius computer. I hugged Layla.

"Ski, are those leads any good?"

"Beats me pal, they trust that machine way more than I do."

"What else do we have?" Ski handed me a thick stack of files.

"These are the seventy some Peters or Peterson's. There are photos of some of them."

I sat down with Layla and went through the pictures. None of the Peterson's was even close to our Pete. Rebecca and Ski went to their office to track down the serial number on the ATV. We began going through the files with no pictures. It was grueling, but there was nothing else to do. We were running out of time. From Layla's description of her fight with Pete, he had several serious injuries. It was the eye gouge that might drive him to seek medical attention. I called Ski with the observation.

Halfway through the no picture pile, I found a picture. It was of the house of a man named Pedro "Pete" Lopez. The photographer only caught a glimpse of a man slamming the door in his face.

"Popi, did you find something?"

"I don't know sweetheart. Find the letter, Pete's letter." She was looking over my shoulder at what I was looking at so intently.

"I don't see anything Popi."

"I need that letter." Layla felt my urgency.

She couldn't find it in the FBI's mound of documents, so she ran to our bedroom and retrieved our copy. I read the important part to her.

"Mi casa es su casa," I read aloud.

"I still don't see, Popi."

"Look at the sign above the door."

Above the door of Pete Lopez's house was a wooden sign with the words, Casa Lopez, burned into the grain.

"Popi, that's pretty thin." Skepticism ruled her cute face.

"It's all I've got, call Ski. We leave in two minutes."

"I'm coming too Popi. Don't try to stop me. Pete attacked me at my home. Mi casa isn't su casa Pete."

"Li'l Freckles, that's it. It might not be Lopez. What if Pete was being literal when he said mi casa es su casa? Maybe Pete lives in my old house."

We now had two locations to hit. Ski left to hit Casa Lopez and Layla and I drove to our old neighborhood. We made the hour drive in forty-eight minutes. I pulled my truck into the familiar driveway. The two car garage was around the back, but I wasn't interested in reconnoitering. I was interested in a blitz raid on my former home.

On the porch with Layla's nervous hands on my butt, I tried the knob. It was locked, but I didn't let that slow me down. Layla held the storm door and I kicked the hard maple door which I'd spent a week finishing and installing twenty some years ago. The jamb splintered.

"Stay with me Li'l Freckles."

You may wonder why I didn't even try to coax her to stay in the car. It's because I'm a fairly bright man who's learned not to waste my time on an unwinnable battle. We cleared the first floor quickly. The home was well decorated by a woman's hand, but was quite messy. Apparently, when Pete's wife left, all housekeeping skills went with her. We went next to the basement, the logical place for holding a captive. Walking down, Layla's hands shifted to my shoulders. Though I hated having my fiery bride in harms' way, I took great comfort in her closeness. At the bottom, to the left, was the modern laundry room that Claire had designed and I had built. It was in disarray and piled with dirty, smelly clothes.

On our right were the two rooms which I had framed and finished on the insides, but had left the outside walls, wiring and all, uncovered. The first was an auxiliary TV room. Layla opened the door and I turned on the light. It was still a TV room, now with a fridge. We moved on to David's bedroom. He was the main reason for the renovations. He never asked, but Claire and I agreed that he had outgrown sharing space with his slovenly brother. Layla put her small hand on the knob, but I held her back. There was a squeaking noise and soft light emanating from under the door.

# Sophie Laughed

If I were to give a piece of advice to the violent men of the world it would be this. Don't ever mistreat a woman while Popi is in the vicinity. You'll be risking your lives. I wasn't worried about Pete's safety. He was lucky to have me because I'm the only force in this universe with a chance of stopping Popi from killing him. We searched the make-out room. Davey and I called it that because the few times we had watched a movie in there turned into wild petting sessions. Like every other room in the house, it was unkempt and filthy.

I opened the door to Davey's old room and Popi walked in first. The light was on. It took a second to take in the situation. Pete was on top of Sophie who was tied to a small bed. He was fully clothed, but Sophie was fully naked. Pete was strangling her. Popi didn't take nearly as long as me to assess the situation. He grabbed the three hundred pound rapist by his hairy face and threw the behemoth to the floor. Popi veered off his expected path.

"Sophie! Don't you dare leave." The urgency in his voice was heart stopping.

Pete was trying to get up and Popi noticed. He kicked him on the chin with his two thousand dollar alligator loafers.

"Li'l Freckles, find a club and keep this prick under control."

I found a short length of two-by-four and tried it out on the grotesque man's head. It performed well. Popi was talking to Sophie again.

"I'll give you air and you can re-enter your beautiful body."

Sophie's body was beautiful. There wasn't a flaw on her except the bruises ringing her slender neck. Popi began breathing into that beautiful mouth alternately applying chest compressions.

"Call for an ambulance honey, then call Ski. He can call Don."

I did those things plus beat the rapist several times while Popi continued his rescue efforts.

"Hurry Sophie, before it's too late. I love you. You're part of my family now. I can't bear to lose you." I was beginning to believe it was over for Sophie.

Popi said, "I love you," again.

Her eyes jolted open and she screamed. Popi kissed her again.

"Popi, if you kiss her one more time, I'm going to beat you with this club."

He, of course, smiled and hugged me. Popi gave me his pocket knife.

"Cut her loose while I play Whack-a-Mole with Pete."

He wanted to kiss me, but I refused him. It wasn't because I was miffed at my heroic husband. It was because I didn't want Sophie to catch a glimpse of Big Popi and thus desire my man even more than she so obviously already did. When I got her left hand lose, Sophie pulled me into a hug.

"Thank you Layla. I can't believe how hard you fought for me in the woods. Now you've rescued me."

"Popi helped a little." Something amazing happened, Sophie laughed.

She was dressed in her sexy running clothes before the cops and EMT's came storming in. The medics tried to look at Pete first, but Popi gently, for him, redirected their attention to the victim and away from the serial killer. In their defense, Pete wasn't looking so good. He had apparently sought treatment for his sore eye and was wearing a black eyepatch. He also had six or seven stitches closing the gash on his forehead and eight scabbing scratches down his cheeks. Finally, were the six lumps on his balding head. The big man was a mess.

Sophie was driven to the hospital by a city cop and the ambulance was used for Pete, two more cops escorting. Ski and Don arrived as the ambulance left. Don went straight for Popi, but Ski pulled me into a big strong hug.

He said, "Great job squirt."

"Thank you Ski, It was the easiest combat mission ever. Pete didn't even put up a fight." Kurt was shaking his head in disbelief.

"Every time you think you know what these psychos are about, they do the most unexpected things."

"How was Casa Lopez?"

"He was a real treat and a certified psycho. When I found out that he was raising five grandkids, under age ten, I cut him some slack."

We drifted the two steps toward Popi and insinuated ourselves into their conversation. The gist was that Don couldn't believe that Popi would illegally raid a citizens' home on such flimsy evidence. It was not rebuke encoded in these words, but admiration. Popi was humble.

"It was a stab in the dark and we got lucky. Layla took out Pete while I worked on Sophie." Don gave Popi an unexpected hug.

"Thank you Walter, I don't know if I could take losing another one. Mike and Jon are on their way to the hospital. I'm going to collect the main evidence and seal the house for the forensic team. Take your brave wife home."

# PETE THE RED HERRING

I did take my brave wife home. On the hour long drive, we were both still on an adrenalin buzz. When Layla said that it had been surprisingly easy, it made me wonder. Why had it been so easy? Pete had been doing this for a long time, yet he didn't give me the madman's twist. I've met my share of these maniacs and they always have a late surprise for you. Mr. Charles scrubbed me from Layla's brain. Horrible Harold came back from being beaten to death and emptied his 44 magnum at us. Caesar Hernandez recovered from my three to his chest for long enough to shoot me and Layla. My point is, it's never this easy. Layla agreed with me to a point.

"You're right Popi, it was easy, but shouldn't we be happy about that?"

"You're right sweetheart. These doubts can wait until we know more. I just wish I had some way to burn off this nervous energy." Layla undid her seat belt and slid closer to me.

She nibbled my ear and whispered, "I've got an idea that would tire you out."

"Oh really, I'm intrigued." I knew that the vixen was teasing me.

"Yes Popi, you can help me inventory and reorganize my stock of fabric." I was prepared for this punchline.

"I don't know baby, my back's been acting up. I figure that I'm good for lifting about 109 & ½ pounds."

"Why, Popi, what a coincidence, that's exactly what I weigh."

Unfortunately, the demands on her time when we got home prevented me from taking my Li'l Freckles inventory. It would have to wait. We did take a shower together which left Big Popi in a rebellious fit. Layla went back to work and I searched out Ski and found him alone in his office. I wanted to try out my pessimistic doubts on the avowed skeptic.

"Hey Ski, do you have any reservations about Pete?"

"You mean besides him seeming dumber than a reality show, can't shoot, can't fight and he looks like a heart attack waiting to happen."

"Don't forget that he was strangling the perfectly rape-able naked woman with his clothes on."

"Walter, I'm waiting for the evidence to come in, but I'm with you, something's hinky."

"Double the guard Ski, I'm worried." Ski stood and gripped my hand.

"Okay pal, good call. I'll make a detective outta you yet."

We talked for a while, but it was all speculation. We needed more facts and were dependent on the FBI to provide them. Those of you, who know me, know how much I hate the feds. All those burdensome rules of evidence and stoic faces were only overshadowed by their mind numbing bureaucracy.

Just before dinner time, as I was about to climb the attic stairs to retrieve my angel from the dress mines, the FBI returned. Sophie raced to me and enfolded me in those long arms, kissing my neck and whispering her gratitude.

"Thank you for bringing me back. I didn't even know that was an option until you said those beautiful words. Did you mean them?"

I have been worrying about my charming line of bullshit lately. It has let me down several times in the past few weeks.

"I'm so sorry honey, but I don't even remember what I said. I usually mean what I say though." Sophie's whole demeanor and body language abruptly changed. She went from gushing with love to professional stoicism.

"Well, thank you again Walter."

I knew that my words were the wrong things to say, yet I said them. I felt bad for the girl, but the beautiful agent was already on Layla's radar.

"Everyone go get cleaned up, dinner in twenty minutes."

I continued with my previous mission, but I was worried that I'd handled that badly. These people would be gone in a day or two, but I had to stay and it would be much more comfortable with my unscratched out eyes.

Layla was of course the only one left in the massive design shop. Also, as usual, I got to watch my wife toil at her work station. She was sketching on water color paper and looked as if she were having a difficult time transferring her beautiful mind to the page. She ripped the unfinished artwork off the pad and threw it away. She was frustrated.

"If you don't want that, can I have it?"

By the time I was finished speaking, Layla was up and kissing me.

"No Popi, I won't share my failures. Is it dinner time or are you looking for other pleasures?"

"Dinner can wait, but the FBI is back and I want to pick their brains."

"Is Sophie back?"

"Yes."

"Then, by all means, we mustn't delay your drool session." I thought, uh oh.

Layla needn't have worried because Sophie wasn't speaking to me. Only the full time members of the household were present. Chrissy, Mary, Ski, Rebecca, Gabrielle and Michael plus, of course, the FBI were here. With the two teenagers and the five year old present, discussing the serial killer was inappropriate, so we discussed my trip to Mary's school. Though that visit was just this morning, it seemed to be the ancient past to me.

Mary said, "Daddy you're now a legend at school. People are saying that you kicked Assistant Principal Dyer's butt without throwing a punch. Is that true?"

"Let's just say the punk wasn't nearly as tough as he acts. I did like the Principal though and Lois too."

Layla's ears perked up at the mention of another female. This Sophie thing has her hyper-jealous.

"Mary, who is this Lois?" Mary looked at me, worried that she'd said the wrong thing.

"Don't worry mom. She's just an old evil battle-axe who daddy tamed with his charming smile." Layla enjoyed being called mom so much that she calmed right down.

"Mary dear, put yourself in her lonely shoes and you might understand her a little better."

"Yes ma'am, the rumor is that after you slapped Mr. Dyer silly, Principal Welling fired him for covering for the violent jocks. Is that true daddy?" I considered this for a moment.

"In the end, it wasn't my doing. It was beauty that slayed the savage beast. It was you, Mary, who gathered the evidence and cared enough to go against the popular kids. You should be the legend. There may be some pushback from the jocks, but never let that stop you from doing what you know in your heart to be right."

Ski said, "He's right Squirt and we're all proud of you." Mary blushed.

"Mary you're a hero. Next year we're going to get you elected President of the student council," said Chrissy, with a warm hug for her sister.

After dinner, I asked Don and his team to give us a briefing on the evidence in my office. Once settled with a drink in our hands, Don started.

"Walter, it's a slam dunk. We have Pete's DNA and fingerprints on the letter and eight of the fourteen bodies. We have two very credible eye witnesses to his kidnapping and attempted murder of a federal agent."

"I agree with everything you're saying Don, but there are some anomalies that need explanation." Don looked resigned to listen because he felt he owed me one.

"Okay Walter, let's hear it."

"First some questions, who is Pete, what's he do for a living and is he as dumb as he looks?" Don smiled and nodded to Mike.

"Peter Ray Vaughn, born November 13th 1963 in Houston Texas, he's 6'2" 328 pounds. Pete has worked in numerous fields over the years, mainly in janitorial and grounds keeping. In 2000 he got his current and better paying job at a large Cincinnati Cemetery. It's unclear what his duties are. As for the last question, the simple answer is yes. His High School rated his IQ at 76." They had a lot so far.

"How could he afford my old house? Claire sold it three years ago for 210,000 dollars." Jon took over.

"He apparently came into a large sum of money in 2012. He paid cash for the house."

I was ready to summarize my misgivings.

"Thank you all for your hard work and dedication. Yes, Layla and I found Pete and Sophie, but it was your research that guided us. It's obvious that Pete is a major part of this fifteen year long series of gruesome murders, but I don't believe Pete is fit enough or smart enough to get away with this for so long on his own. Why didn't he rape Sophie?"

Sophie stood and angrily said, "How do you know he didn't rape me? You didn't even ask." I considered my next comments carefully lest I make the situation worse

"Sophie, I know you went through hell, but I've known victims of violent rape and you didn't show any signs of that horrible trauma. Why didn't he rape you? Pete had his incredibly beautiful victim at his mercy, yet he wasn't even aroused while he was killing you. I believe that the brains of the team normally does the raping of his living victims and the strangling. He then cleans all traces of himself off the body and turns her over to Pete, who is now very turned on by the poor dead girl. He has his perverted way with the corpse, leaving the evidence that will rightfully get him a death sentence." Don appeared to be intrigued, but unconvinced.

"So why wasn't Mr. Brains there today? He had a beautiful victim naked and tied down. According to your theory, he should have been present to strangle and rape her."

Ski, in my defense, said, "He may have been spooked by the botched plan and may have even found out that the FBI was on his trail. He may have instructed Pete to eliminate Sophie."

Don stood and pulled out his phone.

"Goddamn it Walter, I already called the Director and told him it was all wrapped up." The angry cop made the difficult call.

# THE REJECTS

Sophie wouldn't even look at Popi much less speak to him. I took this to mean that Popi had clumsily let her know that he was unavailable for anything other than a platonic friendship. I felt bad for her even though she was after my husband. I know how it feels to desire someone so much that your moral compass goes askew. I also felt bad for Popi because I knew he had no desire hurt Sophie. He only made her angry to soothe my irrational jealousy. Still, his tactics worked and made me feel good. I know that sounds selfish, but I can't help it. One feels what one feels.

The FBI was staying for a few days. Don didn't want to move twice so he was waiting for the incoming evidence to guide his next move. He also made it clear that Popi and I were not going to be involved in his investigation.

"If you're good, I'll give you a nightly briefing."

Popi was okay with this. Besides, Popi and I would be very busy for the next two days, though he didn't know it yet. Eight Rejects were spending the weekend, Jacob Smoot and his friends.

Jacob had sent me an email with a group photo attached, giving me an instant idea of the work involved. They would need new clothes, hair and makeup or rather, in one case, a few pounds less makeup. They would need personal hygiene, grooming and social skills classes. The four girls had it made because I had enlisted the aid of four fashion models to assist me. The boys had as a role model, only Popi. I had considered asking Kurt to help, but I was afraid that he'd shoot them. Just kidding, I didn't think he would have the patience.

I had not told Popi about the makeover camp because I knew that he'd be against it. Don't get me wrong, Popi loves to help people. It's just that he is opposed to trying to change them, holding that their freedom of choice has made them the way they are. I had a different theory. I think these good kids desired to change into more mainstream teens, but they were being held back by their family's lack of knowledge and money. We had the knowledge and tons of money. I would have to sweet talk Popi tonight.

In bed that night, Popi only wanted to talk about Pete's phantom partner. He was still in his disturbingly predictable overprotective persona. I knew that I would have to handle him delicately.

"Popi, if Pete does have a partner, he doesn't have the skills to come after us. His MO is to study his prey and have his henchman do the dangerous part. He's a coward."

"You're right Sweetheart. I'm going to try to be patient and let Don's team ferret the punk out."

"Good idea, will you read me another letter? We're almost done with them."

With an evil grin, Popi said, "Okay Li'l Freckles, but remember, if we get another psycho, it may negate the Zen state you just guided me into."

I was busted yet still it worked.

Dear Layla and Popi

My name is Sylvia. You don't know me, but I was a close friend of Holly Hendricks. I was with her at the mall on June 26th 2011 when we were approached by Harold Sparks. Holly and I just had our hair cut and dyed the previous weekend. We were trying to look like Li'l Freckles. Holly was more successful because she was short and petite. Harold said that he really loved our look though I could tell he was mostly focused on Holly. He told us that he was Li'l Freckles' publicist and that he had a meeting with her that evening.

He showed us some pictures of her hugging and kissing him. He wrote down his address and said he would get us a short meeting with our idol at eight that evening. We laughed and fantasized all the way home, giddy with excitement.

Holly, with a dreamy look, said, "Syl, maybe Popi will be there too."

We both went home to get permission from our moms and made a pact, either we both go or no one goes. My mom of course said no way. I put up a small fight, but knew it was futile. I called Holly with the bad news.

"I'm sorry Holly but my mom is being a big dick."

"You told her we were going to meet Li'l Freckles? I just told Elvira that we were going to the church festival."

I reminded her of our pact and she promised to honor it. It was the last time I talked to her. The next day we learned that Holly was missing and my mom convinced me to keep this all a secret, which I have until now. I didn't hear about the three girls, almost four, the monster killed after Holly until you two killed him. When I saw the pictures, I knew that keeping quiet was not only wrong, but criminal. They all looked just like me trying to look like Li'l Freckles.

Please believe me. I still love you guys, though I no longer pretend to be you, Layla. I don't blame you for anything, but I do blame myself. That is why I've decided to leave it up to you, Popi and Layla, whether I live or die. It is April-Fools Day as I write, but please don't be fooled into believing that I'm not serious. Please call me by May first or your message, in your silence, will be perfectly clear.

With love, your fan, Sylvia Lyn Cooper

"My God Popi that's today. What time is it?"

"Oh shit, it's 11:45." Popi was furiously dialing his phone. "DeeDee listen, find Sylvia Lyn Cooper. I think she's in Tampa. She is threatening to commit suicide if Layla or I don't call her by midnight tonight. I need her cell ASAP."

Popi stayed on the line as Triple D did his research and the minutes ticked by. Popi told me to get my phone ready and I dialed as he said the numbers. It rang. I looked at the time, 11:56. After the second ring Sylvia picked up.

"Hello, is it really you Layla."

"Yes and Popi's here too. You're on speaker."

"Sylvia."

"Yes Popi."

"You were just a child. Don't be so hard on yourself. We all make mistakes in judgement once in a while."

"But Popi, some of those girls may have lived if I had just told the truth." I couldn't remain silent.

"Sylvia, we'll never know if that's true or not, but it doesn't matter. What matters is what you do the next time you have a dreadful decision to make." Popi finished my thought.

"Honey, if you're gone, who is going to save the next people at risk?"

We talked with the poor tortured young lady, she was eighteen now, for almost two hours. She agreed to visit Triple D in the morning so we could help her in her journey of atonement. Popi and I were emotionally spent, it was after two and I still hadn't told Popi about the impending reject invasion. Of course, I was grateful that we got to the letter in time, but my sneaky manipulation of my Popi's mood was thwarted. I made slow patient love to my man as he drifted off to sleep with a sweet smile.

# DIABOLICAL AMBUSH

I awoke at eight on Saturday morning. I was alone. I yawned and stretched, unsure if I was ready to rise. I did rise and looked out the window. The weather was fair, so why wasn't I running. I put on my fancy old swimsuit and headed down to the kitchen. Only Briggs and his team, except Jon, were there drinking coffee. I filled my cup and sat at my normal spot. When Sophie saw that I was staying, she hurriedly left the room.

Don asked. "What the hell is up with you two?"

"I don't know Don, but she may be embarrassed that I saw her naked."

"I'd think that saving her life would make up for that." I shrugged.

"Do you have anything new on Pete and his associate?"

"We're going to Pete's workplace this morning. Hopefully we'll identify his known associates. If there is a Mr. Brain, he shouldn't be hard to spot. According to our profile, he'll be a small forty to fifty year old white guy. He'll be neat, tidy, smart and unimposing. Mr. Brain is a college educated, well paid and maybe even rich man, with a wife and kids."

"Wow, Don, it sounds like he's as good as caught. Have you interrogated Pete yet?"

"First of all Walter, identifying Mr. Brain and proving it are two separate things. We can't talk to Pete until the doctors say he is recovered from the concussion he got from your sweet tempered wife." We both laughed at that.

"Have you seen Layla this morning?"

"Ski and Rebecca took her and the Angels shopping in Dayton. I sent Jon with them for added security."

Something was up. Layla never leaves the property without telling me. I wasn't worried about her safety, but something was definitely up.

"When they get back, we'll be packing up and leaving for a hotel closer to Cincinnati. I'm leaving one agent here to keep an extra eye on Layla."

"Thank you Don. You're welcome back any time."

I picked up my paper, topped off my coffee and headed to my usually picturesque reading room, the indoor pool. I strolled, in innocence, into the room, only to walk into a devious ambush. Mary and Chrissy were in the pool. Mary was diving from the two meter board and Chrissy was floating on a blow-up mat. They were both, as usual, looking cute in their skimpy bikinis. This was normal, but all was not normal, not by a long shot. Standing near the small changing room, gawking at my daughters, were Jacob Smoot and his three misfit friends, the Rejects.

I yelled, "Smoot!" He flinched and looked at me. He was terrified. "You Knuckleheads get over here." The awkward boy rallied his crew and they shambled their way to me. I gave Jacob the key to my den.

"Take your wolf pack to my office and sit there quietly. Don't touch anything." I turned my attention to the girls who now stood nearby. "What the hell is going on here and why are you teasing those weird boys."

"We weren't teasing daddy, we were swimming," Mary said earnestly.

"Daddy, we can't help the way we look. Boys are crazy about us." Chrissy was less earnest.

"Okay Cupcake I'm sorry. Who invited those girl crazy boys here?" Both of my daughters kissed my cheek.

"I don't know Daddy," they said like an echo, as they giggled and jiggled out the door.

I called Layla and got her voicemail.

"Hi this is Layla. I can't talk right now so leave a message unless you're Popi. Popi, please see to my guests while I'm away. If you want to make yourself useful, teach Jacob and his friends how to be honorable Marines. I love you Popi. I'll be home at one."

The minx had hijacked me into some misguided plan to civilize these odd souls whether they wanted it or not. She felt that all kids wanted the same things, the things that she wanted as a girl. I knew better. I knew that their very identities as humans depended upon their differences. The problem is that they, like me, are ensnared in Layla's trap. Now that they have seen the beautiful women in my home, women who treated them kindly, they were hooked. Their natural balance has been upset.

I entered the den and found the four odd kids sitting quietly as instructed on my sofa. I eschewed the desk and sat in the overstuffed leather chair.

"Men, why are you here?" They all looked at each other and finally, silently, picked a spokesman. He was the scrawniest.

"Mrs. Lemon invited us to spend the weekend, Popi."

"What's your name son?" I was grumpy.

"Gordon Bean Popi, but my friends call me Flash."

"Bean, my friends call me Walter, but you guys aren't there yet so you can call me Mr. Lemon. I won't stand for any disrespect toward my daughters or any other females in my home."

Jacob Smoot hesitantly said, "Mr. Lemon, we didn't mean any disrespect. We just have never had such beautiful girls treat us so nice, except when some cheerleader was setting us up for a beat down." This took me aback.

These kids were marginalized and preyed upon by the jocks and their girlfriends. I softened my rigid stance.

"Okay, I know Private Smoot and Private Bean. What are you others called?"

"I'm Private Wood sir," stuttered the fat one."

Private Wood wasn't really fat. He was a few pounds overweight, but the others were so thin that he appeared obese sitting next to them.

"I'm General Funkhauser," said the last one who earned my grudging admiration for his smart-assed introduction.

"Okay General, you're in charge. What did Layla say was the reason for spending the weekend?"

"She said she wanted to teach us how to get along with our peers at school."

"Do you-all think you need to be taught how to survive in society?"

Jacob Smoot said. "Popi, I mean Mr. Lemon, these are my dearest friends and I think we are smarter and better than those violent snobs. We wouldn't want to befriend them even if they begged us."

"What about the girls?" Smoot grinned.

"We would love to have girlfriends, but intellectually, we feel the same about those evil, pretty witches. The smart girls treat us better, but they know that they'll be shunned if they go out with us, so we keep our own council and dream of the days when those people or people like them are working for us."

"I know Jacob and Flash, what's your first name Funkhauser?"

He said, "Otto."

"And you Wood?" I cringed at his unfortunate handle, Hardy Wood. "Private Wood, do you agree with everything your squad has said?"

"Most of it sir, but I'd suffer a score of beat downs for one night with Missy Goodwin." The others chuckled at that.

"Bootcamp is over Marines, so we'll now be on a first name basis. You can call me Walter or Popi and I'll call you Jacob, Otto, Hardy and Flash." They all chose Popi.

"One at a time, tell me why you dress the way you do."

Jacob said, "I wear whatever my mom buys for me. I work on our family farm and my dad gives me fifty bucks weekly allowance. I spend my money on books and scientific equipment. I'm saving up for a new telescope."

Flash said, "I have three older brothers. Like Jake, I have a job and could buy my own clothes, but I prefer to take advantage of the perfectly serviceable free hand-me-downs."

Otto defiantly said, "I buy my own clothes. I dress how I want, which is totally and purposefully different than the stuck-up posers." Only Hardy had reasons beyond his control.

"My dad died two years ago. He was a great man, but he left us in poor financial shape. I work six days a week at the diner and I give all of the money to my mom so she can take care of my little brother and sister."

"We have a big problem, men. My adorable wife thinks you all are in need of her fashion and beauty advice. She has enlisted me to turn you into men. I think you'll be fine without my help, but what I think isn't going to slow her down one bit. I want you guys to go with the flow and accept all the help that she offers. That way I'll be her hero and you-all will be pampered by those five beauties."

Jacob spoke for the Rejects.

"Popi, as you know, I adore your wife and I have great respect for you, but it would be a betrayal to myself and my friends to act like we need someone to change us or to make us better in the eyes of the, quote, normal kids." I had no answer for him.

I drove the boys to Dayton and treated them to an early lunch. They told me about their lives and thanked me for standing up for them against Eli Dyer. I found them to be smart, hardworking and genuine. Yes, they dressed shabbily and could stand a little better grooming, but I admired their pride in their individuality. After lunch, I treated them to a couple of hours at the video arcade. By the time we returned, the girls were back. Layla and the four fashion models, Simone was at the Zoo, looked worn out. The four nerdy girls looked mildly irritated. None were wearing new hairdos, make up or clothes.

# LAYLA REJECTED

I carefully slipped out of bed at six, not wanting to disturb Popi. I was sleep deprived, but excited about todays' activities. At six fifteen the gate guard called as I stepped out of my shower.

"Hi, Harold, are they here?"

"Yes ma'am and they're quite a sight."

I met them at the front door and received pleasant introductions from Jacob. I showed everyone to their rooms. This was the first time that every bedroom in the house was occupied. While they were getting settled, I roused the Angels, who would be spending the day with me and the four girls.

Abby was the smallest. She was 5'1" with unkempt light brown hair. She wore huge, black rimmed glasses which magnified her pretty gray eyes to an uncomfortable degree. She was also Jacob Smoot's cousin and shared his taste for farm fashion. Grace was anything but graceful, being six feet tall and thin as a beanstalk. She wore a baggy flannel lumberjack shirt over baggy jeans. Her face was pretty without make-up.

Barbara, "Call me Babs," Barber was overweight and didn't even try to wear clothes that flattered her figure. Instead she wore a tight blue denim mini skirt over torn black fishnets with motorcycle boots. She had on a top that failed to fully contain her enormous breasts and left her generous midriff bare. Worse than this, she wore a ton of pale white foundation accented with thick black lipstick and eye shadow.

The fourth girl didn't belong here, not because she was black, but because she was pretty, even beautiful. She was dressed in normal teenage fashion, tight blue jeans, a BP&LF t-shirt and bright yellow Nike's. Her name was Tabitha. Before we girls left, I led the boys to the indoor pool.

"You guys can swim and raid the refrigerator, until Popi gets up."

The stretch Limo showed at 7:30 and the adventure began. I was so happy. First we went to the Sheraton for the best brunch buffet in town. Breakfast was great. Listening to their high school stories didn't bring back many memories. Looking back, this was my first clue that things weren't quite as they seemed. Anyway, I was clueless, so step two of my plan began, the mall. Each Angel paired up with a Reject, Kelly with Abby, Charlie with Grace, Jordon with Babs and Brooke with Tabitha.

I said, "Girls, go with your model and pick out two complete outfits. One you choose by yourself and the Angels will pick the second. I'll be bouncing between the groups to observe. Have fun. The teams scattered and I was feeling smug, satisfied and like the great benefactor. I sent Rebecca ahead to report on the progress while I had coffee with Kurt and Jon, who both refused to leave my side.

The mall goers began to gather around us, so I spent my time giving autographs and selfies with the boys and girls. Ski and Jon had to chase away several touchy men.

Rebecca texted me, "Babs has taken Jordon into a small shop called Lady Goth. Jordon looked horrified."

"Not a surprise, Jordon will have to get creative with her choice."

A forty year old grabbed, kissed and groped me in a sneak attack. Kurt punched and floored him then Jon handcuffed him, his knee on the man's neck. He called for a cop who dragged the deranged man away, but we had to move because the onlookers were getting overbearing. My squad fell back to the waiting limo and I let the rest of the Platoon know that I would run things from HQ.

Kelly messaged me, "Abby has purchased bib overalls, a red tube top and three hundred dollar hiking boots."

I replied, "I think you should make your choice very feminine."

Brooke wrote, "Tabitha has selected a wool skirt in light gray, a lacy white top, a cute red sweater and three inch heels. She looked so cute that I want to let her pick her second outfit too."

"Okay, I trust your judgement." I wondered why Tabitha considered herself a Reject.

Finally, Charlie reported in.

"Grace couldn't find anything she liked in the women's sections, so she went to the men's department at Bass Pro Shop and picked out a camouflage duck hunters outfit, including waterproof boots."

"Hang in there honey, A-line skirts and bold print tops look great on tall thin girls."

Over the next few hours the girls returned, laden with their purchases. The enthusiasm from this difficult morning was waning. After a quiet lunch, we headed home. I was unsure of the feasibility of phases 3, 4 and 5 of my failing plan. As we drove through the gates Popi and the boys pulled in behind us. They looked happy.

# GOOD MOURNING SUNSHINE

Layla ran to me.

"Oh Popi, I've made a mess of everything." She was nearly in tears.

Her tears let loose so I took her into my arms, lifting her, kissing her.

"It's okay sweetheart, let's clear the air." I waved Jacob over. "Get everyone into the dining room, the Angels too." As the crowd headed that way, I said, "I take it that your makeover isn't going so well."

"Popi, they're resisting every step of the way. I don't understand what I'm doing wrong." My wife didn't suffer failure well.

"You're incapable of doing wrong. You're perfect in every way, but you don't know everything."

I led my perfect bride to our huge dining room. We entered hand in hand. The Rejects were sitting silently on the left and the Angels, on the right, were attempting to reason with them. I seated Layla on the beautiful side and myself, at the head of the thirty seat mahogany table. I started.

"I get it. You-all are proud of your Reject status, but does that mean that you can't accept generosity from people who want to be kind to you? My Li'l Freckles is the sweetest and kindest person I have ever met and you have made her cry. What was so awful about her, possibly misguided, attempt to help you guys?" No one spoke so I pointed to the large girl with the ghoulish clown make-up.

"You," I pointed, "Introduce yourself and give me an honest answer."

"I'm Barbara Barber. We don't need or want your help. We were looking forward to being your friends, but not the condescension." I looked at my sad Angel.

"Were you condescending toward these people honey?"

"I don't think so Popi, but if they feel that way, I don't know, maybe I was." I pointed to the tall one who looked as though she had something to say.

"I'm Grace Smith. I don't think that Layla was intentionally condescending, but we are very skeptical of do-gooders who think that we are clueless about the way we choose to live our lives."

"Thank you, Grace." I pointed to the cute African-American. "Dear, why are you a Reject?"

"My name is Tabitha Washington. I'm the only black girl in my class. When I enrolled in school last year, I found it very difficult to make friends. There was no overt racism, but all of my attempts to blend in were rewarded with decidedly cool receptions. The Rejects observed this and invited me to sit at their cafeteria table. I was very grateful and soon found these dear sweet, smart kids were the most accepting, non-judgmental people I'd ever met. They have never, not even once, tried to change me, yet they have changed me. They have instilled in me a great pride of who I am."

Jacob Smoot raised his hand as if he were in class.

"Okay Jacob, speak."

"Layla, we all love you and appreciate that you care, but if you can't take us as we are, you join a very long list of people who can't accept us as real people. You become our enemy. You become another assault on our hard earned pride in our Reject selves." Layla was crying again.

"I'm so sorry that I assumed that you guys needed my help. I do want to be your friend and I'll never make you feel unaccepted again. Will you forgive me and give me another chance?"

Of course they all did, and after many hugs all was forgiven. We ended up having a fun filled day, playing games, swimming and eating like teenagers. The reject girls even lightened up enough to put on a fashion show. Layla was thrilled.

In bed that night, Layla was wearing her blue silk pajamas. She asked for my forgiveness for the hectic day.

"Of course, honey, I'd forgive you anything except falling out of love with me." Even though this was my stock answer to that question, it, as usual, melted her heart.

"I knew you would be against interfering with those kids, but my stubbornness convinced me that they needed my help. I still believed this until Tabitha spoke. I then realized that what you have been telling me for years is true. You can never judge a person by his appearance."

"Don't feel bad Li'l Freckles, I've been guilty of the same thing many times."

With all forgiven, I began the dance, the ballet, our lovemaking. I say, I began, because I coaxed my dear Li'l Freckles to lie still while I caressed and kissed every square inch of her perfect body, relishing the sweet feel of her warm flesh through the cool silky fabric. When I kissed her bare little toes, she rightly took this as the signal to become more actively involved. She went wild on her Popi and my alter ego, Big Popi. She didn't let up until Big Popi failed to respond to my enchanted wife's intoxicating kisses.

Layla kissed me awake the next morning. Big Popi's bout of exhaustion was a distant memory. We ran, but my legs felt weak and I lost by a hundred yards. Layla wasn't buying my excuses.

"Take your beating like a man Popi. You sound like a little princess."

"Wow! You don't pull any punches champ." I further drained my lower limbs with sweaty sex before our showers.

With the FBI, Claire and Stump gone, the kitchen was a lot less active. Claire was living in Paris, Stump was living with Sally above the Feed Mill and the FBI had packed up and left. I remembered that Briggs said he was leaving an agent here to protect Layla. I wondered which would stay, though in afterthought, I bet you, my readers, could have guessed. Sophie entered looking beautiful with a cool, nay, icy expression on her lovely, if foreboding face. Being an avowed jackass I said what I knew would cause a rise in the atmospheric tension.

"Good morning sunshine, you're looking extra pissed off this fine day." My happy grin was cruel.

"Save it Lemon, I'm here to protect Layla and nothing more." Her mood was sour.

"Why did Don pick you and why in hell did you accept it?" She was about to answer honestly, but Layla walked in talking.

"Popi, did you make coffee? Oh, I'm sorry. Am I interrupting?"

"No sweetheart, Sophie was about to tell me why Don left her here to look after you and why she chose not to fight that stupid assignment."

Layla and I turned to Sophie in anticipation, Layla expecting the truth and I expecting a lie along the party line.

"I am not in the habit of questioning nor disobeying orders." She took her coffee and briskly left the room.

"I recognize that attitude from the many other women that you have infuriated. You have to fix this Popi."

"She has no reason to feel the way she does. I'll not apologize to sooth her hurt feelings at me not falling hopelessly in love with her." Layla seemed to like the sound of that. I liked the sound of what Layla said next.

"Okay Popi, I'll have a talk with her."

"Thank you sweetheart, remind her that I saved her life twice."

She asked, "Twice Popi?"

"Yeah, once by finding her and then by coaxing her back from four."

"Popi, Hardy Wood's mother is a cook and housekeeper. I want to interview her for a possible job of taking care of some of Claire's duties."

"Sounds good honey, do you want me to tag along?"

"I did, but now I'm thinking that Sophie should start earning her pay."

"You're as devious as you are gorgeous," I said in prelude to a big kiss.

Layla and Sophie left and I retreated to the pool with my coffee and paper. I hoped Mrs. Wood worked out because since Claire left everyone's workload had increased significantly. Stump, though no longer living here, hired some young people he trusted to take care of the property and the outdoor pool. I had taken over the indoor pool. Layla and Gabrielle were doing all of the cooking and though they both loved to cook, it was too much. It would become impossible from September to march, the winter fashion season.

# SOPHIE CRIES

I found Sophie in her room. She answered my knock after a long thirty seconds. Tears were still streaming from her pretty eyes. I hugged her.

"Sophie, will you drive me to an appointment to interview a lady for a cook and housekeeping job. It's not far and afterward we'll go to the diner for a late breakfast and a heart to heart talk."

"Layla, I'll go, but there is nothing to talk about." I felt her dark mood.

"We'll think of something."

The short drive was spent in silence, but for the severe voice from Sophie's GPS. It was hardly a necessity in this rural farm land. The Wood house was in need of a coat of paint, but the grounds were well kept and neat except for a few toys in the front yard. Mrs. Wood met us on the large front porch and introduced herself as Debra. She was a strong stout woman of about forty with a ready smile and short brown hair. She wore a bright red dress, probably her best. We sat in her neat living room on her well-worn, but high quality furniture.

"Debra, I'm looking for a full-time housekeeper, laundress and cook. The cleaning will entail only the kitchen and the common areas. The biggest job is the laundry, but we have a huge laundry room and can handle four loads at the same time. The residents are responsible for picking up their laundered clothes and taking them to their rooms. Still it's a hard job and we'll make sure the person we hire is very well compensated. Do you think you're up to the task?"

"I've been doing this sort of thing since my husband Hardy died over two years ago. As for cooking, I have a culinary arts degree from the University of Dayton and will look forward to using my skills. The biggest problem is my young children. They've lost their father and I need to spend as much time with them as possible."

"How old are they?"

"John is twelve and Cynthia is six."

"I've been thinking about that. I propose that we also hire Hardy to look after the kids, including six year old Michael who is my personal assistants' adorable almost six year old son. We have a small groundskeeper's bungalow which we will make available to your family so you can spend time with your children throughout the day.

When can you start Debra?" I was already sold on the nice woman.

"Monday, thank you Layla." The grateful woman hugged me. "I'm so excited."

Sophie drove to the diner after the hour long meeting with our new employee. I refused to think of her as a servant and hoped that she would naturally meld with our strange, lovable family. At the diner, Sophie balked at going in to discuss her feelings.

"Honey, its' only a lunch and you don't have to talk about anything uncomfortable. You may think that I'm the jealous wife with some agenda, but that's not it. I just want peace in my house and family."

"We're not family Layla." That hurt a little, but maybe she didn't know about the BP&LF family.

"Come in and I'll explain why we're now related." She was intrigued enough to accept a free lunch.

"Why are you being so nice to me, Layla? I practically tried to steal your husband."

"I can't say that I wasn't jealous of you at first, but I know in my heart how much Popi adores me. I trust him completely. There is no woman in the seven realms who could take him away from me."

"Layla he's a man. In my experience, they're all dogs who can't help but stray."

"My Sophie, I can tell you've been hurt many times, but still, it must be hard living without hope of finding the perfect man for you." I failed to break through her darkness.

"I did find that perfect man, but he's rejected me."

"Anyway, the BP&LF family is a large group of people who have all been hurt by people who've tried to kill Popi and me. Your brother Sam is a member and is very active on our web site. You are one of us now. Triple D will be in touch soon with the details and your account information."

"I don't want your money. You don't have to pay me off to go away."

"It's out of my control. If you don't spend the money, it will still keep coming until you die. Tell me why you are so mad at Popi." She began weeping again.

"He told me that he loved me, but a few hours later, he didn't even remember it. I wish that I'd just stayed dead." This moved me.

"Don't say that. Popi loves a lot of people. He doesn't want to be their lovers. Besides, he only said he didn't remember to sooth my jealous fury. Try forgiving him. I'd bet it wouldn't be ten seconds before he loves you again. After all, you're smart, courageous and beautiful, three of his favorite things." Sophie cried.

Back at home, Sophie promised to consider everything we discussed. I think she wanted to forgive Popi, but was afraid that he would treat her coldly again. I knew Popi and I knew that he would be thrilled to have another adoring, beautiful woman in his stable. Popi loves to be loved and admired by anyone, but most especially by beautiful women. I don't really consider this a character flaw, but more of an endearing trait. He hates when people dislike him.

I was thinking about tracking down my husband to clue him into my talk with the damaged girl. Instead I decided to let the drama play out without further interference from me, the cause of the problem. I say this because Popi only denied his affection for the girl whose life he saved, to make me happy. Though it worked, the collateral damage was unacceptable. Popi didn't even flirt with Sophie until he was trying to urge her to return to her dying body. I certainly don't blame him for this. I went to work and let the chips fall where they may.

# CHARMING LINE OF BULLSHIT

I read my paper, drank uncountable cups of coffee, and swam with several beautiful, flirting women while Layla and Sophie were away. Ever since Sophie let me have it for my denial of feelings for her, I've been thinking about my need to be loved by these women in my life. In my youth, I didn't feel this way. I could care less for people's opinion of me. When I met Claire, I was a bit of a player. I was dating girls who I really didn't care about except for the things that I wanted from them, sex. Claire was a game changer.

Although I fell instantly in love with her, I didn't really change my flirtatious ways and Claire was surprisingly okay with this. She had absolute confidence in my love for her so I felt no pressure to change. By the time I fell in love with Layla I was, at forty-eight, thrown into a situation where thousands of girls and women began eagerly trying to bed me. I have always been a loyal boyfriend and husband with one glaring exception, my betrayal of my vow to Claire.

I have forgiven myself for this because of the extraordinary circumstances, serial killers, supernatural beings and of course the spectacular nature of my coconspirator, Layla. Now I'm questioning my behavior. Maybe I need to modify my flirtatious ways. Maybe I'm being selfish. I do get pleasure from the devotion of others, men and woman, but have never considered that I may be hurting them. I have had to step in several times and quash the over emotional desires of a few girls who sought to claim me for a sexual relationship, most notably Jordon Woo.

I'm a confident man who doesn't shy away from difficult situations, but I'd rather fight a Tiger barehanded than face a love-struck woman who believes that I want her for a lover. Let me make this perfectly clear. There isn't a woman who, in the entire seven realms, could ever tempt me to betray Layla's love for me. Layla knows this, but like most women, she has an ingrained jealous streak. I try not to trigger this, occasionally unsuccessfully. Instead of standing up to my dear wife's jealousy, I foolishly and selfishly rebuffed the traumatized FBI agent when she needed tenderness and empathy. This is on me and if Layla can open the door, I'll carry Sophie and me to the other side and make this right.

I called the gate guard and asked if Layla had returned.

"Yes sir Popi, about fifteen minutes ago."

I took this to mean that I was on my own. Layla was rightly bowing out. I took my time on the long walk to room twelve. I was not looking forward to this charged situation. I began to plot a strategy, but stopped myself, knowing that there wasn't a chance in hell that I'd follow my own plan. I got to twelve and took a deep calming breath. I realized that I was barefoot and wearing just my damp swimsuit. I did the breath thing again and lightly rapped on the solid mahogany door. Sophie threw open the door. She threw herself into my arms and kissed me ferociously.

"Popi, I forgive you. I'm sorry I got so angry." I kissed her quiet.

"No Sophie, please don't apologized, this is completely my fault. I do remember what I said to bring you back and I did mean those words."

"But Popi, why did you lie?" We were in her room now. I was afraid that she was guiding me toward the bed.

"I lied because I didn't want you to believe that we could actually be together."

"If you love me, why can't we be together?"

"You know why sweetheart, Layla. The love I have for her trumps my love for everyone else all put together." Sophie smiled.

"Okay Popi, relax. I'm just pulling your chain for being so insensitive, but since you saved my life, I'll let you off the hook."

She hugged me again then held out her hand and asked, "Friends?" I took her hand and pulled her into my arms?

"Not handshake friends," I kissed her and matched the ferocity of her kiss with mine, "Kissing friends." She was a bit taken aback by this.

"Wow, I like being kissing friends. Are you sure you love Layla that much?"

"Yes I'm afraid so. I want you to help me catch the shithead who tried to take Layla and I'm sure that it wasn't that knucklehead Pete. Will you help me?" She thought about this for a few moments.

"Are you sure that he actually exists?"

I knew that the FBI found it inconvenient that there was a ghost evil doer and wouldn't search for long.

"I'm Positive. Is there any chance that I could talk to Pete?"

She laughed. To me, her laughter sounded like confirmation of her forgiveness.

"Pete has lawyered up and won't be talking to the law."

"Can you get me the name of his lawyer?"

"Why do I feel that if I say yes my career will be over, but yes?"

At lunch, I was in the catbird seat between Layla and Sophie. Both types of tension were gone, Layla's jealousy and Sophie's feelings of rejection. I think my charming line of bullshit is back.

"Li'l Freckles, I'm driving to Cincinnati this afternoon and I need you to come along?"

"Why are we going, Popi?"

"We are going to see Pete's Weasel attorney to ask him to let us talk to Pete."

Sophie asked, "Why in hell would he do that?"

"If I'm right, Pete will be facing one count of attempted murder and fourteen counts of abuse of a corpse, no murder charges." Layla was appalled.

"But Popi, Pete could be out in ten or twenty years."

"Pete is sick and dangerous, but Mr. Brain is a psychotic killer who won't quit until we put him down. If we can't at least find evidence of his existence, many more will die."

"The FBI will find him if he exists," Sophie said.

"Sophie, don't you see that if nothing jumps out at you guys, you'll just assume that Pete acted alone."

"Isn't it possible that he did?"

"That's another reason to talk to Pete. Maybe he's not as dumb as he looks and acts."

"Popi, you're putting me in a tough spot. I'm honor bound to report this to SSA Briggs."

"I would never ask you to compromise your honor, sweetheart."

So off we went to downtown Cincinnati. Layla was dressed as I had asked and she really looked cute in the clothes she hadn't worn in years. After a minor meltdown, Don told Sophie to stick with Layla and to report in frequently. I was formulating a strategy to convince the slick attorney that it was in his interest to talk to us. All I had was his name and firm. It was a large, well-known local Partnership, Barnett, Feingold and Klein. The most loyal of my readers will recall those lawyers from my first book. I killed both Feingold and Klein or rather the men who impersonated them.

Their front desk lady was a lovely, but strict Sergeant at Arms and refused to get me an unscheduled meeting with the grand Poobah, so I settled for a junior attorney named Jerrod Knotts. He was my real target, Pete's lawyer. I wasn't expecting a twenty-year-old kid, but he turned out to be one of Layla's biggest fans. We were in like Flint, Layla and me that is. Sophie had to wait in the lobby. Jerod was fawning all over my wife, completely ignoring me.

"Mr. Knotts, we want to talk to Peter Vaughn."

"I'm sorry Mr. Lemon, but you are both witnesses against my client. I can't possibly allow that."

"What if I told you that we believe that Pete is not guilty of the fourteen murders with which he is about to be charged?"

"I'd say that you are crazy, but I'm definitely interested. Mr. Klein assigned me to this case because he believes that it's unwinnable. If I were to get him off, my career would be golden."

"Pete is definitely guilty of kidnapping and attempted murder of a federal agent and we will testify to that. I believe that he is innocent of the murders of the fourteen girls, but I need his help to prove this. As an added incentive, I'll provide a sworn statement admitting that I illegally broke into his house."

Jerod was sold and immediately made the call to the County Courthouse lock-up for access to his client for him and two consultants. We met Jerod there two hours later. Sophie came along, but had to wait outside the interview room with the guard. She was able to observe through the small window in the door. Layla also waited outside the room until I was ready for her. Pete was handcuffed to a steel ring attached to the bolted down table. He was still sporting the injuries inflicted on him by my fiery bride though he no longer wore the eyepatch.

"What do you want?" He was surprised to see me.

"Mr. Vaughn, I want to ask you a few questions. I've guaranteed your lawyer that nothing you tell me will be recorded or used against you in court." He looked at his mouthpiece who nodded.

"Okay Popi, I wanted to thank you for saving that poor girl. I didn't want to hurt her. I've never wanted to hurt her. I never wanted to hurt nobody."

"Then why were you killing her when I found you?"

"I can't tell you that or he'll kill me." I ignored this.

"Did you write me that letter?"

"Yes, it was the only letter I ever wrote. Was it good? Did you like it?"

"Yes Pete, it was very nice, but there was one thing that I didn't understand. What did you mean by mi Casa es su casa?"

Pete put his clumsy fat finger to his lips and whispered, "Sssh, it's a big secret."

"You don't know what it means do you Pete?"

"No, but he says it means that I live in your old house in a secret language."

It was time for Pete to meet Layla, so I went to the door and invited her in. Pete saw Sophie in the hall. Laya walked in wearing, according to Pete's letter, his favorite outfit, her red leather miniskirt and white button down shirt with a matching red leather necktie and platform shoes. Pete ignored the fetching Li'l Freckles.

"The girl's here? Will you ask her if she'll talk to me?"

I looked at the lawyer who shrugged. While I went to the door Layla spoke to Pete.

"Do you like my outfit Pete?"

"Yes, it's pretty, you're pretty too. I watched you for the longest time. I don't blame you for hurting me. You were just trying to protect you and your friend."

"Thank you Pete, that makes me feel better." Sophie was hesitant and Pete tried to put her at ease.

"Come in miss. I won't hurt you no more. Even without the chains, I won't hurt you no more." Sophie wasn't mollified.

"Why did you hurt me the first place and why didn't you rape me?" Pete started crying.

"I'm so, so sorry. It weren't my idea and I would never rape no one. When he found out that you was a cop he said that I had to kill you. I'm glad you're alright. I'm glad that Popi and she saved you. Will you forgive me?"

Sophie, ever the cop, said, "If you admit to all the bad things that you have done, I'll forgive you."

"I will Miss, I promise." Pete looked relieved.

He also looked completely unimpressed with Layla and her youthful sexy clothes. I asked Sophie to leave the room.

"Pete I need you to tell me the name of the man who told you to kill Sophie."

"I can't do that 'cause he'll kill me and send me to hell."

"Pete, there is a hell, but there is also a place where people who do evil things can earn forgiveness. When you die, you'll be given the chance to be a good person in your next life."

"How do you know if that's true?"

"I've been there and It's kinda gray and boring, but not scary. Besides, if you don't tell me, Sophie will never forgive you." The thought of this horrified the large, dumb, dangerous man.

"He's my boss, Marcus, but it weren't really him. It was his dark shadow who only comes out every year at tax time."

Pete went on to say that the shadow demon came every year, but only between mid-April and Late May.

"The Demon only leaves Marcus alone after he brings him a pretty young girl. That's what Marcus needs me for, not picking the girl, but only for catching her. He pays me real good and even bought me a new house."

"Have you seen this Demon?"

"It just looks like a puff of black smoke, but I seen the way Marcus changes when the Shadow goes into him and it ain't pretty. He is very mean to me."

# The Spontaneous Ejaculation

I met Popi for lunch and was cautiously happy to find him laughing and joking with Sophie. She was glowingly beautiful and I automatically had a jealous thought. What can make a girl glow like that? I told my jealous mind to pipe down and enjoy the peace in my house.

"Hi Sophie, you seem so much happier." Her reply was telling.

"I decided to take your advice and forgive your stray dog."

Popi didn't understand the inside joke, but he astutely did not comment.

We all went downtown to find Pete's lawyer at Feinstein and Klein. I watched as Popi used, not his charm, but reverse psychology to get the high powered receptionist to guide us to Pete's lawyer, Jerod. The young lawyer was very sweet and handsome. Popi convinced him that talking to Pete could help his despicable client. We went to the jail where Sophie and I waited in the hall while Popi took a crack at Pete. He said he'd call for me after a few minutes, but Sophie was barred from the room.

When Popi opened the door and asked me in, I was expecting a reaction from Pete. After all, I was wearing the outfit that, according to the letter, drove him mad with desire for me. Pete looked past me at Sophie. He asked to talk to her. I was miffed.

"Pete, do you like my outfit?"

He said it was pretty and so was I, but he was actually focused on Sophie. He did forgive me for hurting him. Now I can sleep at night. He also asked Sophie to forgive him. She agreed if he would fess up. He seemed relieved.

Popi asked Pete to name his partner, but he refused, claiming fear of being killed and sent to hell. Popi used his experience in the second realm and the threat of withholding Sophie's forgiveness to get him singing like a canary. I really didn't believe that Pete had a partner until he failed to react to my sexy clothes. Popi saw that this upset me, but had a ready answer.

"I know you're shocked that Pete didn't start drooling when he saw you looking so sexy. Hell, I was drooling. Now that we know that Mr. Brain is Marcus, I can guarantee that he won't be able to hide his lust for you. He's gonna have a spontaneous ejaculation." I felt better.

It was almost five when we arrived at the offices of Sweet Haven Cemetery. It was an idyllic pastoral setting. All the markers were bronze plaques which were flat on the ground, giving unobstructed views of the lovely green, rolling landscape. My mood was further elevated by the wolf-like leers cast at me by the office workers fleeing for home. The modern offices were bright and cheery. The pretty receptionist manned her post though her squad had deserted her. As I say, she was pretty, so this was a job for Popi.

"Hello Linsey, Walter Lemon to see Marcus, is he still here?" He had to do or say no more.

"Oh Popi, I can't believe it. My, you're so strong." The girl was all over him.

She had wrapped herself around my sexy husband. Popi finally got her calmed down enough to ring for Mr. Marcus Samson, the President.

"Mr. Samson, Walter Lemon to see you."

While we were waiting Linsey volunteered that Marcus was

always in because he had an apartment on the grounds. She also acknowledged Sophie and me for the first time.

"Oh, are you with Popi?"

Linsey sent us back to Mr. Samson's office and Popi planned.

"Li'l Freckles, you wait outside the door again until he throws us out. Sophie, don't show your creds unless its' necessary."

Popi and Sophie walked in without knocking, leaving the door ajar so I could eavesdrop. There was some small talk, but soon Popi got to the point.

"Marcus, I've just been to see Pete and he had some interesting things to say about you."

"Walter, you must know that he's a disturbed man. I took him under my wing because he, as much as he tried, couldn't make a single friend here."

"So you didn't know that he was murdering those girls?" The tiny man bristled at this.

"Of course I didn't know and I'm still not convinced that he killed anyone." Popi had intentionally pissed off the unseen man. He wanted him on edge.

"Pete also said that a black shadow takes over your body every spring and that it makes you bring him a young girl."

"That's preposterous. I want you both out. I've already talked to the FBI and I'll not answer to the likes of you, get out." I took this as my cue. Marcus was set up for an honest reaction. I pushed the door open and strutted into the fray. Marcus Samson was not what I expected from his voice and his name, my only clues. He was about 5' 3" 110 Lbs. with slicked back receding black hair and sporting a cute well waxed handlebar mustache. Marcus wore a beautifully tailored black three piece suit and expensive Italian shoes. He was a miniature Snidely Whiplash. I'd bet he has a tiny black top hat and cape stashed somewhere. Two things happened when I came into his view. First he suddenly acquired a stammer.

"LaLaLayla wawawhat are you dododoing hehehere?"

The second thing was really two, his black wool trousers pitched a tent and he was forced to sit, too late to hide his discomfort. Popi was right, Marcus wrote that letter. He's the one who wanted to rape and kill me. He needed Pete because most teenage girls could easily kick his butt. Popi was sarcastic.

"Wow Marky-Mark, you seem a bit smitten by my cute wife. Wouldn't you just love to get your hands around her graceful, supple neck?"

The little man was staring at me. He was taking in the very essence of me and his predatory eyes visited every inch of me. I was no longer happy that we had exposed him. That's how he made me feel, exposed and laid bare before that savage hunger inside of him. He wasn't insisting that we leave any longer because he knew that I'd leave too. Popi kept baiting him.

"Do you want me to tie her down so she can't hurt you? Come honey, the great Samson needs help getting you under control."

I took it upon myself to go off script and walked over to the seated, excited man. I put my arm around his neck and kissed him on his sweaty cheek.

"Don't tease him Popi, I think he's cute."

I accidentally on purpose, knocked a pen off his desk and bent over to retrieve it. This gave him a good look at my butt and again two things happened. He squeezed my butt and grunted. Yes, you guessed it. He erupted into the mythical spontaneous ejaculation, soiling those expensive wool trousers. I consoled him.

"That's okay sweetie. Not everyone can be Big Popi." This comment reignited his ire.

"That's it, I'm calling the police." On cue, Sophie pulled out her FBI ID.

"That won't be necessary Mr. Samson. The FBI is about to turn your life upside down. We are going to make you wish that you really had a black shadow to blame for this." Marcus regained his composure.

"My life is an open book, but for now I'll have to ask you to communicate through my Lawyer."

He handed me Jerod's business card, stroking my hand at the exchange. We both shivered, he from extreme desire and I from a bad case of the creeps. This is when the investigation went from maniac serial killer to something far more dangerous.

# THE SHADOW

In my mind, we had enough evidence to prove that Marcus Samson was the serial killer, but I knew that the FBI would need a lot more. By the little perverts' reaction to Layla and his uncontrollable need to touch her, I knew that once he chose a victim, he was totally fixated on her. This, of course, sealed his fate with me. If the Feds couldn't at least put him away for his crimes, I had enough to act on my own. Just before we left, we heard a rustling from his closet.

"Who is hiding in your closet, Samson?"

"That's none of your business Lemon. Get the hell out." I went to the closet door. "If you dare open that door without a warrant, I'll sue you and the FBI." I was undeterred, but Sophie warned me.

"He's right Popi." I thought about this.

"Sophie, maybe you should leave." She stayed.

I whipped the door open. I was expecting to find someone lurking, but nobody was there. I saw relief on the miniature perverts' face. The closet had just the normal clutter, an umbrella, a camel hair coat, a cashmere sweater and scarf and several pairs of expensive footwear. There was nothing that could have made that noise. I looked to the top shelf and saw nothing but shadow. I was about to close the door when

I had a thought. The room was fairly bright so that shadow shouldn't be nearly so dark.

I took the umbrella and poked and rattled it around that top shelf. First there was a growling hiss then the shadow leapt into my face. I reeled backwards, feeling that filthy, evil being trying to enter me. It was unsuccessful. Layla screamed and Sophie pulled her weapon. I grabbed the shadow and threw it against the wall. It hissed again and flew around the room. Finally, having no ready escape, it flew into Marcus Samson's mouth. He acquired a big maniacal grin.

"This is going to make you look like a bunch of crackpots when you put it in your report," said the demon through those cocky grinning teeth.

Layla and Sophie were clinging to me.

"Samson, what the hell was that?" He ignored the question. He was leering at Sophie.

"When that corpse fucker Pete told me how juicy you are, I definitely wanted to give you my goodbye and good fuck." Then he said what landed me in jail. "Layla, I haven't given up on you. I can't wait to fuck you to death."

I knocked the demon out with the first punch, but I was not satisfied with that. Sophie and Layla were able to stop me before I killed him. Layla snuck in a kiss to my face because she knew that the spell would quench my killing colors. Linsey had called the police, who were not swayed by Sophie's credentials. I was arrested and Marcus Samson was hauled away in an ambulance.

"Sophie, Layla, keep the spooky stuff to yourselves and don't let each other out of your sights. I mean it, not for a minute. Call DeeDee, Ski and Briggs. Tell Lilly that I need to see her."

I wanted to give them both a little kiss, but with my hands cuffed behind me, I wouldn't be able to hide Big Popi. Such is my charmed life. I was processed, booked and transferred to the county lock-up where I shared a small cell with two other men in the four bed dungeon. Being a late comer, I got a top bunk. Both of my roommates, a white guy named Steve and a black guy named D'Ron, were here for trafficking in drugs. I wasn't about to judge these men, having just severely beaten a tiny man who was seventy pounds lighter than me. Still, I found their chosen profession repugnant.

Having missed dinner, I lay on my upper bunk and tried to sleep through the constant cacophony of hollering from the disgruntled criminals. I eventually drifted off, dreaming of the black shadow. In the midst of tearing the unclean phantasm to shreds, Lily appeared in her fifteen year old body wearing a corrections officer's uniform.

"Prisoner 57069-0516 front and center." I dropped the tattered demon and came to her.

"Lilly dear, are you here to spring me?" She hugged me.

"No Walter, you'll make bail after your arraignment in the morning."

"Do you know what the hell that thing is, the one I was just killing?"

"Can you conjure him for me again, whole like you first saw him?"

I closed my already closed eyes and tried to recall my whole interaction with the shadow. It wasn't difficult. The incident was seared into my mind.

"Is it some sort of demon, honey?"

"Walter, there are no demons in the strict sense of the word. There are only insane and evil spirits who have escaped from the second realm. This is rare, but not unheard of. They are usually caught by the second realm security force and sent to one."

"This guy has been killing for fifteen years."

"I think I know what is going on here. This rogue spirit has found a living confederate on three who has invited him to hide inside of him. This can only happen with the sick permission of the host, so the man is just as much to blame for the evil done to others. He just doesn't have the courage to do it himself." I took my dear friend into my dream arms and gave her a big kiss.

"Thank you Lilly, now I don't feel so bad about beating that little man."

"That evil spirit can only stay inside the man for a short time, an hour at the most, so he must leave almost all of his energy with the host or risk detection by the authorities. The spirit appears as a shadow because he's powerless to project any solid looking façade and he can't appear completely invisible because that takes energy too. If he becomes completely drained he'll be automatically pulled back to two."

After a breakfast of runny scrambled eggs, soggy toast and a small carton of room temperature milk, all of which I gave to my cellmates, I was taken in handcuffs to the county courthouse. Triple D was there.

"Walter, did you really beat that midget?"

"That midget has killed fourteen teenage girls and has threatened to make Layla next, so yes."

"Okay brother, you must plead not guilty or they may just keep you locked up."

"You can't let that happen DeeDee, that mutt is still after Layla and Sophie."

"Sophie?"

"It's a long story, but she's an FBI agent who was very nearly victim number fifteen. Layla and I rescued her just in time."

Outside the courthouse, the press was there in force. I eschewed my normal reticence to speak to the free press.

"Popi, did you beat Samson and send him to the hospital?"

"My lawyer has told me to plead not guilty, so that's what I'll do. The man in question is Peter Ray Vaughn's boss and coconspirator. When he threatened to rape and kill Layla and my friend, Special Agent Sophie Templeton, I did what I did."

The Pete story was very much in the public eye, so I knew that my statement would destroy Marcus' life. In the courtroom, I was lucky. The judge was an attractive woman who smiled at me. When the bailiff read the charges, she looked chagrined.

"Popi, say it ain't so. You are a role model for my children."

"I can't say it ain't so, but when my reasons come out, I think I'll still be an appropriate role model for your kids and you too beautiful." She blushed.

"Counselor, how does your client plead?"

DeeDee said, "Not guilty your honor."

The grinning woman turned to the young prosecutor who stood.

"Your honor, due to the violent nature of the crime, the county requests that the defendant be remanded into our custody." DeeDee fought back.

"Your honor, Walter Lemon is an upstanding member of the community. We request ROR."

"Mr. Lemon may be an upstanding member of some community, but not ours. Bail is set at 100,000 dollars cash. Are you prepared to post at this time?"

"Yes ma'am."

DeeDee, in a dramatic show of strength opened his brief case and removed a large stack of bills, only a small fraction of its contents." The cute Judge smiled.

"By all means, see the clerk and you are released with a warning. Stay away from Mr. Marcus Samson."

# HERE WE GO AGAIN

When Popi was arrested, I cried. Although Popi beat the much smaller Marcus, he brought it on himself. He should have known better than threatening me or any other woman in Popi's presence. On the way home I called Triple D who promised to be on the next flight. I told him a little bit of the story and he had some encouraging words.

"Don't worry too much. If that man is proven to be evil, these charges will go away. It will be months before a trial is held or longer if that's what Walter wants. He'll be out in the morning as long as he cooperates with me."

While I talked with Triple D, Sophie talked with her boss, Don Briggs. He wasn't happy and was heading to our house for a full report. Sophie was upset.

"Don blames me, but he wasn't there. He didn't see that hideous creature and probably won't even believe it." She was right.

"You can't tell Don about the shadow, he'll never believe."

"But Layla, I have to, it's my sworn duty."

"Sophie, I understand, but if you don't want to lose all of your credibility with your team, you'll break that vow."

I tried to call Kurt, but cell service became spotty for the last fifteen minutes from home. I left Sophie to her awful decision. I told her on the ride that I intended to fully disregard Popi's order that we spend every second together.

"I'm not afraid of Marcus Samson and I'm not afraid of that disgusting shadow either."

She didn't believe me, but it's the truth. Neither he nor the shadow had enough physical power to try to subvert the security. Their only chance was to recruit some living muscle. Then they would still have to get by Kurt.

I took a shower, glad to be clean and rid of that now cursed red leather mini-skirt. I'll never wear it again after that creep touched it. Though it was only a bit before eight I dressed for bed in my blue silk pajamas, Popi's favorite. I went downstairs, first to see what was left over from dinner then to the security office where I found Kurt and Rebecca. He was watching the output from the twenty-four video cameras on the six screen control panel. She was going through all of her computer news sources, undoubtedly looking for any news on Popi and me.

"I'm back, but Popi was arrested for defending me." They both mugged me.

"We were worried to death, Squirt."

They, of course, knew that I was back, having watched me enter the gate and the back door. They had patiently waited for me to clean up.

"How did you even know that something was wrong?"

Rebecca said, "It was only on the national news."

I briefed them with everything I knew, including the shadow. Kurt sighed.

"Aw Jeez, here we go again."

Rebecca said, "Poor Popi has to spend the night in jail. It's not fair. Who'll look out for him?"

"I'm going to have a snack and go to bed. Don't stay up too late. We may have a busy day tomorrow." They both hugged me again, their concerned lips kissing my damp hair.

Before bed, I called for Lilly. She didn't answer, but I trusted that she'd heard. I could expect her to visit my dreams. Embarrassingly, I was dreaming of making love with Popi when she appeared. She stood and smiled at us until I shook Popi.

"Popi stop, Lilly's here." He not only stopped, he disappeared. I finally realized that I was dreaming and that she was here for me. "Lilly, Popi has been arrested. He asked me to ask you to visit him tonight. He's in the Hamilton County Jail."

"Okay sweetheart, I'll take him a cake with a file in it."

"That's not necessary dear. Triple D is on the way and will bail him out in the morning."

"Go back to your excellent dream Layla." I did.

The next morning, Triple D told me to be at the courthouse at ten. I brought Kurt and Rebecca. We sat in the gallery and had to watch two other arraignments' before Popi's. The judge was a nice looking woman in her forties. She didn't smile even once and she was very harsh to the two men before her. She set a high bail for one and denied bail for the other. I was worried. I should have known better. Popi charmed the icy woman with a practiced ease. She did set a high bail, but I'm sure she knew it would be no problem for Popi.

Popi hadn't seen us yet, so when he turned around, a free man, I attacked him. I jumped into his arms and we kissed to a series of flashes from the court photographers. One of those pictures graced the front page of Popi's inky old newspaper the next morning. Popi and I made out like teenagers the whole way home. When we arrived, Don and his whole team were waiting for us, Including Sophie who seemed nervous. Don immediately tore into Popi.

"Damn It Walter, what in hell were you thinking. You've jeopardized our case. This joker could walk." Popi was calm.

"Don, if I hadn't done anything, there wouldn't even be a case. You would have shrugged your shoulders and pinned it all on Pete. I know how the FBI thinks, no evidence, no crime. Pete was a perpetrator, but also a patsy. Samson made several incriminating statements in front of your agent. Surely you can see the good in that." Don calmed down.

"Okay, Okay, I believe that Marcus Samson is Mr. Brain, but how can we prove it?"

"We let him think that you buy into the black shadow defense, make him believe that he can skate if he helps us trap the demon."

Don was skeptical, but having no better Idea agreed to listen. Popi told him that he needed to talk to his expert on supernatural entities and we should meet tomorrow at his hotel. Don agreed, but I didn't get the feeling that he was up for any of Popi's shenanigans. I presumed that Popi wanted to talk to Lilly again. Popi left to shower and the FBI, except for Sophie, left for the city. I gave Popi a five minute head start and crawled into our bed naked. He walked out of the shower naked, but for the towel he was using to dry his short brown hair. He didn't see me at first and grabbed some boring blue boxers from his chest of drawers. Popi turned and faced me, still unaware.

"You won't be needing those for a while." No more words were spoken.

My darling Popi made me feel like the most loved woman in the world and I did my utmost to return that love. Afterward, we went our separate ways, I to work and he to his daily routine.

"I need coffee. I hope they haven't tossed my paper."

When I arrived at work, the designers, seamstresses and Gabrielle were all gossiping about Popi's arrest. I gathered them around and gave them the sanitized version of the story, leaving out only the black shadow. We went back to work.

# TRIAL BY FIRE

Being married to Layla has paid off again. Using her Zen techniques and my charming line of bullshit, I gently guided Don to accept my plan to trap Marcus Sampson. What Don didn't know was that he was also going to help trap the insane black spirit. I needed to talk to Lilly. I would only attempt this if she agreed that it was safe and feasible. I got my coffee and paper and pretended to read, but was actually plotting. I needed to convince the bait to put her life on the line again.

I went back to room twelve, dressed exactly the same as I was yesterday. Sophie answered my soft knock. She was dressed, barely, in a towel. I don't know why these things always happen to me, these trials by fire.

"Popi, your timing is unfortunate, can I do something for you. I have a video conference with Don in ten minutes." She dropped the towel and began to dress.

"I'll come back after your call."

She had her fancy undies on now and was brushing her long blonde hair bare breasted. She was amazingly beautiful and sexy. I couldn't avert my hungry gaze.

"It's okay, nothing you haven't already seen."

By the time she was squirming into her black lace bra, I had regrouped.

"Sophie, I want to use you as bait to capture this black demon." Her face went from her amused, teasing one, to her horrified desperation one.

"Popi, please don't ask me to do that. Why ask me and not Layla?"

"Because you're the trained Federal agent and I need Layla to lure in Samson."

"I don't think that I can do this." She began to weep and I took her into my arms.

"It's okay sweetheart, you don't have to do anything that you're not ready for. I won't put you into any danger." Sophie looked up from the damp spot on my left shoulder.

"Popi, that beast scares me to death."

"That beast is hot for you and Layla, but Samson is obsessed with only Layla. We've got to think of a way to offer each of them what they want without risking your safety."

"Popi, Layla claims that she isn't afraid of either of them."

"She knows that Marcus is a wimpy loser and that rogue spirit is too weak to do anything physical on this realm without Marcus."

"I see. I guess that's why they needed Pete. Is there a chance that they have someone else to be their enforcer?"

"I don't know honey, but I have a secret weapon."

Sophie had to scramble to put on her shirt for her video call. I watched from stage right as she reported to Don and her team in her pretty underwear. After her call, I told her about Lilly. I could tell that she didn't want to believe my strange story, but after her encounter with the shadow, she did believe.

"I'm going to talk to Lilly tonight, so I'll know more in the morning." She rose and kissed me.

"I still like this kissing-friends concept of yours."

Staring into the beautiful young lady's eyes, I saw her hidden pain, her love for me and her aching need to be loved. I kissed her again.

"When this is over, I'm gonna cure that broken heart of yours."

Back in the kitchen, I met Mrs. Wood for the first time. She was busy preparing lunch for the family and Layla's Petites staff.

"Hello, you must be Mrs. Wood. You can call me Walter or Popi." I took her hand and waited for her to regain her composure.

"Popi, I promised myself that I wouldn't behave like a star struck fan when I met you, but I can't help myself. You're just so handsome and brave. I'm sorry. I'm babbling like a lovesick teenager."

"That's okay sweetheart, it never gets old being admired by beautiful women."

"Layla warned me about you and your charming line of bullshit, but that'll never get old with me either."

Debra coaxed me into trying a bowl of her freshly made chicken and dumplings. It was absolutely delicious. By the time I was done, the kitchen was rapidly filling with the lunch crowd, including Layla, so I stayed.

"How goes it in the dress mines sweetheart?"

Layla kissed me, but since I was seated, Big Popi lurked under the granite countertop. This also facilitated her confirming the condition of the spell. It was unbroken.

"I'm still painting, but it's coming along nicely. How is your project doing?"

"It's stalled until I talk to Lilly."

I was forced to recount my experience in jail for the gossipy Layla's Petites staff. The only sympathy I got amid the chuckles was from missing dinner and the room temperature milk for breakfast."

I found it odd that no one remarked on the beat-down I put upon Marcus Samson. I guessed they had heard of his threats to Layla and Sophie. Speaking of the devil, Sophie entered and kissed me on the cheek.

"Popi, what time do you want to meet at the hotel tomorrow?" The room hushed at the question, but really, it was the familiar kiss.

"I was thinking about ten. Does that work?"

"I'll let him know. Are you coming Layla?"

I looked at Layla because we hadn't discussed it yet.

"Not unless I'm needed." It was my turn and I recognized the need to be diplomatic, about time cowboy.

"I always need you Li'l Freckles, but," I kissed her, "If you're busy, I'll brief you later."

The spirit of the room lightened and again, the spell was unbroken. I hung out until everyone went about their day and helped Debra clean up the kitchen. She didn't even try to turn down my generous offer.

"There is nothing sexier than a strong virile man helping around the house. My husband never failed in that regard."

"How did Hardy die honey?"

"The dear man was helping our neighbor, Fred Kerry, fix his truck. The vehicle slipped off the jacks and crushed him." She began to weep so I hugged her.

"I'm so sorry Debra. I shouldn't have brought it up."

"No, it's okay Popi. Hardy lingered for two days and though it was hard to see him in pain, I was glad to have a chance to tell him how much I loved and appreciated him."

I gave Debra a warm parting hug and went about my day which I spent planning. At this point, all I could plan for was the easy part, luring Samson to my house. I say easy because I knew that he would follow Layla anywhere. Maybe the shadow would follow along. I had ruled out using Sophie as a lure for the perverted spirit due to her fragile state and her complete fear of the weakened phantasm. In bed that night, I planned with Lilly.

# Sophie Dreams

My anger at Popi was irrational and I knew it. It was from his refusal to reaffirm his vows of love for me, vows given under duress while attempting to save my life. Layla talked me down and Popi apologized. I was still in possession of a serious torch for the extremely sexy galoot, but what's a girl to do? In the end I decided that hating him was more painful than loving him, so we became friends, not handshake friends, kissing friends.

When Popi came to my room to ask for help with his plan, I was dressed only in a towel. To punish him or maybe to tempt him, I dropped that towel. I was amused at his stammering discomfort. Popi's capacity to send my mood into a terminal death spiral reared its ugly head when he asked me to be the bait for catching that terrifying black shadow. He was asking too much. I couldn't do it. He was very understanding, but I felt that I had let him down and that maybe I had lost some of his respect. I tossed and turned most of that long night and when I finally drifted off, it was into a very disturbing dream.

I was back in that dingy basement, observing the scene from outside of my body. I was strapped to that bed again, completely naked except the single strip of duct tape covering my mouth. I was apparently unconscious, but still breathing. Pete was pacing back and forth while talking on his cell phone.

"Marcus, I don't think that I could do that. Please don't make me do that. No sir, I don't want to go to hell, but if I kill someone, that's where God will send me."

Pete closed his ancient flip phone, threw it against the wall and turned slowly to face me.

"Don't worry miss, they want me to strangle you, but I won't never do that." The large dirty man, with his war torn face, was crying.

I wanted to thank him and attempt to bond with the dangerous man, but he couldn't hear me so I couldn't employ my training to mitigate the situation. He sat on the edge of the bed and stroked my hair. I didn't know then, but I do now, why he avoided touching my warm flesh. He was only sexually attracted to cold dead flesh.

Half an hour later, Marcus Samson entered the room. Pete was scared to death of his tiny boss. The squirrely man couldn't take his eyes off of me. He was literally licking his chops.

"Peter, go upstairs and I'll get her ready for you."

"Please Marcus, I done promised her that we wouldn't hurt her." Pete cowered.

"I'm sorry Peter, but Broward has already sniffed her. There is nothing I can do for her now." Pete slinked upstairs as Marcus undressed.

Marcus Samson's body was extremely scrawny. He had a balding head on top of his skinny neck. His hairless chest was sunken in, lacking any apparent power. His pale broomstick legs terminated at his tiny, but solidly excited penis. Marcus climbed onto the bed, straddling me and stroking that miniscule yet menacing erection with his tiny, soft hands. The demon slowly pealed the tape from my mouth. He knelt with his pointy knees digging into my restrained arms while rubbing his disgusting junk across my face, eyes and lips. I was helplessly crying and nearly panicked, at my hopeless situation, though my body was calmly oblivious.

He scooted down my body and pushed my breasts together. The pervert began humping them, between them. He was pinching my nipples as he rapidly fucked that soft crevice. In less than a minute, with a dreamy look on his ugly face, he ejaculated. Marcus looked spent and his mini-member immediately shrunk to a laughable flaccid state.

"That was for me alone, so now let me introduce Mr. Broward. He is very anxious to give you his world famous goodbye and good fuck."

The black shadow entered the small room floating. It seeped into Marcus's open mouth causing an instantaneous change in the diminutive rapist. Marcus didn't grow any taller, but in every other measure he expanded. He was suddenly sporting an evil toothy grin and his arms, chest and even his skinny legs grew to a more masculine size and shape. The most notable change was to his tiny, soft penis. It was again rock-hard and grew to a frighteningly, exaggerated, porn star size.

The unholy monster lay on top of me and began nipping at my breasts and sensitive nipples. He lapped up the disgusting mess that Marcus had left on my chest and neck. Shadow Marcus produced a little capsule which looked to be made of cotton. I couldn't figure out what it was until he crushed it. It was an ampule of smelling salts. The Demon wanted me awake. The grinning freak waved it under my nose, causing my body to snort and cough. My floating vantage point disappeared. I was pulled back to my body. My eyes remained closed and my head was suddenly foggy. Pete ran down the stairs.

"He's here. Popi's here." Marcus climbed off of me.

"Peter, you kill the girl and we'll sneak out the cellar door."

I finally managed to open my eyes only to see Pete now straddling me. He wasn't naked and he wasn't excited. Instead, he was sad, crying and conflicted. I was sure that he didn't have it in him to kill me. I was wrong.

"I'm sorry Miss."

He wrapped his huge hands around my neck and squeezed. It wasn't long until I was back to my floating vantage point, watching the reluctant killer kill me. Popi and Layla burst in and I was startled awake back in my bed room. I was sweaty and chilly at once and strangely naked. Not only had I stripped in my dream, but I was also in the position of my dream with my arms and legs stretched out as if I were tied to the bed. I found myself wishing that I hadn't awakened, desiring to relive Popi's words of love. Oh great, now the horrifying nightmare had suddenly turned me on. I fell back into the dream.

"Sophie I love you." He kissed me and I opened my eyes.

He kissed me again and began making love to me. I awoke again, furiously masturbating. I was ashamed, but that didn't stop me. I lustily completed my sexual, sensual humiliation.

I was chanting, "Oh Popi, Oh Popi."

I knew it was a dream, but I also knew it was the truth, not the last part, of course. Popi and Layla had not only saved me from Pete, but from Samson and the Shadow too.

# LILLY

I entered Walter's dream as he had requested, but I didn't announce my presence immediately because he was making vigorous love and I wanted to watch. Layla was not present. Popi was enthusiastically pounding the beautiful Sophie. She, of course, wasn't really there, but I have no doubt that the girl would be thrilled to actually participate in the sexy dream. Alas, Popi is always true to Layla in the waking world. Unlike some of Popi's wild sex dreams, Sophie's beauty was not exaggerated because Walter knew exactly what the sexy girl looked like naked.

After a rousing grand finale, in which the blonde cop screamed and swooned, I spoke.

"Walter, why don't you dream of me that way?"

The sexy man sat up, with a rare self-conscious grin, on his gorgeous face.

"Gee Lilly, you're here now." He stood and took me into his dream arms. "Seriously honey, I need your help again. Is that spirit as weak as he looks?"

"I've consulted some friends of mine and they're of the opinion that his strength plus that little man should not be equal to yours alone."

"That sounds great sweetheart."

"Don't start your victory dance yet, there's more. I just came from Sophie's dream. The poor girl remembers a lot more about the incident in her subconscious mind." I told him about Broward. "Walter, this maniac has been stealing his victims' power as he kills them and storing the excess in Marcus. There is no telling how much strength he can bring to bear."

"How can we trap him without allowing access to his battery pack, Marcus Samson?"

"Popi, I've only been dead for five years. I don't know everything, but I think we may have to back off this one. It's too dangerous."

"Honey, the problem is, we may not have a choice. Even if we leave them alone, they'll come after Layla and maybe Sophie too."

I thought about this for a moment. Popi was right. We were being forced into a battle with Broward and his little buddy.

"Well, I'm a lot stronger here at home, so let's sucker them into our trap."

We planned. I stayed in my dear friends mind for as long as I could.

# Plans Are Just Wishes

Dream time is strange. Sometimes these nocturnal ramblings and wanderings seem to go on forever. Lilly assures me that she can stay inside my mind for no more than a waking thirty seconds, but often hours of productive work are accomplished. I knew a lot more than I did yesterday. For instance, the shadow, Broward, is a lot more powerful than I'd thought. Before, I had wanted to lure them together, but now it seems safer to keep them apart. When Lilly left, Sophie woke and tried to reignite my passion. I was not in the mood, so I awoke.

I paced the floors of my massive mansion for two hours, only returning to my bed after finally deciding that I would not bring this evil to my home. It would be too dangerous for the noncombatant occupants. The downside to this was that Lilly may not be able to help, but frankly, this battle may be hazardous to her too. I was just going to focus on getting Marcus Samson to pay for his evil deeds and hope that Broward would be punished as a byproduct of losing his protector. I crawled back into bed with Layla at four. I pulled her close and slept peacefully until she woke me for our morning run.

I ran well, though I was distracted and winded because I spent the first four laps laying out my plans for Layla. She was nervous at the thought of a more powerful Broward. I gave her the option of not participating in the battle. My courageous wife gave me her standard and predictable response.

"Wherever you are, that's where I'll be."

When Layla picked up the pace for the last quarter mile, I dug deep and was able to stay with her until the last ten yards. She was thrilled to beat me and I was thrilled just to make it a close race. After our showers, Layla dressed for work in tight black leggings under a cute red skirt, a tight white blouse and a black cashmere cardigan. I was bare-chested and barefoot as usual.

We walked into a noisy hubbub of activity. All five Layla's Angels were here plus a few early Layla's Petites employees. It must be Friday because, as far as I knew, the Angels had no business requirements, so they were here to spend their weekend. This was not unusual, but since Claire left, less common.

The reason for the sudden popularity of my kitchen had her back to me. It was Debra Wood, who was cooking omelets and waffles for the hungry multitudes. The five models each stopped stuffing their beautiful faces to greet me with hugs and kisses.

Debra asked, "Where's mine Popi?"

Not waiting for a reply, she wrapped both Layla and me into a hug and kissed our cheeks. I declined to order breakfast and had coffee. Debra didn't complain as expected.

"Far be it from me to tell you what to put into that perfect body." I didn't blush, but it was close.

At eight-thirty, Layla, Sophie, Ski and I met up in the kitchen for our trip to Cincinnati to meet with the FBI. We took two cars and the two security experts agreed that Layla and I should be split. I, of course, rode with Ski. Layla's jealousy of Sophie was in remission, but not completely cured. I briefed my Polish partner on the forty minute drive. The name brand hotel was on the outskirts of the city. It was fairly new and fairly cheap, but most of all, it was fairly close to Sweet Haven Cemetery.

Don and his team were set up in a small conference room with the super computer occupying half of the eight seat table. After a short greeting period, Don started.

"Walter, I want to tell you upfront, I and my team will not be a party to any of your fantastic shortcuts. As much as you hate the slow pace of justice, when we catch them, they won't be getting off on some technicality."

"Now that we are all safe, I agree to your terms."

"Okay then, lay out your crazy plan, but remember, you'll not be permitted to go anywhere near Mr. Marcus Samson." I started with a question.

"Are we allowed to use trickery to get him to confess?"

"Absolutely."

"I propose that we send Sophie, you and Layla in to see Marcus. Pete told us that he believes his boss is possessed by a black spirit named Broward." Sophie looked astonished that I had information from her dream. "I want you to convince Samson that you believe him and that he isn't personally responsible for crimes committed while he was possessed."

"Walter, in my experience, these guys invent these boogieman stories to explain away their actions, but they don't really believe in them." I had that covered.

"Don, it doesn't matter if he believes as long as he thinks that you three do. Sophie can attest to Layla's power over the freak. If she backs your play, he'll follow along like a speckled duckling follows its momma across a busy road."

Don said, "Layla, this nut-job is dangerous. Are you sure you want to play the bait?"

"I wish Popi could be there." She has a lot of faith in me. "I won't have to touch him, will I Popi?"

"No sweetheart, and if he touches you, I'll rip off that comical mustache and shove it down his throat."

Surprisingly, SSA Briggs liked the plan and went about implementing it immediately. He outfitted his team with sound and video recording devices. We all drove the ten miles to Sweet Haven Cemetery. Jon, Mike and I pulled over at the entrance gate. We were in a rental van which they'd set up as a tactical surveillance headquarters. Our three undercover operatives each had small wireless cameras attached to their collars and two way earpieces which could send as well as receive. Ski had an earpiece, but he would wait in the lobby as backup. He had insisted that he be near enough to Layla to protect her.

# SAMSON AND DE LAYLA

Popi nearly beat me again. I had to dig deep to pull out a five meter victory. He is in the best shape of his life, but so am I. I think his worry about Marcus and Broward had him so distracted that he forgot how tired and spent he was. At breakfast, all the girls attacked Popi, including Debra. Popi had his bitter black coffee while the rest of us enjoyed Debra's delicious cooking.

I spent an hour at work and met back up with Popi, Sophie and Kurt to meet with Don Briggs in Cincinnati. Rebecca was there too, but not coming along. I entered the room quietly. It was a new self-improvement project. I was forever entering talking, often interrupting. Popi was talking softly to Rebecca, but he smiled and opened his arms to me as he spoke.

"Honey, see if you can find anything on someone named Broward. All I know about him is that he's evil and dead. Go back a hundred years or more."

Rebecca said, "Yes Popi," and scurried off with grim determination, like an assignment from Popi was the highlight of her life.

I rode with Sophie. I didn't like it nor did Popi, but both Kurt and Sophie insisted. Sophie was nervous and so was I. I didn't want her to know. I wasn't really sure how much she knew about Popi's new assessment of the Shadow.

"You seem nervous Sophie."

"I don't like having to hold back important information from my colleagues." She was very tense.

"If the Shadow shows himself, we'll coax Don out of there. Popi doesn't want to take him on when he can't be there."

"Don didn't mention it, but we have a search warrant for the offices and his residence."

At Sweet Haven's gate Jon, Mike and Popi pulled over. They would have to listen and observe from the van. The rest of us took the scenic trip up the winding road to the office building where we were met by Popi's number one fan, Linsey. Don showed her his badge and she called Marcus.

"Mr. Samson says to call his lawyer and make an appointment."

I said, "Tell him Layla Lemon's here."

He agreed to talk with me alone, but Don said no and Marcus relented. Don hadn't yet noticed our worry. Sophie and I were practically holding hands. Our nervous jittery fingertips were making light random contact. Don walked in and greeted the little man with a handshake.

"Mr. Samson, Mrs. Lemon and SA Templeton have told me a very strange story about their visit to see you."

"How strange Agent Briggs?" He was cocky.

"They say that they witnessed you being possessed by a dark spirit." His cockiness had turned into worry.

"Surely you don't really believe that sir."

"I don't really know what to believe. These women have no reason to lie and Peter Vaughn told me the same thing."

"Tell me Briggs, what law would I be breaking, if this were true?"

"Li'l Freckles, it's time to work your magic," Popi said into my ear, all of our ears.

"Marcus, I know Broward makes you do horrible things."

Marcus was staring at me, taking in all he could. His tiny erection was back, but he seemed not to care that we noticed.

"Layla, you are so beautiful. What is it that you want from me?"

"I want you to come with us so we can protect you from Broward." Don sweetened the pot.

"You know Samson, you can't be held responsible for the things that monster did."

"I'll only go, Layla, if I can stay with you at your house." Popi growled into my ear.

"Over my dead body, tell him no way." Don came to the rescue.

"Marcus, their house is way too big to be secured from a puff of smoke, but Layla will be with you every step of the way."

"Okay, but we better go. He'll be back any time now." We started heading for the door.

Don was leading the way. I was next with Marcus Samson between me and Sophie. As Don opened the door, an evil growl sounded from the closet. Marcus screamed in a high pitched, girly squeal.

"He's here, run!" Don was slow.

He, of course, didn't believe in the shadow, until that is, the black killer, in a cloud, blew into the room from the crack under the closet door. Sophie screamed in fear. The shadow flew around the room again, but it didn't go for Marcus. Instead, he flew at the frightened blonde agent. He flew into her cleavage and into Sophie's cheap suit. She panicked and began slapping at her own body as the smokey menace explored every inch of her body.

Had I not been terrified, the scene would have been comical, especially when Don did what he did next. He began stripping off Sophie's clothes. Kurt burst into the room with his gun drawn. He was looking for someone to shoot. With all this going on, Marcus Samson did something totally unexpected. The little demon jammed his right hand up my skirt. Simultaneously, he ripped my blouse open and attacked my breasts with his mustachioed face. His attack only lasted a few seconds because for the second time in the history of the perverted world, he was overcome with another spontaneous ejaculation.

Kurt growled and grabbed the mini Snidely Whiplash by his scrawny neck and lifted him until his feet were dangling off the floor. Popi burst into the room. He was wild-eyed and looking for someone to clobber. He saw my torn blouse and went for Marcus. I stopped him with my tears and he took me into his arms. Kurt continued to strangle Marcus and Don had Sophie down to her pretty pink bra and panties. Broward flew out of those undies and into Samson's mouth. The change was instantaneous. Marcus grew in size and strength, his soft, soiled wool pants were suddenly skin tight and his stylish jacket popped its buttons.

He was still short, but no longer tiny or effete. He had acquired a creepy evil grin. Kurt dropped him, as if he had suddenly become much heavier. Marcus/Broward turned the tables on Kurt by lifting him and throwing him through the closed window with a violent shattering crash. Popi rushed the demon and delivered a lightning fast flurry of fists to his ugly face. Even with two black eyes, a fat lip and broken nose, he maintained his evil grin.

The demon attacked Popi, but my man was ready. He knew better than to underestimate the little man. Popi sidestepped the rushing demon and shoved him to the floor. He kicked Samson's exposed ribs as he fell. There was finally a break in the demon's smile.

"I'm still going to kill you and fuck your whores to death."

With that, he jumped out the window. Popi and I went to the sill and watched as a recovering Kurt pistol whipped the bloodied demon.

"Hands up pal or I shoot that mangy mouse off your face."

Marcus sprung to his feet and took off running. He was extremely fast and was thirty meters away before Kurt woozily gathered himself into a good firing position. Kurt fired and hit Marcus in his right buttock. He fell, got up slowly and continued to flee. Kurt didn't rush the next shot. He hit the hobbling Marcus Samson in his left buttock, felling the demon for good.

I looked back into the room. Don Briggs had Sophie wrapped in his arms. He was seemingly oblivious of everything except the nearly naked beautiful woman. Their lips were close.

"Kiss her, kiss her now," I whispered.

Then he did and now I was oblivious to all the chaos, except, of course, the chaos of love unfolding before my eyes. Popi saw my glow of happiness and kissed me.

"That's so nice, Li'l Freckles. Let's help Ski."

He cleared away some of the sharp shards of glass, climbed out the window and held out his arms to lift me through.

# THE PREACHER

I lifted my angel through the broken window and was greeted by Lilly. She was fully materialized. She was wearing her fifteen year old body and her favorite tight silver dress.

"Hi Lilly, what are you doing here?"

Layla said, "Popi is Lilly here?"

Lilly hugged Layla and kissed her cheek then whispered into her ear.

"I'm saving my strength. I've come to help with Broward. I see that Marcus Samson is finished." Ski was cautiously approaching the fallen fop.

I said, "Layla call for an ambulance and the local law." We three walked in that direction. "Lilly, where's Broward?"

"I've been keeping an eye on Marcus and I haven't seen Broward evacuate."

Briggs was helping Sophie through the window. She was fully dressed. Layla and I got to Ski and Marcus. He was breathing, but unconscious and bleeding copiously from his two 9mm wounds. Sophie and Don arrived. He still had his arm around her.

Sophie asked, "Popi, where's the shadow?" Fear painted her pretty face.

"It's still in the little creep."

"How do you know?"

"Lilly told me."

Don asked, "Who the hell is Lilly?"

"Ask Sophie later."

The surveillance van arrived. Not only did Jon and Mike join in the circle around Marcus Samson, but Rebecca was here too. She joined Ski and began fussing over the big Pollock's injuries which seemed to be minor scratches and scrapes. I could hear the sirens of the cops and medics.

"Honey, I'm gonna make myself scarce, so I don't get arrested for disobeying that cute judge."

I went into the back of the FBI van where I could observe and listen. Rebecca left her heroic gunslinger and joined me in the hi-tech duck blind.

"Popi, I think I may have found Broward. There was a serial killer in Broward county Florida, but he never went by that name and the timeline of his crimes doesn't fit this guy."

"So did you find this Broward?"

"Not quite, I found a man named Cyril Howard. He was hanged in 1902 in Salinas Kansas for a string of strangulation murders of teenage girls. All of the victims were members of his congregation. He was a Baptist minister who was the charismatic leader of the cult-like group of townsfolk." I wasn't convinced.

"How does he connect to Broward?"

"Because he went by the name Brother Howard and it's not a big leap, considering the time and place that he could have been familiarly called Broward."

"I'm buyin' it sweetheart, good job."

Since the van had no windows in the back, we were watching the screens, which were being fed by the body cameras worn by Don, Sophie and Layla. It was difficult seeing anything, but my wife. Her camera had been jostled and was aiming down at her torn blouse which was being loosely held closed by the one remaining button. The result was a very alluring scene. Jon and Mike were also transfixed.

I tore my eyes from Layla and saw that Don's camera was roving down Sophie's blouse as he kissed the shaken girl on her forehead. Sophie's camera was unwavering. She was one hundred percent concentrating her gaze at Marcus who was being attended to by the EMTs. It, of course, was not the diminutive funeral director who garnered her devoted attention. It was Broward who would be haunting her dreams. Don turned to Ski and I saw that he was similarly vigilant. He, being a tracker of men, was not about to let the wounded man out of his sight.

We also had audio, but not much was being said until Ski spoke.

"Briggs, you gotta send someone with him. If its' in the punk, he'll need to evacuate soon."

"Ski, who should I send? Which one should I expose to that beast?"

"He is under arrest, isn't he? You can't let him out of your custody."

I could hear the conflict in the agents' troubled voice. He knew that Ski was right, but he couldn't assign one of his agents. He also didn't want to leave Sophie alone.

I said, "You go Don. I'll protect her with my life." As the medics loaded the double butt-shot menace, Don climbed aboard. "Sophie, Ski and Layla come back to the van. Jon and Mike try to handle the cops," I said, taking command. "Sophie, walk backward and to keep your camera on that ambulance."

"Okay Popi," she replied, still shaken.

Layla asked, "Popi how's my camera?"

"It's perfect honey."

# THE UNDERTAKER BURNS

Popi can't really help himself. Anytime he senses a leadership vacuum, he assumes command. He ordered Jon and Mike to smooth-talk the local police and the rest to gather at the van. When we arrived, he gave me a loving hug, but deftly avoided my attempts to kiss him. I was disappointed, but understanding until he wrapped Sophie in his traitorous arms and gave her a big kiss on her painted lips. Then he said something which quelled my jealousy.

"Sophie, stay close to me. Don will kill me if I let anything happen to the new love of his life." Sophie acquired a soft glow at that happy thought.

The police left with the ambulance following closely behind, both with sirens blaring. They didn't get more than a hundred feet before the large red ambulance veered left off the roadway and tore across the graveyard. It was going at least thirty, when it slammed into a beautiful weeping willow tree with a mighty crashing thump. The engine compartment immediately caught fire and started billowing thick black smoke. We all took off running toward the catastrophic scene. Popi got there first and opened the rear door. The escaping cloud of black smoke bowled him over.

Popi yelled, "Get back, it may be Broward."

Sophie stopped in her tracks, yanking me to an abrupt halt because, in our fear, we had been holding hands again. Popi rose to his feet and entered the burning vehicle, disappearing from our view. He emerged seconds later, carrying Agent Briggs. He dropped the unconscious man at our feet and turned to reenter the black cloud. Sophie forgot her fear and began kissing and begging Don to wake up. Jon and mike were trying to gain entrance to the front of the ambulance, but they were driven back by the flames filling the cab.

Jon screamed, "Everyone get back! It's gonna blow."

Ski made another attempt to rescue the driver and was successful at removing the flaming man, using his jacket to smother the fire on his clothes. Popi reemerged from the back coughing and hacking. He had the other EMT in his arms. I went to him.

"Li'l Freckles, see if you can save him."

I went to work on the large blonde young man who wasn't breathing. I breathed into his mouth and he immediately coughed. I thought he would be okay. Popi went back into the flaming ambulance.

"Popi No! He's not worth it."

I meant Marcus Samson, who was the only victim left. Popi, as expected, ignored me. Kurt, Jon, Mike and the two cops Dragged the wounded men and we three girls away from the nearly fully engulfed wreck. I abandoned these good people and ran to get my Popi. I was worriedly crying. Popi emerged from the disaster with the mini Snidely Whiplash tucked under his right arm like a football. He ran, scooping me up with his left arm. We were only six feet away when the ambulance exploded.

The hot force of the blast propelled us another six feet and shoved us to the grass. Dazed, I looked at Samson. His upper lip was bleeding and his waxed handlebar mustache was gone. I saw only one curled tip, which was protruding from his tightly closed mouth.

# Come Together

The explosion picked us up and threw us to the ground. I checked on Layla who was staring at Marcus with a glassy gaze, but was otherwise unharmed. My hands were burned a bit and I was still a bit woozy. I stood and gathered up Layla into my arms. I carried her to the others looking them over and assessing their conditions. I knew this was not over, but our platoon was battered and in need of relief. Besides his wounds from his defenestration, Ski's hands were severely burned. Briggs was just beginning to regain consciousness and was being sweetly tended to, by the lovely Sophie.

Jon and Mike had both lost their eyebrows and lashes and both were experiencing vision problems from the flash of fire. The EMT who I pulled from the back of the ambulance was up and alert. He was dragging Marcus away from the flaming vehicle. I didn't know whether Samson was alive or dead and I didn't really care. Yes, I know, I had just risked my life for the little demon. Don't ask me why. I don't know. The most gravely injured man, by far, was the driver. His face and arms were grievously burned. If he lived, he'd have to endure many months of grafts and pain.

I stood before these battered men and women. They all turned over their attention to me. No one was speaking and I really had nothing to add to that, but that's never stopped me before.

"I love when a finely orchestrated plan comes together." Nobody laughed.

Fortunately, the medivac chopper arrived. They loaded up the critically wounded driver and were air born within two minutes. The next in the triage line was Marcus who earned passage on the first ambulance.

We all eventually made it to the Emergency room Including Rebecca, Layla and Sophie who were unharmed. Ski had his hands cleaned and wrapped and about twenty small adhesive bandages plastered on his arms, face and neck. My hands were burned, but not blistered, so they applied a numbing freeze spray and a soothing salve. I also got ten minutes on Oxygen, Don got twenty. The EMT who Layla and I saved got twenty minutes on the pleasant gas and a nights' stay for observation. The Ambulance driver was flown to the Shriners burn institute in Cincinnati. Jon and Mike's burns, like mine, were mild and treatable. Their vision was back to normal.

# MICHAEL'S STORY, AS TOLD TO LAYLA IN HER DREAMS

My Layla alarm went off and, as usual, I dropped everything. I watched helplessly as she ran from the flaming vehicle. It exploded and she and Walter were sent flying. Then I sensed the beast for whom I'd been searching for fifty years, ever since he'd escaped from two. It was Cyril Howard. I knew without any real evidence that he wasn't hiding four. He was hiding on three where he must have been keeping his energy at an undetectable level. It was the only explanation for his prolonged evasion from the Second Realm Security Force.

Though Layla was unharmed, I sent word to the Seventh Realm. I watched the rescue workers evacuate the injured. I very nearly quit my post because the maniac spirit was still loose and Layla was still in grave danger. I would have been fired, but to save her, it would have been worth it. Fortunately, before that happened Goliath and Lincoln appeared.

I briefed the Messengers as we watched the story unfold on three. We also had eyes on the diminutive funeral director. He was in surgery having his two bullet wounds repaired. The ragtag survivors of Howard's attack began to depart for home. They were shambling out the ER's automatic revolving doors while clinging to each other for support. Judging by the way she clung to Briggs, the Sophie problem had been resolved. They stood and waited for their rides. Our attention was suddenly directed to the ICU where Marcus Samson was transferred unconscious to a bed for recovery and removal of his respirator tubes.

When the doctor pulled the device from his throat, he began flailing into a panicky wakefulness. Then Howard erupted out of Marcus and into the small room, blinding and choking the Doctor and two nurses. Howard set off the fire alarms as he breezed into the ICU control center and out the door. Along his path, he triggered every smoke alarm he passed. We all knew where he was heading.

Goliath said, "It's time to tell Dusty." Lincoln concurred.

The One appeared. It should have been my first time seeing the mythical god, but I instantly recognized him. He was the hobo who helped Walter through his emotional breakdown in 2011. The One spoke.

"We will hold back for as long as we can, but nothing will be allowed to harm Layla. Michael show me what lead to this mess."

"Yes sir."

"Call me Dusty."

I showed Dusty the battle at the cemetery.

Back at the hospital, Cyril Howard blew out of the large revolving door and immediately went after Layla, who was snugly entwined in Walter's arms. When the demon came within five feet of Layla, he burst into bright white sparks like a welding rod. He screamed in unholy agony. Layla's invisible aura appeared in bright pink in a dome of goodness which surrounded her and Walter. The beast retreated and went after the others. Walter left the safety of his wife's shield and attacked the evil cloud.

Howard had wrapped the two other girls in two penis shaped arms. Each of the three FBI men tried to rescue the girls and each was thrown ten feet into the air. They landed on the hard concrete ten feet away and were all hurt or stunned. Walter karate chopped the two black penis arms, causing some sparks of his own making. Though Walter did not possess the grand stockpile of red rays like Layla, he had created a substantial arsenal with his courage and sacrifice in the aide of his friends.

The growling man yanked Sophie and Rebecca away from the evil cloud and hurried them to Layla. I saw his plan. He wanted to get them under Layla's umbrella of protection. He checked on one of the young FBI agents and apparently found him too seriously wounded to be moved. Walter checked the other young man and helped him up. The man was able to hobble his way to Layla's protection. Walter went to Briggs who was sitting up, but dazed. Howard attacked and engulfed the two men, smothering the sparks from his contact with the good men.

I was champing at the bit, but the Messengers and the One remained calm. It was apparent that they didn't consider Walter's life important enough to interfere. Walter was my friend and was Layla's chief source of protection. I spoke up, though I was quite nervous in doing so.

"Dusty, we must save them."

"I'm sorry about your friend Michael, but we'll not interfere unless Layla is in imminent danger."

Fortunately, at that very moment, Layla broke free of the circle of survivors and ran toward her dear Popi with Ski fast on her heels.

# THE PINK FORTRESS

The demon couldn't compete with my rays, so he attacked the others, starting with Rebecca and Sophie. Popi charged the evil cloud and somehow wrenched the girls out of his arms. He brought them to me.

He said, "Stay in close contact with Li'l Freckles," and he was gone.

He checked on Jon who wasn't moving. Popi left Jon where he was and helped Mike up, sending him back to me. When Popi got to Don, the agent was already stirring. Popi helped Don get to his feet and turned to return to me, but Broward roared and swamped the men with his inky blackness.

I should have been conflicted. Should I stay or should I go? Although I was terrified, it was a no brainer. I ran to Popi. I was unwilling to lose my man to that abomination. Kurt followed me even though he couldn't shoot or even fight with his heavily bandaged hands. I ran straight into the evil cloud, causing a tremendous amount of sparks. In the light generated by those crackling sparks, we easily located Popi and Don. They were both on their knees and violently coughing.

I grabbed my Popi and Kurt lifted the special agent to his feet and we backed out in a tactical retreat. I saw the spirits of dozens of teenage girls who were bound in chains. They were silently pleading for my help, but I knew that I must get us to safety first. As soon as we left the cloud, I ran smack dab into a large man. It was Michael who took me into his arms and lifted me. He kissed my cheeks. From my raised position, I saw that Popi had similarly bumped into Dusty. Don Briggs and Kurt had the terrifying experience of meeting Goliath up close and personal.

"Michael, all his victims are inside of him. They're in chains."

"We'll free them sweetheart."

Dusty entered Broward. There were no sparks. Broward tried to flee, but Goliath grabbed and restrained him. After about a minute, Dusty came out of the growling beast leading thirty or so naked teenage girls who were all holding hands. Their chains were gone.

Dusty said, "Michael, get a Second Realm security team here to take these kids to safety. Tell them to bring the gateway device."

"What is the gateway device," Popi, who looked to be almost recovered, hoarsely asked.

President Lincoln said, "It is a portable doorway to the First Realm. We don't want to risk transporting this evil scourge."

As Lincoln spoke, the giant Goliath was molding and compressing Broward into a compact shape. When he was done, all that was left of the spirit was a tall thin man wearing a black frock coat over a black shirt and baggy black wool pants. He had a bible in his hands and wore a battered black prairie hat. He spoke as if he were preaching from the pulpit.

"In the name of our lord and savior, I banish you ungodly demons to hell from whence you came." Popi approached the now solid looking man.

"Brother Howard, why did you kill those beautiful girls? Was it for your lustful pleasure?"

"Of course not heathen, I was saving their souls to join my ministry. My flock is much larger than you can imagine. You and your demons will never stop me."

With lightning speed, Popi clobbered the minister with a ferocious flurry of vicious punches to his gaunt face, regardless of his burnt, bandage fists. Broward fell unconscious to the hard pavement. Dusty, Goliath, Lincoln and Michael smiled.

# THE DELIVERANCE

I should have known that Broward was no match for Layla. I got as many as I could under her protective pink aura. Jon had a possible neck injury so I dared not move him. I helped Don to his feet, but the evil mist enveloped us. It was impossible to see within that putrid cloud and breathing was very difficult. Don went to the ground and I went with him. All around us, I felt the desperate tugs from the helpless captive spirits of the beasts' victims. When they got close enough, I saw that they were teenage girls with chains around their ankles. I tried to speak, but the black air was slowly choking me. The dark cloud was suddenly brightly lit. It was Layla. She had come for us with Ski following close behind.

As they led us out of the blackness, I looked around. There were about three dozen naked waifs, silently calling after us, thinking that we were abandoning them. Leaving these tortured souls broke my heart, but I couldn't save them if I suffocated in the poison cloud. We broke out into the clear heavenly air and literally ran into three large men. I bumped into The Dusty, who hugged me. Layla was in the arms of her angelic boyfriend Michael, but Ski and Briggs met a Giant of a man who I assume to be Goliath. He was nearly ten feet tall.

Broward was growling again and tried to flee, but Goliath grabbed him. Dusty went calmly into the beastly mist and retrieved the captive spirits. They looked horribly emaciated and pale, but were smiling, some for the first time in more than a hundred years. I looked around at our surroundings and saw that the people walking in and out of the hospital were completely ignoring the bizarre activities unfolding before their eyes. Dusty must have blinded them to our battle.

My loyal readers will probably guess who made up the Second Realm security force. It was, of course, Romeo and Caesar Hernandez along with Ryan Hoyt, Elephant. These were the first three men I killed in protection of Layla. They drove up in an old blue woody station wagon with three surfboards strapped to the roof rack. Romeo walked straight to Layla and held out his hands. He seemed to be nervous.

"Li'l Freckles, I'm so sorry for the hell I put you through. Can you ever forgive me? I'll understand if you can't." Layla took his hands.

"I forgive you Paco, Caesar and Ryan too." There were no sparks when the once evil spirit touched my evil detecting wife.

Ryan and Caesar wheeled a large ornately decorated bronze box to the tailgate and lowered it to the ground. They tilted it upright. It was about six feet tall, three feet wide and three feet deep with a thick glass front door. This was a portable doorway to the first realm, the gateway device. Dusty led the spirits of Broward's victims to the tailgate of Romeo's car and they all, one at a time, entered and disappeared. Goliath picked up the unconscious preacher from the hard concrete where he lay after I had battered him with my aching fists. He handed him off to Ryan who slapped the condemned man until he awakened. Paco read the sentencing document.

"Cyril T Howard, AKA Brother Howard, You are hereby sentenced to spend eternity in the First Realm for crimes against humanity. Do you have any last words?" The recovering man sneered.

"You ungodly devils have no power over the pure and holy. I rebuke you. Do your worst, but remember I'll be back with my legion of righteous soldiers of God who will lay your evil kingdom to waste."

Caesar opened the glass door, which looked to be about four

inches thick. Romeo attempted to push the evil spirit into the box, but Broward resisted. Ryan punched the skinny man in his gut and shoved him in. Caesar quickly closed the thick glass door and secured the dozen latches.

Inside the box, Broward continued his insane rant, though we couldn't hear. Romeo brought a bronze cylinder from the back of the woody. It was about the size and shape of a football. He attached the small tank to the side of the box and turned to Dusty, who nodded. Romeo opened a small valve on the cylinder and quickly closed it. Through the glass we saw a red ribbon enter and erupt into a beautiful bright flash of light. The evil inside the box soon neutralized the red goodness.

Before Romeo opened the valve again, we could see that Broward had shrunk by half. He was still screaming mad. Again, the valve was opened. This time, instead of a flash, the red ribbon produced a dazzling array of sparks in brilliant golds and pinks. I was transfixed by the magnificence of the display. The third shot of red was smaller and caused a much smaller reaction. There was no more evil energy left in Cyril T Howard, who was now just a limp flat gray puddle of his former self, yet still he ranted. Again Romeo turned to dusty who again, simply nodded. Romeo, in the final act of this deliverance, pulled a small lever on the side of the box. It was similar to the flushing of a toilet. Broward swirled out of the box and presumably straight to the First Realm, never to return.

# FADING NIGHTMARES

After the fiend was gone for good, we got help for Jon. His neck was okay, but he had a severe concussion. When he awoke, we were all gathered around his bed except for Don and Mike, who were busy executing the search warrant on Samson's office and apartment.

"What the hell happened? The last thing I remember is the briefing at the hotel."

Sophie said, "We raided Samson's office and he put up a fight. The little man was a lot stronger than he looked. He picked up and threw Mr. Staniskowski through the window and ran for the hills. It took two rounds in the buttocks to stop him."

Popi and I made eye contact. I could tell that he too was wondering why Sophie didn't say anything about Broward.

Jon asked, "How did I get injured?" Sophie didn't hesitate.

"It must have been a delayed reaction to when you were trying to rescue the driver of the exploding ambulance."

Jon seemed to be satisfied with this, so Popi and I saw no need to freshen their fading memories.

Rebecca asked, "Did we get any evidence that Marcus was involved in the murders?"

Popi replied, "I don't know. He may walk."

Don Briggs entered the small crowded room.

"How are you doin' partner?"

"I feel fine, but my memory's blurry, almost blank."

Don moved into close contact with Sophie who put her arm around his waist.

"Don't worry about the evidence against the pint sized puke. Mike and I found the mummified remains of his wife and two daughters in their apartment. If we can't convict him on all counts, I'll eat my badge." I gave everyone a hug and a kiss. I reconnected with my battered man.

"Take me home old man or I'm going to check myself in."

It had been a very long and trying day though it was only eight in the evening. Kurt and Rebecca were staying for a while to write their statements. Popi told them not to mention the demon, but they looked at us oddly.

I whispered to Popi, "I wouldn't mind a little forgetfulness too."

It was full dark by the time we entered the back door to our beautiful home. We were pleasantly surprised that Debra had left us plated meals of fried chicken, mashed potatoes and creamed corn. It hit the spot and had us yawning, ready for bed.

We showered and both skipped the standard nightclothes as we often did when we went to bed at the same time. The backs of Popi's hands were painfully bright red so I took control. Since we were both dead tired, I made slow patient love to my glorious man as he kneaded and kissed my breasts.

He whispered, "Li'l Freckles, I love you so much. Thank you for rescuing me from that poison cloud. I will do absolutely anything to repay you."

"Just never leave me and always love me."

The love talk did the trick and we simultaneously erupted in sustained waves of rapturous pleasure which went on and on. Still connected, we kissed with an intensity and passion I've seldom experienced. Four years of blissful marriage hadn't dulled that passion one iota.

I knew Popi would be reluctant to do what I was about to ask of him, but since he'd just pledged to do absolutely anything, how could he refuse?

"Popi, there is one last letter in the bag. Will you read it to me?"

# THE LAST FAN LETTER

Dear Big Popi and Li'l Freckles

My name is John Massey and my fiancée is Cindy Cabot. We are jointly penning this letter. We just finished reading your second book, Not a Eulogy and we both loved it. After we closed the book, Cindy rolled on top of me and asked if I would let her lost love consummate their love before saying a final goodbye. I told her that it depended whether or not she would let me make love with Li'l Freckles, my fantasy lost love.

This of course started a spirited debate. She said that if I was as strong, brave and handsome as Popi, she would never desire another man. I asked her if she would love me more if I were shot thirteen times, kidnapped by terrorists and beaten nearly to death several times. By her dreamy look, I knew her answer was a resounding yes.

"What does Layla have that I don't?"

I made the tactical mistake of laughing at the question. As Popi might say, she was miffed. I told her that she was blind if she couldn't see how perfectly beautiful, courageous and talented she is. Don't get me wrong, Cindy is a very beautiful young lady and I love her with all my heart, but I can't get past the idea that she would leave me at the drop of a hat for Popi. She believes that I would do the same for Layla.

In the end we decided that the only way to prove our love for each other is to each make love to our fantasy lover once and only once. We could then dedicate our lives to pleasing each other, knowing that we could leave fantasy behind and have a wonderful marriage.

Hi Popi, this is Cindy. To me, you are the sexiest man in the seven realms and I would give anything for the opportunity to give you the greatest sexual experience of your incredible life. I can't wait until you are ramming your hard cock into my tight, fully shaven pussy. When I say tight, I'm not exaggerating. I do my Kegels every day. I love it when the man takes charge and will do anything to please you. I've never done anal sex, but for you, I would be willing to try it. Please say you'll do this for us. It will save our relationship.

After Dingbat Cindy's part of the letter, I stopped.

"Li'l Freckles, these people are crazy and I don't want to know what Jackass John would do to you, but I would like to see the pictures of these losers."

Layla retrieved the envelope and pulled out the three photos. The first showed only Cindy's shaven genitals. The second showed Johns erect penis and the third showed the couple posing naked. Layla and I both laughed. John was a balding forty year old with pasty skin and a pronounced paunch. Cindy was skinny, saggy and missing a few crack stained teeth.

"I've changed my mind Li'l freckles. I think we should help this sexy young couple fulfill their fantasies after all."

"Ha, ha Popi, do you think they really believe that they're a young attractive couple?"

"I don't know, but if they do, love truly is blind."

# IFS ANDS OR BUTTS

Popi stopped reading after Cindy's description of making love to my husband. I knew that he didn't mind the teenagers so much, but balked at the grown men's steamy dreams. He asked to see the photos. We both laughed at the naked pictures of the middle aged dumpy couple and I no longer wanted to complete the letter. I cuddled up with my sexy man, hesitant to ask the embarrassing question that was troubling me.

"Popi, Cindy said that she would be willing to have anal sex with you. Is that something you've ever thought about?" He said the sweetest thing.

"Honey, I can't say that I've never thought about that, but the thought of causing you any pain is an extreme turn-off to me."

This was of course the perfect answer. Thus began round two of our fantastic lovemaking. As usual, it was more passionate and satisfying than round one. I was asleep before Popi was finished, dreaming of our life. Even with the all the danger and close calls, I wouldn't change a thing. As long as I have my Popi to love and protect me, I'm the happiest woman in the Seven Realms.

# CYNWRIG AND FIEDLIMID

I didn't so much drift off to sleep as plunge into that deep dark pool of unpredictable slumber. I was back inside of Cynwrig's head. He was, ironically I guess, shearing a sheep. If his skills at the task were the gauge of time before jumping one winter ahead, we'd both have had much more time to grab our love ones. I could tell the young man was a lot stronger. I searched his mind for his recent history.

When he and Fiedlimid instantly appeared from their year long trip to the exact same place they'd left, it was to blowing snow and freezing temperatures. Cynwrig released his darling Fiedlimid who was shivering and in shock. He removed his sheepskin shirt and pulled it down over her bare arms. They found Ulaid abandoned and in much the same condition it was in after the raid by the north men. Cynwrig kissed his sweet Evergood, sat her down on the foundation of the home and went about saving their lives, now from the killing weather.

He unsheathed his sword and began hacking the charred center post. When he had enough splintered wood to start a small fire, he gathered it into a pile near Fiedlimid. He retrieved his fire starting kit from his little draw string purse and soon had a small blaze going. Sitting around that warm fire, He told her the complete tale of how they came to be in this time and place. Surprisingly, she was not skeptical and trusted her man completely.

After a few days, the weather became much milder and Cynwrig was able to build a shelter of remnant sod and stones from throughout the destroyed village. He had also chopped enough wood to last for several weeks. While Cynwrig worked, Fiedlimid scrounged for food, finding onions and other edible roots. She culled the chaff leftover from the last barley harvest. They barely subsisted on the meatless Spartan diet. She wove the stalks into sleeping mats and scratchy blankets.

I saw that eventually, Cynwrig began taking long all day hikes, leaving Fiedlimid alone in their small hovel with the warm fire, so he could wear the sheepskin shirt. He always left his dagger with her for protection. He was looking for their families. Eventually, he found Balis and the children a half days' walk to the west. They all mobbed him with love and kisses. He borrowed Aine's winter coat and went back for his dear wife. They were all reunited the next day. Balis and family were her poor, but they had a warm home, four sheep and a large garden.

I didn't have to wait long to see Cynwrig's family. Just as he finished bagging the sheared wool from the thirty, now naked sheep, they arrived in a two wheeled cart which was pulled by a large handsome ox. I figured that it must be several years later because the fetching Fiedlimid had a two year old boy and a one year old girl. They were both very beautiful. They all ran to Cynwrig who picked up his children with his strong left arm, saving his right to lift his Breck. He kissed them all.

"Did you miss me my darling wife?" Fiedlimid acquired a sexy impish grin.

"I wanted to make sure that you weren't dawdling away the day instead of shearing the flock."

With another sweet kiss on our lips, I was back in bed with my darling Layla. I pulled her close with a smile on my face and with the sweet scent of my Breck's soft clean hair soothing my mind. I fell softly into a dreamless, healing sleep.

**The End**

CPSIA information can be obtained
at www.ICGtesting.com
Printed in the USA
BVHW030457310820
587607BV00009B/10